PRAISE FOR STE

Wide Awake

"[T]he pacing is brisk and the bloodshed cinematic enough that a first-timer can wolf down this entry without having knowledge of the first two. This sends the series out with a bang."

—*Publishers Weekly*

Coming Dawn

"A deft cat-and-mouse novel that keeps the action moving and the reader guessing."

—*Kirkus Reviews*

Deep Sleep

"Techno-thriller fans will delight in military vet Konkoly's obvious expertise when it comes to the authenticity and intensity of the numerous action sequences."

—*Publishers Weekly*

"A lively, roller-coaster thriller that moves like lightning."

—*Kirkus Reviews*

"Nobody's better at spy craft, action, and intrigue than Steven Konkoly. Thrilling entertainment from the first to the last written word."

—Robert Dugoni, *New York Times* and #1 Amazon bestselling author of *The Eighth Sister*

"Steven Konkoly has blown my mind! *Deep Sleep* is an intelligent, intense, and completely unpredictable high-concept spy thriller. I'm hooked!"

—T.R. Ragan, *New York Times* bestselling author of *Her Last Day*

"Fast paced, suspenseful, and wildly creative. A modern-day masterpiece of spy fiction."

—Andrew Watts, *USA Today* bestselling author of the
Firewall Spies series

"A pulse-pounding conspiracy tale in the finest traditions of Vince Flynn and Nelson DeMille . . . *Deep Sleep* is a must-read roller coaster of a thriller."

—Jason Kasper, *USA Today* bestselling author of the
Shadow Strike series

"Devin Gray is the hero we need in our corner. Relentless in pursuit of truth, vindication, and saving his homeland, he is the perfect protagonist for Konkoly's newest dive into the techno-thriller world. Again Konkoly proves his mastery of the genre, drawing from real-rowed events to create a plausible and frightening glimpse into what's happening underneath our feet and behind the walls of power."

—Tom Abrahams, Emmy Award–winning journalist and
author of *Sedition*

"Steven Konkoly delivers a conspiracy thriller unlike any other and proves he's at the top of his game. With a deft hand and an eye for plot intricacies, Konkoly will take you into a web of deceit that will shake you to your core and keep you turning until the very last page. The Lost Directorate has set a new bar in the world of thrillers, and Konkoly has taken his seat at the head of the table."

—Brian Shea, *Wall Street Journal* bestselling author of the Boston
Crime series and coauthor of the Rachel Hatch series

"A master of action-adventure, Steven Konkoly has done it again, weaving a tale of high-stakes espionage that's ripped from today's international headlines. Plan to stay up very late reading *Deep Sleep*, as he keeps the pages turning!"

—Joseph Reid, bestselling author of the Seth Walker series

"I love a great conspiracy thriller, and Steven Konkoly has conjured one that's utterly chilling with *Deep Sleep*. From the high-stakes setup to the explosive finale, there's barely time to take a breath. Crack this one open and buckle in for one hell of a ride."

—Joe Hart, *Wall Street Journal* bestselling author of the Dominion Trilogy and *Or Else*

Previous Praise for Steven Konkoly

"Explosive action, a breakneck pace, and zippy dialogue."

—*Kirkus Reviews*

"Readers seeking a well-constructed action thriller need look no further."

—*Publishers Weekly*

"If you enjoy action thrillers that have both strong male and female characters, then this may be the series for you."

—*Mystery & Suspense Magazine*

"Exciting action scenes help propel this tale of murderous greed and corruption toward a satisfying conclusion. Readers will look forward to Decker and company's next adventure."

—*Publishers Weekly*

"Steven Konkoly's new Ryan Decker series is a triumph—an action-thriller master class in spy craft, tension, and suspense. An absolute must-read for fans of Tom Clancy, Vince Flynn, and Brad Thor."

—Blake Crouch, *New York Times* bestselling author

A HIRED
KILL

OTHER TITLES BY STEVEN KONKOLY

GARRETT MANN SERIES

A Clean Kill

DEVIN GRAY SERIES

Deep Sleep

Coming Dawn

Wide Awake

RYAN DECKER SERIES

The Rescue

The Raid

The Mountain

Skystorm

THE FRACTURED STATE SERIES

Fractured State

Rogue State

THE PERSEID COLLAPSE SERIES

The Jakarta Pandemic

The Perseid Collapse

Event Horizon

Point of Crisis

Dispatches

THE BLACK FLAGGED SERIES

Alpha

Redux

Apex

Vektor

Omega

Vindicta

THE ZULU VIRUS CHRONICLES

Hot Zone

Kill Box

Fire Storm

A HIRED KILL

STEVEN KONKOLY

USA TODAY BESTSELLING AUTHOR

THOMAS & MERCER

Published by Thomas & Mercer, Seattle

www.apub.com

Amazon, the Amazon logo, and Thomas & Mercer are trademarks of Amazon.com, Inc., or its affiliates.

EU Product Safety contact:
Amazon Publishing, Amazon Media EU S.à r.l.
38, avenue John F. Kennedy, L-1855 Luxembourg
amazonpublishing-gpsr@amazon.com

ISBN-13: 9781662524455 (paperback)
ISBN-13: 9781662524462 (digital)

Cover design by Faceout Studio, Elisha Zepeda
Cover image: © Shelley Richmond / ArcAngel; © kviktor,
© Max Levine / Shutterstock

Printed in the United States of America

To Kosia, Matthew, and Sophia—
the heart and soul of my writing

PROLOGUE

Garrett Mann shook the prisoner's chair from behind, waking her up.

"Ready to talk?"

Elena mumbled through the generous strip of duct tape covering her mouth.

Catalina Serrano ripped the tape away, and Elena winced before yelling at them in accented English.

"You'll kill my family if I talk. And me. That's how it works. I've been through this test before!"

Serrano grabbed the woman's hair and pulled her head back. Not far enough to hit the back of the chair, but enough to make a point—and refocus her on Mann's question. Elena coughed, before taking a deep breath. The sole survivor of the inexplicable program Mann's team had discovered deep underground in the middle of New Mexico, she might be able to help his ARTEMIS task force find the people who had run the facility.

His initial instinct had been to treat Elena as more of a rescued hostage than an adversary, but Serrano set him straight quickly enough. Elena was a *sicario*. A murderer. A hard-core member of the Juárez Cartel. Hard-core enough to be selected by whoever ran that facility. Not someone who would readily divulge information. Mann let Serrano go to work on her.

Thankfully, the results hadn't been as bad as he anticipated. Some facial bruising. A split lip. One of Elena's bare feet swollen—boot prints clearly visible on the top. Serrano had tuned her up a bit, but she hadn't crossed the line. Mann hoped it was enough.

"Elena, we've been through this before," hissed Serrano. "You are no longer working for the Juárez Cartel. The facility was run by a private American corporation, whether you knew it or not. Before that—the CIA ran the site."

"Bullshit!" she said, struggling against the zip ties restraining her to the chair. "I was there for two months, *puta*! That was no CIA or private operation. Juárez ran that place."

"In the middle of New Mexico," said Mann, shaking his head. "You already told us you thought you were in Mexico."

Mann gave Serrano a quick nod, and she let go of the woman's hair.

"They may have outsourced a few things, like the instructors. How else could they teach us to blend in here? They needed authenticity. The real deal," said Elena. "But Juárez was in charge. How else do you explain them bringing in *La Triada*?"

"Alejandro and Raul?" said Mann.

"*Sí,*" said Elena. "We've been over this already."

Mann shook his head. "You must have sensed that something was off overall. Right?"

"*Qué?*"

"You wouldn't have been locked in Alejandro's personal torture chamber, awaiting who knows what, if you were a . . . *cómo se dice en español?*" said Mann, nodding at Serrano.

"She speaks good enough English," said Serrano. "He's asking if you were a team player. *Una colaboradora*. Or were you a troublemaker—*una alborotadora*—that they decided to toss away like trash?"

No reply. But there was more to this than words. She'd started taking shallower breaths. All chest breathing now. Previously, she'd worked hard to fill her lower lungs, to try to lower her stress level. She'd been trained to do that. He'd detected a few attempts at box breathing, the act of inhaling, holding, and releasing in a timed manner—another "skill" she must have learned at the facility.

Every time he saw Elena employ that tactic, he nodded to Serrano, who yanked her hair, denying Elena whatever relief it may have given her. Something about the mention of the torture chamber, which they hadn't brought up before, had triggered a response she couldn't suppress. He'd push this a little further, before changing tactics.

"You know what he was going to do with you, right?" said Mann, giving Serrano the subtlest of glances—time for the bad cop. "You saw the room."

"He was going to take you apart, piece by piece, with piano wire and a bone saw, starting with your hands and feet—slowly and agonizingly moving closer to your torso," said Serrano.

"Keeping you alive the entire time," said Mann.

"Eventually he'd wrap that wire around your neck and pull so hard, for so long, that your head would detach without the use of a saw," said Serrano. "The wire cutting through the cartilage between two of your neck vertebrae."

"We've found several dozen of his victims dumped across the United States. All dismembered the same way," said Mann. "This gruesome method matched hundreds of murders unearthed in and around Ciudad Juárez over the years."

"Shallow pits filled with dozens of garbage bags containing body parts and heads," said Serrano. "My mother was one of his victims."

Elena pressed her lips tightly, a sign that she wanted to open up but just couldn't bring herself to do it. Call it brainwashing. Call it programming. Mann had seen this more times than he could count. A hard block. Time for a different approach.

"I mean, it's not like you're stupid, Elena," said Mann. "They wouldn't have dragged you into this if you were stupid. And I use the term *dragged* on purpose, because I strongly suspect you did not volunteer to be a part of whatever your captors had in mind."

Elena swallowed hard, but her eyes betrayed nothing. Hard-core. Like Serrano.

"The private company running that facility chose you for a reason," said Mann. "I have no idea what you did for the Juárez Cartel, but you got their attention. They had thousands of people to choose from. There's something unique about you, and to make any sense of why you ended up in a former CIA facility deep in New Mexico, I need you to start talking."

Still nothing.

"Whatever you've done, I'm not here to judge you," said Mann.

She didn't look convinced.

"But I wouldn't have hesitated to put a bullet through your head—if we had crossed paths down there—under different circumstances," said Mann. "Everything is different now. You pose no further threat to me, my team, or my country. The moment they handed you over to Alejandro, you ceased to be a threat. And if we're being entirely honest, that was the moment they erased you."

Elena shook her head slowly, her eyes slightly moistening. Barely noticeable, but obvious to someone who had been studying her face for hours. He had what he needed. Hopefully.

"Elena. My job is to figure out the purpose of that facility, and how the program that recruited you, or forced you to participate, presents a threat to the United States. I must assume that you and your deceased Juárez Cartel associates were locked away in that facility for a very specific reason. The facility had a purpose—some kind of combined re-creation of suburban and urban American life. What the fuck was going on down there?"

"They'll kill—"

"Enough of that bullshit," said Mann, locking eyes with her. "I need you to talk. This isn't a trick. You saw what we saw. Every single one of your *classmates*, if that's the right word, was gassed in their sleep. The only reason you survived is that you had been brought to Alejandro's custom-designed torture chamber, which hadn't been connected to the main facility's air system. An oversight that saved your life. The facility's leadership and security team put on gas masks—then pulled the trigger on poisoning everyone underground. Everyone."

"Lucky me," said Elena.

"The only reason you're still alive is that we think you might be useful. If you don't start demonstrating some value, I'll break your legs in several places and bury you in the desert. Alive."

"No, you won't. You're FBI," she said.

"Oh, I won't be the one to do the dirty work. She will. I'll be a few thousand miles away in Washington, DC, filing the rest of my reports," said Mann.

"You have rules," said Elena. "You're FBI."

"Rules? Elena. Nothing about this is official. Nobody at the FBI knows about you. We didn't report any survivors," said Mann, which wasn't true—they'd told O'Reilly. "Your fate is entirely in our hands."

Elena went wild, shaking the chair back and forth enough for it to topple over, smacking the side of her head against the basement's marble tile. Mann and Serrano lifted the chair up, returning her to the upright position. Several seconds later, when she appeared to have calmed down, Mann crouched directly in front of her.

"Elena. I know you've endured worse than this. That you've seen worse. Way worse than you're willing to admit. Far crueler than I'm willing to inflict. But I'm not who you need to be worried about," he said, nodding toward Serrano. "The bottom line is that we can move you around forever. I run an independent task force with no oversight. I can fly you overseas if necessary. Disappear you—without killing you."

Elena took a few deep breaths, before refocusing on him. He caught the faintest glimmer of a softened look on her expressionless face.

"Do you want a better life for yourself? Your family? A life that includes you? And a relocation?" said Mann.

Her demeanor remained stoic, but her pupils constricted slightly. A possible sign of relaxation or resignation. Nothing definitive, but worth pursuing.

"I don't know if you have any family. I'm offering you a chance to make a clean break from your previous life, which for all purposes is over. You can't show up back in Ciudad Juárez after disappearing for a few months and resume work for the cartel. We can help you escape all of this. But we're going to need your cooperation."

Her pupils constricted a little more, breaking the seemingly perpetual "go screw yourself" squint she'd arrived with. Enough to indicate he had her attention, and that she might be interested.

"How?" she said, confirming his observation.

He glanced at Serrano, then nodded at a black nylon bowling bag in the corner of the room behind him. Serrano retrieved the bag and set it down between Mann and Elena. He unzipped the main compartment, revealing tight, rubber-banded rolls of money. A mix of tens, twenties, and hundreds, trending toward the smaller denominations. Elena's eyes widened.

They'd found fifteen of these inside the New Mexico facility. Mann's team had counted one bag's contents, estimating the cash to be worth somewhere between five and six hundred thousand dollars. In addition to the cash, each bag contained fifty prepaid Visa credit cards, each valued at five hundred dollars. Another twenty-five thousand dollars of purchasing power, presumably for hotel rooms, rental cars, or online purchases. Transactions that require a credit card.

"If you cooperate with me, I'll give you one of these bags," he said. "Each bag is worth roughly half a million US dollars. Untraceable."

"I don't believe you," she said.

"Believe us," said Mann before producing a folded envelope from one of his pants pockets. "But even more importantly, I'll give you this."

Elena's eyes flickered between the bag and the envelope.

"What's in it?" she said.

"Arizona driver's license, US passport, apartment lease, utility bill receipts. Keys to the apartment on the lease and a vehicle that I presume is parked near the apartment, not that I'd go near either of them if I were you. They'll be watching both," said Mann. "Buy a car with cash."

"I don't understand," said Elena.

"This is what they planned to give you when you graduated from that program, along with a generous amount of money. We didn't find a bowling bag for everyone that had been gassed in their sleep, but the contents of the bags we found could have floated the entire group for quite a while. Which brings us to the literal million-dollar question. Why?" said Mann, before tucking the envelope inside the bowling bag. "Why did they want to plant you in the United States? Like a seed?"

"I don't know," said Elena. "You keep mentioning *they*. Who are *they*?"

Serrano kicked the side of her chair, nearly knocking it over. When it straightened, Mann zipped the bag.

"We don't know—yet. But here's the deal. In addition to murdering everyone at the facility during our raid, the organization running the place did their best to delete their server data banks. We're working around the clock to retrieve or re-create that database. Until that's complete, all we have is what we can infer from what we've found in the facility," said Mann. "And your testimony, as the sole survivor."

"You mentioned helping my family?" said Elena. "How? I can't go back to Mexico."

He glanced at Serrano, who took over.

"I have people who can get them out. Ex-cops and military," said Serrano. "And with a few of those bowling bags, plus some additional identification documents that we can provide, you can take them wherever you want."

"But just to be clear, Elena," said Mann. "This isn't some kind of official witness relocation deal with the US government. This is my team, handing you more money than any of us, or you, could hope to earn in several lifetimes, plus some additional fake IDs—and you making your own way in the world with the people you care about. Understood?"

"I understand," said Elena.

"Do you?" said Mann. "Because we're not giving you this free ride until you give us everything. We digitally documented the entire facility, and you're going to help us make sense of it all—down to the smallest detail."

"I will do my absolute best to help you," said Elena. "But they kept us in the dark about most things. We trained nonstop. Every kind of training. Language. Weapons. How to shop in a grocery store. Traffic laws. So many subjects. But I don't know why. I just know they wanted us to blend in."

"That's fine, Elena," said Mann. "With your help, we're going to examine all aspects of the facility and shed a very bright light on why they gave you a new life in Phoenix, Arizona. *Somos buenos?*"

"*Sí.*"

"*Bien,*" said Mann, still skeptical. "Rest up. We have a lot of work ahead of us."

He covered her mouth with a fresh piece of silver tape.

PART I

CHAPTER 1

Garrett Mann muttered a string of obscenities, before whispering over the team's radio net, "Keep your weapons out of sight—but be ready for action. Remain in covered positions until I say otherwise. We can't be one hundred percent sure yet, but this looks like a federal team. Or some kind of local LEO outfit."

"How the hell did they find us?" said Jessica Mayer, crouched next to him.

"Good question," said Mann.

They'd been meticulous about digital and cyber security since departing the underground site in New Mexico, limiting the team's external communications to a few seemingly untraceable calls to Deputy Director Dana O'Reilly—who had made it abundantly clear that they were entirely on their own until she could sort things out. Mann didn't need to read too far into her wording to understand what she meant: stay off the grid until told otherwise. But somehow, someone had found them.

He triggered his radio button again. "Baker. They'll probably hit both doors at once. Fingers off triggers."

He'd sent Tony Baker, former FBI Hostage Rescue Team leader, along with Ray Mills and Kim Rocha, into the adjacent room. No reason to give whoever was about to try to kick their ass the opportunity to take everyone down at once, if this turned out to be a kill team like the one sent to take them out in Minnesota.

The two first-floor motel rooms, linked by a connecting door, had served as their headquarters for the past three days, while they meticulously planned their infiltration of the final *Triada* serial killer's home, a sprawling estate northeast of Sacramento.

Raul—the last known living member of the *Triada* identified by Catalina Serrano—lived in Sterling Point, one of the most exclusive enclaves on Folsom Lake. Sweeping views of the forested hills to the north, combined with unrivaled privacy for an estate so close to everything California's capital had to offer. Not an easy place to approach. Certainly not as easy as Alejandro's estate in Minnesota. The wealthiest cohort of California's politicians, business moguls, and trust fund babies lived in Sterling Point, protected by competent and heavily armed security. Plus fast police response times.

Mann's team had determined that an approach through the forest behind the estate would be their best option. They'd have to park close to a mile away, next to the lake, and follow the lakeshore to the closest point of approach to the estate, but it should prove to be the least dramatic and least detectable entrance. Even if they were spotted by locals, the kind of people who lived in communities like this tended to turn a blind eye to FBI-stenciled jackets that didn't veer in their direction or toward their estates.

On top of that, despite all appearances and claims of resident privacy, everyone knew everyone's business in places like this. Nobody would be willing to go out on a limb for a guy they likely assumed was some kind of Mexican drug kingpin.

Neither the community security team nor the local cops would go on the offensive. Mann just needed to get into the house without the kind of hassle that might shut him down. A quick call to Sacramento's FBI field office would be a deal killer. No. His mission was to get into the house and spend as much time as possible searching for whatever scraps of evidence the last *Triada* killer may have left behind.

Mann didn't expect to find Raul there, given the time that had elapsed since their attack on the facility in central New Mexico. It was more than fair to assume that he'd been warned in the aftermath of the raid and skipped town. But they couldn't ignore the possibility of finding some kind of lead that might bring them one step closer to unraveling the perplexing nature of the underground training center ARTEMIS had discovered.

The place clearly had been built for a specific purpose. And from what his team could tell, the facility had been designed to integrate former Mexican cartel members into US society. Reason still unknown. But it didn't take a custom-made tinfoil hat to guess that the objective didn't align with the safety and security of the United States.

"What if they just go ahead and shotgun the door open or toss flash-bangs through the windows?" said Luke Turner.

"Then you light them up," said Mann. "But only if I give the order."

"Understood."

"What are you seeing now?" said Mann.

"Two teams setting up on both doors. Staying below the windows," said Turner.

"Any kind of identification?"

"It's hard to say. They're olive drab from head to toe. I saw some kind of subdued lettering on the front, maybe? But not the back. Can't say for sure."

Turner sat in a room watching over their "headquarters" suite. But there was a catch. Only Mann knew which room he was in. By design. Mann had sent him to the motel a day ahead of the rest of the team to assess the viability of the chosen location and to occupy a room that could be used to defend the team if things somehow went sideways. As much as he wanted to believe that the government was on his side as an FBI agent, the fact that the underground facility had been built and previously used by the CIA triggered a deep-seated paranoia. Turner's vantage point could cover the two rooms they'd occupied on the first floor.

The US government had been more than unhelpful when Mann's soon-to-be fiancée vanished in Mexico when they were in college. The

State Department entirely ghosted her family. One in-person visit and a few back-and-forth phone calls before they faded into the background, never to be heard from again. Then some low-level DEA agents showed up at his dorm and her family's house to "ask" them to back off and "bring the media temperature down"—citing "sensitivities" south of the border. Texas politicians sent aides to "calm them down."

His distrust of greater government agendas ran deep, which was why he wasn't taking any chances. His skepticism even bled over into the FBI, the organization he'd served for more than fifteen years. If the wrong people came knocking on this motel door, Turner would cut them down—no matter what letters were stenciled on their jackets or uniforms. If Mann ordered it. He turned to Callie Jackson, who sat on the floor a few feet away, her back against the wall next to the bed.

"Jax. Any sign they're onto Turner?"

She glanced up from her digital tablet for a moment. "Negative. I don't see any other activity at the motel."

"Can you identify the lettering on their uniforms?" said Mann.

Jax shook her head, clearly frustrated. She had installed several motion-activated, low-light-capable cameras around the motel, all but one of them covering the bigger-picture approaches to the run-down facility. Street front. Parking lot. Fence lines connecting to adjacent businesses. The cameras weren't the high-resolution kind. More of an early-warning system—which had worked as advertised. Her cameras had detected the breach long before the teams stacked up outside their rooms. The heavily armed group had crowbarred through two separate points along the dilapidated stockade fence that separated the motel's rear parking lot from an auto-repair business on the street behind them.

"I just need something," said Mann, off the radio net. "Anything to prevent this from getting out of hand."

"I'm trying," said Jackson. "The drone has a good camera. It's just a matter of getting one of those assholes out there to look up and say cheese."

She had launched their quadcopter drone moments after detecting the fence breach, keeping it out of sight until the team disappeared under the covered walkways leading to the motel courtyard and their rooms.

"Try the street behind us," said Mann. "Maybe there's a tactical vehicle with some agency markings? Assuming this is a government crew."

"I already swept Alveda Boulevard," said Jackson. "Nothing stood out."

"Did you check for government plates?" said Mann.

"It's been exactly ninety-three seconds since I detected the breach. So. No. I didn't have time to microscopically examine every license plate on the street," said Jackson.

He started to respond, but she held up a finger. "I have eight SUVs pulling into the front parking lot from Central Avenue. The last two vehicles in the convoy are well marked. One is Sacramento PD. The other is a Sacramento County Sheriff's Office vehicle. The others are unmarked."

FBI, most likely—with the locals bringing up the rear. Mann had forgotten to notify the Sacramento Special Agent in Charge (SAC) that he planned to raid a house within the Sacramento field office's jurisdiction. And not by accident. The last thing he needed was any additional layer of bureaucracy or scrutiny right now. He gave her a thumbs-up, before triggering his radio.

"All stations. Let's take it down a few notches. We have a convoy turning into the motel parking lot, anchored by local law enforcement," said Mann. "I'm guessing that the Sacramento field office caught wind of our plan."

"They could just walk up to one of the doors, show a badge, and ask to chat with a fellow federal agent," said Kim Rocha from the adjacent room.

"That should be the move," said Mann. "But every SAC I've ever met views the job as one of several stepping stones to DC. Those stones being the heads of nearly every agent below them. And sometimes they like to trample a slightly stained stone far above them."

"O'Reilly?" said Mayer.

"Yeah. She's not exactly a favorite at headquarters," said Mann.

"Our patron saint," said Baker.

"The patron saint of ARTEMIS," said Mann.

"Amen," said Turner.

Mann sent a quick text to Serrano.

CHAPTER 2

Several miles away, Serrano snatched her phone off the desk and read the message from Mann. Shit.

"Neva. Launch the drone," she said. "Mann's team has uninvited guests."

"What kind of guests?" said Neva, before grabbing her digital tablet.

"Still unknown," said Serrano. "But it looks like some kind of federal raid."

"Mann's FBI. Right?" said Neva, the sarcasm of her statement not escaping Serrano.

"As far as I know," said Serrano.

"That's not funny," said Sofia.

"He's FBI," said Serrano. "Very FBI."

"Then why would they raid his room?" said Neva. "Treat him like a criminal?"

"That's the big question," said Serrano. "Get the drone up. If we have uninvited guests, we stay put and let ARTEMIS sort this out. If the coast is clear, we leave in less than five minutes and head to the backup motel."

Neva launched the drone every hour to take a 360-degree picture two hundred feet above the motel. Any discrepancies were immediately investigated with the drone. Nothing had given them any prior concern.

"The drone is airborne. I'll have a good picture of our surroundings in about ten seconds," said Neva.

"We're just looking for any evidence that the motel is under surveillance," said Serrano. "Be meticulous. Mann said to check license plates for government markings."

The search shouldn't take long. Their dingy, mostly unoccupied motel was located west of Sacramento in Davis, just off Interstate 80. Less than a quarter of the parking spaces were occupied. Quick business for Neva's drone. The backup motel Serrano'd arranged was an even more obscure place, twenty or so miles to the west, in Vacaville. Prepaid. Keys in her pocket. As much as she wanted to be closer to the action about to go down in Sacramento, Serrano couldn't justify the risk.

She was in the US legally, and so was her entire team of former Mexicans, but their status didn't include direct participation as shooters in an FBI task force's takedown of a secret espionage facility in the middle of New Mexico. Help is help from a practical standpoint. But from a legal one, the involvement of her colleagues could prove extremely problematic—for both Mann and Serrano's people. Which was why she didn't argue with Mann when he suggested that they maintain a much lower profile for now.

Deportation wasn't an exact science. More like a game of "who don't I like and how will this affect my reelection," which was essentially stacked against Serrano and her crew. Despite her status, the wrong people could send her south. She'd come too far for that kind of bureaucratic bullshit. If they sent her back to Mexico, the Mexican government would likely put her in jail, or severely handcuff her. Prevent her from re-entering the US somehow. She could always return, but that would require her to give up her legal status and hire a coyote to smuggle her back across the border.

She was here to stay, for now. Keeping her distance from the powers that be in the US was a small price to pay to find and eliminate the last living member of *La Triada*. Then, and only then, would she be sure that the man who killed her *madre* had been brought to justice. Three of them had been part of the murder spree. Two were dead. Only one to go. The house in Sacramento represented their only lead.

Kim Rocha, their resident computer forensic expert, had done her best to vacuum everything possible from the underground site's computer network. It took four days to sift through the data and come up with the Sacramento address. The information was hidden deep. But Rocha had the skills to pay the bills. They identified a property likely owned by the sole remaining *Triada* survivor. An exclusive enclave north of Sacramento. A property very similar to the one occupied by the killer located just outside Minneapolis.

Serrano really hoped that Mann could negotiate his way out of whatever mess had descended upon him. The rest of their investigation depended on it. There was obviously way more to this whole mess than a few serial killers. The site they discovered in New Mexico suggested a conspiracy that none of them had yet grasped. That said, her number one priority was snuffing out the third serial killer of *La Triada*. She'd gladly help Mann with anything beyond that, but her focus was on finishing what she'd started years ago. Avenging her own mother, and the sisters and mothers of all her Mexican colleagues.

"Cata? You with me?"

She'd gone into her own mind for too long. "Sorry. What are you seeing?"

"From a big-picture perspective, I don't see anything unusual," said Neva. "Same vehicles I marked an hour ago. And the many hours before that."

"Then we need to move before that changes," said Sofia, emerging from the bathroom, dragging two bulky duffel bags containing their small contingent's heavier weapons.

A few military-style rifles. Two UMP-45 submachine guns. Enough ammunition for a small war. A dozen or so high-explosive grenades. All of it taken from the facility in New Mexico. Once they had figured out how to open the underground vehicle bay door, Mann insisted that they transfer whatever remained in the armory to the SUVs parked inside the vehicle bay. They also grabbed whatever they could strip from the facility's dead operatives nearby.

They had driven four fully laden vehicles to the original raid launch point, where they transferred as much as possible to the vehicles they'd brought to the fight. Despite Jax's assurance that she could disable any GPS tracking on the stolen SUVs, Mann didn't want to take any chances. The only things they left behind were the dozen or so AT4 antitank rocket launchers found in the facility's armory.

Most of them, anyway. ARTEMIS had a long road ahead of it, with plenty of roadblocks. And one of those proverbial or real roadblocks would undoubtedly require a high-explosive antitank rocket. She grabbed one of the overstuffed duffel bags and heaved it along the carpeted floor toward the door.

"I think we're clear," said Neva. "I've scanned every license plate in the lot. No government plates."

"We still need to be careful," said Serrano. "Bring the drone back and let's pack up."

Neva nodded, clicking away at her tablet. "Drone inbound. I have it landing on the roof of one of our vehicles."

"That's not too obvious," said Sofia.

"You want to climb up on the roof and retrieve it?" said Neva.

"No thanks," said Sofia, opening the motel room door.

"I'll pass," said Serrano.

"That's what I thought," said Neva.

Serrano paused for a moment to text Mann, who didn't respond. Shit must have been getting real back in Sacramento.

CHAPTER 3

Mann read Serrano's text. Her team was in the clear—for now. He mumbled a sigh of relief.

"Cata's good to go?" said Mayer, who crouched behind the foot of the bed, her rifle lowered.

"From what she can tell," said Mann, before triggering his radio. "Turner. Anything new?"

"Negative. They appear to be in a holding pattern," said Turner.

"Yeah. Holding on for the Sacramento field office," said Mann.

"Why would they send an unidentifiable group of agents ahead of them?" said Turner.

"To rattle us," said Mann. "Jax. What's the status of the inbound convoy?"

"Parked out front," she said. "Nobody has exited any of the vehicles."

"Of course not," said Mann. "They're waiting to see how this plays out."

"How might this play out?" said Ray Mills. "We're federal agents. Unless this is some kind of black ops private contractor group or one of the Mexican cartels, I don't see the problem here. Unless we're being shut down hard by the FBI."

"I haven't dismissed any of those scenarios," said Mann. "Only the last one doesn't end in a bloodbath."

"Jesus," said Mills.

"I'm pretty sure we're looking at the last scenario," said Mann. "Which is going to require some tap dancing. And I'll handle all of that. If this turns out to be a federal raid, push through whoever is outside and pack up the vehicles. We'll be on the road in five minutes. Doing whatever we can to lose these shitheads."

"What about the target house?" said Baker.

"We'll deal with that later," said Mann. "If they don't know about it already."

"How could they know about it?" said Baker. "It took Rocha four days to dig that address out of the facility's data stream, and she's no joke."

"Thank you," said Rocha.

"Who knows," said Mann. "They probably put a room full of a hundred Rocha wannabes on the job."

A hard knock on Mann's door cut off their conversation.

"Immigration and Customs Enforcement!" said an overly gruff and authoritative voice. "Exit both rooms with your hands up!"

ICE. Of course. Someone who didn't like ARTEMIS was playing the immigration card. What a weak hand. Especially since there was nothing here to enforce.

"This is Special Agent Garrett Mann. Federal Bureau of Investigation. Head of the ARTEMIS task force! Authorized and empowered by the head of the Critical Incident Response Group! There are no illegal or legal immigrants present in either room 105 or 106. None at all. State your purpose!"

"While I accept and respect your credentials, Special Agent Mann, we've been ordered to search your rooms for foreign nationals. Their status will be confirmed once in custody."

"I have six FBI agents in these two rooms," said Mann. "All US citizens. There are no foreign nationals present."

"I have my orders," said the ICE agent.

"Slide your badge under the door," said Mann. "I need to verify your identity—and authority."

"That's not how this works!" said the agent, through the door. "You do what I say. Then we sort things out."

"Yeah. That's not going to happen," said Mann. "Take a look behind you."

"At what?" said the agent.

"Just look at the windshield directly behind you," said Mann. "See the blinking red light?"

Mann had placed fake Claymore mines on the dashboards of the team's vehicles, which were parked directly in front of each of their rooms.

"Yes," he said, his voice going flat.

"Do you see what the blinking light is attached to?" said Mann.

"I do," said the agent.

"Can you read the writing?"

"Yes."

"What does it say," said Mann.

"I can't actually read it from here," said the agent.

"But you know what it says. Right?"

"Right."

"What does it say?"

"Front toward enemy."

"Exactly. And the team stacked up on the other door will see the same thing behind them," said Mann.

Several seconds passed. "They see it."

"Good," said Mann. "I'm starting my count. Five . . . four."

"They're on the move," said Turner.

"I can hear the ruckus," said Mann.

"It's a ruckus, all right," said Turner. "I've never seen federal agents move that fast. There's still one by the door."

"Doing what?" said Mann.

"Leaving what looks like a phone outside your room," said Turner.

"You have a phone call!" said the agent outside.

"From who?" said Mann.

No answer.

"He just took off," said Turner.

"I'm heading for the door," said Mann.

A few seconds later, he'd retrieved the satellite phone left on the cracked concrete walkway in front of the room. He waited until he was back into his barricaded position behind the bed before speaking. No reason to make it easy for a sniper. They'd installed a sat phone repeater in each room, which fed through cables into a single antenna on the roof of the motel—with a clear sight picture of the sky. He could use the phone in the bathroom if necessary.

"Mann," he said.

"This is Tara Ragan, special agent in charge of the Sacramento field office."

"It's a pleasure to make your acquaintance," said Mann. "I assume you're in one of the SUVs parked outside our motel?"

A long silence ensued.

"We watched your convoy arrive," said Mann. "Kind of hard to miss."

"Why would we hide from fellow FBI agents?" she said.

"Exactly. So—why send ICE ahead of you?" said Mann. "That's amateur hour."

Jax broke out laughing, then quickly shut herself down. Mayer just shook her head but couldn't help adding a little to the conversation. Loud enough for Sacramento's SAC to hear.

"What a joke."

"This is no joke," said Ragan.

"Yes. This is," said Mann. "There are no foreign nationals in either motel room."

"Our intel suggests otherwise," said Ragan.

"Well. Your intel is shit," said Mann. "Care to place a bet?"

"That's nonsense," said Ragan.

"Twenty bucks. Just a friendly wager," said Mann. "You find a foreign national in either of these rooms, and the next burrito you eat behind your desk is on me."

"I'll pass," said Ragan. "What about the Claymores?"

"What about them?" said Mann.

"Seriously? You know the deal," said Ragan. "Even as an FBI agent, you're looking at a minimum two-year federal sentence for possession of a Claymore mine. They're Department of Defense assets."

"The Claymore mines are fake. Obviously," said Mann. "There's no wireless detonation option. Never has been. It's either a rigged trip wire or a wired, command detonation option. I assume you knew that—even though every one of those ICE idiots didn't?"

"Your dismissal from the FBI is imminent," said Ragan.

"Harsh words," said Mann. "Based on what?"

"Trust me," she said. "Your time is marked by hours."

Shit. She sounded serious.

"Hours?" said Mann. "Why hours?"

"We're about to hit the house," she said.

"Which house?" said Mann, knowing exactly what she meant.

"Funny," she said.

"And why would that signify my demise at the FBI?" said Mann.

"I'm pretty sure your task force's work will be done at that point," said Ragan.

"You think you're going to actually find—" he started, then cut himself off. "What exactly do you expect to find at the house?"

"A serial killer. Or evidence leading us to him," said Ragan.

She hadn't been provided with the bigger picture. Just the serial killer's address, and enough inside information about Serrano and her associates to park a storm cloud of legal doubt over his team. *Inside* being the operative term. As far as Mann understood, nobody outside of Deputy Director Dana O'Reilly and ARTEMIS knew about Serrano or the help she imported from Mexico—which meant one of three scenarios. Each of them presenting its own set of challenges and dangers.

As far as Mann was concerned, the least likely situation was a mole within Serrano's tight-knit crew of former counterparts. Financially, they had more than enough incentive to sell out the operation. Serrano had sent most of them back across the border after the raid, primarily so they didn't lose their jobs. Decent-paying work was hard to come by in Mexico, and Mann didn't anticipate needing their help again for a while. No reason to jeopardize their ability to earn a real living. But Mann wasn't naive. If called upon again by Serrano, they'd most likely lose their jobs. And the prospect of any kind of financial payout working for ARTEMIS seemed unlikely. The FBI certainly wasn't going to pay them.

But they weren't in this for money. They'd all suffered from the scourge uncovered at the underground facility. Closure was first and foremost on their minds, and the raid brought them one step closer to that goal. He'd be surprised if the leak came from Serrano's crew. The biggest obstacle being contact. How would one of Serrano's people get in touch with the right people in the US government to bring down an ICE raid on his head? It wasn't impossible. Just very unlikely without O'Reilly catching word.

That left his own team of misfit FBI agents, which he didn't see as a threat. Mann had handpicked every member of ARTEMIS, all of them already on the outs with the FBI. He couldn't envision any of them betraying the team. Or was that wishful thinking? Could one of them have sold out the team to improve their situation and standing within the FBI? He hated the fact that he was even entertaining the possibility, but he couldn't discount it out of hand.

Which led to the most obvious and awkward question. Who could he trust to investigate his own team? Certainly not anyone on the team, for obvious reasons. The most evident being that he had a one in six chance of picking the informant to run the investigation, assuming ARTEMIS had been compromised. Not exactly good odds. The only way to objectively re-vet his team was to enlist outside help—and he didn't exactly have a handy list of independent investigators.

Maybe O'Reilly could help. She'd vaguely mentioned a few private groups that had previously worked in-line with the FBI to solve problems that required "outside the box" thinking. Exactly what he needed—on a few different levels. First, to scrutinize his team and make sure ARTEMIS wasn't compromised. Then to augment the team. He certainly couldn't take on an expansive, well-funded conspiracy with the gallery of FBI agents and Mexicans who had survived the past week. They'd need serious backing, and from what he'd heard, O'Reilly's contacts had no problem mixing it up with America's enemies.

All that said, Mann also had to consider the possibility that his communications with O'Reilly had been compromised. That was the third, and in his opinion most likely, scenario. They'd taken serious precautions to prevent any kind of eavesdropping, but he couldn't discount the possibility that someone had somehow bugged her office or phone.

Outside of ARTEMIS, O'Reilly was the only person who knew about the Sacramento house—or their motel's location. If the leak didn't come from his team or Serrano's people, it came from O'Reilly's office. Until they resolved this mystery, he'd have to exercise extreme caution if he planned on enlisting O'Reilly's extrajudicial assistance. But he still needed help, and he needed it now. He dialed O'Reilly's office phone.

CHAPTER 4

Jaw clenched, Gerald McCall pressed the phone tightly against his ear. Damn, he hated this woman. Actually, what he hated was the fact that Clara Furst was just a messenger, who treated him like a fast-food cashier who had messed up an order. That's what got under his skin. It wasn't her fault. She served as the sole nexus to their biggest client. The only client that truly mattered to AXIOM, as far as he was concerned.

And they had clearly given her specific marching orders, which did not include a hint of civility or respect. Just a cold, hard "what have you done for me lately" approach. It had been this way from the start. AXIOM's most recent setbacks sharpening her already near intolerable tone. He waited until she had clearly finished her diatribe.

"Yes, ma'am," he said. "Your product will be delivered uninterrupted— yielding the same impact. You have my word. The recently lost shipment was just a backup. Unfortunate to lose, but ultimately having zero impact on our overall ability to deliver what you ordered."

"Let's hope so," she said, ending the call.

He placed the phone receiver in its cradle before muttering a few choice obscenities. Time to spread some of his client's cheer. McCall got up from the small conference table and made his way to the SCIF's only access point. He pressed his thumb against the biometric pad next to the door and entered a six-digit code randomly generated for him every time he entered the building. The code was sent through an encrypted application on his phone. Once he opened the application, he had ten seconds to memorize the code before it vanished. Nobody got into or out of this room unless he personally escorted them.

McCall opened the door and nodded at the group seated around a larger conference table. He used this room when he knew or strongly suspected that some of the topics discussed might go above some of the attendees' clearance levels, requiring the SCIF, or the entire conversation might veer into territory better contained in a room invulnerable to any forms of electronic eavesdropping.

"Grab a seat. This shouldn't take long," said McCall.

Jeremy Powell, whom McCall had chosen to run the DOMINION operations, led his entourage into the SCIF. Gary Litman briefly nodded at McCall, his left arm in a sling from the bullet that had torn through his shoulder. He had to give Litman credit for getting Alejandro out of the lake house in Minnesota, even if Alejandro's escape may have led to the downfall of the LABYRINTH facility. The guy had proven himself resourceful and clever as Powell's tactical operations leader. He returned Litman's nod as a sign of respect, despite his desire to keep this meeting as uncomfortable as possible.

Kerry Conway trailed Litman. Conway served directly under Powell, overseeing the domestic implementation of the DOMINION plan—the product McCall intended to deliver to their client. She glanced at him as she passed, her blank expression reflecting the obviously grave implications of McCall bringing in all of DOMINION's top leadership directly on the heels of a catastrophe.

The last to enter was Oscar Marino, a stocky, zero-nonsense-looking former Green Beret, selected by Conway to run the crews that directly interacted with the DOMINION teams created by LABYRINTH and deployed nationwide. Watching over hundreds of "graduates," all former cartel members, while simultaneously keeping them in line and "on program," took a special set of skills and capabilities. Marino had so far proven to be the right person for the job.

When they had all settled in, he shut the door, which locked and sealed automatically. He remained standing in front of it.

"I just got off the phone with our DOMINION client, and they have concerns about recent setbacks," said McCall, letting his statement hang in the air for several seconds. "Which I assured them would not impact the delivery of our product."

The product being the delivery of on-demand political leverage, scalable up or down and executable through various methods. Violent and nonviolent. All aggressive and guaranteed to achieve the client's desired results. He couldn't promise the outcome their client desired, but the client agreed that the product, created and pitched to them by AXIOM, met their threshold requirements. The only question now was whether they could still deliver the same level of service, and if so, what could be done to prevent any further setbacks that could jeopardize his promise.

"Is there any reason for me to call them and backpedal?" said McCall. "Especially now that LABYRINTH is dead in the water?"

"No," said Powell. "Ms. Conway assures me we have more than enough teams planted nationwide to deliver."

He shifted his attention to Conway.

"The class that we just lost was overflow," she said. "I had planned to spread them out among the currently existing teams. Not because any of them had gaps or weaknesses. Just a little extra padding to bolster their capabilities. Given the client's imminent timeline, we only had plans for one additional class, which would have been held in reserve at LABYRINTH for any final pushes our client had in mind. Less sophisticated work."

"Less calculated violence and mayhem," said Powell.

"And you're certain that we can deliver with what we have?" said McCall.

"Yes," said Conway. "If we do develop a gap on any of the teams—"

"How would that happen?" said McCall.

"One of the graduates goes 'off program' and has to be removed," said Conway, glancing at Oscar Marino.

"We've only removed four graduates so far, out of three hundred and seventy. None of them deemed a critical loss," said Marino. "My group is watching them closely. Constantly reminding them of the consequences, while at the same time rewarding them. I don't anticipate losing more than a few between now and go-time."

"And your contingency plan if we start to lose graduates once the festivities begin?" said McCall. "I know we're talking about hardened killers, loyal to an enterprise they believe is sanctioned by the Juárez Cartel, but when the news starts dropping—some of them might have reservations."

"Sir. I have a very dedicated, handpicked crew of contractors that we can use to fill any gaps," said Marino.

Conway must have read his mind. She spoke up before he could ask the most obvious question.

"They have no ties to AXIOM," said Conway. "They were hired through a proxy, trained by third parties hired through different proxies. They're patriots just waiting for the green light."

"Except they're not Mexican," said McCall.

"They'll be used for standoff, lone-wolf jobs," said Conway. "Low risk of capture."

"I can shift current graduates' assignments around at the last minute if necessary, to make that happen," said Marino.

"Sounds solid enough," said McCall. "On to more pressing matters. ARTEMIS and any fallout from LABYRINTH. Jeremy. Do you have anything new to report?"

"ARTEMIS tried to drop off the grid, which leads me to believe they were directly involved. The FBI and pretty much every three-letter agency in the US government is sifting through the site as we speak," said Powell. "Fortunately, we have a source inside the team."

"That's great news!" said McCall. "Still. The fact that the FBI is digging deep makes me nervous."

"My contacts at these agencies and electronic surveillance operations currently confirm that no link has been made between AXIOM and the facility. The working assumption is that one of the Mexican cartels is responsible for the construction and staffing of the site. Part of a sophisticated operation aimed at further infiltrating the United States and facilitating the flow of drugs."

"Feels like a thin line between the concept of infiltrator and sleeper," said McCall.

"Yes and no. But the current assumption will put the DEA behind the bulk of whatever investigation emerges. That'll slow things down significantly, even if the FBI throws them some resources," said Powell. "My main concern is Garrett Mann's task force. ARTEMIS has proven to be surprisingly resilient and resourceful. Our contact has confirmed this, though they've been a bit cagey about providing details."

"Do you think they've made a connection?" said McCall.

"I suspect we'd already know if they had," said Powell.

"Nobody has kicked the doors in yet, so I suppose you're right," said McCall. "Keep pressing that contact. What do we have on them?"

"Kidnap situation," said Powell.

"Jesus," said McCall.

"We had no other options," said Powell. "The team is a bunch of misfits, but they're not dirty. No gambling debts. Just a bunch of screwups. My guess is that they're lying low because they overstepped their authority by raiding LABYRINTH. But I obviously can't discount the possibility that they may have found something that could take their investigation forward," he added. "Regardless of why they tried to hide, I'm working on several options, ranging from low to high bloodshed when they resurface. In fact, I have something in progress right now that might remove ARTEMIS from the picture with minimal bloodshed. I'm waiting on an update."

"I don't care about bloodshed, as long as it can't be tied back to AXIOM," said McCall.

"Understood. But if we can take them off the board without kicking the FBI hornet's nest too hard, the less likely the FBI gets further involved," said Powell.

"We just need to get past election day. Three and a half months," said McCall, hearing his own words. "Which feels like a long time. Don't hesitate to draw blood, Jeremy. The stakes are too high."

"I won't," said Powell. "I've drawn up a few options that fall more into the clean sweep category than targeted removal. Especially since we know they're still in the game."

"Whatever it takes," said McCall.

"Good to hear. Litman has procured the services of a very skilled mercenary team for any direct-action work."

"I hope they're better than the previous teams," said McCall.

"They're some of the best in the business. Expensive for a reason," said Litman. "I won't underestimate Mann again."

"Cost isn't an obstacle," said McCall. "And speaking of obstacles. Our client indicated that they might add a few names to the cleaning list at some point in the late fall, when this DOMINION business is over. A deep clean apparently."

"We'll still have a small army of sicarios at our disposal. Some of them frighteningly skilled at assassination—and more than eager to get back into that business," said Powell. "I don't think we'll have a problem fulfilling that request. In fact. I have the very best of them working on one of our biggest obstacles right now."

"O'Reilly?"

"She should be out of the picture within the next twenty-four hours," said Powell. "Without her support, Mann's task force should be kneecapped."

"Stay on top of everything. Extra vigilant. We're in the home-stretch, ahead of the pack," said McCall. "Let's not end up like one of those long-distance runners in YouTube videos that starts their victory lap early and gets blindsided."

CHAPTER 5

Deputy Director Dana O'Reilly feigned a smile as her boss and a sizable entourage entered her office—completely unannounced and uninvited. Not that her boss needed an invitation. But the fact that she somehow bypassed O'Reilly's very loyal admin staff and waltzed in with the head of the Department of Justice's Office of the Inspector General felt like a violation of O'Reilly's position. Not to mention her privacy.

She called Garrett Mann as Director James and her posse formed up in front of her desk. O'Reilly hit the speakerphone button, making sure to increase the desk phone's volume. She'd received a call from him a few minutes ago with a "complaint." Her boss's arrival wasn't a coincidence.

"Garrett. You're on with Deputy Assistant Inspector General Jeffrey Walker from OIG and Executive Assistant Director Camilla James."

Mann's voice echoed through the office. "OIG? What's that?"

"You know exactly what OIG is," said Walker. "And what we do."

"I really don't. I've never dealt with your office in the past," said Mann. "But I suppose I could venture a fairly accurate guess what you do."

"The DOJ's version of internal affairs," said O'Reilly. "Office of the Inspector General. They dressed the name up."

Mann laughed. "Lipstick on a pig. Got it."

"That's not funny," said Walker, turning his head to address O'Reilly. "Do you have any control over your agents?"

O'Reilly shrugged. "I'm not following."

"He's being disrespectful," said Walker.

O'Reilly opened her desk drawer and removed a box of tissues, placing them on the desk.

"Jesus," said James.

"What's this?" said Walker, slightly distracted by a few stifled laughs behind him.

"A box of tissues. In case you start to cry," said O'Reilly.

"Didn't realize I was walking into a pit of vipers here. A little warning would have been nice," said Walker.

"I figured you could handle it," said James. "Goes with the territory in my branch."

"Speaking of warnings," said Mann. "I have some ICE agents wanting to kick down my motel door—and half the Sacramento field office backing them up. A courtesy call would have been appreciated. Not that I'm crying about it or anything. No need to rush any tissues my way."

Walker mumbled a few obscenities under his breath, while most of the room did their absolute best not to laugh—or even smile. None of them doing a good job of containing their amusement.

"I would have given you a heads-up—sans Kleenex," said O'Reilly. "If I had any idea something was brewing."

"I know," said Mann.

"We're up against a timeline," said agent Tara Ragan, whom Walker must have added to the conference call.

"Hey, Tara!" said Mann. "Didn't realize you were on this call, too. Can I end our other call?"

"I suppose so," said Ragan.

A loud, repeated crunching sound filled O'Reilly's office.

"You didn't have to crush the phone," said Ragan. "That's FBI property."

"Didn't want to take the chance that you might be spying on me," said Mann. "You know. Given the fact that you're undoubtedly spying on me."

"Nobody is spying on you," said Ragan.

"Sure. You just happened along with ICE and found my motel," said Mann.

"Maybe I should smash the phone in my office and start using my personal cell phone, or an off-the-shelf satellite phone for future communications with my field teams," said O'Reilly.

"Is this how you run your branch?" said Walker.

James turned to the OIG inspector. "Another crack like that, and you're out of here. Nobody talks to me like that."

"You don't have the authority—"

"Yes. I. Do," said James. "Bring it up with your boss if you don't like it. Who I happen to know very well. We were roommates in college. Howard University. Class of 1987."

"Why is he even there?" said Mann.

"Garrett. I don't need any shit from you, either," said James.

"Yes, ma'am," replied Mann.

"But seriously—and respectfully—why is OIG here?" said O'Reilly.

"I'm guessing it's the same reason I have ICE agents outside my motel door?" said Mann.

"More or less," said James. "Our office received information that you have embedded foreign nationals, specifically Mexican foreign nationals, within ARTEMIS. And that those foreign nationals participated in the raid on the underground facility in New Mexico."

Walker added the rest. "Not to mention the foreign national that's been parading around as an FBI special agent for over a year. Does the name Special Agent Serrano ring a bell?"

"Anyone know a Special Agent Serrano?" said Mann.

After several muffled background responses, Mann answered, "Nobody by that name here. Maybe the surveillance footage from the New Mexico facility can shed some light on this allegation."

"The surveillance hub at the facility was torched, destroying all footage," said Walker. "Convenient. Wouldn't you say?"

"The facility's security team released a poison gas that killed every employee trapped underground. Not to mention the fact that someone else escaped the facility and appears to have personally gunned down the head of the complex and the few remaining security officers, who had nearly escaped," said Mann. "I don't think it's unreasonable to assume that whoever escaped would go to any lengths to destroy as much evidence as possible. Including footage that could identify them."

"And we found no evidence of a secondary team in or around the facility," said O'Reilly.

Walker shrugged. "Well. Your team certainly took its time reporting what you found."

"I don't like what you're implying. We engaged in a thorough sweep of the facility to best assess the situation," said Mann.

"Without notifying your superiors," said Walker.

"To make sure we didn't miss or lose time-sensitive evidence," said Mann. "But yes. In hindsight, I could have handled it differently."

"Should have," said Walker.

"Do I need a lawyer, or can I explain my reasoning informally?" said Mann.

"I'd like to hear it, but it's up to you, Garrett," said James. "This conversation isn't protected in any way. Not with OIG in the room."

"Dana?" said Mann.

"I don't think you have anything to hide," she said, aware that her response was a lie on at least half a dozen levels.

Not exactly new territory for her. She'd been party to a number of under-the-table, or entirely illegal, operations in her days with the FBI—thanks to a certain off-the-books, CIA-backed black ops group she'd spent several years quietly supporting. Mann's operation barely crossed the line, as far as she was concerned. He had taken some "less than legal" liberties for sure, but nothing compared to what she'd indirectly and directly taken part in over the years. O'Reilly not only believed that his investigation had serious national security implications, but she was willing to stick her neck as far out as necessary for him to get to the bottom of it.

What he'd unearthed made the hair stand up on the back of her neck. She knew that ARTEMIS was onto something big. Something important enough for her to blatantly lie to her boss and the director of the FBI's internal affairs investigation group. Lies that could land her in jail and strip her of everything she'd earned after putting in close to thirty years with the FBI.

And that's what set her apart, as far as she was concerned. O'Reilly didn't give a shit about the consequences—and never had. She'd never wavered in the past, if the path forward felt clean. This core conviction had propelled her further than she ever imagined possible, thanks in no small part to principled leadership that shared her convictions. Particularly, former FBI Director Ryan Sharpe, who had not only believed in her but shielded her from more than a few career-killing torpedoes. O'Reilly had worked closely with Sharpe for the better part of two decades, dismantling some of the nation's gravest threats—and bending just about every rule in the book to get the toughest work done.

CCRSB Director James seemed to be cut from the same cloth. No guarantee, but Sharpe had aggressively promoted her during his brief tenure as FBI director, and Sharpe had seen enough of the shady underbelly of federal law enforcement operations to know that he had an obligation to put the right people in the right positions to counter the tide working against the Department of Justice. O'Reilly didn't expect James to cut her any slack at all, but she did trust that James would give her the benefit of the doubt—and shield her on some level from those dark forces. She'd extend that same protection to Mann, who didn't hesitate to answer Walker's question.

"Agreed. But I understand the tightrope we must all walk in our position," said Mann. "The reason for the delay was twofold. First and foremost, we were dealing with poison gas, and I wasn't about to risk any of my team to any level of immediate exposure, despite having acquired gas masks during our initial raid. I figured the concentrations would be extremely high at first, possibly limiting mask effectiveness."

"I still don't see why you didn't call this in the moment you exited the facility," said Walker. "Or why you didn't report your discovery and wait for backup before entering. I'm sure the FBI could have mustered a small army within a few hours."

"Which leads me to part two. Ego. Selfishness. A desire to prove myself?" said Mann.

James raised an eyebrow, while O'Reilly struggled to keep a straight face. Hopefully nobody in Walker's entourage noticed. Mann was good. Almost too good. She couldn't wait to see how this blast of bullshit played out.

"What are you talking about?" said Walker.

"Look. There's a reason I am where I am right now," said Mann. "A couple reasons, actually. And I'm not implying that I've made it to the pinnacle of any career. Yes. I have my own task force, which might be considered enviable—but let's be real, nobody thought this would amount to anything. Deputy Director O'Reilly indulged my idea, for which I'm grateful. I'm not sure if I'd still be carrying an FBI badge if she hadn't given me this opportunity. That said, I'm not sure she thought ARTEMIS would go anywhere."

"The premise sounded solid enough to move forward," said O'Reilly.

"I appreciate that," said Mann.

"Anyway," said Walker. "What's your point?"

Wow. He'd waded right into Mann's rapidly rising stream of bullshit. She wished she could text Mann right now. He'd probably just send her a bunch of laughing emojis.

"The point being that I finally, after years of feeling minimized, unearthed something notable," said Mann. "Not only notable, but very likely a direct threat to our national security."

"Let's not get ahead of ourselves here," said Walker. "It's not like organized cartel operations on US soil is something new."

"Exactly," said Mann. "But this looked and felt different, which is why I wanted to keep it for myself. For as long as reasonably possible. It's not often that an FBI agent stumbles on something truly significant. I thought—and still think—there's so much more to this than what we found in New Mexico. That's why I delayed my reports. But after searching the facility, I realized that we'd hit a wall. There's only seven of us now. Dr. Torres and Special Agent MacLeod were killed in Owatonna. We simply don't have the resources to continue pursuing any leads that might come out of the New Mexico facility."

"I say no harm, no foul here," said O'Reilly. "Mann's initial search of the facility, under the real threat of inhaling poison gas, was nothing short of admirable. Stupid, to be honest. But commendable. That—combined with a far more thorough exploration, when the poison levels had somewhat abated—represents the kind of commitment to the job that I've never seen in my career. And I've seen some shit, as I'm sure you've all heard."

"Can I add something?" said Mann.

Jesus. Asking for permission. He was laying it on thick.

"Yes," said Walker.

"I called this in immediately after our initial postraid investigation of the facility," said Mann.

"He did," said O'Reilly. "And we dispatched teams from far and wide."

"But yes," said Mann. "Our postraid investigation was delayed by a few hours, which was my call. I wanted to give the poison gas enough time to dissipate so I could be the first to thoroughly search the site. I should have called Deputy Director O'Reilly immediately after the raid."

"Yes. You should have," said Walker. "You unnecessarily exposed your team to a biohazard."

A few moments passed before Director James turned to Walker. "Are we done here?"

"No," said Walker. "Everything we just discussed is a sideshow. There's still the matter of foreign nationals working for ARTEMIS."

"I'm fine with field agents from the Sacramento office searching our motel rooms," said Mann. "But not ICE. That's just insulting."

"I don't see the problem," said Tara Ragan. "We're all federal agents."

"FBI only," said Mann. "Unless you want to wager a little money on whether they'll find a foreign national in any of these rooms. A hundred dollars."

"Let me get this straight," said Ragan. "If I agree to this stupid little bet, you'll let ICE search your rooms?"

"Correct," said Mann.

"And I win a hundred dollars if they find a foreign national."

"Yes. But if they don't," said Mann, "you pay me a hundred dollars. And I expect payment within the hour."

"This guy is unreal," said Walker.

"You have no idea," said O'Reilly.

"Are we on?" said Mann.

"We're on," said Ragan. "I have better things to do right now. We're about to hit the house."

"Can you slide the money under the door, before ICE enters?" said Mann. "If you're headed out to personally oversee the house raid that we handed you, I'm worried that you might forget."

"I won't forget," said Ragan.

"Neither will I," said Mann. "Or any of the witnesses, which are numerous at this point."

"This is entirely inappropriate," said Walker. "Just in case anyone was curious."

No response.

"Exactly what I thought," said Walker.

"Good luck at the house," said Mann. "And be careful. Seriously. The occupant isn't someone to be taken lightly. I doubt he's still there at this point, but I wouldn't be surprised if he left a few surprises behind. Expect trouble."

"We're well equipped to handle trouble—" said Ragan.

Walker interrupted them.

"You can sort this out later. All I care about right now is searching those motel rooms for foreign nationals posing as US federal law enforcement agents. That was the sole complaint I received. Special Agent Mann, are you ready to let ICE agents into your rooms?"

"I suppose so," said Mann. "But all weapons must be holstered. Rifles left in the vehicles. We're all federal agents—like you said. Same rules will apply to my team. We'll exit with our pistols holstered and rifles lying in plain sight on the beds. ICE searches and leaves. End of story."

"I can live with that," said Walker. "Ragan?"

"Fine," she said.

"Excellent. We're all in agreement," said James. "And there will be no hundred-dollar bet. Not on my watch. And take down those fake Claymore mines. You should know better than to pull something like that."

"Fair enough," said Mann. "Agent Ragan. Are you sure you don't want any help with the raid? We had a solid plan. Pretty low key. Once our rooms are searched here, which should take ten seconds, we'd be happy to accompany your SWAT team."

"I don't think so," said Ragan.

"Suit yourself," said Mann. "But like I said—be careful."

"Thanks for the helpful advice," said Ragan. "Can we get this over with so my agents can get on with business? The only reason I'm here is that I knew you'd throw a fit and hassle ICE."

"We're opening the doors and walking out," said Mann. "And I have an agent in room 207, who was covering the doors to our rooms. You know. In case the bad guys showed up."

"Funny," said Ragan. "Make sure he or she follows the same procedures."

"I will," said Mann. "Hanging up. It's all in ICE's very competent hands now."

Keep a straight face, O'Reilly kept telling herself.

"Coffee while we wait?" she said, pointing to the Nespresso machine on top of one of her filing cabinets.

"I'm fine. Thank you," said Walker.

"Don't mind if I do," said James.

"The pods and paper cups are in the top cabinet," said O'Reilly, before grabbing the tissue box.

Walker's eyes followed the box as she put it away. Time to make nice.

"Sorry about the tissue thing," said O'Reilly. "I get a little over-protective of my people. And I'm not exactly the most tactful—ever."

"Trust me. I've been on the receiving end of far worse," said Walker. "We're not the most popular show in town."

O'Reilly nodded. "I can imagine. A thankless job."

"Pretty much," said Walker, momentarily distracted by his phone. He scrolled through a message, before looking up.

"ICE didn't find anyone but FBI agents at the motel. Looks like ARTEMIS is in the clear—for now. My team still needs to interview any of the police officers or deputies Mann's team interacted with in Minnesota. Maybe even further back. Review video feeds at the various sites they visited. Dot my i's and cross my t's."

"The hallmark of a true professional," said O'Reilly.

Walker stifled a laugh. "I honestly can't tell if that was a dig or not."

"Hard to tell with her sometimes," said Director James.

"Nice," said O'Reilly. "But it wasn't. Let me know how I can help. I'm certain that Special Agent Mann would like to put this inquiry to bed, sooner than later."

"I don't doubt it," said Walker. "I'll be in touch, via your director, if we require any further assistance. Sorry about the intrusion and thank you for your time."

When Walker's entourage closed the door behind them, James sat down in front of O'Reilly's desk.

"Thoughts?" said James.

O'Reilly slid a legal pad in between them, before removing a pencil from the top drawer of her desk.

"Special Agent Mann has run ARTEMIS by the book. I'm not the least bit concerned," said O'Reilly.

"That's what I figured," said James, before taking a sip of her coffee.

O'Reilly wrote on the pad and turned it in James's direction.

EITHER MY OFFICE IS BUGGED OR ARTEMIS HAS A MOLE.

James nodded.

"Good coffee. I need to get one of these Nespresso machines," said James, taking the pencil from O'Reilly. "I thought the company hyped these up by hiring George Clooney."

"No. It makes damn good coffee," said O'Reilly, before reading her reply.

SWEEP REGULARLY? CAREFUL ABOUT COMMS INSIDE AND OUTSIDE HQ?

"And I'm *very* particular about my coffee," said O'Reilly, nodding. "Had some bad experiences in the past."

"Nothing worse than a bad cup of coffee," said James, scribbling.

ARTEMIS IS LIKELY COMPROMISED. BUT STILL—NEVER KNOW ABOUT HERE.

"I couldn't agree more," said O'Reilly. "That's why I'm so careful with my coffee. And very picky about where I get it on the outside."

Another quick note from James.

DO I NEED TO BE WORRIED ABOUT MEXICAN INVOLVEMENT?

"And why I'm even more picky about bean sourcing," said O'Reilly, taking the pencil. "Ethiopian beans are kind of the gold standard, but Central America and Mexico have been producing some nice blends lately."

QUICK MEET TONIGHT ON THE OUTSIDE? COFFEE OR SOMETHING STRONGER.

James nodded and grabbed the pencil.

YEP. SOUNDS LIKE I MAY NEED SOMETHING STRONGER.

"Mind if I take this to go? Busy day ahead," said James.
"Not at all," said O'Reilly.
"I'll be in touch," said James. "And make sure Mann understands that he can't interfere with the Sacramento field office's operation."
"I will," said O'Reilly, thinking, *Not even Mann is that preposterous.*
Then it hit her. James wanted her to warn Mann about the possibility of a mole on the team. Among other things. Like Mexican foreign nationals.

CHAPTER 6

Raul's phone chimed a sound he'd specifically programmed for a moment he understood to be inevitable. They'd found his house in Sacramento. A real shame. The shame being that he had unnecessarily rushed out of the house, taking little more than a few suitcases of clothes and a few of his more portable and valuable possessions with him. He should have known that it would take whoever his minders had originally suspected to have hit the New Mexico site no more than a few days to trace the property.

He wasn't a serious collector of art or curios by any stretch of the imagination, but Raul had surrounded himself with pieces that meant more than money. Both symbols of his success and unique displays that made the house an aesthetically pleasant experience for himself and neighbors who didn't seem to care that his lifestyle might be funded by less-than-legitimate activities headquartered south of the border. If only they'd known that their guesses were off by about two thousand miles—north of the border.

That said, why leave any kind of paper trail? Nosy neighbors could identify moving trucks. Moving companies could be investigated. Moving truck destinations identified and surveilled. Unnecessary risks in the grand scheme of things. No. He'd made the right call. He had several long-haul stashes located throughout the Southwest, even a few in the Midwest. Each storage unit contained a vehicle with current plates—and enough money, identity documents, disguises, and weapons to last months, if not more than a year. Plenty of time to get back in the game after a setback, and in on the next hunt.

Raul had long ago embraced the fact that attachment was his enemy, though he'd admittedly let that mantra slide a little with the Sacramento house. He'd spent too much time there. And put far too much mental effort into the illusion of creating a permanent home. Foolishness. He wasn't in the type of business that afforded that luxury. He should have spent his downtime bouncing between several locations. None of them would have been shabby. His paycheck was excessively generous. Not to mention the money he'd pilfered from the safes of several high-profile targets.

A hard lesson learned. Time to move on. Do their bidding. Finish what he started and then make a clean break—as promised. Easier said than done. Both with his previous and current employers. But if he could escape the strong gravitational pull of the Juárez Cartel, he could certainly get away from the big-money, think-tank-wannabe paramilitary corporation pulling the strings at the New Mexico facility. When the time was right.

A part of him still thought that right time should have been the moment he hung up the phone with Mr. Clean, while enjoying the last sunny afternoon poolside at his Sacramento house. Hit one of his stashes and get out of the country. He had plenty of monetary assets in accounts he could access overseas. Book a flight to Southeast Asia and never look back. Maybe Spain or Central Europe. Definitely not Central or South America. The Juárez Cartel's tentacles reached farther than most would think throughout the Americas—particularly south of the US-Mexico border. He wasn't worried about US reach: Raul had enough dirt on the CIA to bury DC and most of northern Virginia. Mutually assured destruction.

But he couldn't make a clean break yet. He'd committed to one more job, and if he didn't deliver, his current employer would make his life a living hell, no matter where he tried to settle. Not that he trusted them to leave him alone once his services were no longer required. He wasn't naive. Which was why he'd collected enough evidence to bury them, too. They thought he hadn't figured it out. That the intentionally unbranded nature of the facility and the use of cutouts or anonymous payment schemes had kept him from identifying the company behind the operation. Wishful thinking on their part. He'd put the pieces together within the first few months of the facility's transfer from CIA to private ownership.

Once he completed his current assignment, which could be as early as tonight, he'd lay those cards on the table. Literally a killer hand. If AXIOM tried to eliminate him, the company would quickly cease to exist, and a long line of its top executives would spend the rest of their lives either in jail or on the run. To soften the threat, he'd give them the option of bringing him back into service—on occasion.

Raul could accept that. Even embrace it. He understood that he was wired differently. That sipping drinks on a warm Mediterranean or subtropical beach for the rest of his life wouldn't work. He just wanted to get out of his current, involuntary contract and go the freelance route.

Raul wasn't like the rest of the *Triada*. He regarded the work as a means to an end. Juárez leadership needed a distraction, and he'd been asked to join forces with two prominent sicarios to deliver the unthinkable. A seemingly unending string of murders in and around Ciudad Juárez. Women, mostly. Innocent and vulnerable factory workers. A far cry from the work he'd mastered over the previous years: the torture and murder of the cartel's enemies. But orders were orders, unless he wanted to end up beheaded in the same kind of shallow grave he'd dug for countless victims.

The cartel selected three sicarios to carry out the killings. Two of them embraced the carnage. One was sloppy and undisciplined. A former Chihuahua State Police officer managed to track him down, with the help of sympathetic colleagues, and kill him a few years into the murder spree. Alejandro, the other converted serial killer, was meticulous and cautious enough to evade the vigilante cops, but not careful enough to avoid the attention of a very different group interested in his work.

The CIA had grabbed a tequila-infused Alejandro while he chatted up an equally drunk local woman in an El Paso dive bar—no doubt saving her life. Three days later, three Black Hawk helicopters descended on Raul's Land Rover on a long stretch of road outside Ciudad Juárez, swooping him away to the United States and leaving behind the charred remains of "Raul Cabrera" and his security detail inside the smoking chassis of his SUV.

The CIA kept them locked down at the facility full-time. Mercifully, the program changed hands, and the new management viewed their service differently. Work at the facility shifted drastically. They no longer focused on training captured cartel members to return to Mexico and work against their former bosses. Quite the opposite. He never fully grasped the program's new direction, but whoever ran the place clearly had one goal in mind. To convince the facility's "students," all captured Juárez Cartel members, that they were still working for the cartel—and that they were being trained to infiltrate the United States.

Raul and Alejandro seemed to serve a single, chilling purpose in this new scheme. As feared legends in the cartel, they convinced the students that they had been hand-selected by the Juárez Cartel for a higher purpose, and if they rejected their new reality or failed the training, they'd be brutally murdered, along with their families. The strategy worked better than he expected. Few questioned the legitimacy of the program, and those who did suffered fates worse than death—in front of their class.

In between training sessions, Raul and Alejandro were free to live their lives as they saw fit under the new system, with generous salaries. Having little in common, other than the work at the facility, they went their separate ways. Raul accepted contract assassination work from his new employer. All US-based. Alejandro went on murder sprees in the Southwest United States, unable to suppress what had likely always been his nature.

Raul had warned his employer about the risks associated with Alejandro's appetite for wanton murder, but they'd assured him that the situation was under control. That Alejandro didn't take unnecessary chances. That he hadn't attracted the wrong kind of attention—yet. *Yet* being the operative term. Because he clearly had attracted some attention, which was why Raul's laptop screen now showed at least two dozen FBI agents swarming his Sacramento house. He set his espresso down.

Raul had navigated to an encrypted site that displayed several cameras placed in his Sacramento house the moment his phone chimed. So, now what? He could do nothing, which sounded boring but couldn't be dismissed. Why kick the hornet's nest. Not that they could find him. Certainly not before he executed his current mission. Then again, maybe sending a message would make his current job easier. Fluster his target. Contrary to popular belief, paranoia didn't sharpen your defenses. It dulled them, scattering your fear in every direction, preventing you from focusing on the most logical and obvious threats.

With that thought in mind, he returned to sipping his espresso and waited until the bulk of the FBI agents had breached the house—kicking in doors and scurrying through the hallways. Raul hoped this was the same team that had raided the LABYRINTH facility. He had little doubt that Mr. Clean would alter the terms of their final agreement after Raul took care of the FBI deputy director—and turn his talents against whatever team had managed to find Alejandro. Finished with his drink and satisfied that most of the agents who had arrived were either inside the house or close enough, he dialed a number on his phone and selected option two. The camera feeds on his screen vanished a few moments later.

Raul closed his laptop and surveyed the street beyond the coffee shop's floor-to-ceiling window—his gaze focused on the apartment complex in front of him. Northwood at Falls Church. Based on the crystal-clean faux brownstone facade facing the street, he presumed that this was one of the more expensive apartment options in the area. Hard to say. The website provided no pricing information, but it did give him quite a detailed view of the apartment layouts. It was incredible what you could find online—barely lifting a finger.

CHAPTER 7

Mann's phone rang. O'Reilly. Now what? They'd only minutes ago untangled themselves from the motel debacle. The ATF showed up immediately after the FBI and ICE departed, asking questions about some of their weapons—which, admittedly, the government had not issued to his team. They'd added to their standard-issue gear along the way, a few of those additions turning the tide at the underground facility in New Mexico.

The ATF agents focused their attention on the rifle Luke Turner brought down from his overwatch position, in a room on the second floor of the motel. The rifle was a heavy-barrel, automatic version of the HK416, similar to the M27 infantry automatic rifle recently adopted by the US Marine Corps and issued to all infantry Marines. Capable of fully automatic, sustained gunfire, nothing like this existed in the FBI's inventory at the field agent level.

The FBI had experimented with them at one point with a few major metropolitan-area SWAT teams, but ultimately decided against fielding a weapon originally designed to replace the Marine Corps belt-fed M249 light machine gun—a serious weapon of war. The specter of negative public opinion trumped utility and dampened the FBI's desire to procure the weapon.

Turner reluctantly surrendered the rifle. More accurately, he pretended to be reluctant. Mann's team had picked up two in the cornfield outside the motel in Owatonna, and three more from the New Mexico facility's armory. Fortunately, the remaining four automatic rifles sat in the cargo compartment of Serrano's SUV, along with a few other goodies that the ATF would have undoubtedly confiscated. All headed to a backup location only he knew about.

The big question was how the hell did the ATF know about the weapons Mann's team had confiscated? The ICE tip-off could have come from a number of sources. Someone in the Owatonna Police Department. Someone spying on Deputy Director O'Reilly. One of Serrano's Mexican counterparts, though he highly doubted that. They seemed loyal to a fault. Or even a member of his team. A possibility he'd pretty much crossed off the list until the ATF showed up.

The only people who knew about the automatic rifles taken from the New Mexico facility were the Mexicans and ARTEMIS team members. He hadn't mentioned looting the underground armory to O'Reilly. And they'd been discreet about taking the two automatic weapons from the shooters positioned in the cornfield to the south of the Owatonna motel. In fact, they'd taken M4 rifles found in one of the hostile team's trunks and tossed them in the cornfield next to the two bodies. The weapons fired the same caliber. Magazines and ammunition drums totally interchangeable. Only the most observant of deputies could have put that together this quickly, and they had their hands full with one of the biggest shoot-outs in the county's history. No. Mann had a problem. And all signs pointed to it being an internal one.

He grabbed the phone and answered the call, instantly regretting the attitude he threw at O'Reilly.

"More good news?"

"You didn't hear?" said O'Reilly.

"No. I just untangled myself from the ATF," said Mann. "I'll tell you about it later. We're headed out of town to regroup and cool off. I have a bunch of pissed-off agents on my hands right now."

"Shit. You really don't know," said O'Reilly.

"Know what?"

"I'm throwing you right back into the fire," said O'Reilly. "The FBI raid at Raul's house in Sacramento went sideways."

"As bad as the lake house raid in Minneapolis?"

"Worse," said O'Reilly. "As in, several pounds of C4 worse. Every agent that entered the house is down. Nineteen confirmed dead. The rest in bad shape. Pretty much the entire Sacramento field office's primary SWAT team. Another dozen or more agents outside the house were either killed or injured. Only the SWAT snipers and the rapid response backup team parked down the street escaped unscathed. Someone was expecting you."

"That's one way to look at it. More on that later," said Mann, making a vague reference to the possibility of a traitor in his ranks. "You want us at the house?"

"What's left of it. Just don't get in the way. The place is going to be packed with federal, state, and local forensic people. You'll have full authority to search the property and retrieve evidence related to ARTEMIS's ongoing investigation by the time you arrive. Director James is on the phone right now squaring this away. If you run into a problem, call me before you react. Good to go?"

"Yes," said Mann.

"You're not a one-word-answer personality, Garrett," said O'Reilly. "Are we clear?"

"Crystal."

"Garrett," said O'Reilly.

"Crystal clear. Two words," said Mann.

"Asshole," said O'Reilly.

"Isn't that why you gave me the task force?"

"Pretty much," she said. "Please tread lightly at the house. It's a mass-casualty event, with everyone focused on—"

"The casualties," said Mann. "I understand. We won't get in the way of that, and we'll be respectful while carrying out our duties."

"Thank you," said O'Reilly.

"That could have been us. Probably intended for us," said Mann.

"The thought had crossed my mind."

"Watch your back," said Mann. "My spidey-sense is tingling."

"Mine, too," said O'Reilly. "Give me a ring when you're on scene."

"Will do," said Mann, before ending the call.

Jessica Mayer, seated next to him in the driver's seat, hit the left-turn signal.

"U-turn? I assume we're headed back?" she said.

"Yeah," said Mann.

"The whole place blew up?" said Tony Baker from the row behind them.

"That's what it sounds like," said Mann.

"Jesus," said Callie Jackson, seated next to Baker—behind Mann.

"Jesus take the wheel," said Mann, nodding at Mayer. "We're back in business. A shitty, no-holds-barred business, apparently."

◆　◆　◆

Serrano read Mann's text and took in a deep breath. The explosion had been meant for ARTEMIS. No doubt about that.

"What's up?" said Neva, who had just pulled them into their backup motel.

"Raul rigged his house with explosives," said Serrano. "Killed pretty much the entire Sacramento field office SWAT team, plus others."

She didn't mention that Mann had slipped a long-ago-established code word into his text, which now made sense given everything that had transpired over the past hour. He'd slipped *serpiente* into the message. *Snake. Traitor.* In other words: *Watch your back.* First ICE. Then the ATF looking for unauthorized weapons? Only Mann's FBI task force and her Mexican colleagues had known about those rifles.

Not to mention the explosion meant to wipe ARTEMIS off the map. Until around an hour ago, Mann's team had planned to breach Raul's mansion without the Sacramento FBI field office's help. Without their knowledge.

Where did this leave her? Serrano trusted the crew she'd selected to come north with her life—which was the price she was willing to pay. She'd rather die than betray ARTEMIS or her Mexican colleagues. But could the same be said about everyone else?

"That could have been the end of this. Everything and everyone we've sacrificed," said Sofia, from the second row of the SUV.

"*Sí*. But we got a second chance," said Serrano. "Mann wants us to head to Phoenix. I think the gloves are about to come off."

"Elena?" said Neva.

Serrano nodded. "Yeah. She's been holding out on us. Feeding us enough to keep Mann from bringing out the blowtorch and sticking it where the sun doesn't shine."

"I like the analogy," said Sofia. "We definitely need to turn up the heat on Elena."

"Not an analogy," said Serrano. "I'm literally going to take a blow-torch and—"

"We get the picture," said Sofia.

"Thank you," said Neva.

"This is gonna get ugly," said Serrano. "I'm not fucking around this time."

"Mann has his limits," said Neva.

"Mann is going to be busy for a few days. Maybe longer," said Serrano. "I intend to make good use of that time."

"Remind me not to get on your bad side," said Neva.

"Everyone is on my bad side, including all you *pendejas*," said Serrano.

"Bitch," said Sofia.

"Damn right," said Serrano, praying that the traitor wasn't on her team she'd brought to the US.

CHAPTER 8

Garrett Mann's overwhelming first instinct when his feet hit the street was to render assistance, aid—whatever first responders needed. The absolute last thing on his mind was their investigation. He knew this would be bad, but nothing could have prepared him for the devastation and carnage that unfolded as his convoy wove through the red-and-blue flashing tangle of fire trucks, police vehicles, and ambulances.

Paramedics rushed bloodied and wounded FBI SWAT agents on gurneys toward the nearest available ambulances. Sacramento Police Department SWAT officers helped the few federal agents who could walk under their own power through the gate leading to the mansion. Geared-up firefighters dragged hoses and other equipment along the street and through the gate. Uniformed police officers were everywhere. A Sacramento PD Explosive Ordnance Disposal team was suiting up in olive drab, armored gear next to their vehicle. Smoke billowed in the distance, superimposed against the orange-tan, tree-spotted hills.

Three white body bags lay outside the ornate stucco gate. Just the beginning. If the blast had been as destructive as O'Reilly described, and he had no reason to doubt her information, the rest of the bodies would take time to "assemble," before more bags could be filled. He approached a woman in a suit, who appeared to have taken charge of the chaotic scene outside the gate, holding out his badge.

"Special Agent Garrett Mann. FBI. ARTEMIS task force. How can we help?" he said, the rest of his team catching up.

She pointed up the driveway. "An agent named Spencer is running the show up at the house. I'm just trying to fix shit down here."

"Can we help? Here?" said Mann, looking around.

"You can help by getting out of my way," she said, flashing the badge affixed to her belt. "Senior detective. Homicide. No offense, but I have enough people down here to handle this, and they all know I'll kick their asses if they mess things up. All the feds are up by the house."

A gurney surrounded by several paramedics barreled past, carrying an FBI SWAT agent who appeared to be missing his legs. They halted several feet past the gate, a flurry of activity ensuing. Terse orders barked by the lead paramedic indicated that the agent didn't have a pulse and had stopped breathing. Mann had the distinct impression that the scene would get worse the closer they got to the mansion.

"Go," said the detective. "I got this."

Mann nodded, before motioning for his team to follow. They passed a few more teams of paramedics urgently escorting gurneys carrying wounded FBI agents to the street. The winding, oak tree–lined driveway eventually led to a group of SUVs flashing their emergency strobes. A group of agents in suits clustered around the open liftgate of one of the vehicles. One of the agents broke free and approached Mann's team.

"Special Agent Mann?" she said.

"Yes," he said, his eyes immediately darting to two Sacramento PD SWAT officers appearing next to the SUV with a body bag.

Turner grabbed Baker and approached the two officers, offering to carry the body bag away.

"No," said the agent. "I need your team here."

"Where's Ragan?" said Mann.

"Killed instantly. That fucker rigged the pottery lining the inner driveway circle with Claymores," she said, extending a hand.

He shook her hand briefly. "I assume you're in charge?"

"Special Agent Tanya Presser. Assistant special agent in charge," she said. "I'm the senior agent on the scene. I was on the street when everything went to shit."

"I don't know what to say," said Mann, his eyes darting back and forth between opposite sides of the driveway.

"I know what you're thinking," said Presser. "We're pretty sure this area is clear."

"Pretty sure?" said Turner.

Mann shot him a *stand down* look. Diplomacy was the first order of the day here. The Sacramento field office had just lost over twenty agents.

"It's okay. I get it," said Presser. "But we scoured the area. Unless there's an IED buried somewhere, we're good to go."

Mann still couldn't see Raul's mansion, though he presumed it lay under the cloud of brown smoke rising toward the sparsely clouded, light-blue sky.

"Have you accessed the house?" said Mann.

"Yes," she said. "But only to retrieve bodies and the few that survived the main explosion. Only three survivors so far—and they're barely hanging on, from what I'm told."

He didn't have the heart to tell her that one of them most likely had died just outside the gates.

"What can we do?" said Mann.

"Ragan gave me a quick rundown on your task force's objective here," said Presser. "Do whatever you need to do to get to the bottom of this."

"I'm sorry about Ragan," said Mann. "And everyone else you lost today. This was meant for us."

"No time to dwell on any of that," said Presser. "What do you need from me to do your job?"

"Is the house on fire?" said Mann.

Presser shook her head. "Not really. Some heavy, localized smoldering around the C4 points of detonation, but most of the damage resulted from the explosive's shattering effect. A few firefighters have been inside and assessed the likelihood of a sudden blaze to be minimal."

"I saw EOD suiting up," said Mann.

"I'd say it was just a precaution, but who the hell knows," said Presser. "We can't rule out secondaries."

Baker stepped forward. "The house should be clear of secondaries. If the initial blast occurred after most of the agents had entered, it's fair to assume that the interior of the house was under remote surveillance—and the blast was initiated remotely. Given the fact that you haven't been vaporized yet, I think we can safely assume that whoever set off the explosion is not watching us right now."

"Big assumption," said Callie Jackson, their electronic surveillance expert.

"True," said Baker. "But here we are. And here we remain. Plus, any surveillance devices or additional explosives in the house would have been rendered useless by the initial blast. Assuming it's as bad as it looks—from here."

"Oh. It's bad," said Presser. "I'm not sure what you're going to recover from the structure."

"I say we press forward, before any of those hot spots spread and create an inferno that destroys everything," said Baker.

Mann shrugged. "This is strictly voluntary. We're taking a big risk here."

"You're kidding, right?" said Jessica Mayer. "New Mexico wasn't a big risk."

"Just saying," said Mann. "This whole place could go up and burn us alive."

"At least we won't need gas masks," said Mayer.

"Fair point," said Mann. "But we might need basic firefighting gear. Oxygen masks and tanks?"

"We've been in and out of the structure," said Presser. "Without masks."

Mann didn't want to say what he was thinking.

"But you need to spend more time inside," she said.

"A lot more time," said Mann, thinking about the tequila bottle label Serrano had deciphered that had led them here.

"I'll let the Sacramento Fire Department know that you need seven air packs," said Presser. "What about gloves?"

He glanced at Ray Mills, their forensic expert, who nodded. "Whatever they can spare. In case we need to move hot stuff around."

"Coming right up," said Presser, before returning to the team of agents huddled around the tailgate of the SUV.

Kim Rocha spoke up, quietly enough that it was unlikely that Presser's agents could hear her. "We're persona non grata here, aren't we?"

"I get the feeling that Tara Ragan didn't mention the fact that she jumped ahead of the line to get to Raul," said Mann. "On some level, they probably think this is our fault."

"Still the Island of Misfit Toys," said Mills.

"Yep. Get used to it," said Mann, before pulling out his phone to call O'Reilly.

She needed to know the full extent of what had happened here. If Raul, or whoever pulled his strings, had no qualms about murdering a few dozen FBI agents to keep their bigger secret in the dark, they might not have a problem hitting even higher up the chain of command.

CHAPTER 9

Dana O'Reilly parked on the street, the clock on her dashboard reading 10:03 p.m. A first for her at the apartment she'd called home for more than twenty years. Mann's suggestion that she not take her safety as a deputy director at the FBI for granted had spooked her. And she'd witnessed some seriously nefarious, nobody-is-safe shit in her career. The difference today being that the insanity she'd seen before rarely consumed FBI agents.

CIA officers and mid- to lower-level directors? Yes. Corrupt government officials, all the way up to the director of national intelligence? Sure. Former military black ops personnel? By the dozen. But FBI agents? It was a line rarely crossed, because it rained fire and brimstone down on your head. Mann was right. Whoever crossed this line didn't seem to care, which was why she chose not to park in her climate-controlled garage tonight.

She would start to modify her daily routine, to include the routes she took to work, coffee shops or restaurants she frequented, and the times she returned. Basic counterintelligence and counterterrorism tenets. Except she wasn't stationed in Pakistan, driving back and forth every day to the embassy from a guarded compound. She lived in Falls Church, Virginia, minutes away from Washington, DC.

"Screw this," she muttered, hitting the button on the key fob to lock her BMW sedan.

To put a quick end to whatever mayhem the sponsors of that underground training facility had in mind for the United States, and anyone who stood in their way, she'd go to her boss tomorrow and request an enhanced funding package and more agents to support Garrett Mann's task force. And as much as O'Reilly loathed the idea, she'd ask for a protective detail. Why take any chances until the threat had been thoroughly and permanently neutralized.

She would have asked James tonight, over a drink or two, but the ambush in Sacramento put those plans on hold. O'Reilly considered a glass of cabernet at one of her favorite wine bars, a few minutes' walk down the street, but immediately scratched the idea. She could be found there a few times a week after work, enjoying a generous pour of whatever the owner recommended that night. Off-limits until Mann got to the bottom of this mess.

O'Reilly removed a keycard from her coat pocket and pressed it against the street entrance to her apartment complex. The light above the reader turned green, and the door clicked. She walked through the lobby, past the mailboxes and darkened sales office, to the automated sliding glass door that led to the complex's outdoor common area.

A brightly lit, kidney-shaped pool ringed with padded outdoor lounge chairs and umbrellas anchored the center of the space. A grilling area sat on the opposite side of the courtyard, covered by a wide pergola. Nothing fancy, but certainly not a bad perk on weekends, when all she wanted to do was read a book in peace and take in a little sun.

The complex didn't rent units, so most of the people living here were middle-aged couples or single professionals like herself, who had been living on good salaries for decades. Many of those salaries were provided by the Central Intelligence Agency or nearby think tanks that catered to the intelligence community. In other words—quiet people who mostly kept to themselves. Her favorite kind of people.

She noted the pool area was empty as usual. In two decades, she could count on two hands the number of times she'd seen anyone down here after returning from work—and still not use all her fingers. Maybe she'd bring a glass of wine down by the pool and enjoy the warm evening air tonight. Why not? Relax a little after a long day of trying to make sense of Sacramento. She shook her head as she approached the staircase leading up to her second-floor apartment. Who was she kidding? She'd be half-asleep by the time she changed out of her suit.

A few minutes later, she stood in the foyer of her apartment, half wondering whether she should have searched the doorknob and dead bolt keyholes for the subtle signs of a picked lock or the immediate hallway for a trip wire. She settled on looking for trip wires, because she was exhausted, and hated feeling paranoid again. O'Reilly hadn't looked over her shoulders like this in years. Not since True America had run amok and nearly ruined the country. And even then, she wasn't really a target. Her boss at the time, who would go on to run the FBI after True America fell, had shielded her from most of that.

She turned on the light. No obvious trip wires in the hallway. Once out of the hallway, O'Reilly took a few moments to scan the main living area. Nothing appeared out of place, and she'd know if anything had been moved. A lamp. Couch pillow. The salt and pepper shakers sitting in the middle of her dining room table. She had a tidy, knickknack-free home, which she kept in order. Not in an obsessive way, but a consistent one. For a reason. Every time she walked in the door at the end of the day, she could count on her apartment as a constant. A safe space free from the more-than-occasional madness of her job.

O'Reilly let her shoulders relax for a moment. Shouldn't she check her office, spare bedroom, and owner's suite? Dammit. This was getting ridiculous. She'd request an executive protective detail first thing tomorrow morning. The detail would not only follow her home but send an advance team out a few minutes ahead—to enter her apartment and make sure it was safe. They might even post a team outside her complex overnight. It was the last thing she wanted, but O'Reilly had seen enough in her career to warrant the request.

She returned to the hallway to hang her suit coat in the closet, only realizing her mistake the moment she opened the door. O'Reilly didn't feel the knife blade punch through her abdomen. Only the force of the hand that had jammed it in. She lowered her head instinctively to deliver a headbutt, unintentionally stopping the attacker from lodging their forearm against her throat and slamming her backward against the wall. The move kept O'Reilly in the fight, her trachea still intact.

Years-old training kicked in. Hand-to-hand fighting in a tight space never ended well, particularly when you were on the defensive. She lurched to the right, toward the end of the hallway, and dropped to the hardwood floor, raising her legs to fend off her attacker. The initial knife strike felt like a punch. The pain came a few moments later. Like a hot poker had been inserted in her stomach.

Somehow, she managed to draw her service pistol before she hit the floor, but before O'Reilly could insert her index finger in the trigger, her attacker kicked her hand. The Glock 19M disappeared in a flash, sailing somewhere far out of reach behind her. She slammed her right leg into his stomach, stopping him momentarily. He punched the knife into her calf, sending a shock wave through her body.

Holding her right leg in the air with the knife, he quickly and effort-lessly produced a smaller knife with his other hand. Her attacker was no ordinary killer. This had to be Raul. The very brief delay gave her time to reach the Glock 43 subcompact in the holster attached to her left ankle. She didn't bother pulling it all the way out. The moment her finger felt the pistol's trigger, she pressed repeatedly until the magazine ran empty.

Six 9mm hollow point bullets left the barrel in under a second, punching straight through the holster and stitching her attacker's right leg from top to bottom. He screamed and staggered backward toward the apartment's front door, giving her enough time to scramble on her back into the kitchen—a knife protruding from her right calf.

She spotted her service pistol under the dining room table but decided against going for it. If he carried a firearm, he'd drill her full of holes before she reached it. Instead, she scrambled for the guest bathroom just inside the hallway leading to the bedrooms. The attacker popped into sight around the entryway corner, leading with a pistol.

She crawled into the bathroom, her legs taking a few bullets before she got them inside—and locked the door.

Her immediate priority was putting more than a flimsy door between her and the bullets that were soon to come. She heaved herself into the tub, catching the knife in her calf on the edge and nearly blacking out from the pain. Moments later, the door splintered from rapid gunfire, most of the bullets hitting the floor where she'd lain moments ago or thunking against the hard plastic tub.

Lying on her back, O'Reilly realized she still had the Glock 43 subcompact in her hand, its slide locked back. A literal death grip on the pistol. Pushing through the agonizing pain in her stomach, she twisted to the right and retrieved one of the magazines for her service pistol situated on her left hip. Glock magazines being interchangeable, she inserted the fifteen-round magazine into the subcompact, then depressed the slide lock lever, chambering a round. She was back in business.

Playing it safe, she fired four bullets straight through the door, starting low and ending at average chest height. O'Reilly then shifted to the walls next to the door and fired two bullets into each side—one low, one stomach level—before sinking down into the tub. *Your move, asshole.* Several seconds passed. Nothing. She waited a few more before removing her cell phone from her suit coat pocket and sending a short text to a number she'd committed to memory years ago. Then she dialed 911 as her blood pooled in the tub.

CHAPTER 10

Raul backed up and watched from a safe distance. Several bullets punched through the door and walls. No surprise. His target had proven more skilled and resilient than expected. Far more skilled than he'd been led to believe. Eight shots. Her Glock subcompact held only six. She'd switched over to her service weapon's magazines. His target knew what she was doing. Impressive for a high-level FBI director. Mr. Clean hadn't done his homework, or the bald fuck had withheld information.

It didn't matter at this point. He didn't see a cell phone on the floor. She still had her jacket and didn't carry a purse. Raul had to assume that she'd called 911. Local police were on the way, possibly more than just a local response given her position at the FBI, and time wasn't on his side. Even if her cell phone lay on the floor and she couldn't call 911 for help, one of the neighbors was sure to call soon enough.

Not to mention the three bullets she'd put into his leg. None of the wounds were immediately life threatening, but it wasn't exactly a "sit back and wait it out" situation, either. He was slowly bleeding to death, and he needed to get out of there while he could still think clearly. Especially if the police were on the way.

His only offensive option right now was to grab her service weapon and blast away at the bathroom with two full magazines. Thirty bullets. Fifteen from her G19M and fifteen from his SIG SAUER P365. Hopefully that would do the job, but she was probably in the bathtub or curled up off to the side somewhere. Bitch would pop a few rounds off and stop him cold. No. He'd messed up by not shooting her dead the moment she passed the closet.

His overconfidence left him with no choice but to withdraw from the scene, having failed to complete the job. A first for Raul. He just hoped that the over-the-top explosion he'd orchestrated at his former residence in Sacramento had wiped out the team responsible for locating and shutting down LABYRINTH. That should be enough to get him off the hook with Mr. Clean after tonight's failure.

But if he'd instead killed a few dozen unconnected agents, Raul had a tough decision to make. Stick around and face the music, which could just as easily result in his immediate execution as it might yield a chance to redeem himself. Or he could disappear. He had everything he needed in his nearest storage unit—roughly a two-day drive away—to vanish forever. Or try, at least. Better than walking in front of a firing squad.

If Mr. Clean offered him what sounded like a genuine opportunity to make amends, he'd take it. A life on the run was barely a life at all, which was why he hadn't already gone poof. Of course, he'd perform extreme due diligence evaluating the offer. Raul wasn't naive. He'd assassinated exactly 193 people on Mr. Clean's behalf over the years. That was a lot of research and data points. Enough to draw some conclusions about LABYRINTH's purpose, and the overarching goal of Mr. Clean's organization—AXIOM.

Which led him to his third option. One he could execute by simply taking a seat in the living room and waiting for the authorities to arrive. Then again, after killing a few dozen FBI agents in Sacramento and attempting to murder an FBI deputy director, how much leverage could he possibly have to strike a deal with the Department of Justice? No. He'd need to approach that option from a distance. Deny that he planted the explosives. Claim he had no idea his target here was FBI. Hire the best lawyer in the business. Get some signed and sealed assurances before turning himself in.

All those choices seemed so far away at the moment. His first order of business was to get out of this building and go to ground. Find some competent, off-the-books medical care, and take the time to recover. He was effectively useless to Mr. Clean until he could prove he was back up to speed, which could take one to two weeks—minimum—depending on the extent of his wounds.

Raul exited the apartment and started down the hallway to the elevator. The stairs were the safer option, but the less strain he put on his legs right now, the longer he'd last on the streets. The last door in the hallway opened to his immediate right, revealing an unassuming man dressed in sweatpants and a Georgetown T-shirt. The man's eyes immediately shifted to the bullet wounds along Raul's leg. Then the gun in Raul's hand.

"What happened?" said the man, the *oh shit* look on his face signing his death warrant.

Raul shot him twice in the face and closed the apartment door, before pressing the elevator button. A minute later, he slipped out a back door labeled No Exit and paused behind one of the apartment complex's trash dumpsters. Still no sirens.

One block to the north, he opened the rear driver's door of his G-wagen SUV and crawled inside, shutting the door behind him. The backpack on the seat next to him contained a robust first aid kit, along with spare ammunition for his various firearms and a few high-explosive grenades—which would have come in handy in O'Reilly's apartment. Overkill, but he would have accomplished the mission.

Now he lay bleeding all over the leather seats of the luxury vehicle that had cost him close to one hundred fifty thousand dollars, hoping he wouldn't have to apply a tourniquet to stop the bleeding. A tourniquet meant he'd need to seek immediate emergency care, most likely at a hospital. Unless he could quickly arrange something through the dark web, which was a long shot at best. Presenting himself as a gunshot wound victim at any emergency room was a serious gamble. Almost a guarantee that he would face the "turn witness" option.

He took off his pants and went to work on the wounds, first removing the two bullets—without anesthesia. The third wound had been a through-and-through, the projectile embedded in the hallway door or wall. He poured antiseptic into every hole, which hurt more than plucking out the bullets, before packing each opening with hemostatic powder. Hemostatic gauze pads came next, followed by a thick white gauze pad and tape.

He waited a few minutes to see whether the blood soaked through the white pads. Only the through-and-through showed a little seepage, which he'd expected. Based on the blood loss he'd observed, the bullets had done some serious damage, but they hadn't hit an artery or major vein. He could take his time seeking care. But first things first. Get the hell out of Falls Church. He'd left a blood trail that even a rookie uniformed cop could follow.

Raul put on his pants and gently exited the SUV, before getting in the front seat. Just pressing the brake to start the vehicle felt like jabbing small knives into his right leg. He was in for a long night. His objective being a reasonable chain motel ten to twenty miles out of DC. A place where his SUV wouldn't stand out and the night manager wouldn't pay too much attention to his limp. He'd regroup in the room, accessing the dark web to find an off-the-books medical provider who asked no questions and reaching out to Mr. Clean through the encrypted channel AXIOM used to pass along target dossiers. No way was he going to use his phone or any standard means of contact anytime soon.

CHAPTER 11

McCall sat up on the plush, deep-brown leather couch in his office—his phone buzzing. A quick glance at the phone told him two things. First. That he'd been asleep for only about thirty minutes. He'd assumed this would be a long night and had decided to take a short nap around ten o'clock. Second. He'd made the right decision. Powell buzzing him at 10:37 p.m., after this catastrophe of a day, couldn't be good news. He'd be up all night putting out various fires.

"Where are you?" said McCall, after answering the call.

"Downstairs in the SCIF," said Powell.

"Give me a few minutes. I'll call you from a secure line."

"I can come up if that—"

"I'll call you when I'm ready," said McCall, ending the conversation.

The abrupt hang up and summary rejection of an in-person meeting with someone two minutes away felt a bit petty, but he was in no mood to see Powell right now. Especially if he had more bad news. Things were messed up enough already. He gripped the decanter on the marble-topped table in front of him and poured a few fingers of Scotch that cost more than most Americans made in a day into a crystal tumbler that cost more than most Americans made in a month. McCall took a restrained sip and savored the cherry and oak notes. He'd save the rest for what promised to be an unpleasant report.

Once inside his SCIF, he sat down at the head of the conference table and picked up the phone receiver. A single button press later, Powell was on the line.

"Give it to me straight," said McCall. "I'm in no mood for platitudes."

"I don't even know what a platitude is, so here we go," said Powell. "I just heard from Raul. We have a real shit show on our hands."

"Your hands," said McCall. "And now mine. The number of dead FBI agents just reached twenty-five. Three more lives hang in the balance. Not exactly what I had in mind when you gave your little speech about minimal-bloodshed options."

"I didn't know he planned to detonate enough explosives to take out half of Sacramento if an FBI team came knocking at his door," said Powell. "I orchestrated the Sacramento field office takeover of the raid to sideline ARTEMIS. He assumed that whoever arrived at his house would be the key to continuing the investigation—and took matters into his own hands."

"Well. That didn't work out. Did it?"

"No," said Powell. "And it gets worse."

McCall downed the glass in one swig, no longer contemplating the complex flavor notes or cost. "How?" he said.

"O'Reilly proved more resilient than expected," said Powell. "The glaring gap in her FBI history profile blindsided Raul. She survived the attack."

"Wonderful," said McCall. "And Raul? Has he driven out to a remote quarry in West Virginia and blown his brains out—for the cause?"

Maybe the Scotch had hit him a little harder than expected. He rarely drank more than a finger of hard alcohol in any setting.

"Uh. No. He's seeking off-the-books medical care," said Powell. "Took a few bullets to his right leg. Nothing life threatening. He's under control."

"Under control?" said McCall. "Did you tell him we can take care of his wounds?"

"Yes," said Powell. "But he prefers to stay in the cold for now."

"He doesn't trust us," said McCall. "So not under control."

"I suppose not," said Powell. "But he indicated a desire to return to work, when he was mission capable again."

"How long?"

"A few weeks," said Powell. "He could come in handy later down the line."

"Or he could become a liability sooner than later down the line."

"Do you want him out of the picture?" said Powell.

"If it can be done with one hundred percent certainty," said McCall. "It sounds like he's having some doubts about our intentions. If we try to wipe him away, and he survives—he might examine all his options. One of which exposes us to direct FBI scrutiny."

"Understood," said Powell.

"I hope so," said McCall, lingering over the call.

He'd just received an encrypted message from their client on his cell phone.

"You haven't hung up," said Powell.

"Observant," said McCall, accessing the encrypted application. "Give me a moment."

His phone, which had been specially configured to receive and send messages from this single application, revealed the message. CONCERNED ABOUT SACRAMENTO AND FALLS CHURCH FAILURES. EXECUTE ORDER 66. SIMULTANEOUS IF FEASIBLE. Order 66, a *Star Wars* reference his client had previously connected to a request he hadn't expected to "execute" until at least late November.

"Jeremy?"

"Yes?"

"I'm going to send you a list of targets. O'Reilly must somehow be connected to our client. They referenced Raul's failed assassination attempt, along with the Sacramento fiasco," said McCall. "We're in clean-sweep mode."

"Got it," said Powell. "I'll set the machine in motion."

"The sooner the better," said McCall. "And the closer together the better. Per our client's request."

CHAPTER 12

Mann surveyed the ruins of what had once been a several-thousand-square-foot Spanish villa–style home with vaulted ceilings and twenty-foot-high windows facing the hillside to the north. It had taken first responders most of the day to sift through the near-total destruction for the remains of the agents consumed by the devastating explosion. The good news was that they'd recovered all the bodies. The bad news was that only two of the two dozen or so agents who had entered the structure that morning had survived, and one of those two was still fighting for her life at a nearby hospital. At least a half dozen agents who had been just outside the house, on the circular driveway, faced the same uphill battle. So, for all practical purposes—not good news.

Which was why he made sure his team didn't show any signs of excitement or cheer when they found Raul's computer, mostly intact, in the rubble. Rocha placed it in a weatherproof duffel bag and casually walked it back to their vehicles. They'd spent the rest of their time so far searching for thumb drives, hard drives, spare phones, paper logs. Anything that might shed some light on the role Raul played and where they might find him. Fortunately for everyone involved in the explosion's aftermath, the detonation had not resulted in a fire that would have burned the structure to ashes. Interestingly, Raul had shut off the gas to the house. Another data point to ponder.

His phone buzzed in his hand. He'd been using it to take pictures of the wreckage and their removal of any evidence. A quick glance at the phone screen surprised him. Director James. Shit. ARTEMIS was finished if James bypassed O'Reilly.

"Director James?" he answered, hoping it was O'Reilly using her office phone.

"How are things out there, Garrett?"

Not exactly the question he'd expected.

"Bad. Worse than it looks in the media," said Mann.

"That's what I figured," she said. "Are you making any progress?"

"We found a computer with an intact hard drive, but I don't have an update on what it contains. We're still looking for anything else that might point us in the right direction," said Mann. "The sun is about to go down. They're setting up lights so the various forensic teams can work through the night."

"I need you back in DC immediately," said James.

"So, this is the end?"

"End of what?" said James.

"ARTEMIS."

"No. You didn't hear?" said James.

"Hear what?"

"Shit. I thought you'd been contacted. My bad," said James. "Dana O'Reilly was attacked inside her apartment about an hour ago. She survived but sustained life-threatening injuries. Before she passed out, Dana told police officers that her attacker was either a Latino or Hispanic male in his midforties. Possibly early fifties. She used the words *professional hitman* to describe him."

"Raul?"

"If that's the name of the man who owns the Sacramento house— sounds like a match," said James.

"She never mentioned the name Raul?" said Mann.

"O'Reilly kept things close to the vest when it came to your task force," said James. "Probably for the better. A little plausible deniability isn't a bad thing now and then."

"I suppose not," said Mann. "So. You're not dismantling ARTEMIS?"

"The opposite. I'm expanding your budget, authority, and roster. But I need to talk to you in person," said James. "Dana wanted to meet me outside tonight, instead of talking about ARTEMIS in either of our offices."

"I think I understand why," said Mann. "Today's explosion—"

"Save it for our face-to-face," said James.

"When?"

"I'm in the process of arranging an executive jet to fly you out of Sacramento International Airport. Head there right away. I'll pass you the details shortly. I'm headed to the hospital now to check on Dana," said James.

"All right. I'm on my way," said Mann. "What are Dana's odds?"

"It's hard to say," said James. "She was stabbed in the lower abdomen, which appears to be the primary concern. Her attacker also stabbed her straight through one of her calf muscles. She crawled away with the knife embedded."

"Jesus," said Mann.

"She also took two bullets to her other leg," said James.

"How the hell did she survive?"

"Apparently, she managed to fire the pistol in her ankle holster, hitting her attacker at least once. Probably twice. Police followed a blood trail one block north to an empty parking space on the street," said James.

"Ankle holster?" said Mann. "I didn't know that was still a thing."

"Neither did I. Especially for a headquarters agent."

"She's one tough cookie," said Mann. "I've heard some stories."

"We all have. See you when you land," said James, ending the call.

Five minutes later, he was on the road, heading to the airport with a random FBI agent from the Sacramento field office at the wheel. Not only did Mann want to keep his entire team working on evidence retrieval, but he also needed to discreetly reach out to Serrano without their knowledge. He couldn't risk the chance that the team member driving him to the airport, and listening to his conversation, was working against him somehow. Mann called Serrano, who answered immediately.

"Are you at the new location?" said Mann.

"Yes. We just settled in," said Serrano. "Are you sure this was necessary? The last place was perfect. This isn't ideal."

"We can work on a more ideal situation later," said Mann, keeping his conversation as generic as possible.

"Is someone with you?" said Serrano.

"I'm on the way to the airport to meet with Director James," said Mann. "Deputy Director O'Reilly was attacked in her apartment tonight. James says it might be connected to today's bombing."

"Raul. Understood," said Serrano. "Is ARTEMIS done?"

"James is expanding every aspect of the task force," said Mann.

"That's good news," said Serrano. "But where does that leave me and my team?"

"I'm going to test the waters with James. If the water feels warm, I may read her in to the full situation."

"Be careful with that," said Serrano.

"I will," said Mann. "For now, you should sit tight and make the best of your new situation. If all goes well tonight, we'll get it fixed."

"We'll be fine," said Serrano.

"I figured you would," said Mann. "One last thing before I let you go. With the department's renewed focus on the task force, I anticipate the need for more assistance in the field. Can you think of any volunteers willing to spend some time with us?"

"I can think of a few," said Serrano.

"Excellent," said Mann. "We'll take good care of them while they're with us."

"I hear that bowling is a popular team activity," said Serrano, indirectly suggesting they use the money they'd found at the underground facility to incentivize them.

"I couldn't agree more," said Mann. "Make sure to mention it."

"Watch your back," she said, before disconnecting the call.

Watch your back. Hadn't he said the same thing to O'Reilly earlier today? He gave the driver a quick glance. Nothing. Same poker face. The guy hadn't said a word to him, which told Mann everything. The narrative circulating through the Sacramento field office somehow allocated some of the blame for today's tragedy to ARTEMIS. Maybe they were right. Maybe someone on his team had tipped off the FBI—along with ICE and the ATF—not knowing what awaited whoever showed up at Raul's house.

He'd crossed Serrano's people off the list. If one or more of her colleagues had turned on ARTEMIS, they would have shot Serrano and whoever else wasn't involved and disappeared with the money-stuffed bowling bags. Unless Serrano had pulled off the greatest deception of all time and had answered his call from Mexico a few million dollars richer, one of the task force members was behind today's inexplicable string of setbacks. But why? Money? The same theoretical scenario applied. At any point in the last few days, the traitor could have killed everyone while the team's guard was down and run off with the bowling bags.

Was anyone on the team that desperate? Was three to four million dollars worth a lifetime of looking over your shoulder? It wouldn't be hard to figure out who wasn't in the pile of bodies. Unless the plan all along had been to lure them into Raul's mansion and blow up the team, the conspirator hanging back at the last moment for some reason. That would require some level of complicity and cooperation with Raul or the people behind the underground facility. Why let the massacre proceed if ARTEMIS had been sidelined and replaced by the Sacramento field office?

No. That couldn't be it. So back to the original question: Why? Had the organization behind the facility somehow orchestrated a leverage operation against ARTEMIS within a few days of their raid? Their roster wasn't exactly a secret. If this still-unidentified group had managed to turn one of his agents so quickly, ARTEMIS was up against a power-house with the confidence to blow up a few dozen FBI agents and sanction the assassination of an FBI deputy director. The kind of confidence generated by unlimited resources, reach, and influence. The opposite of what Mann had at his fingertips.

PART II

CHAPTER 13

Audra Bauer raised the pair of binoculars she normally used for bird-watching to check on the speedboat that had slipped into her creek about an hour ago and anchored a few hundred yards east of her dock. No change. She'd been up since O'Reilly's message arrived five hours ago, sipping espresso and keeping an eye on the approaches to her house. She hadn't spoken with O'Reilly in a few years. Hadn't seen her since David's funeral. O'Reilly had stood as far back in the cemetery as possible while Bauer's husband was lowered into the ground, but close enough to catch her eye.

That's how O'Reilly worked. There—but not there. Which was probably how she'd not only survived but thrived for so long at the FBI. Especially during the True America years, when anyone not deemed loyal to the party was either fired or demoted. Some had been out-right targeted for murder, which was how Audra's husband had died. Protecting her from True America's wrath. She'd been on the short list of people who knew too much about their past. And when push came to shove, they sent an assassination team to erase her. Was she facing the same situation tonight?

She didn't know. Bauer was literally and figuratively in the dark, at three in the morning. O'Reilly wasn't taking her calls or answering her texts. Maybe she should reach out to Farrington for help. Or was she just being paranoid? No such thing in her experience. And the boat had arrived around two in the morning. Nothing normal about that. But it still crossed her mind. The human brain had an infinite capacity to try to dismiss the obvious. To play Bob Marley's "Three Little Birds" in the background, on repeat.

Don't worry. About a thing. Except she was worried. O'Reilly wouldn't have triggered this alert without a reason, or without answering her calls and messages. Until proven otherwise, she had to assume her life was in jeopardy. Maybe she shouldn't have been sitting so close to the window overlooking the water. Then again, thermal imaging couldn't see through cameras, and she'd never turned a light on in the house after receiving O'Reilly's message. Bauer had been seated on this recliner, facing southeast, for five hours, minus the few times she slinked away to make another espresso—in total darkness.

She sipped the last of the latest round of espresso, which had gone cold in the small cup, before raising her binoculars again. The boat was headed in her direction. Shit. Her first instinct was to get in her car and drive away, but wouldn't they have thought of that? One shooter standing a few feet outside her garage could riddle her car with bullets the moment she backed out. Even a team of idiots could pull that off without much thought.

Or was she overthinking this? If they didn't know about the distress message sent by O'Reilly, they'd have no reason to assume she'd suspect any danger. She should be asleep in her bed, protected by the usual array of break-in deterrents. Maybe a few motion-activated exterior lights. A smart enough team would send someone to the front of the house, just in case she managed to slip out. She needed David. He'd know what to do. He knew exactly what to do when True America came knocking several years ago—and it cost him his life. He'd willingly paid that price to keep her alive. She'd never forget that. Which was why she had no intention of backing down.

Bauer had honored his death by doing her duty and destroying the scourge that had infected the country. Or so she had thought. If True America was back, she'd face it head-on. Like her husband had. She slipped out of the recliner and grabbed the CZ Scorpion EVO 3 submachine gun on the couch next to her, along with a small backpack containing spare magazines and a set of night vision goggles.

She exited the house via a side door unobservable from the water and threaded her way along the western edge of her property to a position where the long dock met land. If they were stupid enough to tie up to her dock and approach the house, she'd engage them here—at point-blank range. If they had a brain cell among them and beached their boat on the far eastern side of her property, she'd open fire on them as they moved across her backyard toward the house.

She'd practiced extensively with this weapon at ranges well in excess of the forty feet or so to the other side of her property. If they landed out of sight on either of the properties adjacent to hers, she'd disengage and slip into the water. Live to fight another day. Shortly after crouching in the bushes, she spotted the boat's dark silhouette plying through the silky black water—headed straight for the end of the dock. The boat moved silently, undetectable over the low din of crickets and other nocturnal insects. They must have switched to an electric motor for their final approach.

Three people dressed in street clothes and wearing black watch caps hopped off the boat the moment it pulled alongside the front of the dock, one of them aiming a suppressed rifle toward the house, while the other two tied the boat to the end posts. Once the boat was secured, they unrolled and lowered the edges of their caps, turning the head covering into balaclava-style, eye-and-mouth-hole ski masks, and moved in a tight wedge formation up the dock. Could this be some kind of rescue mission? They reminded her of Farrington's people. Swift. Efficient. Quiet. Professional. The last thing she wanted to do was kill friendlies sent to help. But why would they have waited? And why the masks? They could have knocked on her door or called first. One familiar face and she would have welcomed them with open arms.

She waited for them to pass, before removing her phone and navigating to her home-management app. A few screen presses later, a light on one of her nightstands illuminated her bedroom and part of the second-floor deck. All three of the intruders crouched, shifting their rifles toward the light, two of them frantically whispering back and forth in Spanish. She didn't catch the full conversation, but she heard *mate a la puta*. Kill the bitch. Which sealed the deal. They weren't friendlies. Bauer triggered the IR beam transmitter attached to one of the Scorpion's rails and a green beam shot forward, mimicking the trajectory of any bullet she fired.

They took a few moments to coordinate whatever attack they intended, before setting off for the house. Once they were in motion, she emerged from the bushes and fired three bullets into each of their backs, knocking them to the grass. Knowing full well that the Scorpion's 9mm bullets wouldn't penetrate body armor if they wore it, she advanced on them, firing two bullets at a time into each of them, pinning them to the ground, as they tried to crawl away—until she was close enough to hit each of them in their unprotected head.

Four rounds. The first two hit their marks, the bodies immediately stopping. The third killer rolled onto his back at the last moment, and her shot thudded into the ground next to his head. While he tried to bring his rifle into the fight, her fourth bullet struck home, switching the killer off like a light bulb.

"Don't move!" hissed a voice behind her.

She wasn't going out like this. Even if they riddled her body with bullets, she would get at least one of them.

"Bauer. Lower your weapon," said a sort-of-familiar voice from the bushes just feet from where she had previously hidden herself. "It's Enrique Melendez."

"Rico?"

"*Sí*. We've been watching over your property for a few hours," said Melendez. "Apparently, you didn't need any help."

"Who said I needed any help?" she said, lowering her weapon and turning around slowly.

Melendez, still recognizable to Bauer, emerged from the brush. "Mind if I do the final honors?"

"Please," said Bauer.

The black-ops operative she'd known for close to two decades, though they'd met only a few times, walked among the three men lying on the lawn, firing a single suppressed bullet into each of their heads.

"Can't be too sure," he said, before pulling out a satellite phone and typing a quick text. "Incoming call. You'll want to take it."

Her phone buzzed, a text containing a familiar code appearing. No shit. A call came through a few moments later from an unknown number.

"Karl. What the hell is going on?"

"It appears O'Reilly hit a nerve," said Karl Berg. "After her warning, I put some people I pay well out here on high alert. They intercepted some newcomers at the local airport about an hour ago. They arrived by private jet and got into an SUV that had been delivered to the airport about fifteen minutes prior to their arrival. The SUV was intercepted on the long, empty stretch of road leading to my sanctuary. Upon close inspection of their bodies, we found signs of serious tattoo removal. Like hundreds of hours of work. These people were inked up like circus freaks at one time."

"Cartel sicarios," said Bauer, making her way over to Melendez, who motioned for her to get out of the open.

"Hard to draw any other conclusion," said Berg. "But why erase their ink? And why send them after me?"

"I don't know," said Bauer. "But it's undoubtedly connected to whatever O'Reilly was working on. The facility out in New Mexico."

"Did her crew hit the facility?" said Berg.

"Word on the backstreets is yes," said Bauer.

"You haven't talked to her about it?" said Berg.

"No," said Bauer. "I haven't been able to reach her since she sent the warning."

"Shit," said Berg. "She would have answered or texted you back."

"I agree," said Bauer. "Something is off."

"Damn. I hope the CIA had the good sense to remove their seals from the doors and any agency stationery they were using back when they thought this might be a good idea," said Berg.

"Nobody seems to be panicking," said Bauer.

"What about Ritter?" said Berg. "Assuming he isn't taking a dirt nap right now."

"That's not funny," said Bauer.

"Kind of is, considering how big of an asshole he's been over the years."

"Anyway. So why is Rico here?" said Bauer. "I assume he didn't just happen to be in the area tonight, when cartel heavies showed up on your island."

"Who said it was an island?"

"You're not as invisible as you'd like to think," said Bauer.

"Clearly," said Berg. "To be entirely honest, I got a little bit spooked by your call a few days ago. The underground facility in question was one of the agency's most deeply guarded secrets—"

"But you heard of it," said Bauer. "And provided the coordinates to an entrance even its newest owners didn't know about."

"What can I say?" said Berg. "I like digging into any domestic programs the CIA has its hand in. And people like me."

"No they don't," said Bauer.

"Regardless," said Berg. "People generally open up when I suggest that things tend to go sideways when the agency works on US soil. A few expensive bourbons later, and nobody wants a repeat of what happened before. Sounds like this place falls squarely in that bucket."

"Under new ownership," said Bauer.

"Maybe," said Berg. "If a private entity took over the facility, they either did it with the agency's blessing or got coerced into turning it over. Maybe it failed and someone else saw some potential. Either way, someone either currently or formerly associated with the CIA facilitated whatever transition occurred. Ritter had a hand in the original program, whatever it was. If he's still alive, he's still involved. If he's dead, like you and I should be, this is something entirely different."

"Always full of good news," said Bauer.

"Old habits," said Berg. "What about you? Are you going to jump back into the fire or ride out the storm in safety? I have guest rooms. Warm tropical breezes. Bath-temperature water. Fresh seafood for breakfast, lunch, and dinner. Not a bad way to spend a few months until this blows over."

"What if it doesn't blow over?" said Bauer. "What if this is True America?"

"There's only so much you can do without getting yourself put on psychiatric leave," said Berg. "It's time to turn this fight over to another generation. A younger generation with the energy and will to make a difference."

"Are you dying?"

"No, I'm not dying. I just don't have it in me anymore, Audra," said Berg.

"We have a duty to help this new generation," said Bauer. "Most of them have no idea how close we came to losing everything a few years ago."

"Do you still have access to Langley?"

"I spend two to three days there every week. Advising," said Bauer. "It's a very loose arrangement."

"Not gonna lie. I miss that place," said Berg.

"It grows on you."

"Not enough to yank me out of here," said Berg. "But I have a digital Rolodex of numbers I can call, and a hard drive full of dirt on the people on the receiving end of those calls."

"Any chance you could call a certain senator?"

"I heard she retired from government service," said Berg.

"She didn't donate her fortune and go work at an orphanage in Central America," said Bauer.

"No. She didn't. But she's still in the game. On the board of every think tank and major organization in DC," said Berg. "I'll give her a call."

"Please. The FBI task force running the show is in over its head," said Bauer. "They're going to need some outside help."

"Rico and Emily are at your disposal," said Berg.

"Emily is here?"

Rico nodded. "She's out front. Looks clear."

"No offense, but they'll need more help than two operatives," said Bauer.

"I'll let you guys work things out for now," said Berg. "My first call this morning will be to the senator. I'll see what I can send your way."

"Thank you, Karl," said Bauer. "I owe you one."

"Sounds like you had things under control, but I've never been one to turn down a favor owed," said Berg, ending the call.

She shook her head and muttered, "Karl fucking Berg," before turning back to Melendez. "Who else do you have with you?"

"Gupta," said Melendez.

Bauer stifled a laugh. "Anish is still around?"

"He lives for this shit."

"Would be good to see him again. And it's good to see you," said Bauer, going in for a hug. When she let go, she asked, "What's the status of the rest of your people?"

"Spread out across the world," said Melendez. "It's a shell of what it used to be, but we still pack a punch."

"How many could you assemble?"

"One. Maybe two," said Melendez. "Most of them are either in deep cover or deep shit. I could reach out to LA."

"Decker's people?" said Bauer.

"Garza and Rip might be available," said Melendez. "But I have no idea if they've kept up to speed. They've moved on—to more survivable work."

"I can't blame any of them," said Bauer. "We've all done the same. What's Rich up to these days?"

"Holding the last remnants of Sanderson's program together," said Melendez. "Not many of us left. It's been quiet out there since our last get-together. People have moved on."

"That's always what our enemies count on, isn't it?" said Bauer.

"That's why I'm still here. Same with Emily," said Melendez. "These traitors are like cicadas."

"Except there's no predicting when they'll emerge again," said Bauer.

"Right. But they always come back. That's the one thing we can count on."

"Just in time for the election."

"Damn. I didn't even think of that," said Melendez. "Maybe we should set an alarm one year out from every election. Start shaking the trees to see which scumbags fall out."

"If only it was that easy," said Bauer. "Where's Gupta?"

"On his way," said Melendez. "He's been listening to our conversation."

"I need him to find O'Reilly," said Bauer. "That's where we'll start. Figure out how we can assist the FBI task force working on this."

"He just found her," said Melendez. "Inova Fairfax hospital. Level-one trauma center. She's in bad shape."

"Then let's get moving," said Bauer. "She needs all of the support we can give her."

CHAPTER 14

Garrett Mann followed Executive Assistant Director Camilla James onto
the elevator. She'd met him in the lobby a few minutes after the Escalade
that had picked him up at Dulles International Airport dropped him
off at the main entrance at 3:45 in the morning. The hospital made an
impression, the entrance lobby a three-story atrium of blue-green tinted
glass illuminated from the interior. The rest of the hospital, a modern-
istic structure reaching several stories high, was lit from the outside.

With an array of exterior colors and more glass than most city sky-
scrapers, it looked more like a sprawling, multibuilding corporate headquarters for a Fortune 500 tech company. But Inova Fairfax Medical
Campus in Falls Church was anything but a fancy day care for upwardly
mobile Millennials and Gen Z'ers. It was a state-of-the-art medical
treatment center.

Dana O'Reilly had without a doubt made her own luck tonight,
escaping an expert assassin through sheer determination, endurance,
and skill. But the fact that her apartment sat less than two miles from
Inova's level-one trauma center had probably saved her life. From what
James had told him, paramedics lost her vital signs while pushing her
through the emergency room doors. The expert doctors and nurses
inside brought her back to life less than a minute later. Things had been
touch and go ever since.

"How is she?" said Mann, now that they were alone.

"Not good, but better," said James. "Slow improvement. The doctors said this was a good sign."

"She's a fighter," said Mann. "If the stories about her out there are even half-true, she'll pull through."

"That's what everyone keeps telling me," said James.

"Who's everyone?"

"You'll see," said James.

Interesting. When they reached the ICU floor, two FBI SWAT agents dressed in full tactical gear approached the elevator door as it opened. They immediately stopped and backed off the moment they saw James. Several more agents, some fully geared up like the two who guarded the elevator, others in suits or plain clothes, made themselves obvious up and down the hallway from the elevator lobby. Another cluster sat or stood in the hallway to their right, three doors down from the elevator.

"Glad to see the FBI is taking this seriously," said Mann.

"You have no idea," said James. "This has been a day like no other."

"I assume she's still under sedation?" said Mann.

"Yes. This'll be a short visit," said James. "We have business to discuss. But don't let me rush you out."

"I'm not the sitting-vigil type," said Mann. "More like the 'pay your respects and get out of the way' type. Shit. Maybe that wasn't the best choice of words."

The agents crowding the door made room for them.

"I know what you were trying to say," said James, before opening the door.

Two more agents in tactical gear, rifles at the ready, eased up when the door revealed James. They weren't taking any chances. Despite the fact that agent after agent had likely reported that they were en route, they had orders to vet the situation with their own eyes. Communications could be spoofed.

"Not taking any chances, are you?" said Mann.

"Nope," said James. "My orders."

Mann turned his attention to the ICU bed, where O'Reilly lay attached to dozens of wires and tubes. Something felt off.

He glanced around the room, noting a floor-to-ceiling curtain along the wall at the far-right corner of the room.

"That's not her," said Mann.

"Impressive," said James. "We had the hospital cut a doorway into the adjoining room. A highly unusual request for one of our more unusual days. Dana is in the adjacent room. Follow me."

One of the agents in tactical gear spoke quietly into her radio, presumably granting them access. James pushed the curtain aside and led him inside, revealing a mirror image of the room they'd just left. Mann immediately stopped, surprised to see former FBI Director Ryan Sharpe in a chair next to O'Reilly's ICU bed. He vaguely recognized the woman standing next to Sharpe. CIA. He wasn't sure how he knew that, but he'd seen her face before. The sole SWAT agent in the room made his way past them, disappearing through the curtain. Mann glanced at the door to the hallway, noticing that it had been reinforced with ballistic plates and a variety of anti-entry mechanisms.

"Former Director Ryan Sharpe. Audra Bauer. This is Garrett Mann. ARTEMIS task force leader," said James. "As we discussed, he reported directly to Dana. And his recent discovery out in the middle of New Mexico appears to have unleashed this latest rash of unprecedented attacks against the FBI."

The two nodded.

"We'll give you some time alone, if you need it," said Bauer.

"She's gonna pull through this. I'd rather get down to business, so we can make whoever did this pay," said Mann.

Ryan Sharpe stifled a laugh. "No wonder O'Reilly took this guy under her wing. They're like bookends."

"They are," said Bauer.

"Is that a good thing?" said Mann. "And pardon my manners, Director Sharpe. The FBI is a better place because of you. I think I speak for all of us—"

"Platitudes are not one of Dana's strong suits," said Sharpe, cutting him off. "But I appreciate your words. And to answer your question, it's a good thing. Dana's no-nonsense, fair approach to her job served the Bureau and the country well. We worked together for most of her career. So, keep it up."

"Thank you, sir," said Mann.

"Just keep him off the cocktail party circuit," said Sharpe. "Dana has a way of clearing a room with her frank observations and blunt conversation style."

"Sounds familiar," said James.

"All right. I'm gonna head out," said Sharpe, getting up. He put a hand on Bauer's shoulder. "I'll make sure they provide the best security possible for you."

"I appreciate it," said Bauer, patting his hand. "Good seeing you again, even under these circumstances."

Sharpe made his way over to the curtain, where he shook Mann's and James's hands. "Don't hesitate to reach out for help. I don't know what I can swing these days, but whatever I can do to help you get to the bottom of this—count me in."

"If this is what I think it is," said Bauer, "we may ask you to swing for the fence."

"Batter up," said Sharpe.

"Thank you, sir," said James.

Mann nodded, repeating James's words, before Sharpe slipped through the curtain. Bauer broke the silence a few moments later.

"I may be able to offer you some help. Off-the-books kind of help, if that's something you might be interested in."

"Let's go somewhere else to talk," said James.

"Agreed," said Bauer.

"Yes," said Mann, wondering how this help might impact Serrano's crew.

Her team had proven to be a serious force multiplier and decisive success factor when it came to taking down the New Mexico facility and moving the investigation forward, but if the evidence at Raul's house hadn't been irretrievably damaged . . . the investigation might stop dead in its tracks if Rocha couldn't pull any more information from the corrupted and spotty files taken from the underground facility, and Serrano's team would no longer serve any purpose.

"Give me a minute?" said Mann.

"Take all the time you need," said Bauer.

Mann took a minute to stand next to O'Reilly, wishing her a speedy recovery. What else could he do? Words of encouragement? Could she hear them, even unconsciously? If she could, he had a message for her.

"We're going to mess these people up, Dana," said Mann. "Like seriously fuck them up. You have my word on that. Stay strong."

He squeezed her hand, careful not to dislodge any of the tubes keeping her alive. How the hell had she survived? Mann rejoined James and Bauer in the adjacent room, before the three of them made their way toward the elevator lobby. They passed the elevator and entered a room designed for the families of ICU patients. Comfortable couches, recliners, a soft drink dispenser, a complimentary snack bar, and the kind of coffee maker that you find in fancy hotels. Any drink you want, at a digital screen finger press. Mann made a beeline to the coffee machine and hit "Cappuccino," the machine whirring to life.

"We didn't kick anyone out of here, did we?" said Mann.

"No," said James, nodding at the SWAT agent standing in the doorway, who shut the door.

Audra Bauer didn't waste time. "I'm retired, but still consult at Langley a few days a week. I was deputy director of the National Clandestine Service at one point, under Thomas Manning. Among other things.

"Camilla. Garrett. The bottom line is that I was attacked tonight, similar to Deputy Director O'Reilly, except she passed along a warning a few hours earlier that saved my life. The same warning was passed along to another career CIA officer who worked directly under me within the NCS. An attempt was made on his life as well, but they never got close to him."

"What the hell is going on?" said James.

"I don't know, but there's a common thread to these—" said Bauer, suddenly going quiet.

"What's wrong?" said Mann.

"Ryan Sharpe. Shit. I'm an idiot. You need to scramble a team to secure Sharpe immediately," said Bauer.

"He wasn't attacked," said James.

"Just trust me," said Bauer. "He knows more than O'Reilly."

James bolted for the door, yanking it open when she reached it. "Who do we have in the main lobby?"

"Nobody," said the agent. "We have a rapid response team sitting in an SUV just outside the main entrance."

"Deploy them immediately," said James. "They need to grab former Director Sharpe the moment he steps off the elevator and bring him back up to this floor."

"Copy that," said the agent, before barking an order over his radio.

In all the excitement, Mann almost missed Bauer making a call.

"Sharpe is on his way down."

Wait. What? Mann drew his pistol and pointed it at Bauer.

"What are you doing?" said James.

"She has people on Sharpe," said Mann. "She just made a call."

"What?" said James.

"I can explain," said Bauer.

"Code Red. Lock it down," said James.

Three agents burst into the room and converged on Bauer, who protested verbally, but didn't resist physically. *Jesus. An inside job?*

"I'm on Sharpe," said Mann, already on the move.

He joined five SWAT agents waiting for the next elevator, while James cursed at her phone.

"Does anyone happen to know Ryan Sharpe's phone number?" she said.

"I do," said Audra Bauer.

Of course you do.

CHAPTER 15

Emily Miralles put down her lukewarm coffee and grabbed the backpack lying next to her, unzipping the main compartment. She got up from her seat in one of the hospital lobby's more tucked-away seating areas and headed for the elevator lobby just beyond reception. A quick nod from her partner on the other side of the vast, glass-enclosed atrium told her he was ready to back her up. He'd started moving toward the wide, sliding entrance doors to the lobby, to intercept any trouble.

So far, so good. She had made it past reception without drawing any attention. Not exactly a difficult feat at four in the morning. Sharpe should be stepping out of one of the elevators at any moment. She shifted the backpack forward so she could quickly access the compact submachine gun inside. Four spare magazines for the MP5K sat tucked into interior pouches next to the weapon. A fifth was tucked into her rear pocket, covered by her windbreaker.

She stopped just inside the elevator lobby and slipped into the shadows of a doorway labeled MAINTENANCE. Out of sight from both the elevators and front desk, she waited. One of the elevators dinged a few moments later. Footsteps clicked against the tile floor, and the elevator door shut. She pressed against the wall. If he noticed her, he might bolt. He was a former director of the FBI, not some unassuming relative of someone in the ICU heading outside for a smoke.

A deep crunch hit her ears, followed by the sound of shattering glass. An explosive shock wave rippled through the elevator lobby, changing the air pressure and popping one of her ears. She instantly processed the series of events. A bomb had detonated outside the main entrance. Miralles sprang into action, turning left out of the doorway to find Ryan Sharpe crouched low and repeatedly pressing the elevator button. The moment they locked eyes, he reached for his left ankle. She had the compact MP5K out of the backpack and aimed at him before he could lift his pant leg. Miralles didn't bother extending the folded stock.

"Director Sharpe? I'm working with Audra Bauer," said Miralles. "She just called me. I'm going to make sure you get onto that elevator safely. And that's all. You go straight back to the fourth floor. Understood?"

"Who are you?" said Sharpe.

"I'm Emily. I work with Richard Farrington. Enrique Melendez is covering the main entrance. Do you remember that name?"

"Yes. I remember yours, too," said Sharpe. "What the hell just happened?"

"I think someone just blew up the SUV carrying the FBI's rapid response team."

"Shit. They're cleaning house," said Sharpe.

"Who?"

"True America," said Sharpe.

The reception area's automatic entry doors slid open, a team of four wearing ski masks rushing inside in a tight formation. Miralles turned the MP5K in their direction and fired several short bursts, emptying her magazine. The elevator door next to Sharpe opened, followed immediately by another one closer to the reception area.

"Go!" she said, dropping her weapon.

From the limited briefing she'd received from Bauer, she understood what was about to go down. Nobody who stepped off that elevator would be happy to see a Latina woman holding a submachine gun near the former FBI director. She raised her hands as Sharpe stepped into the empty elevator. The door closed, moments before five SWAT agents and a suit rushed out of the other elevator. They immediately tackled her and pinned her to the ground. More accurately, she let them do it.

"We have a suspect in custody in the elevator lobby," said one of the agents into his radio. "Proceeding to secure the main entrance."

"It's not safe," said Miralles. "They took out your team in the SUV."

The agent essentially sitting on her pressed his rifle to her temple. "Not another fucking word out of you."

The agent in the suit glanced toward the reception area, then back to her.

"Cuff her and get her upstairs," he said. "The rest of you secure the main entrance."

"I'm telling you—" she started, before all hell broke loose.

CHAPTER 16

Automatic gunfire erupted in the reception area, bullets snapping through the elevator lobby, ricocheting off the walls, and skipping along the tile floor. Heavier caliber—7.62mm if Mann had to guess, and they didn't seem to be worried about counting bullets. He turned to face the reception area. One of the agents headed toward the reception area spun in place, the other agent quickly grabbing him and pulling him to the elevator they'd just exited and pounding the button next to the door with his fist. Mann drew his pistol and searched for targets.

Behind him, the woman yelled, "I'm with Bauer! We're friendlies. Sharpe can confirm this!"

"We have a breach at the main entrance," said the agent on top of her. "Rapid response team is down. I say again—"

Mann glanced over his shoulder in time to see the agent go limp, slumping to the side. The woman under him scurried to the closest elevator door and pulled out a phone. Bullets punched the air inches from Mann's head, forcing him to take cover with the agent who had just dragged his wounded colleague into an open elevator. He risked a look into the hallway, seeing the woman pull the dead agent who had fallen off her toward the limited cover provided by the recessed elevator door. He raised his pistol but didn't have a shot—a hail of bullets pressing him back into the elevator. The door started to close, but Mann jammed his foot against one of the door bumpers, keeping it open.

"Is he stable?" said Mann, nodding at the wounded agent.

"I don't know," said the agent. "He's losing a lot of blood."

"We'll send him up to the ICU," said Mann. "Can't think of a better place. Unfortunately, that means we give up the elevator."

"Let's do it," said the agent.

"Let them know he's coming," said Mann, peeking out of the elevator toward the reception area.

He caught a quick glimpse of a man firing an AK-style weapon. Mann couldn't resist. He snapped off two shots, the bullets striking empty space where the man had just stood. A long burst of gunfire replied, a few of the bullets striking the metal doorframe above his foot. The downed agent's radio crackled to life.

"This is Emily Miralles, reporting from the elevator lobby. Audra Bauer requested my presence here tonight, to bolster security. The FBI rapid response team outside has been neutralized by an explosive device. I placed Ryan Sharpe in an elevator and sent him back up to your position on the fourth floor. The FBI team sent to secure Sharpe has been reduced to four agents. None of which have made it out of the elevator lobby. They're holding on for now, but the volume of gunfire coming from the reception area is intense. AK-47s. Possibly drum-fed weapons. Do not send any more agents down the main elevators. They'll get stuck like the rest. Seek an alternate approach."

"Copy," said a female voice that sounded like James. "We have reinforcements on the way."

"Make sure they don't charge in like cowboys. Things are chaotic down here," said Miralles.

"Should I cut this off?" asked the agent next to him.

"No. I want to hear this," said Mann.

A long pause ensued, before James came back on the net. "Copy that. Is Bauer clean?"

"Who is this?" said the woman hiding behind the elevator door next to them.

"Dana O'Reilly's boss. Camilla James."

"Yes. Bauer is clean. We saved her from an assassination attempt a few hours ago. Well. She actually saved herself, but we were there," said Miralles. "She didn't mention that?"

"No," said James.

"Fucking CIA and their secrets," said Miralles. "It's a miracle any of us are still alive."

"Are you sure you don't need immediate backup?" said James.

"Yes. I have a colleague in the reception area, ready to spring into action with the agents you already sent. At the minimum, we can prevent them from accessing these elevators," said Miralles. "Just pass the word to your people. They tried to arrest me. We can clean this up in a few minutes if your agents give us tactical control of the situation."

"Do it now. All stations. This is Executive Assistant Director Camilla James. The operative with you in the elevator lobby, along with any colleagues she identifies, are to be considered friendlies. Listen to them. They know what they're doing."

A few moments after the agents still in the fight acknowledged James's statement, a woman piled into the elevator, carrying a bloodied M4 rifle and a few rifle magazines—presumably taken from one of the downed agents in the elevator lobby.

"I'm Emily," she said. "We need to get out of here before they start tossing grenades."

He hadn't thought about that. Grenades in this tight space would shred them to pieces if they didn't shut the doors and flee, surrendering the elevator lobby to the hostile force.

"And this guy needs medical attention," said Miralles.

"We were about to send him up," said Mann.

"We'll send him as soon as we break out of here," said Miralles, placing three rifle magazines on the elevator floor next to him. "You might want to trade your pistol for this agent's rifle. And grab his radio."

"Right," he said, disconnecting the agent's rifle from the one-point sling connecting it to his body armor.

Mann removed the radio from the pouch on the upper back of the agent's vest, disconnecting the wire connected to the headset.

"Rico. What's your status?" said Miralles, after tapping her watch.

"Who's Rico?" said Mann.

"Rico Melendez. My colleague in reception."

She listened for a few seconds, before nodding.

"He's waiting for them to make their move toward the elevators before he engages," said Miralles. "He counts four hostiles. AK-47s. All drum-fed."

"That's a lot of firepower," said Mann.

"Yeah. But we can even the odds," she said. "He can drop their numbers in half without a problem."

"Can he hold his own?" said Mann. "They might have backup waiting outside or flanking. Hard to imagine they left their six exposed."

He sensed some hesitation before she answered.

"He can hold his own," said Miralles. "Even if they throw another team into the fray."

"Then we should take the initiative," said Mann. "Force them to react. Before they start tossing grenades."

"I have an idea. You and I will swap positions with the two agents across the hallway. I'll drop halfway across, behind one of your downed people, pretending to take a hit. The movement might get them to make a hasty decision to charge forward. My guy will cut most of them down the moment they move."

The agent hesitated, spending time they didn't have on a decision.

"Look. If my guy opens fire first, he'll reduce their numbers, but they'll just tighten their position and call in their reinforcements. If they have any," said Miralles. "That's the gamble. If they bring in another four-person team, he'll have his hands full."

"But he can hold them off," said the agent. "Until backup arrives."

"I suppose so," said Miralles. "Both options seem solid."

"No offense, but I like the option where we all don't run through a wall of bullets," said Mann.

"I hate when I might be wrong. We'll do this your way," she said, before triggering her radio. "Rico. Count to ten and take down as many as you can. We'll press forward and take better positions in the reception area. We're essentially useless in here."

She paused for her colleague's reply before addressing Mann and the agent.

"I need you to listen closely and pass this on to the other agents. When I yell *go*, we press forward and seek covered positions outside the elevator lobby. Shoot and scoot. Do not stop. Be ready to focus our fire on reinforcements coming through the entrance. My guy will keep the rest busy."

"Got it," said the agent, before passing along the gist of their plan to the SWAT agents across the elevator lobby.

Miralles started counting out loud as Mann pocketed the rifle magazines and flipped the rifle selector switch to semiautomatic.

"Three. Two. One. Go! Go!"

The sharp cracks of Melendez's 9mm submachine gun joined the fray, immediately stopping the storm of bullets flying through the elevator lobby. Mann followed Miralles out of the elevator, followed by the FBI SWAT agent hugging the wall. A hostile appeared to the right of the bullet-peppered main entrance sliders, firing in Melendez's direction. Mann placed the rifle sight's red dot on the target's upper thoracic area and pressed the trigger twice, just as Miralles fired a short burst. Their target tumbled backward over a chair—the lampshade next to him turning bright red.

"One target KIA," said Miralles.

The two agents on the other side of the elevator lobby fired several times, one of them turning to Mann's group. "Another one down."

"Rico. We took down another," said Miralles, before picking up the pace. "He said that's the last one inside the reception area. Let's get into position and form a perimeter to cover the entrance and the flanks."

Mann reported their progress over the FBI tactical net, receiving a quick acknowledgment from James. The group exited the elevator lobby and started to spread out, Mann following Miralles to the left, behind the reception desk. He turned to check on the agent following them, who had just turned the corner.

The agent made it a few feet, then slammed into the wall behind him. He bounced off the wall, leaving a bright-red bloodstain the size of a couch pillow. One of the larger windows to the left of the main entrance doors shattered at the same time. Mann froze in place, unsure what had just happened. Instinctively, he started to move toward the downed agent to render aid, not that it would have done any good, based on the soccer ball–size hole punched through the back of the agent's tactical vest.

Miralles yanked Mann backward by his collar and pulled him flat against the floor, moments before a second projectile exploded through the back of the reception desk, passing several inches over them. The fifty-caliber bullet took out most of the workstation, spraying them with wood and metal fragments. Staying flat against the tile floor, they crawled forward.

"Sniper. Heavy caliber. Relative gun target line three-four-zero if facing the main entrance," said Miralles. "One agent down. Report that! And tell the other agents to stay low and out of sight."

Somehow, he remembered everything she said, and passed it along.

A third bullet slammed through the reception area, covering them with debris. They kept going until they reached an open door to their left. No coordination between the two of them was necessary at this point. They slithered inside and kept crawling until they reached a second room, where they remained flat on the ground. Two hospital employees, presumably from the reception desk, lay curled up in the far corner of the space. A fourth explosion echoed through the room but didn't seem to be aimed at them.

"Rico. You still there?" said Miralles.

Mann had to infer what they discussed, which wasn't difficult.

"One is down hard. Just outside the elevator lobby," said Miralles. "The other is with me. We crawled into a back office behind reception."

Pause.

"I have an M4 with a red dot sight. Not exactly a counter-sniper weapon."

Pause.

"I'll ask," she said, before nudging Mann. "Report that the sniper is likely located approximately three-four-zero degrees relative, when directly facing the front entrance—from the inside. Angle of elevation, approximately thirty degrees. That should help them figure out where to look. And they might want to hold off on bringing in reinforcements through the front door until the sniper is neutralized."

"Got it," said Mann, before passing along her assessment of the sniper's general location.

He then addressed the two other agents, who had split off to the right when the group exited the elevator lobby, confirming that they had survived—and were hunkered down. Several long minutes later, a brief exchange of gunfire echoed in the distance. Several sharp cracks, immediately followed by a deep boom. Then a few more cracks. Mann's radio came to life.

"The backup FBI team entered through the north side of the building. They made their way to the roof and took out the sniper," said James.

"Any chance there might be two?" said Mann.

"No. They scanned extensively for heat signatures before engaging," said James. "Local law enforcement SWAT teams are a few minutes out. Head up to the fourth floor as soon as they arrive. Bring Miralles and Melendez with you. They're to be treated as friendlies."

"They are friendlies," said Mann. "Trust me on that."

CHAPTER 17

Mann felt like he might pass out. He was beyond exhausted at this point. No way he'd risk sitting down. Camilla James handed him a small paper cup filled with a thick, dark shot of espresso. The lack of any cream told him it was hospital coffee. Not that he expected anyone to venture outside to fetch anything better. Within the past two hours, the Inova Fairfax hospital had been converted into one of the most protected sites in the United States, second to the Pentagon and White House. For a good reason.

The four men who blew up the FBI team outside the hospital, and tried to assassinate Ryan Sharpe, were quickly identified as former Juárez Cartel members. Two of their faces instantly popped up on a DEA facial recognition ID program. The other two were assumed to be graduates from the New Mexico program.

"You ready?" said James.

"Yeah. So, what is this, exactly?" said Mann.

"A very informal discussion about what's what," said James. "And how we move forward."

"I need more than that."

"What do you need?" said James.

"First. I need to know where you stand," said Mann. "With O'Reilly out of the picture."

"I stand where O'Reilly stood," said James. "Fully in support of ARTEMIS."

He considered how to proceed. Full support of the task force was good, but was it good enough? He considered the presence of Miralles and Melendez. Maybe they presented an opportunity to sanction Serrano's involvement.

"Have you ever heard the name Serrano?" said Mann.

"As in the pepper?" said James.

She was either a masterful liar or had no clue about the help the task force had received from Mexico.

"No," said Mann. "What are your thoughts about Bauer's friends?"

"I'm not sure how to classify them," said James. "That part of O'Reilly's history has been erased, and Sharpe isn't exactly shedding any useful light on the subject, other than to assure me they can be trusted."

"Do you trust them?"

"I do," said James.

"Based on what?"

"Sharpe and Bauer," said James. "They vouched for them."

"How well do you trust me?" said Mann.

"O'Reilly trusted you implicitly," said James. "I trust you the same."

Here went nothing.

"The New Mexico raid required some help," said Mann. "Non-FBI help."

"Local law enforcement?" said James. "I know you formed a solid bond with the Owatonna Police Department, and other departments nearby."

He shook his head. "The serial murders throughout the Southwest shared certain characteristics and methods seen south of the border. Specifically, in and around Ciudad Juárez."

"O'Reilly briefed me on that," said James. "We didn't get any cooperation from Mexican city or state police."

"No. But we did get some help from former city and state police officers. Plus, some former members of their military," said Mann. "The New Mexico raid wouldn't have been possible without their assistance. And sacrifice."

"I didn't hear that," said James.

"I didn't say it," said Mann.

"And you'll never say it again, in front of anyone but me—and only if I bring it up first," said James.

Message received.

"Yes, ma'am."

"We're set up for a chat with Bauer and Sharpe down the hall, in one of the family lounges."

"Just Bauer and Sharpe? What about the director?"

"I don't see any reason to get Director Shale involved," said James. "Unless we want to handcuff ourselves."

"Are you saying the gloves are off as far as you're concerned?"

"The gloves are off," said James. "But we need to be smart about it. The more we can outsource, the better—for now. Which is why Bauer's off-the-books friends, and your south-of-the-border acquaintances, will be critical assets."

"They'll appreciate hearing that," said Mann.

"My name won't be mentioned. Understood?" said James.

"Understood," said Mann.

She motioned for him to follow her. "Time to try and make sense of as much of this as possible."

James led him to a lounge where Miralles and Melendez, the two operatives he'd fought alongside downstairs, sat next to Bauer and Sharpe on a functional but uncomfortable-looking, dark-blue sectional couch. He took a seat across from them. James pulled a chair from the table and set it next to Mann.

"First off," said Mann, locking eyes with Audra Bauer. "Sorry I doubted you—and pointed a gun at your head."

Bauer shook her head. "I would have done the same. You have good instincts. Almost feel like you'd be a better fit at Langley."

"Mann isn't going anywhere. We need him right where he is," said James. "Let's get down to brass tacks, as they say. How does any of this relate to you? And I don't mean that in a condescending way. You're clearly attached to tonight's events. I just want to know how you're connected, and how it relates to Special Agent Mann's task force."

Bauer turned to Sharpe, who sighed deeply before speaking.

"Being retired and having purposefully stuck my head in the sand since retirement, I don't have any specific intel to share. But I can attest to the strong likelihood that a coordinated, direct targeting of myself, Audra Bauer, and Dana O'Reilly on the same night suggests an attempt by whatever form True America has recently assumed, to erase their history. The three of us know everything there is to know about True America's multiple attempts to undermine our democracy. Each attempt more sinister than the one before. Karl Berg, a career CIA officer who worked closely with Audra Bauer to thwart their efforts, was also attacked tonight. The big question is—why now?"

"They're up to something again," said Bauer.

"I thought True America was gone?" said Mann. "There's no way they're coming back into power. Not after the hearings, investigations, and convictions. That party is dead."

"The party itself might be dead, but the idea clearly isn't," said Sharpe. "If I had to guess, they've either reinvented themselves or attached themselves to another movement—and they're afraid one of us might recognize the signs and sound the alarm."

"If there's a link between the purpose of the facility in New Mexico and this new version of True America, understanding their ultimate goal might help me connect the dots," said Mann. "What's their ultimate goal?"

"Political upheaval or worse," said Sharpe. "Fracturing the country so badly that they can seize permanent control. They've been at it for nearly two decades. Probably longer than that."

"That's truly frightening," said Mann. "Because what I saw down there is starting to make more sense."

"How?" said Bauer.

Mann didn't pause for a moment. He'd thought about this long and hard over the past several days.

"The facility was a training center designed to integrate cartel sicarios and soldiers into US society. Either to help streamline the flow of drugs through trouble spots along their main routes, by putting key tasks in the hands of loyal members who don't draw as much suspicion, or in the scenario we're discussing, to be unleashed at some point to cause chaos in the streets. If we're talking about the latter, the question is when and why?"

"With True America, it was always about political power," said Bauer.

"Chaos before the upcoming election?" said James. "Immigration reform is a top issue, for both sides of the political spectrum."

"They could re-ink and start a crime wave," said Mann.

"Re-ink?" said Bauer.

"The cartel members found dead inside the training facility showed signs of significant tattoo removal," said Mann. "Most sicarios and soldier types in these organizations have elaborate and extensive tattoos covering much of their upper bodies, often extending to the neck and face. The tattoo removal we saw focused on obviously visible parts of the body. Arms, necks, upper chest, and neckline. The face. If they were called into action to commit political violence or instigate a perceived crime wave, they could get new tattoos just before going into action."

"I thought I was done rooting out sleepers?" said Melendez.

"Think of them more like counterfeit money. If you know what to look for, you can detect a fake twenty with a specialized pen. They've been given just enough training and resources to pass as US citizens or legal immigrants—until they were activated by whoever is behind the operation. They'll do everything possible to follow the rules and not draw attention to themselves. Anything from a verbal altercation at the grocery store resulting in police involvement to a speeding ticket could ruin the show. Or we could all be overthinking this, and the Ciudad Juárez cartel is behind the current operation at the facility, trying to stay a few steps ahead of the US government's efforts to stem the flow of drugs into the US."

"They're always a few steps ahead of us," said James.

"They play the long game. There's no doubt about that," said Mann. "And depending on how long that site has been churning out graduates, they could have several hundred planted across the United States."

"Tell us more about the facility," said Sharpe. "How could one of the cartels, or any organization with bad intentions, build something like this right under our noses?"

"The CIA built it," said Bauer.

"That explains things," said Sharpe.

Bauer grimaced. "Unfortunately, I don't have specific details. Just what I was told by a very reluctant source. The program run by the CIA lasted for only a few years. The agency thought they could kidnap low-level cartel soldiers and turn them into informants. Create a network of snitches that would ultimately unravel the cartels. It didn't work. Within a year, the program showed signs of serious decay. Informants sent back to Mexico started to disappear within days of crossing the border. They either turned on the CIA or were killed. Either way, the pace picked up. By the end of the second year, it had become painfully clear that the program was no longer viable. Nearly all the informants sent south in the last few months of the program never contacted their CIA handlers, and those that did provided information that led to the death of several CIA contacts inside Mexico. The final straw was a raid to capture a major cartel boss, which turned out to be an ambush. Two CIA officers and eight SEALs went in at around two in the morning. Only their heads made it back, dropped in a contractor bag on the street outside the FBI field office in El Paso. This happened about four years ago, so it's fair to say that whatever that place became, it can't be more than three to four years old."

"I never heard about this," said Sharpe. "And I do believe I was the director of the FBI at the time."

"Neither did I," said James.

"Nobody did. The bag was intercepted before anyone working in the field office found it. The CIA knew they had a disaster on their hands," said Bauer. "And for the record, nobody here has heard about this—if you catch my drift. I was just told about it earlier tonight. I didn't know, when I passed along those coordinates."

Mann just nodded, taking her cue. The less anyone knew about the specifics of the raid, the better. Though he suspected that the more this group knew, the better. Particularly if the New Mexico facility turned out to be more than just a cartel drug trafficking investment.

"So. Fast-forward to the present. At some point over these past four years, presumably earlier than later, a private entity purchased the facility from the CIA and repurposed it. Juárez Cartel or private corporation. Unknown."

"And we're sure the CIA is no longer involved?" said Sharpe.

"As far as I know," said Bauer.

"I didn't get a sense that the CIA had a hand in what was going on down there," said Mann.

"But you're certain that the facility had been repurposed to send cartel members north," said Sharpe. "To pose as Americans, or legal immigrants? I know we've gone over this. Sorry for the redundancy."

"No need to apologize, sir. This is insanely complicated. So. To answer your question, yes," said Mann. "I've confirmed this outside of just observational evidence documented during the raid."

"What does that mean?" said James.

"Can we leave it there, ma'am?" said Mann.

Melendez chuckled. "Sounds like there may have been a survivor."

"Wait," said James. "O'Reilly never mentioned a—"

"I filed a full report with O'Reilly," said Mann. "And personally briefed her on everything we encountered, to the best of my memory."

"To the best of your memory. Understood. If you happened to remember anything you unintentionally omitted, we can discuss it later," said James. "For now, let's move on. O'Reilly and I spoke briefly yesterday. Before the explosion in Sacramento, she said your team was prepping to move on the house of a cartel member directly connected to the New Mexico facility. The next chain in stopping the rash of serial killings in the Southwest and Midwest."

"As far as we could tell, he was the last remaining serial killer we had been hunting. Part of a triad, or *La Triada*. The first had been confirmed dead by one of my highly trusted contacts in Mexico. The second member, known only as Alejandro, killed by my team in the facility. His screwup along an obscure rural road in Minnesota is what unraveled this whole thing. We pulled data from the facility server pointing to the Sacramento house, presumably owned by the third killer."

"No longer a presumption," said James.

"Correct," said Mann. "The killer's name is Raul, and we're pretty sure he's the one that attacked O'Reilly tonight."

"And set the explosives that killed our agents," said James.

"Either he set them, or whoever is behind the facility came in and prepared the trap," said Mann.

"Why would they risk this kind of exposure?" said Miralles. "He could have sanitized his house and moved on. Dead end for you. Right? Have you pulled anything else from the servers and devices in the facility? Anything useful?"

"Not yet," said Mann.

"They really wanted to take you out," said Melendez. "And everyone else in this room. I think we're looking at the True America revival tour theory. The fewer witnesses to the past and present—the better."

"Should we escalate this higher?" said James.

"No," said Bauer, without hesitation. "If this is related to some kind of political revival or reinvention for True America, we need to keep this as close to the vest as possible. Trust nobody outside this room, plus O'Reilly and a few others that spent most of their careers fighting this fight. If we've learned anything about them over the years, it's that they don't make big moves without laying the groundwork first. They corrupt, recruit, and infiltrate before acting."

"Shit. That kind of leaves me hanging in the breeze," said James.

"I wasn't going to say anything," said Bauer. "But I already did a deep dive into your background, finances, recent travel . . . the works. We developed a program over the past few years for this very reason. To vet government employees for extremist red flags."

"And?" said James.

"We wouldn't be talking with you right now if you hadn't passed with flying colors," said Bauer.

"This is some kind of CIA vetting program?" said James.

"What program?" said Bauer.

James laughed. "I can't remember my question."

Everyone else chuckled except for Mann. "This is all well and good, but where does that leave my task force? We started out hunting serial killers, and there's still one serial killer on the loose."

"With serious injuries," said James.

"But he's likely just a cog in the machine," said Bauer. "We need to expand our focus. Look at the bigger picture."

"Agreed," said Mann. "But we need to make a genuine effort to capture or kill Raul. If not, we risk losing the support of some critical assets. We can't ignore the last member of *La Triada*. Trust me when I say that this is important, for more reasons than the one I just mentioned. Once he's healed up, he'll be back in action—and none of you will be safe."

"How bad was he injured?" said Miralles.

"O'Reilly fired six bullets through her ankle holster," said James. "At least one hit home. Probably more, based on the blood trail he left."

"Do I need to ask the obvious question?" said Miralles.

"No. We issued alerts to every hospital within a two-hour driving distance of O'Reilly's apartment and came up empty," said James. "DC was busy as usual, but nobody even remotely matching Raul turned up in any of the ERs seeking medical care."

"He went underground," said Miralles. "The dark web. That's where you need to look."

"My experience with the dark web is limited," said Mann. "But I don't see how we'd do this. Anonymity is the key feature of the dark web."

"True," she said. "But we could start reaching out with requests for medical treatment. See who's out there. Maybe we'll get lucky."

"It's not a bad idea," said James. "But how many of these off-the-books doctors exist? What are we looking at in terms of personnel needed to investigate?"

"I have no idea," said Miralles. "But we have someone who can navigate these murky waters. Hack into the system and see who they're all talking to."

"Anish?" said Bauer.

"The man, the myth, the legend in his own mind," said Miralles. "If anyone can dig up something, it'll be him."

"Who are we talking about?" said Mann.

"How much help do you need taking your investigation to the next level?" said Bauer.

"A considerable amount," said Mann.

"Then you might meet him sooner than later," said Bauer. "If your boss approves."

"The more the merrier," said James. "I'm starting to see the value and genius behind outsourcing."

"As long as you don't hang any of us out to dry," said Melendez. "No offense."

"None taken," said James. "Trust is earned, and you don't know me on any real level. I'm just O'Reilly's boss, and she spent the past two decades securing your trust. I'll gladly let your guy, Anish, monitor all my communications. I'll also keep my nose where it belongs. I don't need to be involved in the day-to-day, hour-by-hour operations. But I need to be kept in the loop, only for big-picture stuff, or whatever you're comfortable sharing. I'll get you what you need, if I can. My branch doesn't have the biggest budget, but I do have some leeway. And some unique resources."

Miralles shook her head. "Someone tell me she's not cooler than O'Reilly. Please."

"I'm not cooler than O'Reilly," said James. "But until she's mission capable, I'll do my best to support all of you. Speaking of which. I have a few candidates for your team. Agents you know well, who have requested to be transferred to ARTEMIS in the past but were denied."

"Like you said. The more the merrier," said Mann. "Wallace? Vincenzo?"

"Kerri is one of them," said James. "Frank, too. Plus Chad Lianez."

Kerri Wallace worked a desk in the Chicago field office, yanked from the field and her position as second-in-command of the field office's primary response SWAT team after a bank robbery suspect she'd chased into a nearby building fell seven stories to his death. No witnesses. Just her testimony that he'd backed up in a panic after being cornered and toppled over the edge. The fact that the ledge was four feet tall and the suspect was just under six feet tall, making it virtually impossible for him to accidentally go over the side, put her behind a desk.

Frank Vincenzo worked with Jessica Mayer as a Special Surveillance Group investigator in Washington, DC, the two of them outing a Turkish diplomat who turned out to be a serial killer in the making. Mayer, being the more outspoken of the two, was put on indefinite administrative leave in the aftermath of the diplomatic fiasco, where Mann found her. Vincenzo had been retained as an investigator, but relegated to a windowless room at FBI headquarters, where he reviewed hours of video and audio collected by SSG, a task normally assigned to an investigative analyst.

Chad Lianez was a surveillance tech, like Callie Jackson, but his specialty was breaking and entering to install devices. A few years ago, he'd entered a Georgetown residence to install several listening devices and cameras, when the couple under surveillance returned hours earlier than intelligence had suggested. The SSG investigator in charge of the surveillance operation failed to warn him in time, and Lianez found himself stuck inside the target couple's brownstone. A fight broke out between the couple shortly after their return, which turned violent according to Lianez, who "felt compelled to intervene"—and beat the husband senseless.

The wife didn't press charges, or the issue, with the State Department. They left the country for Greece shortly after the altercation, where they ate grapes laced with Novichok at a restaurant near their apartment a few months later. The couple, plus five employees of the restaurant, succumbed to the nerve agent used exclusively by Russian foreign agents. Lianez was considered a legend in the business at the time, which kept him on the FBI roster, but he was sent to Des Moines, Iowa, where he kept tabs on organized crime capos who had been similarly exiled.

"I'll give them each a call and see if they're still interested," said Mann. "And make sure they truly understand what they're getting into."

"I already reached out to them, and they all said yes," said James. "I've arranged transfers and flights for them to come to DC in a few days. I just wish you or O'Reilly could meet with them when they get here."

"I'll send Jessica Mayer back to bring them up to speed," said Mann. "She worked with Vincenzo within the Special Surveillance Group. I might be here when they arrive, but I really need to get back to the rest of the team. I'll head back myself once we have a better sense of what moving forward looks like. If everyone's hunches are right, I assume we're expanding ARTEMIS's mission?"

"Only if you want to expand it," said James. "You and your *associates* have gone above and beyond the call of duty."

"I do," Mann said.

"I may be speaking out of turn," said Bauer. "But I think our friends here might be willing to lend a hand—if you decide to expand and take on the impossible."

"The impossible is our specialty," said Melendez, turning to Miralles. "Right?"

"I don't see any reason to turn down the impossible," she said. "But to be entirely frank, this sounds like a job that will eventually require more than an FBI team mostly staffed with surveillance techs, spook investigators, and forensic experts. And I say that understanding that your team managed to take down a heavily protected, covert facility. I'm just used to bringing more firepower to the party."

"I agree," said Mann. "I currently have two very skilled shooters. Operators. Whatever you call them. We leaned heavily on outside help. Competent and trustworthy help. Volunteers from Mexico. All former cops or soldiers. All victims of the horror that *La Triada* inflicted on hundreds of families in or near Ciudad Juárez."

The room went silent.

"Sorry," said Mann, looking at James. "I know I told you I wouldn't. But we all need the most accurate assessment of our capabilities, particularly to address the task force's weaknesses."

"Garrett. I understand. No need to apologize. But let's keep this and any other similarly nonregulation aspects of your task force to ourselves," said James, before turning to Miralles. "So, who can you bring to the fight?"

"Not as much as I'd like," she said. "We're spread thin. Commitments that can't be broken—easily. We have a heavy weapons specialist available. He can be here by midmorning. And our tech guy, who is actually somewhat of a legend—"

"I can attest to that," said Bauer.

"Same," said Sharpe.

"He's sitting in a van somewhere outside the hospital right now, making sure nobody makes a move on us," said Miralles. "Unfortunately, we didn't have him deployed earlier. That was my fault. He would have detected the teams before they attacked. Especially the sniper. I'm sorry about that."

"No need to apologize," said James. "I took precautions, but I didn't post snipers on the roof."

"No blame here. It is what it is," said Bauer. "Any chance our LA connection might be able to provide some help?"

Melendez shrugged. "I'll ask Farrington to reach out to them, but I wouldn't get your hopes up. Rip and Garza have settled into comfortable lives out there."

"Who are we talking about?" said Mann.

"Friends that recently answered the call," said Bauer. "And are probably still licking their wounds. I wouldn't count on them ponying up."

"It's a long shot, but worth reaching out," said Melendez.

The room quieted, everyone exhausted from the night's events. Mann eyed one of the couches, wishing he could lie down and wake up tomorrow—this whole issue resolved. Instead, he raised the paper cup he'd been holding for the past several minutes nearly upside down, willing the last remnants of espresso down the side of the cup and into his mouth. He understood how it must have looked to everyone else, but desperate times called for desperate measures. The cup gave him a dribble of caffeine.

"I plan on heading back to Sacramento later today," said Mann. "Any chance the crew based out of LA would drive or fly up to meet with me in Sacramento? I'd be willing to fly to LA, if that's more convenient for them. We're going to need all the help we can get."

"I'll get the ball rolling," said Melendez. "Hopefully, I'll hear from them before you head out. It's still zero-dark-thirty over there."

"Thank you," said Mann. "My team's plan for now is to dig through the data recovered from a computer we recovered at the Sacramento house, along with the limited data our computer forensic expert managed to salvage from New Mexico. And try to figure out where to focus our resources. I'm not gonna lie. We don't have much to go on. Capturing Raul in Sacramento was supposed to be our next stepping stone."

"Can I make a suggestion?" said Miralles.

"Sure," said Mann.

"Is it fair to say we're working together now?" she said.

"That's up to you," said Mann.

"We're working together," said Miralles. "Before we leave for the West Coast, I'd like to give our computer guy some time to look into medical providers offering their services on the dark web. If we can nail this Raul guy before he skips town, we'll satisfy your associates, which I presume will free them up to help us take the next step."

"It should," said Mann. "But I can't guarantee they'll all stick around. They have lives. Families. Children. They're in this for revenge, along with a sense of duty. But life in Mexico isn't easy for them. They've been discarded by the system, which didn't treat or pay them well in the first place. It's a big ask to suggest that they continue fighting for another country."

A country that doesn't care about them any more than their own country. He could sense where the minds in the room were going, based on his last statement. He'd investigated all the options available. Short of the State Department granting these heroes—along with their family members—green cards or some kind of instantaneous citizenship, they'd remain in limbo up here. Protected by Mann and his team, but constantly threatened by the kind of harassment raid that ICE launched on them in California. Which brought him to his next concern.

"And there's another issue," said Mann. "A critical one."

"Oh boy," said Bauer.

"Yeah. It's not good," said Mann. "I strongly suspect that a member of my team might be compromised."

"That's more than 'not good,'" said James. "That's a showstopper."

"I could be wrong, but I've dissected the events leading me to this conclusion—every way I can," said Mann. "At first, I thought O'Reilly's phone might have been tapped or her office bugged. Or maybe one of our phones had been hacked somehow? I mean, the Mexicans aren't going to turn themselves in, right? But just before we were about to leave our motel, to raid the Sacramento house, ICE shows up and threatens to kick the door in to search for illegal immigrants. They bring the FBI with them, and I speak with the SAC, who informs me that the Sacramento field office will take over the house raid."

"Holy mother," said Melendez. "Somebody saved your team."

"Not intentionally," said Mann. "Not five minutes after ICE leaves the motel, having found no illegal immigrants, the ATF shows up, looking for non-FBI-registered firearms or explosives. Admittedly, I placed fake Claymore mines on the dashboards of SUVs facing our doors, to serve as a deterrent, but I highly doubt ICE or the FBI could have scrambled a six-vehicle ATF convoy in the short time they spent at the motel. And I showed ICE that the Claymores were fake. Someone tipped them off, and it couldn't have been O'Reilly."

"Tipped them off about what?" said Sharpe.

Mann hesitated.

"Whatever you say in this room, stays in this room," said James. "We all agree. Right?"

Everyone nodded, including Sharpe, who added, "I'm retired. Not to mention the fact that Dana O'Reilly and I didn't exactly do things by the book all the time."

"True America would be running the country like the Taliban right now if you hadn't taken, how shall we say—" started Bauer.

"Let's not say," said Sharpe.

"Fair enough," said Bauer. "All I'll say is that we've all temporarily locked the rule book in the desk drawer—when it was necessary to get the job done. Sounds like this is another one of those times, especially if some form of True America is looking to make a comeback."

"So. Why did the ATF show up?" said Sharpe.

"I may have removed some weapons from the New Mexico facility," said Mann. "I never told O'Reilly, so the tip had to come from my team."

"Or the Mexicans," said Sharpe. "Maybe one of them got arrested at some point between New Mexico and the motel room raids. Offered up information."

"The Mexicans didn't know the timing of our raid. Not the exact timing. ICE arrived minutes before we were about to step off. And only one of them knew our location. There's simply no way she tipped them off. I've worked with her for over a year and trust her implicitly," said Mann.

"Did they find any unregistered weapons?" said Sharpe.

"No. Everything we took from the facility was in a different location—but that was a last-minute decision I personally and exclusively oversaw. So nobody on the team, outside of my Mexican friends, would have known that. Another reason why I think we have a rat on the team," said Mann. "We did have a heavy-barrel HK416 with us. Basically, an M27 IAR equivalent, but the ATF didn't seem to notice. Or care. They were looking for something else."

"And what might that be?" said James.

"Do you really want to know?"

"Do I?" said James, turning to Bauer and Sharpe.

Bauer shook her head, and Sharpe answered. "Probably not."

"Then we'll leave it at that," said James.

Melendez got up from his seat on the couch. "Let me get our guy working on the dark web issue. If we can nail down this Raul guy, that'll get us somewhere. He can also help you identify your mole, if you have a mole problem. He's disturbingly good at his job."

"I'll take any help I can get," said Mann. "For now, we're looking for that next step. Something to move us past the Sacramento disaster. One of my techs designed a virus that daisy-chains across devices. We traced one of the survivors from the facility back to Roswell, New Mexico, where the team that snatched Alejandro away from us in Minnesota landed a day or so before our raid. That's how we eventually ended up at the underground facility. This survivor must be linked to AXIOM."

"I wasn't aware of any of this," said James.

"I'll fill in the gaps when we're done here," said Mann. "O'Reilly played her cards closer to the chest than I do."

"Apparently," said James.

"So. The virus transmits location data via Wi-Fi or cellular connections," said Mann. "But the survivor, who we suspect is linked to AXIOM, destroyed their phone at the Roswell airport. The signal ended, but the virus managed to infect two other phones. We're still following those around the country. So far, neither has stopped anywhere interesting. Strip malls or bland, nearly vacant office buildings. If we don't get something juicier, we'll turn our attention to those locations. We're hoping that one of them will eventually make their way somewhere more consequential."

"Like the White House?" said Bauer.

Mann shrugged. "It would be informative."

"That's an understatement," said Sharpe.

James's phone rang. She took the call, listening while nodding—before shaking her head. When the call ended, she shared the news.

"No ID on the four shooters who entered the hospital. All look like former Mexican cartel soldiers. All with signs of tattoo removal."

"Jesus," said Mann.

"It gets worse," said James. "We identified the sniper. Harry Frye. Part of a very high-end mercenary crew based out of the UK. As in very expensive. They're on an extremely sensitive no-fly, no-entry list. Whoever brought them in isn't fucking around."

Bauer stifled a laugh.

"What?" said James.

"You sound just like O'Reilly," said Bauer.

"I was thinking the same thing," said Sharpe.

"I did my research before hiring her," said James. "CIRG can't be run by a yes-man or woman. It's the most diverse and unique branch of the Bureau. Hostage rescue and negotiation. Aviation units. SWAT. Behavioral analysis teams. Violent Crime Apprehension Program. Armed surveillance teams. ARTEMIS. It's a jumble of highly specialized agents working across a few dozen disciplines. She's perfect for the job, based on her personality and experience."

"But who's running that show while she's out of action?" said Mann.

"I am," said James. "So, if you need something—ask and you shall receive."

"Okay," said Mann. "Marching orders. I'll stick around a little longer and see if we can find Raul. If we find him, we transport him to our safe house out west. I'd like to put him in the same room with someone he tormented in New Mexico. See if we can play them off each other."

"Once again," said James. "No idea what you're talking about."

"You probably don't want to know," said Miralles.

Mann continued, turning to Melendez and Miralles. "Next step is cleansing ARTEMIS. I'll take any help I can get vetting my people. Once we have a clean team, we can turn to figuring out where to focus our attention—to get ahead of whatever insanity that facility was designed to unleash on the United States."

"Sounds reasonable to me," said Melendez. "Once we get our tech guy working with your team, he'll quickly sniff out your internal problem."

"Why do I get the impression that I'm just going to have to take a back seat and let this all play out," said James.

"That's kind of how it has always worked," said Sharpe. "All they require is a light touch from time to time, to remind them that there are limits."

"We've been doing this for as long as I can remember, ma'am," said Melendez. "We won't hang you out to dry. We just ask that you give us the same consideration, when things get ugly."

"Agreed. Sounds like I'm in good hands," said James. "Even if my chances of a promotion, or simply remaining employed by the FBI, have just been cut in half."

Sharpe shook his head. "Don't count yourself out. This current crew is ten times less toxic than the one that salvaged my career and cleared the way for me to be appointed director. I honestly never expected it, but having a direct hand in taking out the trash tends to attract attention. Especially when that trash threatens the very fabric of our democracy."

"Keep me in the loop, Garrett," said James. "I don't care how bad you think the news might be. The only way this works is if we work together. We're past the point of keeping secrets. I plan on keeping Audra Bauer and Ryan Sharpe close. I've never navigated murky waters like this before. I'm going to rely on their counsel, and Dana's, after she's recovered enough to return to limited duty. Everything done up until this very moment is in the past, as far as I'm concerned. Clean slate. But if I tell you no at any point moving forward—that means no. No interpretation or wiggle room. Hard stop. Is that clear?"

"Crystal clear, ma'am," said Mann.

CHAPTER 18

Jeremy Powell took a few minutes to compose himself. Box breathing was his preferred method. A four-second inhale. Four-second breath hold. Four-second exhale. Four-second hold. Repeat. All through the nose. Box breathing was supposed to help return your breathing and focus to normal levels under stressful situations. Mostly, the minutes he spent box breathing served to keep him from throwing computer monitors, bottles of bourbon, or other blameless objects around his office. The strategy had proven effective so far, but this morning had tested the limits of box breathing. He'd just been told that not one of the three assassinations he'd assured McCall would be "child's play" had succeeded.

He engaged in a few more rounds of box breathing, before storming down to his floor's SCIF to contact McCall, who he assumed hadn't gone home. The man had peppered him all night with cryptic texts. They'd likely both spent the entire night at AXIOM's headquarters building. Not that he would actually know! Despite the two of them essentially being attached at the hip with DOMINION, AXIOM's most important "deliverable," McCall insisted on keeping him "just out of reach," one floor below. Powell couldn't get on the elevator down the hallway and head upstairs to meet McCall in his SCIF. His access to that floor was restricted. Only McCall could authorize his entry, and the man treated that power with the capriciousness of a petty tyrant.

Powell shut the door to the floor's shared SCIF and waited for the green light to appear on the biometric keypad next to it—indicating that the door had sealed and that his conversation could not be easily intercepted. He dialed McCall's office phone.

"Why are you calling me from your SCIF?" said McCall.

No greeting. Nothing but rebuke.

"I need to talk to you privately," said Powell.

"Good news, I hope."

"No. Very bad news."

"Hold on. I'll call you in a minute," said McCall, before hanging up.

He must have sprinted to his SCIF. The call arrived less than twenty seconds later.

"What happened? I thought this was a clean sweep?" said McCall.

"All three assassination attempts failed. Bauer, Berg, and Sharpe," said Powell. "FBI agents were killed at the Fairfax hospital—and somehow, an FBI sniper took out one of the UK mercenaries we hired."

"You hired," said McCall. "And how the hell did that happen, exactly? You didn't send the mercenaries into the hospital, right? I thought that was going to be left to the small army of sicarios we've raised?"

"The Mexicans hit the hospital, but I stationed a sniper from the UK-based team in a building that faced the hospital entrance, in case things went sideways inside—which they did," said Powell. "I think the CIA had a team inside the reception area. Sharpe was in the elevator lobby when the Mexicans entered. They should have been able to push forward and kill him, but they were stopped by automatic gunfire from inside the lobby. One of the Mexicans had entered about five minutes earlier and confirmed that no FBI SWAT agents were stationed in the reception area. They were all upstairs."

"They might have been blending in with other people in reception," said McCall.

"At four in the morning, the lobby was mostly empty," said Powell. "A few people half-asleep on the couches, maybe. Nobody standing guard. They would have had someone in the elevator lobby. And nobody escorted Sharpe down. The team confirmed that, before they took fire. The FBI had no idea he was a potential target."

"And how did we—you—lose the sniper?"

"He started engaging FBI agents sent to the lobby," said Powell. "They must have had a sniper in the team sent to the fourth floor to protect O'Reilly, or an agent qualified as a sniper. The two engaged in a brief exchange, the FBI agent or agents firing from the rooftop."

"Damn it!" said McCall. "Our client is going to shit on my head for this! We needed them dead. Now they're all buttoned up in that hospital—sharing notes. And guess who those notes are going to implicate?"

"Our client."

"Bingo!" said McCall. "Time to take the gloves off. Forget targeting Bauer, Berg, and Sharpe. They don't command assets. I want ARTEMIS taken down immediately."

"What about O'Reilly and Camilla James?"

"Leave them alone for now," said McCall. "ARTEMIS needs to be erased. Special Agent Mann, his crew, and whoever is helping them with their ground game are the real threat. Whatever James and the rest of them are up to is just talk and conjecture. By the time they put together another task force, and that task force starts to scratch the surface of what's happening out there—DOMINION's job will be done. If we have to punch O'Reilly's ticket, we'll give it another go later."

"I have a rather drastic plan to take out ARTEMIS," said Powell. "There's just no way to hit them quietly and be done with it. They're too clever for that, and I wouldn't be surprised if the failed attempts to kill Berg and Bauer enhanced their roster. According to the files, those two have been involved in the past with a group run by retired Army general Terrence Sanderson."

"They have, which is why our client is currently even more nervous," said McCall. "On the verge of pulling the plug—which would tank AXIOM."

"The only problem I see with my plan is that you'll probably want to clear it with our client. Given the training program at LABYRINTH, the plan would essentially cross one of our influence tactics off the list. But it could serve as the first of several shock wave events that occur between now and November."

"I'll pass the plan along to our client," said McCall. "What did you have in mind?"

"You're not going to like it," said Powell.

McCall laughed. "Based on that statement, I think I'm actually going to love it."

CHAPTER 19

Serrano snubbed out her cigarette against the stone wall surrounding the patio. She took a long swig from the mostly empty tequila bottle and considered tossing it across the pool deck. The thought of cleaning up broken glass didn't outweigh the few moments of satisfaction she'd feel as the bottle sailed through the air and shattered. She actually enjoyed spending time in the pool, when she wasn't babysitting their prisoner. Same with Neva and Sofia.

Mann's call had put her in a dark mood. Too many people were involved now. O'Reilly's boss. Ex-CIA officers. A former FBI director. A group of former mercenaries turned private investigators based out of Los Angeles. And some black-ops mercenaries that even Mann couldn't describe beyond "they're good, and everyone here trusts them." Great to hear, but the only question she had was, *Where does this leave me and my friends?*

She'd joined Mann's task force for one reason. Revenge. And she'd coaxed her carefully developed network of former police and military members with the same promise. Revenge against *La Triada*. Obviously, the scope of the manhunt had changed with the raid against the facility in New Mexico. She wasn't naive. There was more to that place than just supporting the two remaining serial killers who had terrorized Ciudad Juárez and the Chihuahua state for more than a decade. But the sudden addition of several new, unconnected entities to the task force's unsanctioned roster worried her.

If she could put the last member of *La Triada* in the ground—in pieces—like the hundreds of women, her mother included, who had been unceremoniously cut apart and dumped into shallow pits south of the border, she'd help Mann and the people he trusted. That said, if Mann cut her off in any way, she'd shut everything down and leave with the bowling bags of money. She'd leave the guns, explosives, and rocket launchers behind for him to explain.

Neva—all five-foot-two and one hundred five pounds of her—appeared out of nowhere and took a seat on the tiled pool deck.

"We have everyone but Daniela coming back," said Neva. "She has two kids, a good husband, and two crazy *putas*, her mom and mother-in-law, telling her she's not going anywhere."

Serrano laughed, for the first time in a while. "I can't blame them. Or her. So. What does the roster look like now?"

"Javier, Zita, Gloria, and Tianna, plus the newbies," said Neva. "I promised the crew that hit the New Mexico facility the equivalent of four years' salary, based on what they were making when they left their previous jobs. Same with Sofia and myself."

"You promised yourself money?" said Serrano.

"I already pocketed the money," said Neva. "Gave Sofia her cut, too."

Serrano laughed. "What if you don't survive this mess?"

"We're going to bury it and record the GPS coordinates, or something like that," she said. "Someone will make their way over here to get it eventually."

"What about the newbies?" said Serrano.

"I wouldn't exactly call them newbies," said Neva.

"You know what I mean."

"Juan Patillo is in," said Neva. "Might take him a few days to disentangle from his current commitments to get here."

That was good news. Patillo was a former *Fuerzas Especiales* officer. The closest Mexico had to the Navy SEALs.

133

"Isa, Maria, and Antonio are on the way," said Neva.

"That gives us some real punch," said Serrano.

The three she'd just mentioned were either former state police SWAT or Mexican Army.

"They asked about compensation," said Neva. "I didn't know what to tell them."

"Let them know they can expect around three to four times their annual salary when this is finished. Maybe more," said Serrano. "Same for the rest of us."

"That's life-changing money," said Neva.

"Same for the FBI agents," said Serrano. "They get paid well, but not enough for the risks they take. Relative to our situation. Standard of living and all that shit."

Neva laughed. "Yeah. Our standard of living is shit. But still."

"I know," said Serrano. "Mann and I have talked about this. Whatever remains will go to the dead team members' families in some way, ours included—then to the survivors."

"Sounds fair," said Neva.

"Garrett is pathologically fair," said Serrano, pulling out another cigarette.

"Then why are you drinking yourself into oblivion out here?"

"Because he's both pathologically fair and single-mindedly mission-focused," said Serrano, lighting her cigarette. "And I'm worried that the mission has changed."

"We knew the mission changed the moment we set foot in that facility," said Neva.

Serrano took a long drag and exhaled, blowing a thick cloud of smoke skyward.

"I know," said Serrano. "But Raul was in DC. If Mann leaves without finding him, we'll never nail the last member of *La Triada*. He'll slip away."

"He's probably gone already. He'd be stupid if he wasn't," said Neva. "And based on the evidence Mann recently shared with us, Raul doesn't exactly fit the serial killer profile. He's no doubt the last member of the *La Triada*, but it seems like he fulfilled a different role both south of the border, and north. A true sicario. An assassin."

"I don't care," said Serrano. "I want that circle closed. He played a role in the terror. Maybe he pawned most of the dirty work off on the other two, while he pretended to be above it all. Bottom line. He's a depraved murderer, who gladly took part in killing innocent people when shoved against the wall. From what we could tell, his very modest kill pattern in Arizona and Southern California took on a certain political slant, which is why we focused most of our attention on Alejandro, who had no such restraints. We guessed, correctly, that Alejandro would be the one to screw up eventually and unravel the whole thing. Which he did."

"I didn't know any of this," said Neva.

"Well. We never convened a big meeting with PowerPoint slides," said Serrano. "Maybe that's what we need when Mann gets back."

Neva checked her watch. "When is he arriving?"

"That's the problem. I have no idea," said Serrano. "And he's not answering his phone."

"Does he normally take your calls?"

"Yes. He always takes my calls. Or texts me back," said Serrano.

Neva smirked. "Sounds like the relationship I had with my ex—before he started cheating on me. Is there something going on between the two of you?"

"No. But I do feel like he's cheating on me. With the FBI or CIA," said Serrano.

"Seriously?"

"What do you mean?" said Serrano, knowing exactly what she meant.

"The two of you have never—you know," said Neva. "Connected?"

"On what level?"

"You know what I'm talking about," said Neva.

Serrano rubbed her temples, the tequila headache already setting in. "He's complicated."

"And you're not?" said Neva.

"Not like him," said Serrano. "He lost a fiancée to these cartels."

"And you lost your mother," said Neva. "I don't know. Maybe I'm wrong, but I've seen the way he looks at you. There's more than just admiration."

Serrano didn't answer.

"Just saying," said Neva. "Don't shut him out, when he approaches you."

"*When?* Not *if?*" said Serrano.

Neva laughed. "Trust me. It's *when.* Not *if.* Assuming you both survive the shitstorm headed our way. If any of us survive it."

"We'll survive. One way or the other," said Serrano. "We wouldn't be here if that wasn't the case. We're like *cucarachas*—but prettier. And smarter. And all that."

"I sure as shit hope so," said Neva, shaking her head while laughing. "I've never been compared to a cockroach before."

"There's a first time for everything," said Serrano.

Neva nodded. "From this point forward, we're officially named *las cucarachas.*"

"Approved," said Serrano. "We are *las cucarachas.* And nobody can make us go away. Not even Garrett Mann and his new friends."

"Oh, for shit's sake," said Neva. "Mann isn't getting rid of you anytime soon, or ever. Professionally or personally."

Serrano hoped she was right. She'd never assumed anything about their relationship. Never pushed beyond the strict professional boundary they'd both established from the beginning. She'd sensed on occasion that Mann wanted more. Perhaps he sensed the same thing, because it was true. But they'd kept things the same for more than a year, despite sharing hotel rooms and spending nearly every waking moment together. A necessary detachment of sorts, to keep their professional relationship firing on all cylinders, and keep the task force focused on catching killers—instead of gossiping.

All that said, she hoped they both survived the upcoming storm, to explore all the possibilities Neva suggested might lie before them.

CHAPTER 20

Dr. Jeff Drummond had just fallen asleep, during the middle of the day, when a persistent beep from his phone woke him. The inexpensive motion sensor he'd installed above the door to his bedroom, which operated independently of the extremely expensive security system supposedly protecting his entire apartment, suggested the presence of a human being in the hallway. Somehow, his most recent patient had skillfully bypassed everything but the thirty-dollar detector he'd installed as a last line of defense. He should have jammed a scalpel through the back of that guy's neck, instantly paralyzing him. But he needed the money.

The divorce had left him with nothing. His ex-wife cleaned him out, before sending digital footage she'd recorded to everyone at the medical practice. Rumors of cheating were one thing. An email linking to hours of footage, viewed by all your colleagues, was another. He was locked out of the building within a few hours of the email hitting everyone's mailbox. At least she'd sent the email a few hours before the practice opened, sparing him the walk of shame out of the office.

But it didn't spare his career as a legitimate surgeon. Word spread fast. His ex-wife made sure of that. And there was more to the story than that. He'd screwed up on more levels than cheating on her. Substance abuse. Prescribing those substances well outside of his authority as a surgeon. Yeah. He wasn't living in hell an innocent man. Unfortunately, the videos had really done a number on him. Worse than he'd thought possible.

Five months into a seemingly pointless job search in the greater DC area, he stumbled upon a way to make ends meet—by offering "no questions asked" medical services on the dark web. *Stumbled* wasn't exactly the most accurate description of how he landed this gig. He'd known about it for years. Heard the rumors. And resisted the whispers.

After five months of living in a shithole apartment, eating processed food and generally deteriorating into the worst-case-scenario patients he'd treated for years, the whispers grew louder. And he started to take them seriously, which turned everything around. He made more money in one year than he'd made in his entire nine-year career as an internist at one of Silver Spring's largest medical groups. His clients, most of them one-time visits, paid a premium for privacy—in cash, or a cash equivalent. In other words, no taxes.

The job did come with a few downsides. One of them being that he had to convert one of his bedrooms into a treatment room. Many of his patients sought care late at night. Meeting them at a rented office suite in a "normal working hours" building at two in the morning wasn't an option. This meant that all his patients knew where he lived. He hadn't yet taken the advice of fellow dark web MDs and rented a separate apartment for his new practice.

An oversight he'd fix this afternoon, if he lived that long. The second downside being that occasionally, one of his patients scared the living shit out of him. He strongly suspected that one of those patients stood outside his bedroom door right now. The patient he saw last night. The guy wasn't outwardly scary, and never threatened him. Drummond just felt it in his gut. He'd never considered murdering one of his black-market patients before, despite having some serious reservations about treating a few of them, but something about that guy's energy—or affect, or whatever— told him it was the smart thing to do.

He opened the top drawer of his nightstand and removed the .45 caliber SIG SAUER P220 he'd purchased shortly after beginning his underworld career. Drummond crouched next to his bed and aimed at the door, before thumbing the hammer back. His hand trembled, the barrel unsteady. He weighed his options. Shoot first, ask questions later? Or the other way around?

"Dr. Drummond? Dr. Jeff Drummond," said a voice that didn't sound like last night's patient. "I'm Garrett Mann with the FBI. We need to ask you a few questions."

He thought it through. They couldn't enter his apartment without a warrant, so either he was under investigation for treating a patient who had been involved in a crime or this was a ruse to get him to let his guard down. Damn. What was he thinking? In his completely exhausted state, he'd forgotten about the tracking device sewn into the patient's pants.

Drummond kept a closet full of clothing, spanning the most common sizes sold by retail stores, including shoes. His gunshot or stab wound clients rarely showed up with an overnight bag full of replacement clothing. He provided the clothing free of charge—but not free of an agenda. That agenda being basic survival.

He'd sewn a black-market tracker, like an Apple AirTag, into every pair of pants in his replacement wardrobe. Pants being the one item that was always replaced. Shot or stabbed in the arm, blood eventually dripped down to the hands, which brushed against the pants. Shot in the stomach? No-brainer. It didn't matter. Even a shallow face cut requiring stitches resulted in a new pair of pants. Hands always touched wounds, and the blood always ended up on the pants.

The black-market version of the tracking device allowed him to remotely activate and disable the tracker at will, so he could "check in" on his more frightening patients during the day or so after treatment. He rarely used the trackers, and most of his patients ditched the clothes he gave them within twenty-four hours, so there was little risk of them finding the embedded tracker. It was a calculated risk, and a tactic he'd come up with on his own. Nobody in his line of business on the dark web would dare suggest using trackers. Anonymity was the key to attracting patients and staying alive. So far, nobody had detected the trackers.

"Can you slide your ID under the door—please?" said Drummond.

A few seconds later, a black badge holder featuring the letters *FBI*, a picture, and a gold badge slid a few inches into the room. He climbed over the bed and approached the badge from the side of the door. No way they could shoot him from this angle—hopefully. He grabbed the badge and backed up, before examining it. He knew what to look for. The various "how to start your own dark web medical practice" documents he'd read on the dark web laid it out for him. The badge passed muster. Shit.

"Okay! Let me get my pants on," said Drummond.

"Please," said the voice.

He made his way around the bed and grabbed his phone, navigating to the app used to locate recently activated trackers. His latest patient hadn't moved from the Motel 6 in Gaithersburg. Or at least his pants were still there. Impossible to say. But at least the system didn't indicate that he stood outside his bedroom door. Once again, impossible to say.

He pressed the trigger de-cocking lever, which sent the hammer back to its original position, before tucking the gun under his mattress, where he kept about ten thousand dollars in cash, several prepaid credit cards, two burner phones, and fake identity documents. A safeguard recommended by all of those "various" dark web documents, which were probably all just copied, pasted, and shifted around to make them look a little different—to induce a bitcoin purchase. Someone who wasn't a doctor doing this kind of work was probably sitting on a yacht in a Saint Maarten bay, living off the proceeds.

He walked slowly toward the door.

"I'm going to unlock the door and take several steps backward, hands on my head," said Drummond. "Your badge is on the bed."

"Let us know when you're ready for us to enter," said the voice.

He was either preparing himself for a quick execution, or a long interrogation. He hoped for the latter. Not that it was up to him.

"Ready," said Drummond.

The door opened to reveal an unarmed man in a dark suit, flanked by two heavily armed and fully geared SWAT-looking types. Bright-yellow letters—*FBI*—stenciled across their tactical vests.

"Are you armed?" said the agent wearing the suit.

"No. I do own a pistol, but it's tucked under the mattress," said Drummond, convinced this was a legitimate law enforcement raid.

"Then why don't you walk forward, and we'll escort you to the kitchen, where we can talk without having to worry about that pistol," said the agent, entering the room and reclaiming his badge. "I'm Special Agent Mann."

Drummond nodded. "Is it okay for me to move?"

"How about you keep your hands above your head, and my agents will come to you," said Mann.

"Okay," said Drummond.

Four SWAT agents rushed in, two grabbing his arms and keeping them raised. One patted him down for weapons. The other kept his rifle aimed at Drummond's chest, the look on his face making it clear that he wouldn't hesitate to shoot if anything went sideways.

"He's clean," said the agent who searched him.

Interestingly, they didn't cuff or zip-tie him.

"One more thing before we head to the kitchen," said Mann.

"Yes?"

The agent held a phone up to his face. Shit. The dark web was supposed to be secure. Anonymous.

"Is this the patient you treated last night?"

His shoulders dropped, and he sighed.

"I'll take that as a yes, but I need to hear it from you," said the agent.

"Yes. I treated him for multiple gunshot wounds to his right leg," said Drummond. "I'm a licensed doctor. There's nothing illegal about my practice."

"Besides the fact that it's not registered with the state of Maryland as required. And I'm guessing you haven't paid taxes on the income produced by your business," said Mann. "Just a quick stab in the dark."

"How can I help the FBI?" said Drummond. "And continue my work. This is all I have after the divorce."

"We're not interested in shutting you down," said Mann. "But we need to find the man you treated last night. We know he paid you through a cryptocurrency transaction, which isn't as secure as one might think. But we don't have that kind of time. He'll disappear as soon as he's able to move around on that leg. Did he say anything that might help us narrow down our search?"

Drummond weighed his options. He wasn't under arrest. Not yet. Not that it really mattered. This agent held all the cards. A few phone calls and Drummond would lose his license to practice medicine. Not that an active license mattered to the majority of those seeking medical treatment through the dark web. Results were what mattered. But Drummond didn't want to spend the rest of his life living in the shadows, answering his door at three in the morning and never truly knowing whether he'd be alive to see the sun rise. His medical license gave him hope. Just enough to face the next day.

"I sewed a tracking device into the pair of pants I gave him," said Drummond. "Standard practice for me, for obvious reasons. The pants are at the Motel 6 in Gaithersburg. I believe there's only one Motel 6 there. I can get you the address if you need it."

A voice called out from the hallway. "That's thirty-three minutes away."

The FBI agent turned his head to address the voice in the hallway. "I'm leaving you and two agents here with Dr. Drummond for now. Have him show you how to access the tracking app, and make sure he doesn't send some kind of warning. I know some of these devices can be remotely triggered to beep."

"Got it," said the mystery voice.

Special Agent Mann locked eyes with Drummond. "If you're fucking with us, or try to fuck with us, you're gonna lose more than your medical license. Understood?"

"Yes, sir," said Drummond.

"Good," said Mann, before nodding at the two agents holding him in place. "Take him into the kitchen and zip-tie him to one of the chairs. He doesn't go anywhere or talk to anyone until this is settled."

A minute later, Drummond found himself firmly affixed to one of the kitchen chairs, sitting across from an Indian-looking guy holding his phone.

"Passcode?" said the man.

Drummond recited the four-digit code, effectively ending his dark web career—in the DC area. He could always take the medical boards for another state and reinvent himself.

CHAPTER 21

Raul woke from a shallow sleep, but he didn't know why. Maybe a shadow or a group of shadows had passed his window? He'd pulled the thin privacy curtains together, but left the black-out shades alone, on purpose. He shifted in bed, his right leg refusing to take part in the move. Not without considerable pain. That had been his experience since he'd checked into the motel late last night. Bathroom trips required the crutches his doctor had provided. He tried that once, and nearly passed out, opting for the geriatric undergarments also provided by the doctor.

Two days, the doctor had said. Two days of doing absolutely nothing before he tried to move around. At first, he thought the guy was full of shit, but once the deep, radiating pain of three bullet wounds and the rudimentary surgery truly began to sink in, he started to accept the reality of his situation. He'd been shot three times. It would take some time to recover. The best he could do was put as much distance between DC and himself as possible. Unfortunately, at two in the morning, pain shooting up his leg every time he pressed one of the car's pedals, he didn't make it very far. Thirty or so minutes north to Gaithersburg.

He grabbed the suppressed pistol sitting on his nightstand and placed it on his stomach, the barrel pointing toward the door. Several seconds passed. Nothing. A minute passed, and he started to drift away, the one Percocet he'd allowed himself dragging him back under. His eyes closed, and when he opened them again, three FBI SWAT agents stood around his bed—two laser dots marking the hand that rested on top of the suppressed pistol. Special Agent Garrett Mann, who he recognized from the photos sent to him by his handler, stood casually at the foot of his bed.

"Why don't you let that hand just slip to the bed by your side," said Mann. "Where it'll stay until we relieve you of that pistol."

Raul did the math. There was no way he could place his finger on the trigger and press it before they switched him off like a light.

"I know what you're thinking," said Mann. "We have no intention of killing you. Your left hand is covered, too. If you don't comply with my orders, or resist in any way, these very skilled agents will render both of your hands inoperable—forever. You won't be able to brush your own teeth without help. Do you understand?"

The doctor had screwed him. That was the only explanation.

"Raul. You're overthinking your predicament. It doesn't matter how you arrived here. You're here. I'm here. Alejandro and the other member of *La Triada* are dead. I don't even know the name of the other member. My Mexican friends don't refer to him as anything but *el primero*. The first that they killed. They call Alejandro *el segundo*. You'll be called *el tercero*, if you mess this up."

"I'll cooperate if you agree not to send me back to Mexico," said Raul.

"Agreed."

"I need that in writing," said Raul.

"You'll have it within the next few hours," said Mann.

Raul let his hand slide to the bed beside him. The FBI team rushed forward to secure him the moment his hand was clear of the pistol. He was on his stomach, wrists secured, within seconds—his leg screaming in pain. They left him there momentarily, Raul sensing that Mann had silently ordered them to back off.

"So. Now what?" said Raul.

"That's up to you."

"I'd like to speak with my lawyer," said Raul.

"You no longer reside in that world," said Mann.

"What?"

"The world of rules, laws, lawyers, and civil rights? All gone for now. Maybe forever," said Mann.

"You're an FBI agent," said Raul. "All of you are FBI agents."

Mann turned to the agent next to him. "Are you an FBI agent?"

"Nope," said the man.

"You?" said Mann, addressing one of the other agents.

"Do you want me to be one?" she said.

"Not really," said Mann. "Shall we ask the other supposed agent?"

"No," said Raul.

What the hell was going on here? Mann was FBI, but who were these people?

"I know you're confused, so let me break it down for you. My new direct superior at the FBI cares even less about criminals' rights when it comes to pieces of shit like you than the agent you tried to kill last night. Talk about bad luck," said Mann.

"There's a record of this somewhere," said Raul. "You can't expect to—"

"Get away with it?" said Mann. "Shit. I thought you were smarter than that. You're in my world now, and the only jury you'll face—if you don't cooperate—will be comprised of the daughters, sons, brothers, and sisters of the women *La Triada* chopped to pieces and dumped like trash outside Ciudad Juárez. Unfortunately, you're *La Triada*'s only living representative, so you'll have to answer for all their crimes, too."

"What do you want?" said Raul.

"I want to know who ran the facility in New Mexico," said Mann.

"Where?"

"The one where you left an empty bottle of Gran Patrón on the nightstand beside your bed," said Mann.

"I haven't been to—"

"We took fingerprints, Raul," said Mann. "I can match them, but who gives a shit about forensics. Remember—we're no longer living in that wonderful realm of evidence, proof, probable cause, the Fourth Amendment. Pesky shit that gets in the way of me transporting you to an isolated house where nobody will hear you scream. Except for the jury I mentioned earlier."

"I'm not a rapist or a serial killer," said Raul. "I'm a sicario. One of the best, back in the day. Which is why the bosses ordered me to join Alejandro and Felix to form *La Triada*. My work was mostly separate from their day-to-day mayhem. I took out low-level politicians, community leaders, and police officers, who the cartel bosses viewed as future problems. I added their body parts to the piles dumped outside the city."

"Mostly," said Mann, and Raul knew exactly where this was headed.

"Mostly," said Raul. "I know how this is going to sound, but I didn't have a choice. Those other two? Alejandro and Felix. They loved it. Lived for it. But I didn't. It was degrading work for someone with my skill, but I did as I was told. This is going to sound even worse, but if your CIA hadn't nabbed me several years back, I would probably be a capo in the Juárez Cartel by now. That's how good I was."

"Well. Maybe we should just fly you back to Ciudad Juárez International Airport," said Mann. "Let your former bosses know you're headed back to take your rightful seat at the table. Why not, right?"

Raul struggled to respond. This guy clearly knew how the cartels worked. Raul wouldn't make it out of baggage claim alive.

"How do I stay alive?" said Raul. "And before you answer, I'm asking how I stay off the plane sending me back to Ciudad Juárez and avoid the jury trial you mentioned. Both of which would result in a very painful, drawn-out death."

"Well. We wouldn't want that," said Mann. "Tell me who you're working for, and I'll fly you out to Los Angeles, where you'll be held as collateral against the information you've provided. If your information turns out to be bullshit, they'll drive you to that jury trial I described. If your information pans out, they'll escort you to the FBI's Los Angeles field office, where you'll be held accountable for detonating explosive devices that killed or injured over thirty federal agents. Not to mention the attempted murder of FBI Deputy Director Dana O'Reilly."

Raul shook his head, about to negotiate better terms.

"At least you'll get a fair trial. I assume you have access to plenty of money. Hire good lawyers, and maybe you'll get lucky. Maybe all this extrajudicial shit I'm pulling right now will be enough to set you free. It's certainly better than the alternatives."

"I suppose," said Raul. "But how about we explore another option?"

Mann shrugged, like he didn't care one way or the other.

"I give you everything I know about the facility. Who's running it and why," said Raul. "And when you've confirmed that I've told you the truth, the people in LA holding me for collateral will take me to LAX, along with the backpack sitting on the desk behind you. Where I'll book a flight to somewhere far away, and never set foot in North or South America again."

"What's in the backpack?" said Mann.

"Identity documents good enough to get me through customs pretty much anywhere in the world. A cellular-capable digital tablet. Burner phones. Enough cash and prepaid credit cards to get me wherever I need to go and keep me afloat until I can access other resources."

"I can't just let you go," said Mann. "Not after the Sacramento explosion."

Interesting. He didn't mention O'Reilly.

"But you'd overlook what happened to O'Reilly?" said Raul.

"Is that how you describe attempted murder? Something that just 'happened'?" said Mann. "The only reason I didn't include O'Reilly in my previous statement is that she's the kind of agent that would very likely put aside what 'happened' to her, to bring down whatever the people who ran the New Mexico facility have planned for the United States. But she can't overlook the dozens of agents you killed in Sacramento. Have you asked yourself why I didn't show up with FBI agents?"

He'd been so busy mentally calculating a way out of this mess, he truly hadn't given it that much thought.

"To keep you alive," said Mann. "Just in case you know something I don't already know. That said, you have my word that I will not kill you or allow you to be killed on my watch—as long as you continue to cooperate. The FBI knows you're here. Do you have any idea what I had to promise to keep them away from this motel and allow you to be transferred away from here outside of FBI custody? Let me answer my own question. Everything. I assured them you'd tell me everything related to that facility. And if I don't get everything, I flip a coin. Heads. Option one. Tails. Option two."

Mann had tracked him down within a day of the attack against Dana O'Reilly. Not only that, but he'd also somehow assembled some kind of extrajudicial team to apprehend him. Raul had no choice but to cooperate at this point. And maybe there was something to what Mann said about hiring good lawyers.

None of this could possibly be legal. If the Juárez Cartel didn't somehow kill him in pretrial detention, he might have a shot at beating the charges. Especially if he could separate himself from the Sacramento bombing and blame it on one of Mr. Clean's teams.

He was starting to see a way out. With the Sacramento massacre taken off his rap sheet, or with enough reasonable doubt to keep him from going to trial, he'd be down to one charge. Admittedly, the attempted murder of an FBI director wasn't a trivial charge. Quite the opposite. But this was where an immunity deal could wipe his slate clean.

"I'd like to surrender to the FBI," said Raul. "But before we get started, I would like to state for the record that I'm willing to testify against my employer regarding the attempted assassination of Deputy Director Dana O'Reilly."

"Are you saying that you were ordered to kill her?" said Mann.

"I'm not saying anything until you promise not to send me back to Mexico or feed me to the coyotes."

"It's wolves," said Mann.

"Coyotes in my country."

"Agreed. And you have my word. But do not screw me on this," said Mann. "That's the other reason I'm keeping you out of FBI hands for now. If you screw with me, these people will not hesitate to activate option one or two."

Raul nodded. "Understood. So. What now?"

"First, a simple question: Who do you work for?" said Mann. "And forget trying the 'I don't really know, they kept me in the dark' routine. You're a professional, who understands the concept of leverage. And the only leverage you could ever hope to hold over them relied on knowing exactly who was pulling the levers."

"I worked for AXIOM, a corporation based out of Tysons, Virginia. The facility in New Mexico was called LABYRINTH. It was originally built by the CIA and used to create a network of informants, all captured cartel members. We called them recruits. Mostly lower-level *narcotraficantes* or human smugglers. The facility was originally designed to mimic cartel bunkers along the border, to confuse cartel members into thinking they'd been selected by a specialized group within the cartel that intended to send them back out to watch and file reports on other cartel members suspected of stealing or betraying the organization. I assisted with this by lending credibility to that story, along with a general sense of terror that kept the recruits in line. I was a well-known and feared sicario. Someone you didn't want to see unexpectedly, because it usually meant I would be the last person you saw."

"Were you captured?" said Mann.

"Yes. I believe one of my fellow sicarios provided the CIA with enough information to snatch me out of my villa in the middle of the night. They staged my death the next day on a road outside of Ciudad Juárez."

"Possibly a member of *La Triada*?"

"It was the only logical conclusion," said Raul. "We didn't hang out and socialize with each other like you see in your American mafia movies. But the nature of *La Triada*'s work put us in regular contact."

"Alejandro."

"I could never prove it. But yes."

"And how long did the CIA program last?" said Mann.

"Roughly two years, though I'm not one hundred percent sure about that timeline," said Raul. "The program was up and running when I was captured and made an offer I could not refuse. Pardon the *Godfather* reference."

"Did the CIA pay for your lavish lifestyle in the United States?"

Raul laughed. He didn't mean to, fully aware that it would most likely just piss off his captors, but he couldn't help it.

"The CIA kept me a prisoner down there for close to a year," he said. "As a member of the faculty, I was allowed outside on occasion, under close supervision. The lavish lifestyle didn't come until AXIOM took over and turned the program's focus north."

"How did you discover that AXIOM was the new owner behind the facility?" said Mann.

"They told me," said Raul, testing Mann a little.

"No, they didn't," said Mann. "I was there. We found nothing pointing to AXIOM, or any corporation, organization, or nation for that matter."

"I tracked one of my sloppier handlers to the source, in Tysons, Virginia," said Raul. "Like you said earlier. Leverage would be my only way out, if I ever wanted to leave the program."

One of the operatives tapped Mann on the shoulder and whispered in his ear.

"We need to get you to the airport," said Mann. "Someone wasn't happy about my decision to pull the FBI back, and there's a bureaucratic storm headed our way. We'll be flying on a private jet arranged by a third party, to avoid a government recall."

"You're coming with?" said Raul.

"Absolutely. I plan to personally hand you off to our associates in Los Angeles, or wherever we end up landing. I may have mentioned LA one too many times around some of the FBI agents," said Mann. "Can't be too careful."

"Special Agent Mann?" said Raul.

"Yes?"

"You didn't seem surprised when I said AXIOM," said Raul.

"The question was a test," said Mann.

Implying that he already knew, which didn't seem feasible. Mann was right: AXIOM had left no traces leading back to them at LABYRINTH, which he assumed was a safeguard that extended to every aspect of the facility's employees. Unless they captured Mr. Clean, the only visitor who he'd ever seen set foot in the facility, the place essentially existed in a vacuum. For obvious reasons. He couldn't imagine that AXIOM didn't apply the same firewall strategy to the teams they put in the field.

Even their headquarters, which he viewed only from a distance, had the tired, concrete-laden look of a building occupied by an insurance company hanging on by a thread. Nothing about it suggested it was the epicenter of a conspiracy to place narcos across the United States. He still didn't have a full grasp of AXIOM's plan, but he had some ideas, which he'd be glad to share with Mann to keep him on track to testify and buy time for his expensive lawyers to get him out of this. Of course, there was always another option: escape his captors in Los Angeles. But he wouldn't be able to assess that possibility until the team there took custody of him.

CHAPTER 22

Mann drummed his fingers on his seat's armrest. He was putting off the inevitable. For a good reason. He risked losing Serrano's support if he couldn't put this entire thing into the right perspective for all parties involved. And how the hell was he supposed to do that! Everyone wanted something different from Raul.

Serrano and her colleagues wanted revenge. Pure and simple. Raul was the last member of *La Triada*, and regardless of what he claimed, the former sicario had played a role in the murder of hundreds of young women in and around Ciudad Juárez. He had the tattoo. Even if he had played mostly an administrative role, or whatever he'd vaguely suggested. Raul had killed some of these women, and nobody on Serrano's crew would rest until *La Triada* ceased to exist. Just the outside chance that Raul may have been responsible for one of their loved ones' gruesome murders was justification enough to kill him.

The FBI wanted their pound of flesh for the Sacramento massacre. Raul's sudden proclamation that he'd testify against AXIOM for immunity was about as transparent as an open window. Narrow his list of crimes down to one and try for an immunity deal. He'd blame Sacramento on AXIOM, which could be true, though Mann suspected it wasn't.

Raul had every reason imaginable to immediately blame AXIOM for the bombing. Get the ball rolling on that theory. Mann couldn't think of a downside to this. But Raul was groggy and maybe a little foggy from the Percocet he'd taken at some point in the early-morning hours, he had three rifles pointed at his head, and he faced being charged with the easiest connect-the-dots attempted murder in the US Eastern District of Virginia's entire history. He'd stumbled and given away his hand. But damn if he didn't hold a strong one.

Now Mann faced the possibility that Raul could get away with everything, if he shifted the blame for Sacramento to AXIOM—not entirely impossible given the fact that the explosives detonated at the house had destroyed nearly every bit of evidence that could connect him to the bombing, other than the fact that he owned the house. They hadn't extracted anything useful from the computer hard drive and slightly melted thumb drives Rocha had salvaged. If the Department of Justice needed him to nail AXIOM to the wall, an immunity deal wasn't impossible.

All of which left Mann inside his own head, fighting his own demons. For all his sicario talk, Raul was a serial killer. He relished murder, actively taking part in the femicide that terrorized Ciudad Juárez for years. Maybe he wasn't as bad as the others, but he was still a psychopath—who was unlikely to stop if he was freed. Eventually, he would return to his true calling. Mann had dedicated the last several years of his life to finding and stopping Raul. He'd formed an alliance and friendship with Serrano, who sought the same thing. Everyone on ARTEMIS was aligned with this single purpose, and he was about to throw it all away for "the greater good."

And he truly believed that it was worth the sacrifice. Whatever AXIOM and this True America group had planned for the United States, it would undoubtedly claim far more lives than *La Triada* ever did. But how did he explain this to the victims' families and friends, some of whom had died in New Mexico under his leadership?

He wanted to scream or pound the teakwood table in front of him, but that would serve only to embolden Raul in some way Mann couldn't comprehend. The man had a reptilian mind, always plotting. Always calculating. He had seen it during the brief interrogation at the motel. Mann had never heard the name AXIOM prior to Raul announcing it. Callie Jackson had passed along tracking data for the two phones her virus still inhabited, but one stopped transmitting in Chicago at the airport, probably smashed in a toilet stall. The other made its way to Tysons, Virginia. The signal terminated in a Starbucks parking lot, either destroyed or placed in a Faraday bag, which blocks electromagnetic frequency transmission and reception. James put the three new members of ARTEMIS on the job, along with Anish Gupta, Bauer's contact. They started from the phone's last known location and spread outward, examining every building nearby.

Tysons, Virginia, was a mix of old and new, many of the buildings just as sad as Raul described. Hundreds of them. None with an AXIOM corporate logo on their building face. Not surprising, since the team couldn't find a company named AXIOM in any state business registry that even remotely resembled the kind of corporation they were interested in. They weren't expecting to see "specializes in military-industrial complex and political conspiracies" listed on any of these companies' websites, but the team was quickly able to eliminate one after another, until none remained.

Hopefully, Bauer's computer-surveillance friend would be able to shed some light on the mystery. She'd insisted that Gupta could work miracles in the magical realm of the internet, which sounded like code speak for illegally hacking into databases and trawling the dark web for traces of an entity that would otherwise never be exposed. Mann hoped she was right, before AXIOM melted back into the background, where they'd hidden for years unnoticed. He forced his fingers to stop. Raul shifted in his seat, his eyes closed, or were they?

"I'm going back to make a call," said Mann.

She gave him a casual thumbs-up. Raul wasn't going anywhere. They'd secured him to the seat using plastic-coated, titanium zip ties. Impossible to snap open. Nearly impossible to saw through without cutting your wrist open and bleeding out. He passed Melendez and Blake Zekry, their team's heavy weapons specialist and the only other operative available on short notice, before reaching the small aft cabin and shutting the door.

CHAPTER 23

Serrano squeezed the phone in her hand hard enough that she thought it might break. Mann couldn't possibly be serious. The thought of leaving the fate of the last living member of *La Triada* to the US judicial system made her sick. And the thought of having to try to explain this bullshit to the women and men who had trusted her enough to risk losing their shitty, poverty-line jobs and make the journey north to seek closure—made her want to cry.

"I trusted you, Garrett," said Serrano. "This feels like a betrayal."

"It is," said Mann. "It's a betrayal of my mission. The reason I formed ARTEMIS. It's a betrayal of the FBI, who lost more than two dozen agents in Sacramento. I don't believe Raul's claim of innocence regarding that massacre. And it betrays you and your colleagues. For more reasons than I can express."

"Then why? Why are you doing this?" she said.

"Because this is bigger than all of us. There was no way for any of us to know that *La Triada* was connected to something massive—before we hit the New Mexico facility. And I still don't exactly know what we're dealing with, but from what I've been told by former senior-level FBI and CIA officials, who were targeted along with O'Reilly, it's bigger than us. So. I have to look at the bigger picture. And I'd like the opportunity to present this bigger picture to you and your team in person."

"I don't think you're going to be welcome here," said Serrano.

"I don't really care," said Mann. "I just need the opportunity to explain my decision. If you and your crew are not convinced by what I have to say, I will give you Raul—after I've gotten what I need from him. I will not turn him over to the FBI. If that's your decision. But you have to give me the chance to talk with your entire team."

"You'd betray Raul?"

"For you, and everyone who has put their trust in you? Yes," said Mann. "I'm in a catch-22 situation here, which you might not understand."

"I read Heller's novel," said Serrano. "We do have an education system that doesn't solely focus on Mexican history and culture."

"Sorry," said Mann. "So. You understand my dilemma."

"I think I do," said Serrano. "And what we found in New Mexico was disturbing."

"The facility is called LABYRINTH. It used to be run by the CIA to reprogram cartel members and send them back south as informants for the US government. Apparently, that didn't work out. At some point, about three years ago, from what I can tell, an obscure US corporation took over. I'm still piecing together how that happened. The bottom line is that they turned the entire operation around, facing it north—into the United States."

"That tracks with what we observed," said Serrano, not entirely wanting to throw her phone in the pool anymore.

"Here's where I stand now. I'm trying to determine if the Juárez Cartel hired AXIOM to create a training facility to better facilitate the flow of drugs through the United States, or did AXIOM create the facility on behalf of an anti-American political organization, to unleash a fake wave of immigrant chaos ahead of our upcoming election. If this is just a drug thing, Raul is yours. If this is an attempt to interfere with this fall's election, I must hold on to Raul as long as possible. As long as it takes to wring every bit of information out of him."

"Let me ask you this," said Serrano. "Can you envision a situation where you don't deliver him to us?"

A long pause ensued. She shook her head and muttered a few expletives.

"Only one," said Mann. "But that would literally be the worst-case scenario. One in which I can't stop AXIOM's plan, assuming it's election-related, without Raul's help."

"Just give me the address in Virginia when you find the building, and I'll kill everyone inside. Burn it to the ground. Problem solved," said Serrano.

"That idea has crossed my mind," said Mann. "But from what I'm told, by the same former senior government officials I mentioned earlier, these groups never run their conspiracies out of their headquarters buildings. They typically go with a more decentralized leadership organization."

"But most of the leadership will be inside," said Serrano.

"Not necessarily," said Mann. "The group running the operation supported by the LABYRINTH facility may be just one arm of the greater organization. We simply don't know yet. And if we're wrong, and they've decentralized, we run the risk of accomplishing nothing—except for giving them advanced warning. The satellite hubs will sever all links to the main hub, and still execute the plan. Think about how the cartels work: Yes, we could drop a GPS-guided bomb on the leader of the Juárez Cartel's head, but that wouldn't end the cartel. There'd be an internal fight to take control, but within a few weeks, or sooner—back to business."

"AXIOM is a US corporation. Not a drug cartel," said Serrano. "Taking out their headquarters would put a halt to operations. Maybe not forever, but long enough to stop whatever plan they had in mind."

"I wish it were that simple, Cata," said Mann. "But if someone walked into a major corporation's board meeting and killed everyone in attendance, before dropping the building to the ground, operations would continue without even the briefest pause. These are complex operations, with built-in redundancies. The cars at GM would still roll off the assembly line. Exxon's oil would still be refined. Maersk ships would still sail with their cargo. United's planes would still carry passengers across the world. We have to assume that AXIOM's 'product' would still be delivered. That's the problem I'm facing: how to target the right part of AXIOM. Or we could go with your plan and just take out their headquarters with a few hundred pounds of dynamite."

She knew he was right, but the thought of letting her friends down didn't sit well with her.

"Raul has to pay for what he did," said Serrano. "And make no mistake—he took part in the killings. He may not have been the most prolific killer in *La Triada*, but there's no way he could have entirely avoided direct participation. Even if it's somehow true that he just killed a few women, there's no way for us to know that we've avenged all the murders, without taking his head."

"I understand. I truly do," said Mann. "Which is why we need to get to the bottom of what AXIOM delivered—in the form of hundreds of cartel soldiers planted around the United States—before we require more help from Raul. The less I need from him, the more leverage I have over him. Has Elena shed any more light on the overall scope of her mission?"

"No. And we've applied some serious pressure," said Serrano. "She's tough, but she's not stupid. She knows she can't return to Mexico. There's no reason to lie to us. She didn't even know where they were going to send her until we showed her the envelope with the documents they planned to give her. Did Mayer turn up anything at the apartment?"

"No. She arrived with Baker and Mills early this morning," said Mann. "Spent a few hours scoping the place out before entering. Nobody was watching it as far as they could tell. Sparsely furnished. A few sets of utensils, plates, and bowls. A few pots and pans. Towels. Bedding. Toilet paper. Nothing else inside the apartment. The SUV was sitting in the parking lot. Registration and title in the glove box. Both in her name."

"There has to be more of them in Phoenix," said Serrano.

"Maybe. Maybe not," said Mann. "We just don't know why they're here, but like I said, some people I met last night, both of them closely connected to Deputy Director O'Reilly, believe people like Elena are being seeded throughout the United States to carry out some kind of attack, or a series of attacks, ahead of the upcoming presidential election. That's why I didn't just shoot Raul in the head and say he resisted arrest. If he knows anything useful, I need to get it out of him."

"You could always bring Raul to me," said Serrano. "I'll extract every last bit of information from him."

"Nice try," said Mann. "That would be my last resort."

"But it's not off the table," said Serrano.

"No. It's not."

"Well. That's good to hear," she said. "I suppose I can justify continuing to work with you."

"Cata. I promise you that Raul will pay for what he did," said Mann. "I just can't promise the kind of revenge you and the rest of the victims seek—and deserve."

"I understand. I don't like it, but I understand," said Serrano. "If you gave him your word, you have to do your best to live up to it."

"As long as he lives up to his end of the bargain," said Mann. "Which is a steep upward climb as far as I'm concerned. Giving us the name AXIOM started him up that hill, but we haven't made much progress. And it's not like he gave us an address."

"I think he's stringing us along, but that remains to be seen," said Serrano.

"My guess is that he'll start sharing more useful information once he settles in with the team assigned to watch over him," said Mann. "And I fully expect him to dole out the information, or as you very aptly put it, string us along. If I detect he's playing that game, I'm told that the team taking custody of him doesn't have a problem turning up the heat."

"Make sure they bring a blowtorch," said Serrano.

"I think the threat of being delivered to you and your friends will be enough to keep him talking," said Mann.

"I'd be happy to pay him a quick visit to assure him that life in prison, or even a slow, painful death at the hands of the Juárez Cartel, would be vastly preferable to what we have in store for him," said Serrano.

"Tempting. But only as a very last resort," said Mann.

"You didn't say no."

"Don't read too much into it," said Mann.

Mann was wise not to take her up on the offer. As much as Serrano would like to believe she'd honor his wishes, she didn't think she could stop herself from killing Raul the moment she saw him. One dark thought triggered another.

"Garrett. Make sure they know exactly what they're dealing with," said Serrano. "I don't know anything about this West Coast team, but if Raul sees an opportunity to escape, he'll take it, along with all their lives. He was the cartel's top sicario. The boss's go-to killer for the toughest jobs. If they underestimate Raul's capabilities or lose focus for even the briefest moment, neither one of us will ever see him again. And if we do—it'll be right before he kills us."

"I've already briefed them on the special nature of their captive, but I'll make sure to repeat what you just told me, word for word."

"Word for word," said Serrano. "Or we all lose eventually. Because he can't help who he is, and he'll never stop killing. It won't happen next month or even next year, but eventually, we'll all see his face, and that'll be the last thing any of us sees."

CHAPTER 24

Mann's phone buzzed a few minutes after the copilot came back to let him know that they were twenty minutes from their destination. Phoenix. Mann had decided that any LA-area airport was too big of a risk given the bureaucracy blizzard—a.k.a. shitstorm—descending on Executive Assistant Director James. Like O'Reilly, there was only so much she could do to shield them from Department of Justice higher-ups, who were worried about one thing, and one thing only: upward—or at the very least, sideways—mobility. But never a backward slide. He checked his phone. Kim Rocha.

"Good to hear from you. What's up?" said Mann. "We're on final approach."

"I extracted a data fragment from Raul's hard drive," said Rocha. "It's very corrupted, but from what I can tell, it was sent a few hours before we hit the New Mexico facility. I think he was supposed to fill a bigger role than we suspected prior to our raid. Some kind of oversight role? But I'm just guessing based on the data fragments."

That lying piece of shit. Playing the victim all along.

"What are you thinking? First impression?" said Mann.

"It's just a fragment, but it's disturbing," said Rocha. "A string of addresses, times, and dates, but only six of them. Five, actually. The last one is a partial. No date."

"Shit. What's the first date?"

"July 25," said Rocha.

"And what are the other details?"

"Just a time and address," said Rocha. "9113 East Ashford Drive. 6:35 a.m."

"That's it?" said Mann.

"Unfortunately," said Rocha. "The address is in a planned community called Rita Ranch, about fifteen miles southeast of Tucson proper, off Interstate 10."

"A safe house?" said Mann.

"Maybe. But why the specific time?"

"Exactly," said Mann. "We'll break all this down tomorrow morning. I'm delivering the guy that tried to kill Dana O'Reilly to a third party in Los Angeles. I'll be back in Phoenix within a few hours. As soon as they can turn this plan around."

"Raul?"

"Yeah."

"Why a third party?" said Rocha.

"Because I'm fairly convinced that Cata and her crew would kill him on sight, given the chance," said Mann. "I need to keep him a safe distance away. For now."

"Shit. I didn't even think of that," said Rocha. "Does Cata know?"

"She knows," said Mann. "She deserved to know."

"That must have been a fun conversation," said Rocha.

"You have no idea," said Mann. "I'm not looking forward to seeing her."

"But normally you would?"

"I'll pretend not to read anything into that," said Mann.

"Just saying," said Rocha. "The two of you seem to get along. Two peas in a pod, or whatever."

"Well. We're about to be two peas fighting in a pod shortly," said Mann. "She wasn't pleased with Raul's arrangement."

"I imagine she wasn't," said Rocha. "Does he have a deal?"

"Nothing official or signed," said Mann. "If he sincerely cooperates with our investigation, I have to hand him over to the Department of

Justice. I gave him my word. And I can't go back on that, as much as Cata will hate me for it."

"Yeah. That's pretty much all we have at this point," said Rocha. "Our word."

"Exactly," said Mann. "Let everyone know I'll be back tonight. I'm not sure how long of a drive I'm looking at."

"About five hours. From LAX," said Rocha. "But I assume you're not flying into LAX. That would be too obvious. Cata mentioned that you might have pissed off some people above James's paygrade?"

"Possibly," said Mann. "And I can neither confirm nor deny where I'm landing. But I'll reach the safe house sometime tonight. We'll go over everything tomorrow."

"I'll keep digging through the data," said Rocha. "I didn't expect to find anything on Raul's computer. Figured they had cut him off, or just fed him the occasional order outside of his role at the New Mexico facility."

"LABYRINTH. They called it LABYRINTH," said Mann.

"Fitting," said Rocha. "I'll do my best to extract whatever hasn't been entirely corrupted. Maybe we'll piece more of this together."

"Sounds like a plan," said Mann. "And I'll have a little chat with Raul. Maybe he can shed some light on why they sent him this information. How did they send it to him? Was it in an email?"

"He downloaded it from somewhere," said Rocha. "Probably some kind of encrypted dark web site built specifically to pass instructions to him. We've seen this before."

"Yes. We have," said Mann. "It's just a little odd that he saved it to his computer."

"I agree," said Rocha. "But we've seen that, too. And I strongly suspect that this was a much longer list of dates, times, and locations. Too much for him to memorize. He likely panicked after we hit LABYRINTH. Left the file on his computer in his hurry to get out of there. Or maybe he thought the entire computer would be destroyed by the explosion. The hard drive I recovered just barely survived."

"I'm leaning toward the latter," said Mann. "One of the explosive devices detonated in his upstairs office. A single point of detonation from what I've been told. Not an antipersonnel blast. I suspect that he thought it would destroy the computer."

"Right!" said Rocha. "I hesitate to call him an amateur—on any level—but a high-explosive blast creates a shock wave that pushes, crushes, and shatters very violently. As in, fucks up everything within a certain range, depending on the amount and type of explosive compound. It creates heat, too, but that's not what causes the most damage."

"The pushing and crushing is what kills," said Mann.

"Exactly. But brisance, the shattering effect, mostly affects hard objects. Like a plastic computer. If he didn't place the explosive inside or directly next to the computer, he ran the risk of pushing the hard drive away, before the shattering effect could destroy it. Unfortunately, he mostly succeeded. Even though the hard drive survived, the shock wave did a number on it."

"At least we have something to go on," said Mann. "We'll take what you recovered and try to make sense of it. I have to go. Time for a little chat with our new friend Raul. See you later tonight."

"Give him our best," said Rocha.

"Oh, I certainly will," said Mann.

CHAPTER 25

Raul's ears suddenly didn't feel right. The aircraft was descending. He subtly adjusted his jaw position by moving it slightly forward and relieving the change in pressure. A simple trick that most people didn't know about. Most people relied on chewing gum, which sometimes coincidentally relieved the pressure. What they didn't realize was that the gum chewing had nothing to do with their relief. The throat and jaw mechanics of swallowing the saliva created by gum chewing accomplished the mission Raul could replicate by simply moving his jaw.

Alas. One of a million facts about the human body that Raul understood, which set him apart from the masses. And the only thing he could do for himself right now to alleviate the misery of his condition. His captors were taking no chances. The restraints were unbreakable. The team assigned to transport him were anything but the casual crew they pretended to be. The woman who sat catty-corner across the aisle from him, the only one he'd seen for more than a few minutes inside the main cabin, seemed lax and disinterested in the whole situation—but she was anything but what she pretended to be. If he somehow broke free of his interestingly robust zip ties, he strongly suspected that she'd kill him before he got up from his seat. All the more reason to stay put for now.

The door behind him opened, and Raul turned his head to see Special Agent Mann strolling casually down the aisle. *Casual* wasn't one of Mann's traits. Something was up. Mann dropped into the seat directly in front of him, placing both hands on the table that should have been packed with luxury food and Gran Patrón Reserve, if Mann had paid any attention to what he'd found in LABYRINTH—and understood anything about the subtle art of interrogating a master interrogator. Instead, two water bottles sat on the table, shaking and shimmering as they descended to whatever destination Mann had chosen.

"You lied," said Mann.

"I need you to be more specific," said Raul.

Mann picked up one of the unopened water bottles sitting on the table and threw it at his head. A crude tactic that Raul hadn't anticipated—and didn't appreciate.

"Your office. Your computer," said Mann, grabbing the second bottle.

As much as Raul didn't want to get hit in the head with another water bottle, he couldn't resist the temptation to piss off Mann.

"Yeah. I blew it up."

The bottle hit him square in the nose, breaking it. Mann had stood up for the throw, a factor Raul hadn't considered. At least that was it for now. He was out of bottles, and Mann hadn't punched him once since he'd been taken into custody. Raul knew this type. They squirmed when it came to using their hands.

"You received instructions from AXIOM," said Mann.

They'd set him up. Shit. This was not good.

"No. No. O'Reilly was my last contract," said Raul. "Period. That was supposed to be my out. I know how this sounds, but the deal was—after I killed her, I was no longer obligated to AXIOM."

The serious-looking Latina woman across the aisle handed Mann another water bottle, which he promptly threw at Raul's chin, popping his jaw out of place. Then the woman placed four more bottles on the table between Mann and Raul.

"We land in about ten minutes," said Mann, picking up one of the bottles.

As much as he didn't want to get hit with another bottle, this was child's play when it came to torture. He could endure this forever. But what would be the point?

"This feels like a setup," said Raul.

"We're setting you up?" said Mann, his grip on the bottle tightening.

"No. *They're* setting me up," said Raul. "My handler called me directly with the O'Reilly job. I never used the computer for work related to LABYRINTH. Maybe they thought I did, and that's why they blew up the computer."

Mann opened the bottle and placed the cap on the table.

"Well. They failed to blow up the computer, so I guess we'll know everything there is to know soon enough."

Raul didn't like the sound of that. He didn't have anything to hide regarding AXIOM on his computer. That wasn't how they communicated. His true worry was that he used that computer to keep track of his worldwide prosperity portfolio—a fancy term for his multilayered "disappear and live like a king if things went sideways" plan. A plan he should have put into place the moment Mr. Clean told him that LABYRINTH had been wiped out. Taking the O'Reilly job had been an utterly stupid mistake. He should have flown out of Sacramento that same night, never to be seen again.

Instead, he was tied to a chair, waiting for a water bottle to be thrown or dumped over his head.

"You going to do something with that?" said Raul, nodding at the bottle.

"Yeah. I'm going to drink it," he said, before downing half the bottle. "Flying dehydrates the shit out of me. Three days."

Mann placed the bottle on the table between them.

"Three days?"

"That's how long a human can survive without water," said Mann. "Give or take a day or two. When's the last time you had a drink of water?"

Raul didn't answer. He saw where this was going. He'd tortured dozens over his career. The one torture that never failed was dehydration. It messed with you in unimaginable ways. And it hurt, slowly. Miserably. He'd rather take a beating or face a knife than be left to dry out.

"I'm guessing eighteen hours," said Mann.

"I swear," said Raul. "I never received instructions from AXIOM on that computer. They're setting—"

"Setting you up?" said Mann.

Raul shook his head. "No. No. They're setting you up! That's the only explanation."

Mann sighed. "So. Now you're telling me that they put stuff on your computer before you blew up your house and dozens of FBI agents?"

"I didn't blow up those agents," said Raul.

"Sounds like you didn't do anything. Ever," said Mann. "I mean. Why are you even in custody?"

"That's not—" started Raul.

Better to say nothing at this point. Something was off, and it was starting to sound like AXIOM had set him up to take a much bigger fall than he'd ever imagined.

CHAPTER 26

Mann stepped off the jet's staircase and onto the blisteringly hot concrete tarmac, the air shimmering in every direction. Why anyone would want to live in the middle of a desert defied comprehension. He shaded his eyes with a hand and peered into the nearest open hangar. Four figures leaned against the front grille of a massive white SUV, arms crossed. One of them waved him over, yelling something Mann couldn't hear over the whine of the jet's engines.

"I recognize two of them," said Melendez, from the jet's doorway. "We're good."

Mann gave the group a thumbs-up, before turning to Melendez. "Let's get this over with. Before my shoes melt to the tarmac."

He headed to the hangar, the group walking forward to meet him but stopping at the edge of the shade. Now he could see them better. Two women and two men. All wearing what Mann called "military contractor casual." Khaki or darker-brown pants with cargo pockets. Thick nylon belts that could support holsters. Untucked button-down safari shirts—sleeves rolled just below the elbow. Earth-toned ball caps. Except this was the Friday-casual version. No body armor or visible weapons, though he had no doubt they all carried pistols in concealed rigs hidden by the untucked shirts.

They all looked serious, but one of the women stood out. Literally. She was taller and blockier than the rest of them, her hair buzzed tight around the sides—the top only an inch thick but standing straight up thanks to copious amounts of hair gel. This had to be Pam. The other woman looked like she could snap Mann in half without breaking a sweat, but this one frightened him. He'd been told that Raul would be in good hands with Pam running the show. They hadn't been kidding.

"Pam?" said Mann, extending a hand.

She uncrossed her arms and smiled warmly, accepting the invitation. "At your service," she said.

His hand escaped the exchange unbroken, though for a moment during the handshake, a few of his fingers felt like twigs on the verge of snapping.

"Thank you for agreeing to do this," said Mann, stepping into the shade. "Hopefully this arrangement won't last long. The tempo of our investigation just picked up. Momentum is the name of the game."

"We understand what that feels like," said Pam.

"And thank you for driving out to Phoenix," said Mann. "I couldn't risk landing anywhere near LA. The man you'll be babysitting is likely responsible for the Sacramento bombing. He most definitely tried to kill Deputy Director Dana O'Reilly."

"Why isn't he in federal custody?" said one of the men. "I'm Garza, by the way."

"Rip," said the other guy.

"Brooklyn," added the woman.

"We're all private investigators," said Pam. "These three are former special forces. Just in case you were wondering."

"I wasn't. If anything, you all look overqualified for the job," said Mann, before looking over his shoulder at the team escorting Raul in their direction. "And to answer your question. He's not sitting in a federal detention center because I found him first, and he may hold the key to stopping a massive conspiracy with national security implications. Once officially in the system, he'd lawyer up and that would be that. We'd lose all momentum. That or the not-so-far-fetched possibility that a pissed-off FBI agent has an accidental firearm discharge during transit to the detention center."

"Accidents happen," said Pam. "Especially after you kill a few dozen FBI agents."

"Exactly. I couldn't run the risk of losing access to him. Yet. O'Reilly's boss bought me enough time to fly him out of DC. I'm still not sure who paid for this plane."

"I have an idea. Especially now that I see those two yahoos," said Garza. "Emily and Rico."

"You know them?"

"We worked together a few years ago, helping Audra Bauer and Karl Berg unravel a big mess," said Garza.

"Bauer arranged for Emily, Rico, and Blake to unofficially join my task force. As far as you know, if anyone were to ever ask—they're FBI agents. They saved Audra Bauer and former FBI Director Ryan Sharpe's life last night. Whoever is behind the conspiracy we uncovered tried to assassinate Bauer, Berg, O'Reilly, and Sharpe on the same night. Three of them are retired."

"I don't know anything about how they were all connected in the past," said Rip. "But a coordinated attack on all four? Something big is about to go down."

"That's what we're worried about, and why I need to get moving," said Mann. "I'm not sure how much time we have left on the clock."

"How's O'Reilly doing?" said Garza. "I heard some stories about her. Dodging kamikaze drones and kicking in doors during the National Mall attack. Sounds like she's moved up in the world."

"She's doing better," said Mann. "But she's still in critical condition. Stabbed in the stomach. Took a knife through her right calf and three gunshot wounds to the legs. She's a badass. That's for sure."

"And that piece of shit did all that to her?" said Brooklyn.

"Yes," said Mann. "Which brings me to the point where I very likely insult your intelligence and unintentionally cast doubt on your professional capabilities."

"That's one hell of a way to soften the blow," said Pam.

"Sorry. I'll just get it out of the way before he's in earshot," said Mann. "The guy you're holding was the Juárez Cartel's top sicario for more than a decade. Please do not underestimate him for even the briefest moment. He may not look the part, but he's extremely dangerous. As in 'kill you before you know what even happened' dangerous. You'll notice that he's always listening and always watching, even when his eyes are closed. Always plotting."

"How did O'Reilly get away?" said Garza.

"She's even more dangerous," said Mann, cracking a thin smile.

The group shared a quick laugh.

"Any chance of cartel blowback against us?" said Pam.

"No. If I put him on a flight to Ciudad Juárez tonight, he'd be dead before he claimed his baggage," said Mann. "Just don't take a selfie with him and post it on Instagram."

"I'll try to keep that in mind," said Pam.

Melendez shoved Raul into the hangar, tan capture-hood placed over his head, with a smiley face and X's for eyes drawn on the bag.

"Good to see you all again," said Rip. "Been a minute."

"It has," said Melendez. "You guys ready to watch over this piece of shit?"

"Pieces of shit are our specialty," said Garza.

"We specialize in rescuing and protecting abused or at-risk girls and women," said Pam.

"Hear that, Raul?" said Mann. "We picked this group for a reason. They don't have a very high tolerance for men who victimize women."

"Zero tolerance," said Brooklyn, poking Raul in the chest.

"I promise I'll behave," said Raul. "Showers? Bathroom breaks? Meals? I have strict dietary requirements."

"No, he doesn't," said Mann.

"I'm not running a bed-and-breakfast," said Pam. "No showers. Period. So don't soil yourself. You'll have just enough mobility, with the cuffs we've designed, to pull your pants down to piss and shit in a five-gallon bucket. MREs for meals—heating element removed. This isn't our first rodeo. Does he understand what that means?"

"I get it," said Raul.

"Good," said Mann. "Here's the last thing I'll say. If he tries to escape. Kill him. If he tries to take one of you hostage. Kill him. If he tries to attack one of you—"

"Kill him," said Raul.

"No. Smash his nuts with a hammer or whatever hard object you have available," said Mann.

"Can I squeeze them until they pop?" said Brooklyn.

"Yes. I'll allow that," said Mann, winking at her.

Raul didn't say a word or move. A first since they'd become acquainted earlier this morning. A good sign? Hard to say with a psychopath.

Pam handed him a satellite phone.

"Encrypted. We're the only number saved," she said. "Reach out anytime."

"Thank you. Seriously. We owe you one. Or two," said Mann. "Don't ever hesitate to ask."

"Good seeing you guys again," said Miralles.

"Same. Same," said Rip.

"You still single?" said Garza.

Brooklyn straight-armed Garza so hard, he fell over.

"Jesus. Sorry," said Garza, shaking off the sudden drop. "I was just making conversation."

Brooklyn kicked Garza while he was down. Not a hard kick, but enough to make a point.

"Looks like someone is trying her best to make you a better man," said Miralles.

"Don't forget to invite us to the wedding," said Melendez.

They all laughed while Brooklyn helped him up.

"He's a work in progress," said Brooklyn.

"Like the Sistine Chapel," said Pam.

"Can we move this along?" said Raul, his voice slightly muffled by the hood.

Everyone went silent, as Mann approached him. Four rapid, alternating gut-punches later, Raul dropped to his knees. Mann followed up with two quick, light jabs to Raul's nose.

"Shit. I didn't see that coming," said Garza.

"Damn. I didn't even see what happened," said Pam. "Remind me not to fuck with this guy."

"He's full of surprises," said Miralles.

Mann knelt next to Raul and whispered in his ear. "As far as I'm concerned, you're a dead man. The only way you don't die in their hands is if I'm one hundred percent convinced that you're not holding back anything. Do you understand?"

Raul nodded under the hood.

"I hope so. Because this group may seem like they're all fun and laughs, but they're not," said Mann. "If you screw me over, you'll find yourself in a stainless-steel vat filled with lye. You know how the rest of the story goes."

"These people don't strike me as the types that would do something like that," said Raul.

"Oh. They'll be long gone by the time my Mexican friends arrive with the equipment and chemicals to dissolve you alive," said Mann. "Don't lose sight of your best-case scenario. A federal trial."

"I won't."

Mann got up. "He's all yours."

CHAPTER 27

Jessica Mayer drained the last of her quadruple dry cappuccino. Her third in the last twelve hours. They'd driven every street in Tysons, Virginia, focusing their attention on the Tysons Corner business district located south of Virginia State Route 267 (Dulles Access Road) and north of Virginia State Route 7, while briefly expanding their search into nearby suburban business parks.

Anish Gupta's mobile surveillance vehicle, a totally rigged-out white Mercedes Sprinter van with a faux raised top to accommodate an array of sophisticated electromagnetic frequency (EMF) detection gear, was impressive to say the least. The FBI could take a lesson or twenty from Gupta's setup. She'd spent years in the back of the most conspicuous faux dry cleaning, cable TV repair, or heating/air-conditioning vans—depending on the season—that the FBI insisted would blend into "the background of a big city."

The only thing more conspicuous would be the addition of a neon This Is Not An FBI Van sign on top. And to make matters worse, they were about as comfortable as they looked. Busted air-conditioning. Heating systems with two settings: solar flare or Bic lighter. Of course, you couldn't run any of the systems when the van wasn't running, which was most of the time. A junker van bought at auction by the government, pumping a smoke screen of carbon monoxide into a neighborhood, was suspicious enough during the day. At two in the morning?

The only time she truly felt comfortable doing her job as Special Surveillance Group investigator was when she was following a target on foot through DC. Or in her shitty Toyota Corolla, when her targets took to the suburbs to meet with their handlers or tape a thumb drive to the inside of a restaurant's toilet tank. Staking out targets from an apartment was bad either way. Just mind-numbingly boring—which pretty much described ninety-five percent of an SSG investigator's job.

"This sucks," said Gupta.

"No shit," said Mayer.

She'd been given some background on Gupta. The words *genius* and *game changer* had been mentioned several times, but so far, all he'd done was complain and make jokes.

"We should probably call it quits for the day," said Frank Vincenzo.

"Nope," said Gupta.

"I'm barely awake," said Kerri Wallace, who had been driving all day.

"Lianez?" said Mayer.

Chad Lianez sat next to Gupta, on a slightly unstable stool, staring at the same screens Gupta had been glued to all afternoon.

"I'm good," said Lianez.

"What does that mean?" said Mayer.

"I'm still wide awake," said Lianez.

"You're just in love with this van," said Mayer.

"That's entirely true," said Lianez. "I think I've found my new calling."

"We're always interviewing," said Gupta.

"Is anyone hungry?" said Mayer.

Everyone said yes, or some form of the word, at the same time.

"Let's find a place where we can sit down and talk without anyone bothering us," said Mayer.

Gupta glanced at his watch. "Denny's."

"Denny's?" she said.

"Or a Waffle House," said Gupta. "But Denny's is a little more spread out, with big booths. And they're usually empty at this hour. The dinner crowd is gone, and the drunks are still a few hours from arriving. We could literally repeat state secrets without a concern."

"What about the servers?" said Mayer.

"You went to an Ivy League college, didn't you?" said Gupta.

"Dartmouth," said Mayer.

"Have you ever been to a Denny's?" said Gupta.

"Maybe once or twice?"

"Night or day," said Gupta.

"Breakfast."

"That's what I thought. You haven't truly experienced Denny's," said Gupta. "The night shift wouldn't bat an eye if you put a gun or switchblade on the table, and they certainly don't pay attention to or give a shit about late-night conversations. Especially in DC."

"Sounds like the FBI needs to start infiltrating Denny's," said Mayer.

"I said that like ten years ago!" said Gupta. "But nobody listened."

"Jesus. I can't tell if you're joking or telling the truth," said Mayer.

"A little bit of both," said Gupta. "I've been at this for close to two decades. I find humor where I can, as annoying as it might come across—because this job can turn to shit on a dime."

"What are you thinking about our current job?" said Mayer.

"I think it's going to take that turn sooner than later," said Gupta. "This isn't my first hunt through Tysons Corner. Bad people like to base their operations here. Close to McClean and everything that comes with that. A short drive to the city. Convenient for a wannabe military-industrial-complex scumbag."

"That's what I think," said Mayer. "Our investigation started out as a serial killer hunt. Admittedly, not an easy one. But it morphed into something entirely different a week ago. AXIOM is behind something far more sinister than bankrolling a few serial killers."

"AXIOM," said Gupta. "A mystery wrapped in—"

"An enigma," said Mayer.

"No. That's cliché. Wrapped in a nondescript concrete building built during the seventies. Or later, to match the background. A form of corporate camouflage."

"Interesting," said Mayer.

"It's worth digging into," said Gupta. "There's no telling how long they've been around, but if this is their first big move, it makes sense that they either recently bought out a struggling company, placing them in a shitty seventies office building, or they built from scratch, trying to melt into the background."

Mayer gave Gupta's theory some thought. She liked the way he analyzed things, clearly the product of his extensive experience solving serious problems for the group he'd worked with for close to two decades. The group had been at ground zero, slugging it out with America's enemies during every major internal threat to democracy over those decades. She almost responded with some half-baked compliment, when a thought crossed her mind—related to something Gupta said.

"Let's take everything you just said, and add another parameter," said Mayer.

"I'm down with that," said Gupta.

"Let's focus on buildings with zero signage," said Mayer. "And no attached or underground parking garages. Like you said. Camouflage. A private garage attracts attention."

"What if they're using a fake company sign?" said Lianez.

"That's a fair point. We have to assume they've thought this through on some level," said Gupta. "But I've taken footage of every building we've passed today. My cameras are always rolling. I can work some magic, and feed every sign into a program that searches the web for Virginia-, Nevada-, or Delaware-registered companies. I can expand that if necessary. Look for shell companies or entirely nonexistent ones. That should narrow things down."

This guy definitely knew what he was doing. Maybe she'd apply for a job with his organization.

"Are you sure you want to stuff yourself with a two-thousand-calorie meal at Denny's?" said Mayer. "That'll knock you out."

"I order salads at Denny's," said Gupta. "I don't have a death wish."

"Funny," said Mayer, taking out her phone. "Siri. Find the nearest Denny's."

CHAPTER 28

Serrano stood at the front door to their rental house with her arms crossed. The second time today Mann had arrived to crossed arms. Unfortunately, this wouldn't be the kind of warm reception he'd received at the airport hangar. Prior to his phone call from the airport, her baseline anger level probably sat somewhere just below the boiling point, thanks to the Raul situation. Once she'd learned that he'd landed in Phoenix instead of LA, bringing Raul within several miles of their hillside safe house—and the revenge she sought—her blood was probably on the verge of creating steam.

"Didn't expect you until later tonight," said Serrano.

"Change of plans," said Mann. "Our sudden departure from DC didn't go over very well with the powers that be."

Serrano ignored his comment and nodded at the three operatives unloading heavy duffel bags from the back of the SUV.

"New friends?"

"From what I've been told, they've played a part in taking down every major conspiracy or direct attack against the US over the past twenty years," said Mann. "Based on what I've seen, I believe it."

Serrano just stared at him.

"Raul is in the right hands for now," said Mann. "Trust me. We need him to vet information we come across."

She shook her head, her grimace slightly relaxing. "I know. And just so you know, I haven't told anyone on my team about this. As far as they know, Raul was taken into federal custody. They aren't happy about that, but they've accepted it. So—I can't stress this enough—make sure you and your new friends are on the same page. Raul is in federal custody in DC."

Miralles passed Mann on the right, carrying a duffel bag that looked like it weighed a hundred pounds more than she did.

"We get it. Trust me. I've bitten my tongue hard enough over the years that I wear a mouthguard during mission briefings—just in case," said Miralles. "I'm Emily, by the way."

"Cata," said Serrano. "Let me help you with that."

"We got it," said Miralles. "Thank you."

"You're joking about the mouthguard thing, right?" said Serrano.

"It's a figure of speech, but there have been times," she said, before looking over her shoulder at Mann. "He did the right thing with Raul. It sucks. But it's the right thing for now."

"Subject to change," said Mann. "At any second."

The other two agents passed by, hauling similarly bulky bags.

"I'm Rico. This is Blake," said Melendez. "We're here to help, not get in the way. I can tell who's actually in charge here, so don't hesitate to let me know if we're getting on your nerves."

Serrano laughed.

"Am I that obvious?" she said.

"You look like a wife standing at the kitchen table when her husband tries to sneak inside the house at two in the morning, after stopping for a few drinks with the guys before dinner," said Melendez.

"Feels that way," she said, before nodding at Mann. "I should show them where they're staying. The walk-out basement is mostly unoccupied, except for where Elena is staying."

"How's that going?" said Mann.

"Let's walk and talk," said Serrano.

They caught up with the three operatives, and Serrano showed them downstairs, into a large room with floor-to-ceiling windows. Luke

Turner got up from the couch, a very compact version of an M4 rifle slung across his chest.

"You're back early," said Turner. "Everything okay?"

"All good. Had to divert at the last minute. Raul is in good hands, headed back to California," said Mann.

"Very good hands," said Melendez.

Introductions followed, appearing to put Turner at ease. Serrano motioned to the five doors that led deeper inside the lower level.

"That door," she said, pointing to the one with the sign that read GUEST, "is occupied by the prisoner we recovered from LABYRINTH. I assume you're familiar with all this terminology?"

"Yes," said Miralles.

"The one directly to the right is a full bathroom. The one to the right of that is our armory. The other two rooms are available to you. Same with the couches in here," said Serrano.

"How long are the shifts?" said Melendez.

"Shifts?" said Serrano.

"Watching the prisoner."

"Four hours," said Turner.

"We'll help you out with that," said Melendez. "Four hours can be a bitch, especially at night."

"Thank you," said Serrano. "It's been a bit of a hassle, since we need to bring a second person down here whenever we open the door to give her food or take her to the bathroom."

Blake Zekry, the mysterious team's heavy weapons specialist, plopped down on one of the oversize leather couches.

"I'll take this couch," he said. "And be that second person for as long as we're here."

"Offer accepted," said Serrano. "What kind of gear did you bring? You're under no obligation to keep anything in our makeshift armory. We just figured it would be easier to keep everything in one place. We do get some hikers in the hills behind us, so we keep the heavy weapons inside the house. Anything concealable is good to go outside."

"Sounds like a good policy. The last thing you need is a 911 call," said Miralles.

"Well. We do have six FBI agents on the property," said Serrano. "But still. Our guest falls into a gray area."

Melendez turned his head toward Mann. "Lots of gray-area activity on this task force."

"The entire thing is in a gray area at the moment," said Mann. "Which means we can't communicate with any other federal authorities outside of Executive Assistant Director James for now."

Serrano grimaced. "That bad?"

"We're on our own," said Mann.

"That's pretty bad," said Turner.

"Welcome to our world," said Melendez.

"Nothing new," said Serrano.

"For any of us, really," said Mann. "Let's get everyone together and start trying to make sense of the data Rocha pulled from Raul's computer."

"I think we've already figured it out," said Serrano. "And it's not good."

"Timeline?"

"Roughly thirty-six hours," she said.

"Target?"

She subtly shook her head. Definitely not good.

"Thirty-six hours until what?" said Melendez.

"We'll brief your team after you get settled in," said Mann. "One hour? Upstairs?"

Serrano nodded. "Rocha is putting together a quick presentation. She should be ready by then. Maybe sooner."

"We're ready when you're ready," said Melendez.

Mann motioned for Serrano to step outside with him, while Melendez's crew settled in. Turner returned to his corner of the couch, flipping through channels on the wall-mounted flat screen TV. Mann shut the slider behind them.

"What's the target?" he said.

"School bus."

"No," said Mann.

"It's the only thing that makes sense according to the information," said Serrano.

"Shit," said Mann. "And our internal problem?"

"Still nothing," she said.

"Triple shit," said Mann. "Is it possible that we're wrong?"

"How can we be?" said Serrano. "It couldn't have been O'Reilly's office or phone. She didn't know about the weapons. Same with James. If it was one of my colleagues, I'd be sitting in an ICE detention facility. You were smart to keep us away from the official side of the task force. Even smarter to keep our location to yourself. And the weapons we took from the facility? Nobody but you knew we had them. I'm sorry, but all evidence points to someone on your team."

"But why?" said Mann.

"Because it can't be anyone else," said Serrano.

"No. I mean—why? Why would anyone on ARTEMIS betray the team?"

"I'm the wrong person to ask, Garrett," said Serrano. "I can think of a hundred reasons based on my experience working for the Mexican state police, but I will say this. Not all of them come down to money—but most of them do."

"We don't have time to audit everyone's finances," said Mann. "You said thirty-six hours. That only gives us one full day to prepare."

"Yes."

"Here's what I think," said Mann. "The ICE and ATF raids were passive ways to slow us down. Neither would have shut us down permanently, but they would have sidelined us for a while. Whoever is pulling these strings seems more interested in slowing us down than taking us out. Otherwise, we would have been hit by another mercenary team, like the motel in Minneapolis. And we would not have been ready for the attack."

"You actually think that's the end of it?" said Serrano. "Look what happened at Raul's house."

"Yeah. But the ICE and ATF raids actually saved us," said Mann. "I believe the bombing and the raids are entirely independent of each other."

"I agree," said Serrano. "But I'm talking about the concept of escalation. They couldn't sideline us with simple moves. What's their next move? And how will the traitor in our midst respond to their escalated request? Will they send us into the meat grinder or warn us? That's the question."

"No. That's the gamble we have to take," said Mann. "We don't have enough time to vet the team."

PART III

CHAPTER 29

Mann absorbed Rocha's presentation like a black hole. Nothing escaped. And when she finished ten minutes later, he couldn't think of a different conclusion. There was no other way to analyze the data fragments she'd recovered from Raul's hard drive. AXIOM's plan to sabotage the upcoming election would kick off less than thirty-six hours from now, in Tucson, Arizona. On a school bus transporting high school students—or so they presumed, based on the time, date, and location presented in the data fragment.

6:35 a.m. July 25. Mann was skeptical. School in July? Could they be targeting a summer camp bus? A quick call to the Vail Unified School District administration office put an end to his doubt. The Vail Unified School District ended their year in late May and started up again on July 22. AXIOM had done their research. But things still didn't entirely add up.

The address taken from the hard drive corresponded with a home at an intersection in Rita Ranch, a planned community southeast of Tucson's city center, about a mile off Interstate 10. Admittedly, the data could represent something different altogether. A drug or weapons delivery. The location of Raul's next victim. A target on a list Raul could pick and choose from. Whatever it represented, the data was too specific to ignore. Too close to the bus pickup time to ignore.

The catch was that the bus didn't stop at that intersection. The high school students would be picked up about a third of a mile away on

Esmond Loop Road, listed on the school district transportation route map for 6:40 a.m. The elementary and middle school students in the neighborhood lived too close to those schools for bus service. They either walked or had their parents drive them a few blocks to school.

Whatever AXIOM had planned for the bus, it would go down near that intersection—and ARTEMIS and its allies would be on board instead of the students. Mann intended to flip this script and send a strong message back to Tysons, Virginia: *Not on ARTEMIS's watch.* He was fairly convinced that all his team needed to do was actively interrupt one of these false flag operations, capture the attackers, and expose the truth.

Once the former cartel members learned that they had not in fact been part of a Juárez Cartel–sanctioned or supported operation but were instead being used by a company affiliated with the American military-industrial complex to facilitate a domestic political coup, Mann imagined they would have no issues testifying about exactly what they had been ordered to do. They also had Elena to explain LABYRINTH, and if the Department of Justice had any intention of knocking AXIOM's overall plan into the dirt, they'd expose the details of the facility itself. Make it crystal clear to the American people that the country was not under attack by the cartels.

Wishful thinking, of course. LABYRINTH was originally built by the CIA, which would present a roadblock. If he'd learned one thing in his FBI career, it was that high-level embarrassment, no matter how stale or old, was one of the most powerful forces in DC. Magnified a thousand times more powerful than the actual blowback itself.

A small scandal in Congress could deny thousands of patients a proven cancer treatment. An inappropriate "business" trip taken by the child of a cabinet member could leave a struggling African democracy swinging in the breeze. Which was why ARTEMIS needed to document everything they'd discovered and create a backup plan in case the government decided to sweep them under the rug. Some kind of fail-safe system that would release everything they'd uncovered to the public if they were "disappeared" before the truth was revealed.

But before any impactful exposé could become a reality, they had about a week of planning to pack into the next thirty-six hours. He had no illusions about the complexity and risk associated with his soon-to-be-proposed concept. And he had no expectations about it surviving the first phase of the planning process, which was about to commence. Mann didn't run a "my way or the highway" task force.

If his plan was unrealistic or too risky, he expected to be told as much right away, so they could move on to another idea. It wouldn't be the first time one of his ideas was swept aside, and it wouldn't be the last. Shouldn't be. He'd put this team together for a reason. They each brought a unique perspective to the table. If anything, his perspective was the least unique out of all of them, which was why he so heavily respected and relied on their input.

"Thank you, Special Agent Rocha," said Mann. "And to everyone else that contributed while I was away. New introductions first?"

Melendez shrugged. "First names only."

"Fair enough. Rico, Emily, and Blake. I dragged along three members of an active CIA black-ops team," said Mann. "A close friend of Deputy Director O'Reilly arranged for them to join us. As far as anyone here is concerned, they are FBI, and will wear FBI patches during the operation. If anyone starts to question their status, send them my way immediately. I'll square the situation away. Given their skill sets and the fact that they aren't FBI agents, I suggest we deploy them away from the intersection, on nearby, unconnected streets. Close enough to reach the intersection by foot in a few minutes—navigating a few backyards. They'll be our surprise if things go sideways."

"I think you skipped a step," said Turner. "You know, the part about what the rest of us will be doing."

"I got ahead of myself," said Mann. "Last introduction before I throw down the first iteration of our plan. Cata's crew. We have four new additions to the team. All former Mexican SWAT, Army, or Special

Forces. Everyone that hit the New Mexico facility returned—except for Daniela. All combined, we have a potent mix of Mexican state police surveillance specialists, National Guard SWAT, Army counternarcotics experts, special forces, and even a Marine."

Zita raised her hand, getting a few hoots from her colleagues.

"They'll wear patches that read US-MEXICO JTF and wear the same olive drab uniforms, tactical vests, and helmets as the rest of the task force," said Mann. "I'll let you all mingle and get acquainted a little later. Right now, we need to get a basic concept of operations in the works."

Mills raised his hand.

"Shoot," said Mann.

"How far ahead of time will we notify local law enforcement? I assume you're thinking about putting ARTEMIS on that bus instead of the students?"

"I am. And even if I wasn't, we couldn't in good conscience allow that bus to proceed along its route with students on board," said Mann. "It's a good question. Probably the most important one. How much notice do we give the school district and local law enforcement?"

"The less time the better," said Baker. "I'm thinking an hour at most. Maybe less. If they have too much time to think about it, they'll just shut down the entire system and tip our hand."

"Which may not be a bad thing," said Miralles. "Your assumption about the hijacking or attack location sounds solid, but it could be a rally point for the team that follows the bus to a far less populated area, where they'll take it down and drive it into the desert. Or follow a different bus."

Mann hadn't thought of that. He'd assumed that AXIOM would be going for full publicity right away. If they managed to hijack the bus and successfully hide it, they could draw this out slowly.

"We identified five other high school pickups at the Esmond Loop location, spanning from 6:56 a.m. to around 8:00 a.m., but the 6:40 a.m. pickup is the only bus that runs down Ashford Drive," said Rocha.

"I called the transportation department and pretended to be new to the neighborhood. I took a chance and said that I heard the bus drives down Ashford Drive on the way to the pickup, and if there was any way the bus could stop at the intersection. They said it used to be a stop, but with the expansion of the school district, they had to consolidate stops to get kids to their schools on time."

"Good work," said Mann. "I think we need to be on that bus."

"Which means we'll have to coordinate with the local police," said Mills.

"Correct."

"But not until the last moment," said Turner. "The last thing we need is for the locals to reach out to the resident agency in Tucson. We'll have the entire Phoenix field office down here within a few hours."

"He's right about that," said Rocha.

"Or the Tucson field office jumping in like Sacramento," said Baker.

"Saved our lives," said Callie Jackson. "Ironically."

"Yeah, but this could be a one-time opportunity to nail AXIOM," said Serrano. "And we have more than enough people to take down a hijack attempt. Especially without any kids in the cross fire."

"We can't ignore local law enforcement," said Mills. "And I assume we're going to coordinate with the Vail Unified School District transportation department, and not just hijack the bus the moment it leaves their bus depot?"

"If you insist," said Mann. "Just kidding. Yes. We need to coordinate this, but I do agree it should be a last-minute thing to avoid any outside FBI involvement. I'll arrange for Director James to make it happen. She just needs to buy us enough time to stop whatever AXIOM has planned and get Cata's people well clear of the scene. Same with Rico's crew. I can keep up the ruse if we're only dealing with local law enforcement, and probably confuse the agents at the resident agency in Tucson long enough to get everyone clear. But once the SAC or ASAC from the Phoenix field office arrives, things will get tense. Especially after Sacramento. Every field office this side of the Mississippi knows that our task force neglected to inform the Sacramento office about our intentions within their jurisdiction."

"Maybe your task force's presence will keep them away," said Miralles. "I imagine word has spread about DC. Getting too close to ARTEMIS might be considered bad luck at this point. Not a bad situation, to be honest. Keeps the fingernail biters away."

"Until you factor in oversize egos and all that crap," said Serrano. "I agree with your overall sentiment, but all it will take is one asshole to take this above Director James's head and ruin what might be a one-time opportunity. If Phoenix FBI swoops in and scares AXIOM away, we're finished. We have to assume that AXIOM has well-placed contacts in every one of your field offices. Some kind of early-warning system. How else do you explain Sacramento?"

Careful, Cata. We may have one of those "contacts" on our team.

"Cata is right," said Turner. "We need to keep this under wraps until the last moment. If James can convince the Tucson PD and Pima County Sheriff's Department that the success of this operation depends on secrecy, plus run some last-minute interference, we'll be able to pull this off."

"The key to this will be convincing local law enforcement and school officials that our operation will not endanger any students, bus drivers, or people living in that neighborhood," said Mills.

"Which it shouldn't," said Mann.

"*Should not* and *will not* are two very different assurances," said Mills. "If the time, date, and address turn out to be a staging point for a hijack mission against one of the Esmond Loop bus pickups later in the morning, we must be able to convince them that we can readjust our plan accordingly. If the 6:40 a.m. bus passes that intersection without incident, then what? They'll be scared out of their minds that another attack is possible. No way we're containing this operation at that point."

"You're right," said Mann. "If nothing happens at 6:35 a.m., we're either looking at a nonevent, some other kind of transaction, or a staging point for a later operation."

"I can have our Albatross drone up, slowly circling the Rita Ranch, at 5:30 a.m.," said Jax. "The drone has a minimum four-hour loiter time. Six max. More than enough to cover the two-hour timeframe covering all the pickups, plus enough juice to follow any of the buses to their high school drop-offs. If the 6:40 a.m. bus isn't intercepted, we can redistribute our teams to several vehicles and watch the house and neighborhood. Follow any suspicious activity headed toward one of those buses. We'll have an eye in the sky, plus boots on the ground. All backed up by local law enforcement. That should be enough to ease their safety concerns. On top of that, my Mexican colleagues can put a quadcopter up if we need a close look at something."

"So . . . what do we think?" said Mann.

"I think the success or failure of this operation is up to Director James," said Turner.

"I agree," said Serrano. "We have all the pieces needed to run this operation safely. Maybe not for us, but definitely for the civilians. I don't see this being a hard sell to local law enforcement. But your director will definitely need to step up. Sooner than later."

"I'll get on the phone with her as soon as we're done here," said Mann.

"We're done here," said Serrano. "I don't think a phone call or two from her will suffice. She needs to be here to talk to them in person, along with her entourage and a few other assistant director–level types. This is going to take every minute of your time, which we shouldn't waste."

Melendez raised his hand, which Mann acknowledged. "I've been at this kind of sensitive, risky-as-shit work for nearly two decades, and I couldn't agree more with Cata. We can try to go this on our own, but if there's any chance of getting James on board and on a plane to Tucson, that's where your focus needs to be."

Mann nodded. "Any last thoughts before I try and summon one of the FBI's top directors out to Tucson?"

No takers.

"Then that's the plan. I'll work on James, while the rest of you come up with the ground-level plans," said Mann.

CHAPTER 30

Serrano followed Mann out of the two-story great room, down the hall toward the office. Once inside the office, she shut the door. He sat down on the black leather sectional couch facing the hillside window view. Serrano made her way to the sliding door leading to the pool deck.

"We're taking an awful risk here," said Serrano. "If we have a mole on the team, this whole thing might be shut down before it gets started. My team will get deported. Your new friends will go through the wringer. Or worse. We'll all end up dead. A bomb planted under one of the couches in the great room would take us all out the next time we gather. Maybe it's already there, and they just wanted to determine what we know, before they send us sky high."

"Endless possibilities," said Mann. "And I've thought about them all. If a member of our team has been compromised, they're being blackmailed for something like excessive gambling debt. Some kind of financial or personal indiscretion. Something serious. And nobody on the team is married, so it can't be infidelity."

"Maybe AXIOM is threatening extended family members?" said Serrano.

"That's possible. Or they could have already kidnapped family members. The thought had crossed my mind," said Mann. "That said, I don't get the impression that AXIOM's leverage, whatever it might be, rises to the level where they'd purposefully put any of us in real danger. The ICE and ATF raids were stumbling blocks in the grand scheme of things, and the Sacramento bombing was Raul's doing. He can deny it all he wants, but AXIOM wouldn't have pulled that trigger, unless ARTEMIS walked through those doors."

"Then what's the point of holding on to him?"

"Leverage," said Mann. "We hold one of the linchpins of the entire AXIOM operation, a holdover from the CIA days, plus the sole survivor of a class of students about to be sent into the United States to wreak havoc. A class that AXIOM attempted to exterminate. And within the next thirty-six hours, we'll have an entire AXIOM 'hit team' in our possession."

"Hopefully," said Serrano.

Mann buried his head in his hands and took a few deep breaths. She stayed silent, turning toward the purplish-orange hills in the distance. She'd never appreciated the beauty of the desert around sunset. Serrano had lived most of her adult life in squalor, crammed into an un-air-conditioned apartment with a view of the slum that surrounded her. Sometimes she wondered why these FBI agents bothered.

They were far from poor, making more money in one year than she'd earned in her entire life. They owned climate-controlled apartments that they could afford to keep without even living in them. The entire team could walk away from this right now, take a five-hour flight, and fall asleep in a comfortable bed. But she hadn't heard one of them speak a single word about quitting or backing down from this fight. From ARTEMIS.

"Without their testimony, LABYRINTH and whatever plan AXIOM has hatched will fade away into the background," said Mann. "Just another conspiracy theory, AXIOM's deep-rooted media and internet scrubbers making it all go away long enough for everyone to focus on the next shiny thing. Maybe a month? Two weeks? What's the average American's attention span for 'conspiracy theories'? AXIOM will wait for the news cycle to settle down, before reactivating their plan, sending Americans into a panic over the border, immigration, and the cartels living among us."

"Cynical," said Serrano. "But realistic."

"Hard to tell the difference between the two sometimes," said Mann. "I'm going to call Director James. I'd like you to be on that call. I get the feeling that Rico and his crew have nothing to worry about. Friends in high places."

"I was wondering about that," said Serrano.

"Your team has a lot more to lose if we get tangled up with the Phoenix field office, ICE, or the Department of Homeland Security. I think I could run enough interference to get you all back home safely, but there's no guarantee. Especially if we have a mole on the team."

"Have you spoken to James about this?" said Serrano.

"Yes," said Mann. "She feels the same way I do. It is what it is, and we won't know exactly what we're dealing with until we make another move."

"A possibly deadly proposition," said Serrano.

"I agree. But what other choice do we have? We have to dangle ourselves out there as bait," said Mann.

She shook her head. "They'll throw you to the wolves if you screw this up. You understand that, right? Even James won't be able to save you. If one kid or parent gets killed in this operation, that's the end of this."

"I know," said Mann, pressing a few buttons on his phone. "Let's get some guidance from above."

"Garrett?" said Camilla James over the speakerphone.

"Yes. And Señorita Serrano is on the line with us," said Mann. "We need your guidance."

"You mean you reached a point where you're about to cross the line, and you need a little nudge in either direction," said James.

"I like her," said Serrano. "Sounds like O'Reilly's sister-in-crime. How is Dana doing, if you don't mind my asking?"

"She regained consciousness about an hour ago and told me that Mann was nothing but trouble and that I should shut down the task force."

"Okay. I think that's a joke?" said Serrano. "But not being from the United States, I may not share the same sense of humor."

"Sorry, Cata," said James. "That was entirely a joke. Except for the part about O'Reilly waking up. She's doing so much better."

Serrano glanced at Mann, who wiped one of his eyes. Then the other. She found herself doing the same a moment later. She'd never met O'Reilly in person but somehow felt a similar connection. Without Dana O'Reilly's support, this task force would never have existed. And Serrano would be working the night shift at a Mexican convenience store, clutching the cheap revolver hidden behind her back every time a customer pushed the door open a little too hard.

"We need your help," said Mann, taking the next few minutes to explain the situation and his plan.

"Shit," said James. "Cata. Do you really think I need to fly out there?"

Mann raised his hands and looked away, not wanting to influence her answer—but sending a strong message, nonetheless. She pointed at him and silently mouthed *bullshit*. He nodded and mouthed *sorry*.

"We do," said Serrano. "But we don't want to alert Tucson's resident agent or the Phoenix field office. If you arrived tomorrow evening and convinced local law enforcement to support Mann's plan, without drawing any wider attention, that would be best."

"If I reach out to local law enforcement tomorrow night, every FBI field office from here to Denver will know something is going down in Tucson," said James. "I'll arrive tomorrow night, you'll brief me on the plan, and I'll contact them around five in the morning. We have a homeland security emergency alert system that should put me in touch with the Tucson chief of police and the Pima County sheriff within minutes. I'll let them know what's going to happen, and how they can support us."

"I think that would work best under the circumstances," said Serrano.

"Garrett. You can resume command of your task force now, unless you've yielded command to Señorita Serrano."

"She could be in charge. Maybe she should be. I mean that," said Mann. "When this is all done, she needs to be fast-tracked to citizenship and given a badge. We need her on our side."

"What makes you think I'd want to give up my Mexican citizenship?" said Serrano.

A long silence ensued. "I'm sorry. I didn't mean it that way. I just meant to say that . . . you're a good cop. A very good cop."

"Sounds like my cue to leave the two of you to sort some shit out," said James. "I'll see you tomorrow. I expect a full briefing when I arrive, to include every option on the table. And I'll be coming alone. Vacation day or something. I don't trust anyone around here to keep this quiet. Which means that you and another agent that looks somewhat legitimate will accompany me when I visit the Tucson chief of police and Pima County sheriff."

"I recommend Special Agent Mills," said Serrano. "He's about as low key and low ego as FBI agents come."

"Cata might be a better choice," said Mann. "Being in charge of the Mexican side of our Joint Task Force."

"Not a bad idea," said James. "We'll work this out when I arrive. I'll send along my travel itinerary as soon as it's finalized."

"Thank you," said Mann. "Is Dana in any condition to chat?"

"She's awake. Not chatty," said James. "Not that she's ever been chatty."

"Well. If it's possible tomorrow, we'd like to chat at her. Wish her a speedy recovery. Something like that," said Mann.

"She'd like that," said James. "Even if she says *hell no*. I plan on swinging by in the morning, around eight."

"We'll be up," said Mann.

"Keep him out of trouble, Cata," said James.

"Oh. I'm on the job. That's been my number one priority for over a year now," said Serrano.

"Good to hear it," said James, the call ending.

Serrano turned to Mann. "How the hell did O'Reilly and James end up in the same chain of command?"

"It wasn't an accident," said Mann. "I strongly suspect that former FBI Director Ryan Sharpe put them together."

"Well. Whoever this Sharpe guy is, he's a genius," said Serrano. "Because if the two hadn't been aligned, we'd both probably be in prison right now. Don't mess things up with James. She's fired up and angry about what happened to Dana, which makes her a very potent ally."

CHAPTER 31

Perfect timing. The sun was a minute or two from rising over the top of the Rincon Mountains. It had already lit up the south face of Mica Mountain, the tallest peak visible from the parking lot, with a deep-orange glow. The eastern sky shifted from dark blue to pale blue as he watched. Most of the stars had disappeared, only the most stubborn still visible high above the horizon. Gone within the next minute, when the sun finally peeked over the mountain range, causing him to shield his eyes.

Dale Evans loved this time of the year. Sunrise coincided with his 5:30 a.m. arrival at the Vail Unified School District transportation hub, easing the pain of the start of a new school year—and the early wakeups he faced for the next ten months.

As the head of the school district's transportation system, he really should get a new car. He'd taken enough ribbing from his staff about the "confidence" he inspired in parents, who trusted their children's safety to a man who drove a rust bucket so old it didn't have shoulder seat belts. But the thought of retiring this trusty contraption didn't sit well with him. He'd driven his late wife to Cabo for their honeymoon in this truck.

He stayed in the driver's seat, pausing for a moment to think about her. Taken a few years ago by some dipshit drunk who had pregamed before her book club, where she probably would have downed another bottle of pinot whatever—if she hadn't plowed into his wife's car at 6:23 in the evening. Helen had stayed at school late that afternoon to sell raffle tickets at a baseball game. She'd long ago given up staying after school to coach volleyball or softball, but she occasionally volunteered to help with things like the concession stand if the PTA found themselves shorthanded.

"Well. Another day. Another dollar," said Dale Evans, shoving open the Ford Bronco's temperamental door.

The moment his feet hit the asphalt, a swarm of SUVs tore into the parking lot, screeching to a halt in the parking spaces on both sides of his Bronco. One stopped directly behind his truck, barely a foot from his rear bumper.

"What the frango?" muttered Evans, wondering if he shouldn't jump back in the Bronco and try to drive through the landscaping in front of the building.

Probably pop a tire on a cactus or get stuck trying to ram through the smokers' picnic table. The door to the SUV directly next to him swung open to reveal a woman holding a badge in front of her like a shield. The blue letters above it—*FBI*—were plain as day.

"Dale Evans?" said the woman.

"Yes," he said, somewhat relieved that she didn't have her gun drawn.

She got out of the SUV, badge still up.

"I'm Executive Assistant Director Camilla James, head of the FBI's Criminal, Cyber, Response, and Services Branch," she said. "I know it's a mouthful. I basically run the criminal investigative side of things at the FBI. And you're not in any trouble. Sorry for the dramatic arrival, but we couldn't run the risk of you seeing us in your parking lot and driving on by, before giving the school district's superintendent a quick call."

"I don't understand," said Evans. "Is someone in the transportation department in trouble? Is this a drug thing? We spot-check for drug shipments twice a month with the Pima County Sheriff's Department. Run the dogs through early morning. Sometimes at night when they're all back. It's been an issue across the state over the years."

"Dale. Nobody's in trouble," said a voice he recognized. "But we need your help."

A small group of men and women stood between his Bronco and the FBI SUV. Shit. The county sheriff himself. Along with the Tucson chief of police and two others he didn't recognize. A man and a woman dressed in SWAT gear. The man's vest read FBI. The woman's read US-MEXICO JTF. He wasn't a betting man, but he'd put good money down that she was the Mexican half of the task force.

"Good to see you again, sheriff," said Evans. "I think?"

"It's all good," said Sheriff Jeff Jones. "But we do have a bit of a situation on our hands, which will require some cooperation with your office."

"Whatever I can do. Just say the magic word," said Evans. "Did I understand you correctly when you said you did not want me to call the school district's superintendent?"

"That's correct. We will notify her, but it's going to be at the very last moment," said the FBI director. "There's a very good reason for that, which we'll explain. But I'm not going to lie to you, Mr. Evans. You're probably not going to like what we're about to propose."

He'd already forgotten her name, the shock of the moment still weighing him down like a soggy blanket.

"As long as it doesn't jeopardize the safety of the kids or the drivers," said Evans.

"It won't. You have my word on that," said the man wearing the FBI tactical vest.

The agent stepped forward to shake his hand.

"I'm Special Agent Garrett Mann. And I'm the reason we've interrupted your morning. My task force identified a possible threat to one of your buses. Specifically, the bus scheduled to arrive at the Esmond Loop pickup location at 6:40 a.m."

"That's one of the high school pickups," said Evans. "It's usually packed to the gills after the 6:40 pickup."

"Well. Today it's going to be packed to the gills with federal agents and members of a special Mexican task force," said Mann, before nodding at the woman standing next to him. "And all the pickup locations will be protected by a small army of Tucson police officers and Pima County deputies, especially the Esmond Loop pickup. The suspected location of the hijacking or attack—"

"Good heavens. Are you sure I shouldn't contact the superintendent?" said Evans. "I would think she should know about this."

"She will," said the tactical agent. "Just not right now. We're going to give you a full briefing, where we can discuss this in more detail, but the bottom line is that the group that may or may not pose a threat to one of your buses today has proven to be very elusive. If your superintendent were to shut down the entire school district right now, these terrorists will melt away and pick a new target. What I didn't get to say a moment ago is that we do not think the Esmond Loop pickup is the target. We were given an address along the route, just a few minutes away from there. Our intelligence suggests that they plan to stop the bus near that address. If they don't, we'll keep riding the bus and my drone team will let us know if any suspicious vehicles follow the bus. If vehicles pull out of that address or any of the houses nearby and follow us, we'll stop before we get to the Esmond Loop pickup and deal with the threat. We will not endanger your students."

"Thank you," said Evans. "But I still think we need to—"

"Dale. The drone is already up and watching the Rita Ranch neighborhood. And my drone team is good at what they do," said Mann. "Do we need to borrow your phone for the next hour or so?"

Evans gave it some thought, before nodding. "Yes. I think you do. It doesn't feel right to keep Dr. Jacobs in the dark. She's responsible for every kid in the district."

"It isn't right, but I assure you it's necessary," said Mann. "And I appreciate your honesty. We'll make sure that the record reflects that we confiscated your phone to keep you from calling the superintendent. I'm not here to get anyone fired."

"My only concern is for the kids," said Evans. "But I do appreciate you keeping the little folks in mind."

"Little folks? You're in charge of, what? A hundred or more buses. Vetting the hundreds of drivers that transport thousands of kids around the district? Maintaining the buses that keep the kids safe? Trust me when I say that your job is more important than mine. I get to make a difference a few times a year, if I'm lucky. You're on the job all year long. That said, I'm going to have to ask you to hand over your phone."

"You're an interesting fella, Agent Mann," said Evans, surrendering his phone.

A U-Haul truck pulled into the parking lot moments later. None of the agents seemed concerned, so he did his best to keep his cool.

"What's that?" said Evans.

"Every mannequin we could round up in Tucson. Compliments of Target and Kohl's. We can't have an empty bus driving around," said Mann.

"Damn. This is something," said Evans.

"It's something, all right," said Mann. "Let's move inside. I get the impression that we don't have much time."

"You're right about that. The driver for that particular bus will be here any minute. She'll enter over there," said Evans, pointing west. "That's the bus farm. She'll swipe in at the automated gate, park her car, and get the bus started. Then she'll check in with my dispatcher, who should also be here any minute. Your director is parked in her spot. James. Right? I couldn't remember earlier. A little shell shocked."

"We'll move," said James, before checking her watch. "Maybe we should all just head over to the bus farm. What time does that bus leave?"

"Six. Give or take a few," said Evans. "She drives east toward the mountains and hits four smaller pickups, before turning toward Rita Ranch. That's her biggest pickup. Only one more on the way out to the high school, but that's a small pickup."

"Does your dispatcher have the key to get in the office?" said Mann.

"She does."

Mann gave him the phone back. "Send her a quick text and tell her that the sheriff popped in with a surprise drug check, or whatever you call it. Make it clear that the bus will run on time, but the sheriff received some specific intelligence about a possible drug shipment hidden in one of the buses."

"Sounds realistic enough," said the Pima County sheriff.

"I suppose it does," said Evans. "But you know Debbie. She's got a tinfoil hat in her purse. She'll know something's wrong within a minute of arriving."

"I'll leave two detectives here," said the Tucson police chief. "To make sure we don't have a problem."

"I can leave one of my task force agents," said Mann. "He's a forensic investigator. We won't need him until later."

"That'll help," said the police chief. "What time will we let them reach out to the superintendent?"

"6:40. If nothing happens by then, I don't see it happening today," said Mann.

"I hope nothing happens. No offense," said Evans.

"None taken," said Mann. "I hope we're entirely wrong about this and the information we intercepted was taken out of context. But if we're right, we'll have saved a busload of kids and one of your drivers."

"And that's all that matters in the end," said Evans. "If you're wrong, a small hiccup won't be a big deal. Just don't leave me out to dry when Dr. Jacobs comes a-calling."

CHAPTER 32

Mann turned the bus left off Rita Road, onto Ashford Drive. If you could call what he had just executed an actual turn. More like a Hail Mary turn of the wheel that clipped the median. Jesus. Whatever they paid bus drivers—here or anywhere—wasn't enough. The captain of the *Titanic* had more control of the maneuverability of his ship than a standard school bus. You literally had to think about how you'd navigate a simple turn blocks in advance of it. His radio came to life. Everyone on the bus, plus the three operatives under Melendez's command, was on the same radio frequency.

"Mann. This is Jax. Ashford Drive looks clear. No cars on the street itself. Plenty of vehicles parked in the driveways."

"Copy," said Mann.

While Jax flew the drone and watched the thermal feed, Neva—one of Serrano's surveillance techs—kept her eye on the overall ground feed. The drone's dual-capacity surveillance pod gave them the simultaneous ability to scan with different sensors in different directions, the only limitation being the direction of the pod. They could use both sensors on one target, spinning the pod 360 degrees, but they couldn't split their attention between targets more than ninety degrees apart.

The bus straightened out on Ashford Drive, somehow not clipping a cyclist or pedestrian. This was the homestretch.

"Thirty seconds!" yelled Mann, slowing the bus.

Luke Turner, who crouched behind him, repeated the thirty-second mark to the Tucson Police and Pima County Sheriff's Department. A few seconds later, Jax reported.

"I have two SUVs backing out of a driveway on South Castle Bay Street. The SUVs have been parked in the driveway since I arrived on station. We did not see anyone leave the house and get in the vehicles. Get ready for a roadblock at the intersection or a tail heading south of the neighborhood."

Turner passed the information along to the locals. Under no circumstance were those two vehicles, if they indeed followed the bus down Ashford Drive, to reach Esmond Loop. And if they did turn and follow the bus, local law enforcement would form a shield around the kids waiting for their bus.

"The SUVs are headed toward the intersection," said Jax. "Good luck."

"Launch the quadcopter," said Mann, focusing on the road ahead.

"Already up," said Jax.

The intersection came up faster than he'd anticipated. More like twenty seconds than thirty. Not that it mattered. Everyone had been ready to pounce since they had left the bus farm. Two teams crouched in the aisle: Serrano in the back row; ALPHA team, two of Serrano's people led by Turner; followed by BRAVO team, comprised of Baker plus three Mexicans.

The plan was simple. When the bus stopped, ALPHA team would deploy from the bus's back door, moving down the left side of the bus. BRAVO would head right, toward the door. Ideally, the two teams would converge on the hijackers at the same time, having been staggered by a few seconds. Serrano would cover the bus's six with one of the drum-fed automatic rifles that the ATF had been looking for.

"Coming up on the intersection," said Mann, before taking a quick look over his shoulder.

Everyone was in place. Everyone but the mannequins, half of which had shifted during the rough ride over.

"Straighten out the mannequins," said Mann.

"Does it really matter at this point?" yelled Serrano, forgoing the radio.

"Probably not!" said Mann.

He resisted the temptation to slow the bus as he approached the intersection. He didn't have a stop sign.

"I see two SUVs waiting at the intersection," said Mann over the radio. "Ten seconds out."

"Jax to Mann. I see a rifle barrel in the back seat of the lead vehicle," said Jackson. "Expect hard contact at the intersection."

"Copy," said Mann, wondering what would happen if and when he slammed on the brakes.

He hadn't asked the bus driver about the bus's stopping distance.

"Our friends are in place," said Jax.

Melendez, Miralles, and Zekry sat in their vehicles waiting for orders. He had purposefully kept their exact locations and purpose a secret from the team. He needed to keep a few surprises away from their mole and out of enemy hands. If the bus safely passed through the intersection and made it out of the neighborhood, they'd drive wherever Mann needed them. If things went sideways in the next few seconds, they'd make their way on foot to the fight, backing up his team from the outside. Force multipliers. Like nothing he'd seen before, that was what Audra Bauer had told him, and given what he'd seen at the Fairfax hospital, he had no reason to doubt her assessment.

"SUVs are on the move!" said Mann. "Hang on!"

The two SUVs pulled into the intersection, blocking the bus's path. He hit the brakes. By the time the bus came to a complete stop, six very serious-looking bald and neck-tattooed men carrying AK-style assault rifles were on the street—one pointing his rifle at Mann as the group rushed toward the door on the right side of the bus. Mann wore an oversize flannel shirt over his body armor, his helmet on the seat bench behind him, so they wouldn't see a tactical agent at the wheel of the bus.

"Six hostiles. All armed with AKs," said Mann, slipping out of his seat and retreating down the aisle.

"ALPHA and BRAVO are on the move," said Serrano.

It was out of his hands for the next several seconds. He grabbed his helmet, which had fallen to the floor, and quickly snapped it in place, before grabbing one of the ballistic shields the Pima County Sheriff's Department had given his team.

ALPHA and BRAVO carried the rest of the shields, two per team to create an impenetrable wall in case the cartel crew decided to try to shoot their way out of this. He couldn't see his own teams through the windows since the bus was high off the street, but one team would be rushing forward along each side of the bus, leading with their shields.

Mann inched forward, until he could see the cartel soldiers through the ballistic glass window embedded near the top of the shield. The sicarios paused, glancing back and forth at each other, before lowering their weapons and backing up. Mann stood and walked to the front of the bus, where he had a full view of the interaction. BRAVO moved right past the bus door, Baker and his team yelling surrender commands in Spanish. ALPHA team crossed the front of the bus, trapping the sicarios in a tight group.

The sicarios dropped their rifles after a vicious exchange of words, kicking them under or toward the nearest SUV as ordered.

"Luke. Bring up our SWAT friends," said Mann. "I'm on my way out."

Rocha, who had remained hidden several rows back, shoved a mannequin into the aisle, before making her way to the back of the bus, where he joined her.

"That was painless," she said.

"Yeah," said Mann. "Almost seems too good to be true."

"The SUVs didn't come from the address referenced by the data fragment," said Rocha. "They came from Castle Bay Street."

"I really don't want to see what happened to the family at that house," said Mann. "These people are savages."

"More than any of us can imagine," said Rocha.

Mann took a moment to check in with their eye in the sky.

"Jax. You got anything we need to be worried about?"

"Negative," said Jax. "I have six tangos marked. No additional movement in the neighborhood."

"Thank you," said Mann. "Keep your eyes peeled for trouble. Never know."

"This ain't my first rodeo," said Jax. "I'll be on station until the batteries run out. Two hours. Don't pick your nose or scratch your ass. I'm watching."

"Wonderful," said Mann.

Serrano slid into one of the back rows to make room for Rocha and Mann to reach the rear exit.

"Looks like the cavalry is on the way," said Serrano.

Mann turned his head, glancing toward the front of the bus. Up the street, a convoy of SUVs raced toward them, emergency lights flashing.

"Perfect timing?" said Mann, before he hopped down to the street.

"This is too easy," said Serrano.

"I agree," said Mann, helping Rocha down. "Stay frosty."

"What?"

"It's military jargon for *stay alert*," said Mann.

"That's stupid. How does that even make sense?"

"It doesn't," said Mann. "But stay frosty."

"Piss off," said Serrano.

"Now that's frosty," said Rocha.

"Right?" said Mann, winking at Serrano, before hitting the street and following Rocha along the right side of the bus.

Rocha stopped halfway and pulled out her phone.

"What's up?" said Mann, passing her.

"Nothing," said Rocha, putting her phone back in one of her pockets.

Mann sprinted ahead of her, reaching BRAVO team a few seconds later. The six sicarios were in various states of surrender. A few with their hands behind their heads and quiet. Others still protesting. The most important thing for now being that they'd kicked their rifles away.

A harsh verbal exchange ensued, Serrano's people demanding that they raise their hands above their heads and turn around, their immediate concern being that the sicarios might be hiding pistols under their shirts. A valid concern, given the circumstances.

"How are we doing?" said Mann, patting Baker on the shoulder.

"I don't know. Six of them. Eight of us," said Baker. "I'd like to wait for reinforcements before we physically engage them."

On cue, three SUVs screeched to a halt on the other side of the sicarios' vehicles, forming a rough perimeter. A dozen Tucson Police Department SWAT officers swarmed the scene.

"What are we doing?" said one of the officers, presumably their commander.

"Disarming these guys!" said Mann. "Can you move in behind them? Their rifles are under the westernmost SUV."

"Roger," said the officer, before issuing orders that set his team in motion.

A dozen SWAT officers quickly moved into position behind the sicarios, their commander giving Mann a thumbs-up. A few more of the hostiles raised their hands, leaving one with his hands still down. Once he put his hands up, SWAT would rush in.

"Garrett?" said Rocha.

He looked over his shoulder. Rocha stared down at the phone in her hand. What the hell was she doing on her phone again?

"What's up?"

She shook her head. "I'm so sorry. I didn't have a choice."

"What are you saying?" said Mann, suddenly realizing exactly what she was saying.

"I swear I didn't know this was a setup," she said. "I just thought they—"

Rocha dropped to her knees, a bright-red blotch striking the side of the bus where she had just been standing. The snap of a bullet reached Mann's ears at the same time. She clutched her neck with both hands, blood spraying through her fingers. A second bullet struck her helmet and knocked her over. Then all hell broke loose.

CHAPTER 33

Luke Turner put his back to the bus's front grille and crouched behind one of the shields, pulling the closest Mexican task force member behind the shield with him. Zita. Javier didn't waste a moment, scooting in tightly against Zita until the shields touched. The three of them huddled together behind the makeshift barricade as bullets cracked against the shields and slammed into the bus around them. The volume of gunfire was incredible. Definitely some kind of drum-fed automatic weapons. Possibly light machine guns.

He took a quick assessment of the situation, trying to determine if they were safer staying here and engaging the shooters, or moving to a more advantageous position. No obvious solution presented itself. The SWAT agents had immediately retreated behind the sicarios' SUVs, a steady stream of gunfire chasing them and pounding the vehicles as they took cover. At least a third of them didn't make it, immediately dropping where they stood or tumbling to the street in the chaos that ensued. The surviving officers appeared to be shooting in several directions at once.

Baker's team had retreated out of sight along the right side of the bus, frantic calls for backup and medical assistance rendering the radio net unusable. The shooters appeared to be firing from multiple directions, preventing all the officers and task force members from finding effective cover from the maelstrom of gunfire. A worst-case scenario. None of them would be standing for much longer, if they didn't take out enough of the shooters to establish at least one safe zone where they could take cover.

"*Los sicarios!*" said Zita, pointing toward the group of six cartel soldiers who had stopped the bus.

A bullet struck her gloved hand before she could pull it back behind the shield. A second tore through her forearm, spraying Turner with blood. He peered through the window in his shield and saw why she'd been concerned enough to expose her arm like that. The sicarios had crawled to their SUV and started reaching under the vehicle to retrieve their rifles. One of them already had an AK-47 in his hands, crouched near the back tire. The moment he raised it, pointing down the right side of the bus, his head snapped back. Blood splattered the side of the vehicle.

If the rest of the team took possession of their rifles, things would go from bad to worse in a matter of seconds. A second rifle appeared, followed by a third.

"Fuck this," muttered Turner. "Open fire on the sicarios!"

Javier didn't hesitate. He'd already started shooting by the time Turner had made the necessary adjustment to his grip on the shield to brace his rifle. He'd slid his left hand through a center strap that allowed him to keep the shield in place and fire the rifle around it. Once he'd stabilized the rifle, he pressed the trigger repeatedly, moving from target to target until the sicarios lay in a bloodied heap on the street. One less thing to worry about.

"All teams. This is Jax. Shooters are located on the second floors of four houses surrounding the intersection. The quadcopter is equipped with an explosive charge. Enough to clear a few rooms. We can knock out one of the houses."

Jax had suggested arming one of their quadcopters with an explosive device. Mann didn't like the idea. He'd seen online videos of the Ukrainians using them against Russians who took shelter in Ukrainian homes they'd occupied. The results? Brutal. Turner was glad Mann hadn't said no. They needed this capability now. The task force was surrounded, taking casualties every second.

Turner searched for the sources of gunfire, rapidly identifying the windows the shooters used to rain down hell on them. From what he could tell, one shooter in each house fired an automatic weapon, probably equipped with high-capacity drum magazines to keep up the prolonged, high rate of fire. The other fired short, automatic bursts.

"Hit the house to the west!" said Turner.

Mann glanced at him and nodded. "Jax. This is Mann. Hit the house to the west of the bus."

"On the way," said Jax.

"We'll do what we can to clear the house to the north. That'll give us good cover on the right side of the bus," said Mann. "ALPHA. Can you move to the right side of the bus?"

"Once that drone hits," said Turner.

"Mann. This is Emily. I'm halfway to the house north of you. Keep firing on it until I tell you to stop."

"Copy. Rico and Blake, what's your status?"

"This is Rico. Same."

"This is Blake. I can see the back of the south house. Give me thirty seconds."

"ALPHA. How is SWAT doing?" said Mann.

In all the pandemonium, he'd completely forgotten about them. He grabbed the shoulder transmitter, attached to his vest.

"SWAT. This is Turner. What's your status?"

"Pinned down between our vehicles. Half my team is out of action," said their commander.

"We're about to take out the shooters to your west," said Turner. "When that's done, focus your fire on the house to the south. But stay on the line. We have a team member moving through the backyards to that house. When they breach, I'll need you to cease fire."

"Understood. SWAT out."

He turned to Zita and Javier. "When we move, we take it slow until we get around the side of the bus. Javier. Change magazines."

Zita started to adjust her rifle to do the same. He wasn't sure how she planned to do that, but the fact that she was even trying led him to believe she could pull it off. She was former Mexican Naval Infantry. Once a Marine, always a Marine. He squeezed her shoulder.

"Zita. Your pistol only at this point."

She nodded. A few seconds after Turner had reloaded his rifle, a buzz cut through the gunfire. Turner glanced up at the house to the west in time to see a gray quadcopter crash through the rightmost corner window. The subsequent explosion ejected glass and drywall dust through both second-floor windows, hopefully taking out the two shooters.

"Let's go," said Turner.

They inched toward the right side of the bus, staying in a low crouch and keeping the shields slightly overlapping to better protect Zita, who didn't carry a shield. When they reached the corner of the bus, Turner made sure his shield remained facing the house to the south until they had backed up past the door. When he turned around to check on the others, he froze in place. Baker lay face up on the ground, two small bullet holes in his right cheek—a pool of blood expanding underneath his helmet-protected head.

Rocha sat against the bus, legs straight out, arms slumped to her side. Blood slowly pumped out of her neck. One of the Mexicans lay face down a few feet past Rocha, his body motionless and contorted at an angle that told Turner one thing. The man was dead.

Mann and one of the new additions to Serrano's team crouched behind one of the ballistic shields, stacked up one behind the other to maximize the shield's coverage. They both fired rapidly at the house to the north. The other Mexican task force member crouched next to the bus's rear tire, firing from behind the team's second shield. Their bullets continuously peppered the two windows, splintering the casements and chipping the adobe walls.

A bullet smacked into the bus next to Turner's head, punching a small hole through its yellow side, just above the school district name and bus number. He repositioned his shield and started firing at the house to the north. Javier did the same. The addition of the rifles must have attracted Mann's attention. He glanced back at Turner and nodded, before reloading his rifle and going right back to suppressing the north house. Some of them might actually get out of this alive. Then his radio squawked.

"All teams. This is Serrano. I have a fast mover inbound from the rear."

"I see it," said Jax. "Pickup truck. Three armed hostiles in the bed."

"Take it out," said Mann.

CHAPTER 34

By the time Serrano sighted in on the approaching pickup truck, bullets struck the bus's doorframe and zipped inches from her head. She lay prone on the floor, the rifle's bipod holding the site's magnified reticle steady. Serrano resisted the temptation to fire at the men visible above the pickup's cabin. She couldn't waste the time. Her priority was to stop the truck from plowing through the task force.

She placed the reticle on the driver's side of the windshield and pressed the trigger for about two seconds. Overkill, literally, but she had to be sure. The windshield in front of the driver turned chalky white, a dozen dark holes in the shattered glass contrasted against a massive red splotch. The pickup truck violently swerved left a moment later, tossing two of the shooters in the bed to the street, where they quickly tumbled to a stop—their rifles skittering along the road.

The pickup plowed over the curb and struck a thick palm tree in the middle of a yard. The third shooter in the pickup bed flew over the top of the cabin, clipping the tree with his shoulder and spinning midair until he hit the garage door. The pickup's airbags deployed, stopping the driver and front passenger from flying through the windshield. Not that it would have mattered for the driver.

She placed the rifle sight's reticle on the lower passenger side of the windshield and emptied the magazine as the airbag deflated—her salvo of bullets having a near identical effect as the burst fired at the driver. Glass showered her from the right, several bullets punching through the brown vinyl seat backs and bottom cushions. Someone wasn't happy. She'd finally drawn the eastern house's attention.

Serrano turned her attention to the two sicarios who had fallen off the pickup. One had turned on his back. The other had managed to crawl halfway toward one of the rifles. She grabbed one of the rifle magazines she'd placed beside her for quick access and swapped magazines. A few more trigger pulls made quick work of the two lying in the road.

"The pickup and its passengers are no longer a threat," she said over the radio net.

Another long burst of gunfire tore through the back of the bus. The eastern house must be out of targets, or they had another surprise on the way. She reloaded again, just in case.

CHAPTER 35

Miralles did something reckless. Something Melendez most certainly wouldn't approve of. But now the task force had vehicle attacks to contend with, and the longer it took her to neutralize the shooters, the more casualties they'd suffer. Based on what she'd already heard over the radio, things were a mess out there. She hopped the brick wall leading into the target house's backyard and sprinted to the patio sliding doors without stopping to take any precautions.

An easy way to get yourself killed, if your adversary had personnel to spare. She'd made a calculated guess that they didn't. They seemed entirely focused on wiping out Mann's people. The only thing out of place in the backyard was a sizable hole dug near the back of the fence.

A wall of vertical blinds blocked her view through the slider, presumably providing her the same courtesy. She didn't have time to guess which way to go, so she contacted Jax.

"Jax. This is Emily. Which side of the house is the garage on?"

"Left side. If you're facing toward the house. There's a regular entry door on that side. The shooters are on the right side."

"Thank you. Breaching in a few seconds," said Miralles, already on her way.

She reached over her shoulder and removed a compact crowbar from the equipment pack attached to the back of her vest. She inserted the crowbar next to the doorknob and said a prayer. If the house had an alarm system, and this crew had been smart enough to activate it, she'd find herself in a gunfight on unfamiliar terrain. *Here goes nothing.* She yanked the crowbar, freeing the door.

The first thing she noticed was the smell. Bodies. Early-stage decomposition. Then she realized that both cars were in the garage. She slid behind them on her way to the door leading directly into the house. School logos and bumper stickers with friendly sayings adorned the back of the minivan. This wasn't a sicario hideout. A family had lived here, likely stuffed in the trunk of the four-door Toyota Corolla parked next to the minivan.

She shook her head as she approached the door. She tested the knob, surprised to find it unlocked. Miralles opened it a half inch and did a quick visual check up and down the opening. There was more than one way to booby-trap a door, but she didn't have time to send in an optic fiber, and these shooters didn't strike her as the motion sensor or laser trigger types. More like the "wire attached to a grenade or the trigger of a shotgun" level. Finding nothing obvious, she crept along very slowly, until she could peek inside. Nothing. She slipped in and drew her pistol.

A quick sweep of the first floor revealed nothing but the mess in the kitchen these beasts had made over the past few days while they waited. Probably got tired of the smell penetrating the door to the garage and started digging a hole before they got word from their inside source that Mann's team was coming.

The gunfire outside continued at a steady rhythm, the occasional long burst from the automatic rifle upstairs and from the other houses breaking up the staccato pattern created by the task force's more controlled semiautomatic fire.

She found the stairs and noted the orientation. She'd turn left at the top. Before heading up, she searched for trip wires. Nothing obvious. They really thought they were going to wipe out Mann's people within minutes and just drive out of here. Unbelievable.

Miralles holstered the pistol and switched to her suppressed rifle before creeping up the staircase. She wasn't worried about creaky steps.

The shooters were essentially deaf at this point, even if they had been smart enough to wear hearing protection. Halfway up, a bullet popped through the top stair riser.

Shit. It was go-time. "Mann. This is Emily. Cease firing. I say again. Cease firing. I'm about to hit them."

"Copy."

The gunfire stopped a few seconds later—and Miralles made her move. She took the rest of the stairs two at a time and turned left into the hallway at the top. The rest was a bit of a blur. Three doors. Two facing the street. One facing the backyard. Miralles leaned into the first doorway and pressed the trigger twice, her bullets striking a woman firing an AK-47 in the right temple.

Miralles moved on to the next room before the woman's body slid to the floor. Two more quick trigger presses and the Soviet-era RPD light machine gun went quiet, the man holding it collapsing on top of a wide sandbag barrier like the one she'd seen in the other room. That explained the hole in the backyard: they had filled sandbags and created reinforced firing positions. No wonder Mann's task force and the SWAT team were having no luck silencing these guns.

"Two hostiles neutralized," said Miralles, before taking a closer look at the man she had just killed.

Blond hair. Blue eyes. Very white skin. Not likely a member of the Juárez Cartel. She ran to the other room and ducked behind the sandbags to examine the woman. Something was off.

"Mann. This is Emily. They reinforced their positions with sandbags. And the automatic fire is coming from RPDs. Drum-fed. One more thing. One of the targets I took down is one hundred percent not—I repeat, *not*—a cartel member. The other shooter fits the description, but she's not inked up."

"This is Mann. Copy your report. Nice work up there. Rico, what's your status?"

"Entering the east house."

"Blake?"

No response. Shit. A sharp, but distant explosion echoed through the room. Followed by a second.

"Just flash-banging some rooms. South house is clear. Found the same setup. RPD. Sandbag barriers," said Zekry. "And I got a pasty white dude and a Middle Eastern–looking guy."

It sounded like a mercenary crew.

"This is Mann. Good job. All units, standby to cease firing on the east house. Let Rico work his magic. Emily and Blake. Hold your positions. Be ready to lay down suppressing fire on the east house if it goes active. I'll send a team up to verify that it's clear when all the guns go quiet."

Miralles crouched behind the sandbag barrier and waited, ready to pick up the RPD and go to town on the east house if it went hot again. A long volley of fully automatic gunfire erupted from the house across the street. She stayed down. No reason to take on a drum-fed light machine gun. When the streets quieted again, two muted but sharp cracks hit her ears. She knew the sound. Two suppressed rifle shots.

"Rico?" she said over the radio net, barely lifting her head above the sandbags to look at the house across the street.

Melendez appeared in one of the corner windows, giving her a thumbs-up. "East house is clear."

CHAPTER 36

A single gunshot broke the silence. "This is Rico. Two targets down. Both Caucasian."

Mann slid next to Turner. "Take Javier to the west house and verify that the drone took out the two shooters."

"Got it," said Turner, grabbing Javier and taking off for the house's driveway.

"All units. This is Mann. Remain in place until we clear the west house."

Sirens wailed in the distance as Mann surveyed the scene. Baker dead. Rocha dead. One of Serrano's people dead. Zita, severely wounded, crouched behind him. A half dozen SWAT officers down. Some down hard. He'd driven them into an ambush, trusting Rocha's information—which she'd undoubtedly fabricated. This was his fault. He'd underestimated AXIOM and overestimated his own plan.

Mann had thought he'd taken enough precautions if AXIOM planned to attack his team on the bus. They'd created a contingency plan to counter that possibility. But he'd been thinking small. His plan could easily have repelled a sicario attack. Four FBI agents, two with significant SWAT experience. Serrano and her team. Six Mexicans with SWAT or special forces military training. Twelve Pima County SWAT officers. Plus three seasoned operatives provided by the CIA. Not to mention full drone coverage. Twenty-five serious shooters, with more standing by, just a few blocks away.

More than enough firepower and experience to easily put down a squad of LABYRINTH-trained cartel soldiers. But just barely enough to contend with a multidirectional, trained mercenary attack employing light machine guns. He was lucky they hadn't used rocket-propelled grenades or grenade launchers. If you considered losing half of the people you put in harm's way to be lucky.

"This is Turner. The team in the west house is down. The drone shredded them. One guy was still moving. He's not moving anymore. We searched the house. It's clear. But uh—these sick fucks murdered the couple that lived here and stuffed them in the back of an SUV in the garage."

"This is Emily. They did the same at the north house. An entire family."

Jesus. How many people had AXIOM killed to get at the task force? No. How many people had *he* killed with his pride? Or were they dead the moment someone at AXIOM got the idea to pass that data fragment to Rocha? Kim wouldn't have concocted this sinister of a plan. She'd said something right before she was shot—when she tried to warn him. They must have known she might have last-moment doubts. It must have had something to do with her phone, which lay next to her, covered in blood.

"Jax. This is Mann. Do you see anything else down here that concerns you?"

"Negative."

"Turner. Let the Pima County SWAT commander know that it's safe to move more officers onto the scene and into blocking positions around the neighborhood. And we need ambulances. At least a dozen."

"I'm on it," said Turner over the radio net.

"All other units can stand down. Rico and company. Clear your houses before joining us at the bus," said Mann.

Mann suddenly felt nauseous and a little dizzy, his vision narrowing. He took a knee and placed a hand on the bus to steady himself.

"*Estás bien?*" said Isa, scooting in his direction—still crouched down.

"*Sí. Un poco mareado,*" said Mann, before taking a few deep breaths and nodding. "*Gracias.*"

He headed over to Rocha's body to check her phone, his legs still feeling a little wobbly. Serrano opened the bus's side door and headed in his direction. Isa said something to her so fast, he didn't catch it. She knelt next to him as he wiped the phone's blood-slicked screen on his pants.

"You okay?" she said.

"Yeah. Just felt a little dizzy for a moment. Sorry about Antonio," he said. "Zita took a few bullets to her hand and arm, but she should be fine. Patillo is patching her up until the paramedics arrive."

"Sorry about Baker and Rocha," said Serrano. "What are you doing?"

"Rocha said something to me seconds before she was hit," said Mann. "She called out to me. When I turned, she was staring at her phone—saying something about being sorry and not having a choice. That she didn't know it was a setup. She started to say something else, but the bullet cut her off."

"Rocha was the mole?"

"Apparently," said Mann. "I want to see what was so important that she pulled out her phone twice while we ran down the side of the bus."

Serrano pulled a few gauze pads out of her first aid pouch and opened them. Mann took them one at a time, wiping away as much of the thick blood as possible. He removed one of his gloves and pressed the screen. Locked. Serrano took it from his hand and stuffed it in the first aid kit before proceeding to remove Rocha's helmet and tactical glasses. Jesus. She then held the phone up to Rocha's lifeless face, before handing the phone back to him.

"Sorry. I normally have more respect for the dead, but we have work to do," said Serrano.

Mann read the text chain that appeared:

TOMMY 6:35 a.m.

They just left the house. Said we're free to go. That you came through. Thank you. I don't know how you did it.

TOMMY 6:37 a.m.

Where r u? The police are on the way. This is for real. Thank you!

"Kim has a twin brother, who has a family. Three kids. His name is Tom," said Mann.

"These people are fucking sick," said Serrano.

"At least they let her brother and his family go free," said Mann. "That seems to be the only silver lining today."

A few minutes later, all the survivors assembled in front of the bus, except for Patillo—one of the new members of Serrano's crew—and Zita. Patillo was busy patching up Zita's wounds, ahead of the ambulances.

"I don't see Blake," said Melendez, before triggering his radio. "Blake. This is Rico. What's your status."

Silence on the line.

"Blake. Click your radio twice if you're in a situation where you can't talk."

Nothing.

"Shit. I'm headed up to the house," said Melendez, taking off—Miralles following close behind.

They returned carrying Blake Zekry's body and placed it carefully alongside the three dead SWAT officers arranged in a row directly in front of one of the SWAT SUVs. Melendez looked up at Mann and shook his head.

"One of the bullets from that last mag the mercenary burned off caught him just below the rim of his helmet."

Mann swallowed hard and was about to say sorry—when Melendez cut him off.

"It's not your fault. It's nobody's fault but the people who ambushed us and the people who sent them—and we're going to burn the people who sent them to the fucking ground."

Mann nodded. "Damn right we are."

CHAPTER 37

Within ten minutes of Mann declaring the intersection engagement area clear and calling in first responders, Rita Ranch became the center of the universe, overrun by every police officer, sheriff's deputy, paramedic, school official, and town or city official within the greater Tucson area. Mann had lost control of the scene, which wasn't his to control in the first place. He was just one of the winning pieces on the chessboard here. A costly win—but what victory didn't come with a price? The problem here being that he couldn't identify what had been gained or won.

Sure. He'd survived to fight another day, which wasn't exactly a modest accomplishment given what had been thrown at his task force. But he'd lost half of the FBI agents he'd brought to the task force. For what? How did this disaster move the fight forward? Or maybe he was asking the wrong question. The right one being, How could he make the best of this disaster to move it forward? The answer didn't come to him like some kind of sudden signal. The skies didn't darken. The winds didn't rise. It just came to him.

"Luke," said Mann.

"Yeah?" said Turner.

"Gather everyone on the team and search the houses again," said Mann. "I want every phone, tablet, and computer you can find. Use the badge to push the locals around if you have to. I want everything that can possibly be used to figure out who ordered this attack."

"We know who orchestrated the ambush," said Turner.

"You and I know, but we need some hard evidence," said Mann. "And I'd like to know how they planned on getting out of here. My guess is that they planned on using the homeowners' vehicles to reach a staging area. Maybe a motel?"

"I doubt they checked into a motel. Rico didn't find a dead family in the east house, the address listed on the data fragment. My guess is that an AXIOM proxy bought that house and one of the original LABYRINTH graduates was stationed there. Or it was rented as an Airbnb until it was needed."

Mann nodded. "Focus on the four houses. This place is turning into a zoo."

Turner left with Ray Mills and Callie Jackson, who had just arrived, along with one of Serrano's people.

"Maybe we should send Isa with them," said Serrano. "I don't know how long this joint task force ruse is going to last."

"Not a bad idea," said Mann.

Serrano spoke a few words to Isa, and she was off, racing to catch up with the others.

"What about you?" said Mann.

"I'm FBI," she said, pulling out her fake badge.

"Might want to switch the patch on your vest," said Mann.

"Good point," she said, turning to face the bus.

When she turned around, the patch on the front of her vest read FBI.

"James is going to have a fit," said Mann.

"Speak of the devil," said Serrano.

Three SUVs approached from the south, slowing down for the SWAT roadblock protecting the core of the crime scene. Even from here, he could read the blue letters on the badges held out to the SWAT officers. *FBI.*

"Shit," said Mann as the vehicles blocking the road backed into the adjacent driveways, admitting his boss to the scene.

"Maybe I should help Turner with the houses," said Serrano.

He shook his head. "She already knows your deal."

The convoy slowly made its way through the crowds of officials, stopping next to the bus, where Mann and his team had essentially remained since the end of the street battle. There was something reassuring about having a fifteen-ton, thirty-five-foot-long steel barrier at your back that had kept him securely anchored in this position.

James opened the rear passenger door of the lead vehicle and hopped out. Her eyes immediately went to the four bodies lying face up on the street next to Mann. She clasped her hands and closed her eyes, presumably saying a quick prayer. When she opened them again a few moments later, she was all business.

"I need to get you and your associates," she said, lingering on the word *associates* while she turned her head toward Serrano, "out of here immediately. For obvious reasons."

He glanced at the bodies next to him. Two "official" members of his task force, plus a Mexican national and a mercenary.

"They'll be handled appropriately," said James.

"Understood," said Mann. "The rest of the team is searching the houses for electronic devices. Anything we can use to possibly trace their movements over the past several days and shed some light on who ordered this attack. Actual evidence, instead of what we know to be true."

"Five minutes," said James. "Not a second more."

Mann passed the word over the radio. A few moments later, the team emerged from the west house and split up to cover the rest.

"I'd ask what happened, but it looks pretty obvious—and the radio traffic didn't leave much to the imagination," said James, glancing around. "Four-direction ambush, giving you no real cover. Light machine guns. The initial roadblock was a ruse to get your team off the bus and into the open. This is fucked up."

"Beyond fucked up," said Mann. "I'm not sure where we go from here."

"Anywhere but here," said James, glancing around nervously. "Where are Melendez and Miralles?"

"Not far away," said Mann. "They didn't want to stick around."

"They should have taken your Mexican friends with them," said James.

Serrano started to protest, but James cut her off.

"No disrespect intended. Seriously. Your team's accomplishments and sacrifice will not be forgotten, but you do represent a complication," said James. "Fortunately, I happen to be the most senior FBI agent within two thousand miles of Tucson. What I say goes. Until someone gets on a phone and reaches someone more senior. I'd like to be out of here by the time that happens. Tucson's resident agent is rip-shit mad right now. I'm sure he's got the Phoenix SAC dialing every number she has at headquarters, trying to go over my head."

"They know you're here?" said Serrano.

James laughed. "Let's just say, I kind of put Tucson's resident agent in a timeout after he threw a fit. Told him that this was a 'need to know' operation and that I'd take a personal interest in his career if he didn't stand down. I'm guessing I bought about thirty minutes before he decides to call my bluff, and another hour or so before the Phoenix SAC finally reaches someone in DC who will take her gripe seriously. Another thirty before I start receiving calls, which I'll ignore for a little while. Basically, two hours—minus the five minutes spent driving here—to get to Phoenix."

"What's in Phoenix?" said Mann, knowing the answer.

"Elena. You're going to transfer her into my custody at the airport, and I'm going to fly to wherever Raul is being held, to take custody of him as well. You and your team will not be accompanying me on that trip. The same jet that dropped you off in Phoenix the other day will be waiting to take you back to DC. Serrano's people will have to make a tough decision in Phoenix. Head home or take the flight to DC with you," said James, turning to Serrano. "I have no intention of denying you and your team the opportunity to see this to the end. Whatever end comes of it."

"Thank you," said Serrano. "That means more than you can imagine."

"The catch is that I can't ensure your legal outcome if you're taken into custody—during whatever operation the task force executes," said James.

"She's in the country legally," said Mann.

"Not as an authorized law enforcement proxy," said James. "I'm just pointing out the risk her team will be taking."

"Can Bauer wave her magic wand and bless her team?" said Mann.

"There's a reason her people split," said James. "They run the same risk."

"I'll discuss this with my team on the way to Phoenix. My guess is that a few will head back to Mexico," said Serrano.

"Director James?" said Mann.

"Now I'm Director James?"

"Two things."

"Even better," said James.

"First. We need to protect the task force's families. I didn't think of that before," said Mann. "Rocha was solid, but they got to her in a way that few of us might have been able to defy."

"I'll get the US Marshals on it immediately," said James. "Number two?"

"Raul. I think you should delay his transfer to DC," said Mann. "The only thing keeping him talking is the hope that he'll be taken into federal custody."

"That's what I intend to do," said James. "Take him into federal custody."

"*Hope* isn't the right word," said Mann. "It's the *prospect* of being taken into federal custody that will keep him talking. I promised him that if he cooperated, I'd turn him over to the US Department of Justice. If you take him into custody now, we won't get another word out of him. He'll lawyer up and take his chances with the system. Maybe we'll convince him to take a deal to testify against AXIOM. Maybe not. Either way, it's going to be a long, drawn-out process, and I don't believe we have that kind of time. Not to mention the fact that I'm not convinced the DOJ can protect him while in custody. Not with the stink of Sacramento on his hands."

James muttered a few choice words under her breath.

"I agree. Based on what I've been told by Bauer and Sharpe, ARTEMIS will have to move fast to derail AXIOM's plan, especially if their suspicions about the true intention of the cartel network turn out to be true. We could be looking at days, not weeks, before this whole thing just melts away, leaving us with a big mess on our hands—and nothing to show for it but a rather far-fetched conspiracy theory."

"And a still intact network of cartel soldiers ready and more than willing to do their dirty work," said Mann.

James nodded, before tapping her watch. Message received. He contacted the team.

"All stations. This is Mann. We're leaving in thirty seconds. Stop what you're doing and return to the bus."

After receiving an acknowledgment from everyone, he turned to James.

"Where are we headed? I need to let Bauer's people know where to meet us."

"Nogales International Airport," said James. "They won't be expecting us to head south. Once the resident agent calls my bluff, he'll have every cop in the city looking for us in Tucson."

"Nogales, Mexico?" said Serrano.

"No. Nogales, Arizona," said James. "Then on to Wickenburg Municipal Airport, about sixty miles northwest of Phoenix. That's where I'll take custody of Elena and you'll meet your ride to DC. So, you better get your people up there moving sooner than later. And whatever you intend to bring to DC needs to be on that plane."

"Understood," said Mann, before transmitting again. "Rico. Emily. We'll meet you at Nogales International Airport. Nogales, Arizona."

"See you there," said Rico. "Where are we headed after that?"

"Phoenix area to conduct some quick business. Then to DC."

"Sounds good," said Melendez. "Any baggage restrictions?"

James shook her head.

"No. Which is a good thing, because I picked up a few items at the AXIOM facility in New Mexico that are probably on the military's no-fly list," said Mann.

"We'll be able to add to that when we get back east," said Melendez.

"I'm not hearing any of this," said James.

"Hearing what?"

"Exactly," said James.

CHAPTER 38

Halfway down the Gulfstream G550's stairs, Serrano overheard Director James issue an order to the cockpit.

"We're back in the air in five minutes."

James seemed to be in a hurry to get out of there, which was informative. If the director of the FBI's most powerful branch didn't think it was a wise idea to stick around for long, neither should the rest of them. She'd make sure to mention that to Mann if he hadn't overheard her order. Serrano stepped onto the concrete tarmac and headed for Maria and Sofia, who held Elena by both arms next to a black Suburban inside the hangar. Mann followed quickly behind.

"Welcome to Wickenburg, Arizona," said Mann.

He was trying to lighten the mood, but she wasn't interested in that right now. "Did you hear what James told the pilot?"

"I did," said Mann. "From what I was told, our ride out of here is on final approach. We won't be too much farther behind James."

"We still need to have a talk with everyone, about their choice to stay or go home."

"I'll let you handle that. Like we discussed," said Mann. "How many do you think we'll lose?"

"Hard to say," said Serrano. "Life is hard for them back home. They've all been persecuted, and continue to be harassed by the cartel, their own former organizations, and local government officials. The hardest part is making a living. It's not like any of them were living luxurious lifestyles on their government salaries, but now that they're essentially discriminated against because everyone is afraid to hire them, they work shit jobs where they can find them. Until the blacklist catches up to them. The money will be hard to pass up. It may be hard to believe, but I can assure you that just a quarter of the contents in one of those bowling bags is a life-changing amount for each one of them."

"I don't doubt it," said Mann. "So. I'll set aside one bag for Elena, if she cooperates with James. That's fourteen bags. To stay off the grid in the DC area, we'll stick to the prepaid credit cards. Maybe use up the cards in a few of the bags, depending on how long this whole thing lasts. The rest will be split between your team when this is over, or now if they decide to go back. Sixteen shares, which includes a share for the families of each of your friends who were killed helping the task force."

"That's one share too many."

"I included a share for you," said Mann.

"I'm not in this for the money," said Serrano.

"None of us are. The offer stands. Take it or leave it in the end," said Mann. "But it could be around a half million per share."

"That's a lot of money," she said, just before they reached the Suburban.

"You can't put a price on what your colleagues have already done for the task force," said Mann.

"We came here to avenge the victims back home," said Serrano.

"And you did," said Mann. "While at the same time helping the US government take on a fight that's not yours. I only wish we had found twice as many bags. You all deserve it."

"We'll see," said Serrano, before nodding at Sofia and Maria. "Did she behave?"

"*Sí,*" said Sofia. "But she's a little confused about this transfer. Says it wasn't part of the deal."

He produced a business card and handed it to Sofia. "Can you show that to her, translate it, and then put it in one of her pockets?"

242

Sofia took the card and held it in front of Elena, reading his name and title. Elena still didn't look convinced.

"Thank you," said Mann. "Cata. Will you translate for me? I don't want there to be any confusion."

"Better than listening to you hack your way through Spanish," said Serrano.

"The agent who is about to take you into custody is a very high-level FBI director. She and I have an understanding. If you cooperate with the FBI, I will hold up my end of the bargain. As far as I know, you haven't committed any prosecutable crimes in the United States. Eventually, the US Department of Justice will release you."

Serrano translated word for word, Elena looking skeptical.

"Contact me when they release you, and I'll personally deliver the envelope with your identity documents, the bag, or bank instructions to retrieve the money. Your choice on how to receive the money. We can help you deposit the money to avoid any legal scrutiny. Each bag contains around twenty-five thousand dollars in prepaid credit cards, so even if it takes a little while to figure out the cash side of the deal, you'll be all set."

Elena shook her head after Serrano's translation.

"What good is your deal if it puts me on a flight back to Mexico and then on some kind of international no-fly list?"

"I'll keep track of your status. If they fly you back to Mexico, I'll make sure you go back with enough prepaid credit cards to keep you hidden until I can arrange a way to deposit the money and send you bank instructions to retrieve it or move it. If the DOJ refuses to let me give you the credit cards, contact me from Mexico, and I will wire you money. Either I or someone I trust will deliver the banking instructions and envelope, with a proper entry stamp from the Mexico side on your passport. You'll be able to reenter the US if you choose, but I suggest you pick a different country. They won't send your profile to Interpol, but you'll be entered into the US Customs and Border

Protection database. And our facial recognition software is more sophisticated than you think."

She didn't look happy with the deal, but she nodded. Director James and two agents arrived at Serrano's side.

"Anything we need to know?" said James.

"She's a former cartel soldier," said Serrano. "So don't take your eyes off her. Not that she's going anywhere at thirty thousand feet."

"They say she's been pretty well behaved," said Mann. "I think she understands her situation well. No good options unless she cooperates. One very good option if she does. My business card is in her back pocket. If she fulfills her end of the bargain, whatever you deem that to be, I ask that she be given the card back when she's released."

"If she's released," said James. "We'll be running her face through every database in existence to make sure she hasn't been implicated or associated with any crimes in the US or against US citizens abroad. But one way or the other, I'll make sure she gets your card. A promise is a promise."

"Thank you," said Mann.

"Señoritas," said James. "Thank you for keeping an eye on her—and for the risks you've taken. It's truly awe-inspiring. I wish I could offer you jobs."

"Señor Mann is keeping us busy enough," said Sofia.

"Sounds like it," said James. "I wish I could stay and chat more with the team, but I'm in a little bit of hot water over the events in Tucson."

Serrano motioned for the women to hand over Elena, who was swiftly taken away by the two agents.

"See you back in DC," said James. "With whoever shows up. Just remember what I said. I can't protect them."

"Understood," said Mann. "Safe travels."

The rest of the team joined them after the handoff, the jet already taxiing away before the aircraft's passenger door had fully closed. They weren't wasting any time. The Gulfstream G550 made a right turn onto the western end of the runway, the roar of the engines reaching her ears a moment later. The jet used up nearly all the airport's 6,100-foot-long runway, before rising into the air. She scanned the sky, trying to locate the aircraft sent to bring them to DC. Mann's phone chimed. He took a look at the screen, before turning to Serrano.

"Our flight lands in three minutes," said Mann. "But we still need to wait for Jax and Neva."

Neva and Jax had driven one of the SUVs from Tucson so the team wouldn't be forced to leave their surveillance gear behind. Especially the drones. They'd maxed out the Gulfstream's cargo capacity with their body armor, weapons, and the personal bags they retrieved on the way to the Nogales airport. She typed a quick text on her phone, getting a reply from Neva a few seconds later.

"Seventeen minutes," said Serrano. "We should probably have that talk now, before they arrive. I can FaceTime with Neva, so she can decide before they arrive. James seemed eager to get off the ground. I don't think we should waste a single moment."

"Yeah. The entire Phoenix field office probably made a U-turn on Interstate 10 and is headed in this direction," said Mann.

CHAPTER 39

Mann let Serrano explain the details to her colleagues. He'd asked his team and the two CIA-affiliated operatives to watch the entrances and approaches to the hangar, keeping them out of earshot. Like the Mexicans, they obviously weren't in this for the money, but a half million dollars wasn't a trivial number. Even to government agents making a six-figure salary or CIA contractors likely making twice that amount. His agents wouldn't and couldn't take the money, but it might make them feel a little resentful.

Or not. They already knew about the money and had probably come to their own conclusions about how it would ultimately be used. The most logical being to compensate those who volunteered without any promise of compensation. He just didn't want to formally put them in an awkward position. He couldn't speak for Melendez and Miralles.

When they'd finished their discussion, Serrano walked over to him. The jet sent to fetch them was slowly rolling down the tarmac toward the hangar. A Gulfstream G650 Extended Range version from what he could tell. Larger than the G550, which was lucky for them. They should be able to load everything on board.

"So. What's the damage?" said Mann.

"Do you mean how much is it going to cost, or how many are heading home?" said Serrano.

"I already know how much it's going to cost," said Mann.

"They're all in," she said. "With one condition."

"Whoa. I wasn't expecting that. I mean . . . I was, but I wouldn't have thought any less of anyone that wanted to head back," said Mann. "What's the condition?"

"That the shares be divided between everyone who took part in ARTEMIS since I started, including the FBI agents lost along the way. Except for Rocha," said Serrano. "And the three CIA contractors."

"My agents can't take that money," said Mann. "And it's better if we don't mention anything about this very generous offer. Same with the contractors. At least for now."

"Can the money be given to their families? Not them directly?" said Serrano.

"I have no idea," said Mann. "I suppose the families of the agents killed in action could accept the money. The only one committing a crime in that case would be me, hiding and distributing evidence without authorization, which I'm already doing. Not to mention the antitank rockets, explosives, and the rest of the stuff we took from LABYRINTH."

"Promise me and my team, that when this is all over, you'll try to get the money to them," said Serrano.

"I promise," said Mann. "Let's get all the gear staged and ready to load on board. I don't want to hold up our ride any longer than necessary."

While Serrano's team unloaded the SUV and moved the task force's personal bags and gear to the edge of the open hangar, keeping everything in the shade, the Gulfstream came to a stop in front of the hangar. Its front passenger door opened moments later, revealing the stairs built into the hatch. Audra Bauer descended the stairs the moment they hit the tarmac.

"Who's that?" said Serrano.

"Audra Bauer. Former deputy director of the CIA's National Clandestine Service," said Mann. "She's more of a consultant now."

"Did you know she'd show? You look surprised," said Serrano.

"I didn't know."

"Should we be worried?" said Serrano.

"No. She's on our side," said Mann. "She arranged the flight. Same with the one that brought me back from DC with Raul. Bauer understands what we're up against, which is probably why she's here. We'll have plenty of time to talk strategy on the way back."

Mann headed out of the shade to meet her on the way over and brief her on the team's status.

"You coming?" he said, looking over his shoulder at Serrano.

She shrugged, before hustling to catch up with him. They met Bauer halfway, the two shaking hands.

"Ms. Serrano. It's a pleasure to meet," said Bauer, shaking hers as well.

"The same," said Serrano. "Thank you for all of this."

"The pleasure is all mine, especially when I'm not footing the bill," said Bauer. "Garrett. Do you have a minute before we start loading the plane? I'd like to introduce you to someone."

"I'll head back to the hangar. Have them start moving the gear to the plane. Jax and Neva should be here any minute," said Serrano.

"Sounds good," said Mann.

"How many are coming?" said Bauer.

"All of them, plus two more," said Mann. "Fifteen passengers. Plus, an Albatross drone kit and some other surveillance gear when the other two get here. They drove up from Tucson."

"I better send the copilot out to help organize the equipment onload," said Bauer. "Make sure the weight is distributed correctly. Looks like we'll be pushing the cargo capacity."

Mann followed her up the stairs and into the gloriously air-conditioned and luxuriously appointed Gulfstream cabin. A deeply tanned man in his sixties with a thick mane of salt-and-pepper hair got up from a brown leather captain's chair. He wore a navy-blue business suit with a white button-down shirt, but no tie.

"Karl Berg. Audra and I go way back," he said, extending his hand, which Mann accepted.

"Garrett Mann," he said, shaking his hand. *This must be the former CIA officer that AXIOM attempted to kill the other day.* "I hope you didn't make the trip all the way out here just for me."

Berg cracked a grin.

"You kind of remind me of a young O'Reilly," said Berg. "No. I thought that given the auspicious circumstances, the flight would be a great chance to catch up with an old friend. Friends, actually. Rico and Emily are here?"

"Yes," said Mann. "They lost Blake in Tucson. Just so you know."

Berg's face went dark. "I never met Blake, but I heard good things about him."

"It's been a rough week," said Mann. "We lost two agents today. Two last week. My Mexican counterpart's team has taken the brunt of it. Four killed in the LABYRINTH raid. One killed today. Another severely wounded."

"Taking on these dark-money, shadowy military-industrial-complex entities is a nasty business," said Berg. "Even nastier when their clients promise them more than just money. And if we're dealing with the client Audra and I suspect, it'll get way nastier."

"True America?" said Mann.

"Or some variation. Call it True America 2.0," said Berg.

"3.0," said Bauer. "This would be their third try."

"You're right," said Berg. "Anyway. Sounds like you have the resources to more or less take matters into your own hands. Along with a boss who's willing to turn her head and look the other way?"

"I'm not sure how far her head will turn, and she definitely won't just close her eyes," said Mann. "But I'd say that's a fairly accurate description. If she's still in charge of CCRSB by the time we return. Today's disaster, coupled with a few other little stunts we've pulled over the past few days, might be the end of her."

"I highly doubt they'll sack her that quickly. The FBI moves slower than mud on a hot Arizona day when it comes to big decisions like that, which should give you time to do what needs to be done."

"What do you think needs to be done?" said Mann.

"I see three tasks ahead of you. AXIOM needs to be destroyed before they pull a Houdini. The scheme they've created needs to be wiped out at the subatomic level. Or True America 3.0 needs to be exposed, with clear evidence that they are connected to AXIOM's domestic plot. Any combination of two out of the three will prevent whatever sick outcome the two groups have been working toward."

"A fourth option would be to terminate True America 3.0," said Bauer. "Hit that goal, and you can skip the others."

"I don't think that falls under Special Agent Mann's job description," said Berg. "It's more of a job for Rico and Emily's group. Something you and I can explore later. For now, we should focus on preparing Mann's task force for the nasty road ahead of them."

"I don't see how it can get any nastier," said Mann.

"If you choose to go down the road we suggest, it most certainly will," said Berg. "The key to your success will be matching their nastiness. For all our sakes, I hope you're up to it."

"I am. I can't speak for everyone on the task force, but I get the strong sense that they're ready for payback," said Mann. "And I don't know if Bauer told you, but I have a crew of nine former Mexican police officers and soldiers who certainly don't give a fuck about the rules."

Berg nodded approvingly at Bauer. "Now that's music to my ears. I think he just might be able to pull this off."

CHAPTER 40

Jessica Mayer took a seat at the small conference table in the business suite they'd reserved at their hotel. The room felt like a waste of money, since it came with an attached bedroom that none of them used, but they needed a space more secure than one of the hotel's small conference spaces or a restaurant table when they analyzed the surveillance data they collected. The room would also give them the ability to work through the night. If anyone felt like taking a nap, they could head into the bedroom and crash on one of the double beds. The two couches in the corner of the business sitting area would also work in a pinch.

"How are we looking?" said Mayer.

"We're going to focus on three specific buildings in the Tysons, Virginia, business district for now," said Special Agent Lianez. "If they don't show any promise, we'll expand to a second tier."

"How many buildings are in the second tier?" said Mayer.

"All of them, except those three," said Anish Gupta. "Just kidding. We'll be able to shave the number down considerably by eliminating easily identifiable, full corporate headquarters buildings. That leaves the buildings with multiple tenants, though I strongly suspect an organization like AXIOM would not be keen on sharing building space. Unfortunately, I say that from a place of real-world experience dealing with groups like this."

"What's the plan for vetting the three buildings of interest?" said Mayer.

"I like that. BOIs. I'm going to steal that, if you don't mind," said Gupta.

"It's all yours. I'll likely never use it again after this operation."

The guy was a little quirky, but he was growing on her. She'd been highly skeptical about working with him at first, thinking that the last thing the task force needed was a murky group of CIA or private-contract operatives poking around in official FBI business. Kind of a ridiculous concern in the grand scheme of things. Nobody had voiced a single concern about Serrano tagging along with the task force. She'd essentially become family to them over the past year. And then there was Serrano's crew from Mexico, whom they'd fought side by side with in the LABYRINTH facility.

Now she was glad she hadn't put up a fight about collaborating with Gupta. His experience and expertise had already proven to be impressive. It would become invaluable if he found the building. Either way, he was a welcome addition to the team.

"Cool," he said.

"Unless I should trademark it," said Mayer.

Gupta paused for a few seconds before responding. "You're messing with me, aren't you?"

Everyone broke out in a quick laugh, the heavy air still present.

"Just a little," said Mayer. "But seriously, what's the plan for the three buildings?"

"I suggest we fly one of my RQ-12 Wasps over each building," said Gupta. "Take a look at the antennae on top of each building. I can tell more than you'd think by what they've installed. If they were out in the boonies, they could lay high-speed cable to a relay station, but in Tysons, Virginia, the land of concrete? They're going to rely on some serious encrypted satellite gear to communicate with their villains around the country and world. Burst transmission stuff. Crazy shit. Way above your heads. No offense."

"None taken," said Mayer. "I assume you can identify this equipment? Even if it's camouflaged? I've read the top-secret bulletins about hiding the type of communications gear you've just described."

"I've read them, too. But nobody here heard me say that," said Gupta, pausing for a moment. "Okay. Here's the plan. Obviously, if one of the buildings has this kind of sophisticated gear on its roof, we list it as high potential and put the camera and telescope people in adjacent buildings."

"Camera and telescope people?" said Mayer.

"That's you, Frank, and Special Agent what's her name—"

"Wallace," said Kerri Wallace.

"She's SWAT and can work wonders with a rifle scope, I assume. Pretty much the same thing," said Gupta. "Sorry. None of this came out right. Our surveillance experts!"

"Nice recovery," said Frank Vincenzo.

"Seriously. Sorry. Moving on. And in my defense, Special Agent Wallace has remained rather tight-lipped since I arrived," said Gupta.

"Sorry if I'm not very talkative," said Wallace. "Surveillance isn't my thing. Protecting the team is my job."

"And you're killing it, lying on the couch," said Gupta. "Shit. There I go again. Sticking my foot in my mouth."

"I can help with that," said Wallace.

Mayer glanced at Wallace and shook her head, signaling for her to knock it off, which she did, returning to a supine position on the couch. Nowhere near the door if someone kicked it in. Not that they were under any kind of threat—yet.

"No thanks," said Gupta. "Anyway. Back to rooftops? If they have fully exposed gear, old stuff, and no suspicious generator boxes or HVAC units nearby, we cross them off the list. I've seen the full spectrum of pictures documenting every possible bullshit camouflage construction, plus I have a catalog of rooftop configurations, so even if they somehow bucked the trend of typical camouflage construction, we should be able to win the 'which rooftop doesn't belong to the other' game. Questions?"

"And you're not concerned with flying a drone in Tysons, Virginia, less than a mile away from the National Counterterrorism Center? Not to mention CIA headquarters just a few miles away."

"I do this all the time. Launch out of line of sight of the building, one pass overhead, then a quick dive and return to base. Never been caught before."

"Three times in a row?" said Mayer.

"I'm not too worried," said Gupta. "If we run into a problem, I can make a call. Your boss is flying back with the former deputy director of the National Clandestine Service as we speak. We go way back."

"Former deputy director?" said Mayer.

"But she's still in the know, if you know what I mean."

"I do, but 'in the know' doesn't always translate into a 'get out of jail free' card," said Mayer. "If you know what *I* mean."

"Yeah. It's one of those gray areas I've learned to live with."

"There's no black and white anymore," said Mayer. "Is there?"

"Never has been," said Gupta.

CHAPTER 41

Mann's phone buzzed. Word from his team in DC. He prayed it would lead to something. They would land at what Bauer described as one of the most discreet landing strips in the entire mid-Atlantic region within the hour. She actually used the term *landing strip*, like they were flying in a single-propeller Cessna below radar, to deliver an illegal weapons shipment. Which is essentially what they were doing, except they were doing it in a fifty-million-dollar private jet.

The recently concluded, hours-long conversation with Berg and Bauer, which included everyone on the aircraft, except for the pilots, made one thing very clear. Their window of opportunity to reach out and touch AXIOM would very likely close within the next seventy-two hours. Maybe sooner, if AXIOM caught any whiff of his DC team's surveillance. The two of them felt confident that Anish Gupta would keep the team's efforts off AXIOM's radar, but there was no guarantee. Especially if AXIOM suspected that Bauer and Berg might be helping his task force.

"Tell me you have something," said Mann. "And—hello. How are you all doing? Should have led with that. It's been a day."

"It's okay," said Mayer. "I can't imagine. We can't imagine."

"I thought I could control the risk level," said Mann. "Even with a suspected mole on the team. I couldn't have been more wrong."

"I know you probably want to hear 'it's not your fault and we're all fine,' but we're not fine, and yeah, the team is shaken by the fact that you let us conduct operations knowing that one of us might be the mole."

"I appreciate your candor. And that's a fair assessment," said Mann. "To be honest, I didn't know what to do, so I just moved everything forward, assuming I could control or contain the problem. I'm truly sorry."

"It is what it is. We're in uncharted territory. Have been for a while," said Mayer. "So. To answer your original question, I think we found AXIOM."

"Seriously? That fast?"

"If we didn't," said Mayer, "then we should send some agents to the building in question. Maybe we'd prevent a problem down the line, because they're definitely up to no good."

Berg raised a hand. "Ask her what she thinks of Gupta."

A faint voice came through the phone. "Screw you, Karl."

"I heard that, and so did Anish," said Mayer. "His response was fairly colorful."

"Oh. I heard it. Hey, I'm going to put you on speakerphone," said Mann. "You're talking to Cata, Luke, Jax, and two former CIA bigwigs."

"One of them is a former CIA bigwig," said Gupta.

"That would be Audra," said Berg. "Good to hear from you, Anish. How are things?"

"Busy as always," said Gupta. "Both in my personal and professional life."

"I meant, what's your assessment of the team?" said Berg, winking at Mann.

"Same as always. Business as usual. They're—"

"Just kidding, Anish. It's seriously good to hear your voice again. Been a while."

"It has," said Gupta. "Good to hear your voice, too."

"I suspect we'll grab a drink within the next day or two," said Berg.

"You know I don't drink."

"You quit Pepsi?" said Berg.

"Pepsi?" said Bauer. "Seriously?"

"Hello, Audra," said Gupta.

"Hey, Anish. Thank you for your help with this," said Bauer. "Even if you drink Pepsi."

"My pleasure. And for the record, I don't discriminate between sodas. I drink Mountain Dew, too."

"I'll make a note of it," said Berg.

"You're all just fucking with me—as usual," said Gupta. "Aren't you?"

Mann tried not to laugh. This seemed like some kind of ritual that Gupta fell for every time.

"What gave you that idea?" said Bauer.

"Never gets old," said Berg, eliciting a round of laughter from the group.

"Anyway. I think I'll leave you with the FBI folks for a few minutes," said Gupta. "There's a vending machine on this floor that dispenses Pepsi!"

"Jessica?" said Mann, once he stopped laughing.

"Still here," she said.

"You found AXIOM?" said Mann.

"We did," said Mayer. "Hold on. Shit. He really left the room. I thought he was kidding."

"He'll be fine," said Berg. "We go way back."

"Okay," she said. "But he should really be here, because he can just rattle this stuff off the top of his head."

"Now I feel bad," said Berg.

"You should," said Bauer. "You know how he gets."

"I'll go get him," said Mayer. "Wait. He's back."

"Forgot I had a six-pack of Pepsi in the fridge," said Gupta. "What did I miss?"

"We were talking about the AXIOM building," said Berg. "But we didn't want to proceed without you."

"But I was only gone for like, five seconds," said Gupta.

"Well. It felt like five minutes," said Berg, rolling his eyes. "What did you find?"

"One of the buildings has an overkill sophisticated communications suite on the roof. They built a faux upward extension to all four sides of the building, creating the impression that there was another floor, but it was just a wall to conceal the gear from ground-level observation or one of the other buildings. It's not the tallest building in the immediate vicinity, but we spent some time on a few geometry apps, concluding that the gear will be concealed from every rooftop. But that really doesn't matter. The drone imagery is conclusive. The gear on that rooftop is on a par or better than what we saw at the APEX building. Just a few blocks away from this one—I might add."

"Tysons is definitely a runner-up for dark money, shady influence capital of the US," said Bauer.

"I don't doubt it," said Berg. "Why spend twice as much on a lease across the river, when you can be a few miles from the National Counterterrorism Center, Langley, and the Pentagon. Not that real estate is cheap over here."

"What city is in first place?" said Mann.

"The city right across the Potomac," said Berg. "Sorry for the interlude. The AXIOM building."

Mayer jumped back in the conversation. "We're going to access the building a few hundred feet to the south of the—"

"Building of interest," said Gupta. "BOI."

"Just. No," said Mayer.

"You coined the term," said Gupta. "And told me I could have it."

"Anyway," said Mayer. "Drone footage from a second pass identified a fenced-off loading dock area."

"What kind of fencing?"

"Ten-foot-high chain-link wrapped in green privacy mesh," said Mayer. "But what really grabbed our attention was the loading bay door. Typically, you see them raised off the ground to accommodate direct, flat offloading from the back of a truck. This loading bay door extends to the ground. We think it's a VIP entrance. The chain-link fence appears to have a motorized sliding section. We'll confirm that when we start a full surveillance workup, in a few hours, from the adjacent building. I'm thinking we go full FBI on that building and set up wherever we want."

"Do whatever you need to do," said Mann. "We'll be on the ground by then, so give me a call if you run into a problem. Director James still has her job, for now, so she can apply some brute force if necessary."

"Perfect. We'll start taking pictures and video of anyone that comes in and out of that loading dock. If we set up on the third or fourth floor of the adjacent building, we should be able to see inside. Unless they created an underground parking garage. I'll also have a team in the parking lot doing the same for anyone using the front door. Never know who might stroll in—or out," said Mayer. "We'll start assembling a portfolio of probe photos to send over the FACE unit in the Biometric Services Section out in Clarksburg. Start putting names to faces."

"I'll let James know to reach out to let them know you'll be sending them some faces, and to bump that portfolio analysis to the top of their list," said Mann. "Pictures of bald men or men possibly concealing their heads with a hat go straight to the team in California. Send those immediately. If this Mr. Clean guy shows up, and Raul positively identifies him—we're in business," said Mann.

"I'll issue a bald-man BOLO," said Mayer.

"Mr. Gupta. Is there any way to intercept their communications?" said Mann.

"Personal or from the communications array?"

"Both."

"You're not going to arrest me if I disclose something illegal, are you?" said Gupta.

"I will not arrest you," said Mann. "If anything, I should be asking you the same question."

"And my lips are always sealed," said Gupta. "So, to answer your question. Yes. I can potentially intercept their personal cell phones.

With the right decryption software and a little luck, I could listen to and record their conversations."

"Stingray?" said Mann.

"Hailstorm," said Gupta.

Hailstorm was one of the latest generations of cell phone intercept technology.

"Impressive."

"It comes in handy. Mostly for tracking, which could still be useful. But most of these big players use satellite phones these days when they're on the move. Very hard to intercept unless they use the same location every time to place their calls," said Gupta. "Regarding the communications array on the rooftop, the answer is a hard no. Unless I misidentified the system, they're using a multidirectional satellite-burst antenna array. All outbound digital traffic is split into an uncountable number of parts and randomly sent to one of the array's fifteen antennae, each pointed at a different satellite. Sometimes there's a bit of overlap, since fifteen might not be available. Anyway, all those bits are then sent to their destination, where they're reassembled. Of course, each bit is encrypted as well. I'd have to position fifteen drones above the building in perfect alignment with the antennae to intercept their signal, which would be useless without the ability to assemble the bits in the right order."

"Same issue with inbound communications traffic?" said Mann. "But in reverse?"

"The whole thing simply isn't feasible," said Gupta. "If the array was in a remote location that wasn't monitored, we could build some kind of dome contraption over it that could intercept the inbound and outbound signals. Of course, then we'd have to decipher it—which is not within the scope of my capabilities. Or anybody's, as far as I know."

"You just need to identify their headquarters and the big players," said Berg. "Rico, Emily, and Anish have done this before. They'll be able to quarterback the team."

"You make it sound easy," said Serrano.

"Oh. It's never easy," said Berg, glancing at Bauer.

"Never. But's it's doable. And the endgame is never the same. What Karl described is the most general description of how these operations have gone down in the past. It's the basic template. Not exactly rocket science," said Bauer. "Like most operations you've ever worked, the devil is always in the details. But in this case, the devil will start nipping at your heels and biting your ankles at the larger-scale level. This group will not be easy to touch. Not if you want to tick off at least two of the three goals Karl laid out for you."

"Exactly," said Berg. "You could always just blow the head shed away with the antitank rockets you took from LABYRINTH, as they drive away from the building in their armored SUVs. But that doesn't kill the plan. Somebody will step up and implement it. Or offer to send it to their client for a price, if they haven't already paid for it. Sounds like the network they created is already in place. Up for anything at any time."

"No doubt about that," said Turner. "They basically threw themselves at us back in Tucson."

"That's what scares me the most about the network they created," said Berg. "The last time we faced something like this, money and personal politics played the two most important roles. Mostly money. These cartel soldiers operate on an entirely different level. I probably don't need to tell any of you that. Ms. Serrano?"

"You're right. Money means nothing to them at this point in their careers. Politics even less. The only political party they know is the Juárez Cartel. Nothing else exists to them. They're driven by one thing. Fear. Fear of being brutally murdered by their own cartel if they don't prove themselves unquestionably loyal and useful. Afraid for their families, too. Depending on the severity of the failure, cartel punishment can go far beyond the perpetrator. We've seen grade school birthday parties massacred. I've seen brains and blood sprayed on an intact piñata."

"That's why the next few days are so critical," said Berg. "A fanatical group like True America 3.0 would figure out how to use this network on some level, even without AXIOM's involvement, which might be enough to accomplish their goal. And they can't be shooting for the moon again. The White House is out of reach for them. But they could sure do some damage if they swung the White House and Congress in their direction—and created another obstructionist block. They've done it before. They held the country hostage for over a year. Fortunately, we—"

"We . . . can't go there," interrupted Bauer. "Part of the agreement we all signed."

"Seemed like ages ago," said Berg.

"They did implode rather quickly," said Mann. "Interesting."

"Don't draw any conclusions, or try to connect any dots," said Berg. "But we know what we're talking about here. Whatever AXIOM cooked up today needs to be thrown out with tomorrow's trash."

"Is that a saying?" said Gupta.

"It is now," said Berg.

"Can I borrow it?"

"It's all yours for a hundred bucks," said Berg.

"Sold."

"I think he keeps a book with all of these phrases," said Mayer.

"I know he does," said Berg. "How do you think I retired to the Caribbean?"

They all shared a laugh, before Mann brought the task at hand back into focus.

"Jess. We'll link up after we get settled. I'm not sure what that's going to look like yet. We have a big group," said Mann. "Hopefully by then, you'll have some actionable intel. Things are going to move fast."

CHAPTER 42

Gerald McCall ushered Powell into the SCIF and shut the door behind them, waiting for the keypad to indicate that the door had sealed. Powell moved past the conference table, toward the compact but luxurious arrangement of leather chairs and teak side tables, basking in the soft glow of green-glass banker's lamps. It was well past the dinner hour, and he hoped for a small nip of something spicy and oaky with the big man.

"This is going to be a quick meeting," said McCall, basically stopping Powell in his tracks.

No bourbon tonight. Or ever, apparently. Powell still wasn't in the club. He turned to his boss and pretended not to be disappointed. Then it hit him. Did the words *quick meeting* mean *end of employment*? Mann had once again beaten the odds and made him look utterly incompetent. All Powell had to show for today's debacle were two dead FBI agents, one of them his mole, and a few still unidentified ARTEMIS allies. Their identification would shed some light on Mann's latest string of successes, but he had paid a costly price for information with limited value. Eleven LABYRINTH graduates dead and his inside source burned.

"Oh boy," said McCall, raising an eyebrow. "You look worried."

"My batting average hasn't exactly been great lately," said Powell.

"Don't beat yourself up over this. You hired the best in the business, and you had an insider lead them right into the ambush," said McCall. "I just got off the phone with a source at the FBI. Mann had some outside help, and not just the Mexicans. He had an ace up his sleeve. Nothing you could have done about that. And apparently, he's not afraid to strap explosives to a drone and use it as a kamikaze."

"That's a whole new level of concern," said Powell.

"It gets worse."

"Is there a new development?" said Powell.

"That's the problem. There are no new developments, which worries me," said McCall. "ARTEMIS, Mann's Mexican amigos, and his new friends have vanished without a trace. The FBI tracked Executive Assistant Director James's Gulfstream flight to Wickenburg, Arizona, about an hour northwest of Phoenix. When agents arrived, everyone was gone. They left two rented SUVs behind. And before you ask— no—they did not get off the jet with James in DC."

"A second jet. Probably the same one that Mann used to transport Raul," said Powell. "Who's paying for these flights?"

"Great question. When you find the answer, let me know," said McCall. "Which brings me to the second nondevelopment. Raul. He hasn't shown up in federal custody, which means Mann still has him."

"Raul won't break," said Powell.

"But will he bend?" said McCall. "In Mann's direction if offered a deal, or a chance to walk?"

"Mann wouldn't dare release Raul," said Powell. "Mann would go to jail for life, if his fellow FBI agents didn't kill him before the trial."

"I agree. But don't underestimate Raul's ability to slither out of this, by shifting the blame for Sacramento onto us," said McCall. "After he spends several days going over the details and purpose of LABYRINTH with FBI investigators."

"Who would believe him?" said Powell.

"A government desperate to convince Americans that they're the only thing standing between democracy and the dark forces conspiring against the nation."

"But they are," said McCall.

"I know that. And you know that. But they've had a hard time selling that notion to the American public over the past few decades," said McCall. "If they can justify blaming AXIOM for that bombing, then they only have to sweep an attempted murder under the rug. I expect Raul to fully cooperate with the FBI when Mann finally hands him over."

"But Raul doesn't know who we are," said Powell. "Nobody at LABYRINTH knew who funded the operation. I'm the only official AXIOM employee who entered it, and I didn't wear a polo shirt with the company's logo when I visited."

"Right. But Raul has had a few other handlers meet him outside the facility," said McCall.

"They took serious counterintelligence measures before and after those meetings."

McCall shook his head. "Raul is craftier than all of us combined. He didn't rise to the top of the Juárez Cartel's sicario ladder on his killing skills alone. I think it's time to move the DOMINION war room to the Georgetown annex. Not overnight. Do it slowly over the next few days so we don't attract any attention, if we happen to be under surveillance. Run exhaustive surveillance detection routes for the first few trips."

"I'll double up the building's countersurveillance team," said Powell. "They'll keep a close eye on our surroundings. We'll know if they're building up to something."

"And I have a few contacts at the US District Court who handle Department of Justice warrant requests. Same with the Fairfax County District Court," said McCall. "We'll know well in advance before anyone comes knocking."

"That's good to hear," said Powell. "Do you want me to start the move tonight?"

"No. But put Litman, Conway, and Marino on notice to begin the process tomorrow morning," said McCall. "Only essential

DOMINION personnel. Enough to run the program for our client if we lose the use of this building."

"Will do. Is there anything else?"

"Actually. Yes," said McCall. "This isn't the kind of job you get fired from. Security doesn't stand over you while you pack up your office, before walking you to the door. Understood?"

"Yes," said Powell.

"Are you sure?"

"My next of kin information is updated," said Powell. "So my personal belongings can be sent to the right place."

"We all signed a deal with the devil when we created DOMINION. The best we can do is delay paying the price."

CHAPTER 43

Mayer zoomed in on the open SUV door and waited. They'd been right about the loading dock. Three minutes ago, a little after 7:00 p.m., the chain-link gate had opened, immediately followed by the loading bay door. Moments after the bay door finished its ascent, a black Lincoln Navigator backed into the deep loading bay. Too deep for her to see the door that accessed the building. Fortunately, the SUV stopped when its bumper cleared the entrance by a few feet, giving her a direct view of all four doors.

She'd guessed that any vehicle that entered the bay would park in the center, since the opening wasn't wide enough to accommodate two vehicles. Her extensive experience tailing VIPs had informed her that executive drivers were sticklers for order and detail. One habit in particular—an obsession with equidistant parking—stood out the most. Whether between lines in a parking lot or between other vehicles while parallel parking, these professionals prided themselves on doing a perfect job, with their only job—driving and parking.

She detected a few shadows. Someone obscuring a light somewhere. She activated the ridiculously high-resolution video camera. Mayer wasn't even sure why she bothered taking pictures anymore. Clinging to the past? Video capture technology, much of it entirely automated once set up, had far eclipsed the "agent snapping pictures" era. Speaking of snapping pictures.

The rear right passenger door was the money shot, which was why she always focused her telephoto lens on that side of the SUV. It faced the curb during streetside drop-offs, so most executive drivers habitually offered that door to their VIP customers, no matter where they picked them up or dropped them off. Habits were hard to break.

She started taking pictures. A man dressed in a suit emerged from the back of the loading bay and headed toward the open door. A few dozen camera shots later, he disappeared into the Navigator, and the SUV raced out of the fenced-in area. Several seconds later, the gate and the loading bay doors had closed. In and out in under a minute. But she'd captured some solid pictures. The only downside was that the man had a full head of hair. Slightly graying, the man was in his early sixties if she had to guess. They'd identify him eventually, but this wasn't Mr. Clean—their direct link to AXIOM.

Mayer stopped the video camera and sat back in the office chair the company had given her. She remembered how much she hated stakeout work, the empty office surrounding her exacerbating the bad memories. But this was something else. She'd set up a floor-to-ceiling, wall-to-wall, dark mesh screen about two thirds of the way from the door to the window. The office had been empty for several months, according to Edgewater Wealth Management, the company that occupied this floor, so she couldn't exactly set up two cameras on tripods in the middle of the space, pointed at AXIOM.

The cameras barely poked through the mesh screen, which was about three times darker than a typical house screen, preventing AXIOM from detecting her presence. Not that they could see into the office during the day. The window reflections foiled most observation. And thermal detection gear didn't penetrate windows. Particularly the specially treated UV windows installed in this building. As long as she didn't accidentally turn on the lights at night, nobody in the AXIOM building, no matter how hard they tried, would be able to identify this office as a surveillance nest. She passed along what she'd just witnessed via text and settled in for a long night.

A few minutes later, her phone buzzed, her screen illuminating. A subtle light, but they were dealing with serious people, who they had to assume would have top-notch countersurveillance professionals on their payroll. She'd change the settings after taking this call. Sunset wasn't too far away.

"What's up?" said Mayer.

"Mr. Clean just walked out of the front door," said Frank Vincenzo, a longtime friend and fellow Special Surveillance Group investigator.

"Confirmed?" said Mayer.

"No. But a bald guy walks out of the building shortly after some head honcho gets the backdoor VIP treatment? Good odds we're onto something. The pictures are on their way to the California team. And Anish has locked onto the guy's phone, so we'll be able to track him later," said Vincenzo. "Do we have any idea what's going on out in California? Sounds a little sketchy to me."

"I haven't asked. And yes, it's way sketchy," said Mayer. "I just know they're holding Raul."

"Crazy shit. This is the most fun I've had in years. Thank you for putting my name in the hat," said Vincenzo.

"Thank Garrett when you see him. He's a fan somehow. I just made sure he didn't forget."

"Garrett and I crossed paths a few times. Not always under the best circumstances," said Vincenzo. "But we always kept it civil, and I sensed a mutual respect. I'm not gonna lie, when Director James reached out to me with the proposition of joining ARTEMIS, I had to contain my enthusiasm."

"That's probably why he kept you on his short list of ARTEMIS candidates," said Mayer. "He doesn't like to work with yes-men or yes-women. We all have skeletons of some sort in our closet. Mann, too."

"Damn right we do. And proud of it."

"I might wrap it up for the night," said Mayer. "Leave the motion sensor on for the video camera."

She had drilled a small hole in the corner of the half-wall window to install the sensor, which didn't reliably work through glass.

"We'll probably do the same, but leave an hour or so from now, so we don't draw any suspicion," said Vincenzo. "I have Kerri in one of the buildings behind our SUV. She'll come out and act like she just got out of work. Hop in the driver's seat and that's that."

"See you back at the hotel," said Mayer. "Hopefully we'll have a response from California by then."

"Sounds like a plan. I might grab a drink down at the—"

"Frank?"

"Holy shit. Just got a reply from the crew in California. Positive ID. That's Mr. Clean," said Vincenzo. "According to Raul."

"We'll see," said Mayer. "I'll give Mann a call. He should be on the ground somewhere in the area by now."

CHAPTER 44

Raul woke to a strobe light. Amateurs. Just one of their cell phones on some kind of strobe mode.

"Yes. Yes. I submit to your will because you pressed a button on a phone," said Raul.

The light cut out, revealing the woman with a permanent limp. She'd suffered an injury to her left leg. He guessed the knee. She'd worked hard to recover and conceal it, but it stuck out like a sore thumb to him. Identifying human weakness was his specialty.

He glanced behind her, at the open door. They'd always had two covering him during any interaction, no matter how trivial. Did they slip up, or was this some kind of ruse to put an end to him? He wouldn't put it past Mann to give this rogues' gallery an unsavory order and try to bait him into killing himself by trying to escape. They looked like they'd follow it gleefully.

She shook her head. "Do you have any idea how clearly you're transmitting your intentions right now? Yes. The door is open. Yes. This is the first time only one of us has come into your cell. And yes, my left leg is still messed up. Took a tracer round through the knee working with these bozos. Kind of hurt. Looked like a laser from *Star Wars* punched through it."

Who the hell were these people? "To what do I owe the pleasure of your company?"

She tossed him a satellite phone, which he failed to catch because of the metal-core zip ties that bound his hands together—and were tethered to what had to be a two-hundred-pound anvil! They had actually brought an anvil with them. His ankles were also restrained by zip ties and tethered to the anvil, which required him to hop if he wanted to move around.

They'd given him enough tether line to awkwardly lie on the air mattress or sit on the camping toilet they'd provided. He had to admit, it was a foolproof method of restraint. And a degrading one. He'd fallen down a few times while hopping over to use the toilet. Fortunately, they had sedated him when he first arrived, and changed him into sweatpants and a T-shirt. The sweatpants were fairly easy to lower with his hands bound.

When they entered the room, he was required to be seated on the toilet, which had been just inside the limit of his tethers, on a four-by-four-foot piece of plyboard that had been securely nailed to the floor. They never walked within ten feet of him. This group knew what they were doing. He hadn't identified a single weakness in their system. Aside from possibly losing their rental deposit if he tipped over the toilet.

"I'm underground," he said, picking up the phone.

One of the men placed a table in the doorway. A boxy, black device sat on top of it.

"A satellite repeater or relay?" said Raul.

"Look at the big brain on Raul," she said.

"Funny. That was a good movie," he said.

"You'll be getting a call shortly," she said.

"A private call?" said Raul.

"No. And don't try placing a call or sending a text message outside of the call."

"Why. Because you'll be listening and watching?"

"No. Because the phone has been configured to only receive calls," she said.

"It's kind of hard to use a phone with these—titanium-core zip ties?"

"I'm sure you'll figure out a way to save your life," she said, before exiting the room.

The phone rang. Wait. What did she mean by that? He took the phone in his zip-tied hands, struggling to get it at the right angle to press the button to take the call. He pressed the green button and searched for the speakerphone option, finding it a few seconds later.

"Hello?" he said.

"Raul?" answered a female voice.

"*Sí.*"

"I'm Deputy Director Dana O'Reilly's boss. Special Agent Mann reports directly to me for now," said the voice. "O'Reilly sends her regards."

"That's one tough bitch," said Raul. "I'm not going to lie, I was impressed. She got the drop on me. Lucky for her."

"Luck had nothing to do with it."

"I suppose not," said Raul. "There's more to her than meets the eye. They never warned me about her. I let my guard down and got what I deserved."

"Not entirely, but that's not for me to decide," she said.

"Not entirely? What's that supposed to mean?" said Raul, lying to elicit a response. He knew exactly where she was going with that statement.

"We both know you were behind the Sacramento bombing, but that's not for me to decide, either. Entirely."

"There's that word again. *Entirely,*" said Raul.

"I promised Special Agent Mann that I would honor the bones of the agreement the two of you worked out."

"Just the bones?" said Raul. "Sounds like you're easing me into a contract modification."

"No. You identified Mr. Clean, which led us to AXIOM, so I intend to honor Mann's side of the agreement. I will bring you into federal custody, affording you every protection available—plus some. And trust me. The 'plus some' will cost me dearly. Word will get around that I'm harboring the man who killed dozens of FBI agents."

"Allegedly. But maybe he was set up by a certain group to take the fall," said Raul.

"Maybe," she said. "But I need more information about AXIOM and LABYRINTH to explore your *maybe* and get you the kind of 'plus some' protection you'll need. Or a deal later down the line."

"Once I'm in federal custody, isn't it out of your hands?" said Raul.

"Nothing is out of my hands," she said. "Or the thousands of hands I can deploy however and whenever I choose."

What the hell was up with this particular chain of command? It was like the FBI had just quit vetting their people and let a bunch of rogue, do-gooder lunatics run the place, instead of a bunch of conflicted, red tape–obsessed bureaucrats. Not a bad plan, actually. Especially if you hoped to accomplish anything meaningful.

"Message received," said Raul. "When do I come in?"

"A jet will pick you up in six hours and . . . twelve minutes," she said.

"Kind of late," said Raul. "Can't it wait until the morning?"

She didn't respond.

"Never mind. A red-eye is fine."

"Glad you don't mind," she said. "The team watching over you now will accompany you on the flight."

"*Perfecto,*" said Raul. "They're great company."

"Raul?"

"*Sí?*"

"I know you're gaming this in your head right now. Trying to figure out the angles," she said.

"Naturally. Who wouldn't?" said Raul. "You're doing the same right now, but on a different level. No?"

"I am," she said. "Which is why I'm warning you. And I won't warn you again. If you fuck with me, I will end you. Period. Are we clear?"

"We are clear," said Raul. "But indulge me in something first. How the hell did you find AXIOM? I barely gave you anything. And I don't mean that I held anything back. I didn't. All I knew, and told Mann, was that my latest handler was a bald guy I called Mr. Clean, and that I tracked a previous handler back to a featureless, concrete building in Tysons, Virginia."

"What can I say? Special Agent Mann's team is . . . uniquely qualified for this kind of work. *Unorthodox* being their strongest characteristic."

"It's hard to contend with this level of unpredictability. That's AXIOM's biggest challenge. That's how I got caught," said Raul.

"We all fall into familiar patterns," she said. "It's our nature, which is why Special Agent Mann has succeeded where so many have failed. He follows no pattern at all."

"Well. I'm at your mercy," said Raul.

"Let's not use that word."

"Why not?" said Raul.

"Because mercy has nothing to do with this," she said. "I'm honoring Special Agent Mann's word—to the best of my ability. I would never have offered you a deal. I would have rendered you to a dark hole somewhere and tortured the hell out of you. Predictably. Maybe effectively. Maybe not. Who knows, right?"

He got it. She'd disappear him if he didn't cooperate.

"Right," said Raul. "Where do we start?"

"From the beginning," she said. "From the day you were captured by the CIA."

"It's a long story," said Raul.

"I have nothing but time, and a digital recorder," she said.

"Lucky me."

CHAPTER 45

Mann unbuckled his seatbelt and gave up "shotgun," which was immediately filled by Kerri Wallace, along with her short-barrel rifle. He'd seen enough of the DC streets from the front passenger seat—for now. They'd followed the two-SUV AXIOM convoy that left Tysons for an hour now, as it wound through the greater DC area in what Mayer described as a "lazy" surveillance detection route (SDR). A true SDR would have taken them out of the city into rural Virginia, Maryland—maybe even Delaware—before heading toward their destination.

No other vehicles had left the Tysons Corner building, so this probably wasn't a decoy. But it was still possible, which was why they had a second team standing by near AXIOM's headquarters. Mann understood the surveillance/countersurveillance game well enough, but Mayer and Vincenzo, both seasoned Special Surveillance Group investigators, were the subject matter experts. Which was why neither of them were in Anish Gupta's tricked-out surveillance van.

The white Mercedes Sprinter van didn't stand out in DC; it was ranked high on the list of "dime a dozen" vehicles in the city. But if AXIOM ran a proper SDR, they couldn't drive it beyond the suburbs, which was why Mayer trailed their van in a midsize, entirely nondescript SUV. Vincenzo sat in a similar vehicle back in Tysons, just in case a second convoy departed.

Mann knelt next to Gupta, who sat in a bolted-down captain's chair in front of an array of computer monitors that took up most of the left side of the van's rear compartment. Chad Lianez sat in the seat next to him, closer to the back of the van, looking like a teenager at GameStop with a gift card.

The right side of the van was a floor-to-roof metal shelving structure that protected and held all the electronics gear that fed the screens in front of Gupta and Lianez securely in place. Mann recognized only half of the equipment, and he was no stranger to FBI surveillance gear. The Hailstorm device stood out, but that was about it, other than racks of server and desktop rigs.

"This van is like a ten- to twenty-year sentence on wheels," said Mann.

Lianez started laughing, along with Serrano, who sat in the captain's chair next to the sliding door on the right side of the van.

"Dude. Sir. It freaks me out when you say shit like that," said Gupta.

"I'm kidding," said Mann. "How many times do we have to go over this?"

"I don't know," said Gupta. "I've worked with the FBI before, but not like this. You guys are always, like, in another car or city. Or somewhere far enough away that I could quickly vanish if things went sideways."

"I get it," said Mann. "I'll try to keep the prison jokes to a minimum."

"Thank you," said Gupta.

"What are we looking at here?" said Mann. "Mayer tells me this is a lazy SDR."

"In the grand scheme of things, yes," said Gupta. "A critical Russian spy here in the US would take their SDR outside the city. Three hours minimum. No way to follow them without being spotted. They'd either reenter the city from a completely different direction or meet their contact along their route. Conversely, an American spy in Moscow would remain in the city, bouncing from train to train, before taking to the streets on foot and trying to dodge Russia's extensive camera network.

I don't think AXIOM is too worried right now. But they're definitely up to something. Driving around the city for an hour isn't normal."

"Good thing you have a Hailstorm device," said Mann.

Gupta shook his head. "See. That felt like a passive-aggressive 'I'm going to arrest you' statement."

"Sorry. I couldn't help myself," said Mann, patting his shoulder. "Trust me. You're in good company here."

"I know," said Gupta. "It's the nature of the business."

"How much longer do you think they'll drive around?" said Serrano.

"Can't be too much longer," said Mann. "Especially if they don't plan on leaving the city."

"And there's no way they know we're tracking them?" said Serrano.

"Not unless they've placed a tracker that I can't detect on our van, and determined that we're following their exact route," said Gupta. "But that would require them to suspect we were following them."

"And we've never seen their convoy, which means they've never seen us," said Mann. "And would have no reason to tag us."

"Unless they employed a trail vehicle," said Gupta. "Which could have spotted us."

"Among the dozens of other white Sprinters on the road," said Mann. "Mayer thinks we're good to go. She hasn't seen anything that piqued her attention, and she's been behind us the entire time."

"I feel confident saying that we haven't been detected, but I'm always playing the devil's advocate in my head," said Gupta. "I just happen to have an audience today. Sorry."

"Don't apologize, and don't keep anything to yourself," said Mann. "Every hunch can be a game changer in this business. Sorry if I'm preaching to the choir."

"You're right. It's just taking me a little time to adjust to working with a new team," said Gupta.

"How long have you worked exclusively with your crew?" said Serrano.

"Almost twenty years," said Gupta.

"Same with Berg and Bauer?" said Mann.

Gupta nodded. "Yeah. We crossed paths with them around that time. It's been a wild ride. Not much downtime."

"I imagine," said Mann.

Gupta stiffened. "I just lost all their signals."

"Location?" said Mann.

"2711 Wisconsin Avenue."

Mann contacted Mayer on his handheld radio and repeated the address. "Check it out. We'll be right behind you."

Mayer's vehicle veered left, cutting across traffic onto a side street. Wisconsin Avenue was three streets over from Massachusetts Avenue.

"What am I doing?" said Luke Turner, from the driver's seat.

"Take the next left," said Mann.

The van came to a stop moments later.

"What happened?" said Serrano.

"They either destroyed all of their cell phones at once, or they turned into an underground parking garage," said Gupta. "My money is on a parking garage."

Mann passed that along, while Turner waited for a break in the southbound traffic. He pounded the wheel a few times, the traffic steady.

"There's no rush," said Mann. "Mayer is on it."

Turner took a deep breath before replying. "Yeah. I know. I know. Thank you."

Turner was editing himself, even if his face betrayed his frustration and anger. Baker's death had hit him hard; Rocha's betrayal even harder. They were down to five of the original nine he'd brought onto the original task force, including himself. The past week had whittled half of them away. The week ahead no doubt promised to claim more lives. Mayer's voice squawked over his handheld.

"2711 has an underground garage. And we saw the gate closing as we passed by. It looks like an apartment building."

"Copy. Head south on Wisconsin and look for parking on the street."

Gupta raised his hand.

"Yes?" said Mann, having a good idea what he was about to say.

"I recommend that we just park the van here and wait. Give them time to settle in," he said. "Unless they have some basement bunker under the building, I'll be able to locate them with Hailstorm."

"Exactly. We should be able to pinpoint their location to a specific floor, if not the exact room, with Hailstorm," said Mann. "And if they spread out inside the building, we should be able to map their entire footprint."

Turner pulled the van into a driveway. "This should do for now."

"It's not like anyone can force us to move," said Mann.

"I don't know about that," said Gupta. "The Russian embassy is just a few hundred yards to the southwest. Never know who lives here."

"Interesting that they'd seek refuge in a building this close to the Russian embassy," said Mann.

"Once we identify AXIOM as a corporate identity," said Lianez, "we should drill into their financing."

"Excellent suggestion, Chad," said Mann. "You didn't see it, but the LABYRINTH facility was extensive—and presumably expensive to operate. Unless AXIOM's founder is a billionaire trust fund baby or the company has already made hundreds of millions of dollars under the radar, they'd need a serious outside capital investment to keep the place running. Who better to fund chaos in America than the Russian Federation."

"You sound like one of those conspiracy bloggers," said Gupta.

"What?" said Mann, before realizing what had just happened.

"Just messing with you, Special Agent Mann. Payback's a bitch," said Gupta, the entire van breaking into laughter.

"Touché," said Mann, stifling a laugh. "I think this arrangement is going to work out fine."

"Yeah. I think I've figured you guys—" he started. "Hold on. I have two. Three. Six signals again. They must have moved aboveground."

The Hailstorm system had grabbed all six of the cell phones in the two-vehicle convoy when it departed Tysons Corner. The phones were all encrypted, which Gupta said he'd work on later. His sensors had detected EMF transmission in the satellite communications frequency range shortly after their departure. They were using satellite comms in transit, which would be impossible to intercept. But for now, they could use Hailstorm to pinpoint their movements within the building.

"We need to get closer," said Gupta. "Without being too obvious."

"Luke. Let's find a parking space closer to the target building. 2711 Wisconsin Avenue," said Mann.

Wallace typed the address into the van's navigation screen while Turner backed out of the driveway. A few minutes later, they were tucked into a parking space on Edmunds Street, exactly 393 feet away, perpendicular to the target building. The most important factor being that they couldn't see the building, which meant nobody in the building could see their van. About ten minutes later, Gupta swiveled his chair to face them.

"Top two floors," he said. "They've made a few trips up and down. Looks like they're setting up shop."

"Or moving," said Turner.

"Because we dropped off the radar?" said Mann.

"That would be my guess," said Serrano. "They know we're laser-focused on finding them. And they know we have, or had, Raul."

Mann didn't want to get into the Raul discussion with her right now. She wasn't happy that James had him in custody now, essentially preventing her from closing the loop on *La Triada*—her sole reason for joining ARTEMIS. He made eye contact with Serrano, acknowledging the injustice he'd created. She looked away, keeping a neutral face, which was her way of saying, *Let's move on—for now.*

"This could just be AXIOM taking a preventative measure, based on the two factors Cata just highlighted," said Mann. "If that's the case, this could work to our advantage. They'll feel safer here, and if we don't tip our hand, they'll never suspect we discovered their little hideout.

When the time is right, we can swoop right in and clean house. I'm guessing that they've moved the most critical aspects of their domestic chaos operation here."

"Only time will tell," said Gupta. "If they make a few more of these runs today, then we can start drawing conclusions. This could be one of the executives moving his office out of the line of fire. Still a high-value target worth taking down, but maybe not the most important. Let's give this some time."

He continued. "I have a Kingfish I can loan to Mayer. I'll transfer the tracking data, so she can babysit them. If they head back to the building in Tysons, she can follow at a very safe distance, confirming their return. We should head back now to support Vincenzo. If a second group leaves, he won't have to risk detection."

"Sounds like a plan," said Mann.

"No arrest joke about the Kingfish?" said Gupta.

Kingfish was a handheld version of Hailstorm. Neither device was technically illegal to possess outside of law enforcement, if you were willing to spend a few hundred thousand dollars and could convince the manufacturer to sell it to you—which made this exchange amusing.

"Do you want one?"

"No."

"Your loss," said Mann.

"Loss of what?"

"It's just a saying," said Mann.

"Sounded like you wanted to say *your loss of freedom*, or something like that," said Gupta.

"My work is done here," said Mann. "You're making your own arrest jokes now."

"Shit. Did I just—I did," said Gupta. "Didn't I?"

"Welcome to ARTEMIS, Anish," said Mann.

CHAPTER 46

Clara Furst got on his nerves. Partly because she talked down to him. Mostly because she was now making demands knowing full well that her organization had yet to make a single payment to AXIOM for access to DOMINION's services. He could tolerate the abrasive treatment, but until they made the sizable deposit originally agreed upon, she had no right to make demands.

McCall had invested a significant chunk of AXIOM's cash reserves, not to mention a few eight-figure loans, into repurposing and operating the former CIA training site in New Mexico, along with maintaining its product—the DOMINION network. And he'd yet to see a dime from Furst. Promises of lucrative government contracts, favorable tax laws, and a seat at the table when the political winds filled his client's sails was attractive, which was why he had offered them a generous discount.

But promises of future reward didn't pay today's bills. And there was still a risk that those political winds might never arrive. They needed to start transferring funds before they got to play with his shiny new toy. He sure as hell wasn't going to give them immediate access to the entire network, as Furst had just suggested. He'd have to think of a different approach, other than the outright rejection of her demand. AXIOM had only one client interested in DOMINION, Clara Furst's, which put him in a precarious position. He needed them just as much as they appeared to need him.

DOMINION had a very limited list of potential clients. Few groups needed a small cartel army at their disposal, and even fewer had the kind of money McCall would charge to lease it. Then again, if Furst dumped him, he may have to start thinking a little smaller, to keep the lights on and the network maintained, until he could land another big client. Their neighbor just a few blocks south on Wisconsin Avenue might be interested, if he could arrange a meeting.

"Ms. Furst. I appreciate your concern—"

"I'm not sure you do," she said, cutting him off. "You call me with news that you're taking precautions to safeguard DOMINION, which includes key staff moving from your Tysons headquarters to another location—and you didn't think that we'd be concerned enough to want to safeguard the project?"

Safeguard it by placing it in the client's hands—leaving McCall with an IOU for three hundred fifty million dollars? No thanks. Oh, he most certainly knew it would give them some cause for concern, which was why he'd told her in the first place. To give her a nudge by making her a little nervous. Perhaps create a little urgency around transferring the initial deposit. It was also why he put in those terms, leaving out the details. If she knew the full story, it could potentially kill the deal, though he doubted they'd bail out that easily. It wasn't like her organization could run out to the store and buy another domestic influence operation.

"I believe in full transparency, which is why I reached out to you immediately," said McCall. "And I think I can appreciate your concern. We've spent a considerable amount of money and devoted an incalculable amount of time and effort to create a product ideal for your organization. For true American patriots willing to do whatever it takes to save the United States and set the country back on the path toward greatness."

"Save the flattery," said Furst. "So. In the spirit of transparency, what exactly caused you to run and hide?"

Damn. She was good. Right under his skin. He had to give her credit.

"It's a precautionary move related to the problem in Tucson. We lost a wide variety of pieces in that attack. My biggest concern being the mercenary crew we hired. They are—or were—supposedly the best in the business, so I can't imagine a scenario in which they left any whiff of a trail leading back to AXIOM, but it's better to be safe than sorry," said McCall. "And we were long overdue for a live continuity-of-operations drill. It's all been in-house drills until now. Our capability to quickly shift locations, while maintaining control over DOMINION, is critical to both of us."

"Next time lead off with an explanation. Don't make me ask," said Furst.

"Fair point," said McCall. "We're conducting the move over a few days. Taking it slow to work out any bugs. We'll run another drill within a month. Ideally, we will be able to move our war room in under an hour. I have well-placed contacts at the federal and state district courts covering this area, who can notify me if any US agency submits a warrant request. We'll have plenty of time to protect DOMINION."

"Why not keep the backup location operational at all times, so all you have to do is scramble out of the building," said Furst.

He'd had enough of this.

"Because money doesn't grow on trees around here," said McCall. "And it presents double the risk of losing the program."

"You make it sound like it's in a briefcase," said Furst.

McCall had no intention of taking that bait, even if her statement was nothing more than another one of her digs. The less she knew about how they ran DOMINION, the better, because if her organization couldn't pay the agreed-upon price or, even worse, turned out to be nothing more than an insolvent gang of grifters—he could see them trying to acquire DOMINION by any means necessary. They knew AXIOM's Tysons, Virginia, location. He had no choice but to show Furst that he wasn't some guy holed up in his mother's basement, trying to squeeze money out of them, or an FBI agent looking to burn what she'd helped build to the ground.

But they didn't know anything else about the inner workings of DOMINION or the precautions McCall had taken to assure continuity of operations, without magnifying their risk. She'd almost hit the nail on the head with her briefcase statement. DOMINION was managed through a software program developed in-house, specifically to handle all the tracking, logistical, and communications demands of running hundreds of LABYRINTH graduates. It wasn't the most complex program his developers had designed, but without it, the massive DOMINION database would be useless.

He'd designed the DOMINION control system like this specifically for continuity of operations. If the FBI kicked in their front door right now, the war room could transmit the database to Georgetown, where they could load it into computers containing the DOMINION software program and pick up right where they left off. Likewise, if the FBI somehow jammed their outrageously expensive satellite communications array, depending on the circumstances, they could either carry the database with them if it was safe to drive out, or hide it in one of the purpose-built, impossible-to-find concealment points within the building, for retrieval later.

And just in case both the Tysons and Georgetown locations were hit at the same time, they had an alternate backup location in Montana that contained a computer loaded with the DOMINION program that was connected to the same type of satellite communications array found at the Georgetown annex. Far simpler and less expensive, but one still capable of decrypting the inbound signal and preserving the data for future use. No matter what happened, DOMINION would survive. The trick was for McCall to survive, which was in everybody's best interest, his own being the most obvious. He'd built a fail-safe into the entire system.

Every month, at any time between 12:01 a.m. on the twelfth and 11:59 p.m. on the fourteenth, McCall had to log on to a dark web site and enter a code that he could generate in his head based on a not-so-complex—but impossible to replicate without his brain—decoding system. If he failed to enter the code in time, which was transmitted directly to all the sites harboring the software program, the program would instantly delete itself, rendering the database entirely useless to whoever possessed it. McCall had no intention of being sidelined, whether by illness, arrest, or malfeasance.

"It's where it needs to be. At all times. To keep it secure," said McCall. "Speaking of briefcases. Is that how we're going receive the agreed-upon deposit? A briefcase."

"Tucson didn't inspire a lot of confidence," said Furst.

Interesting. Time to put his foot down.

"DOMINION wasn't designed for that job," said McCall. "We threw about a dozen of our assets at the situation, hoping the mercenary team would do the heavy lifting, but it didn't work out that way."

"I'll take that back to the—"

"Sorry. I wasn't finished. But thank you," said McCall. "Here's what you should take back to your organization. If a combined total of fifty million dollars doesn't hit the four accounts I gave you two months ago within the next six hours, the total price of DOMINION rises to a half billion dollars. And nothing gets delivered until the total price is met."

Silence. A good sign.

"I can pass along the routing information again if you need it," said McCall.

"We have it. You'll have the deposit before the six hours has expired," said Furst.

"Thank you."

"But we're going to need something after we send you the deposit," said Furst. "Two things, actually."

"A show of faith?" said McCall. "Once the check clears, I will be more than happy to kick off your proposed operation. Phase One? Get the country's juices flowing. The election is only three and a half months away. No time like the present."

"Phase one is a good start," said Furst.

"And the second request?"

"I'm sending someone over to Tysons," said Furst. "They'll confirm firsthand that your drill is successful and remain in place until the drill is finished. This is nonnegotiable. We have to protect our investment."

"As long as whoever you send doesn't mind wearing a hood during the trip over and back, plus submit to a search. Both electronic and, shall we say . . . somewhat invasive?"

"That's completely understandable. Our person will be over shortly," she said, ending the call.

He hated how she did that—every single time.

CHAPTER 47

Mann scanned the team, looking for any signs of disagreement, disgust, or contempt for Karl Berg's final words. They'd briefed two full mission options for tomorrow. One went extremely hard, as in no-holds-barred, direct-confrontation hard, which could land all of them—the ones who survived—in jail if things went sideways. The other was far more nuanced, relying on a combination of softer approaches. They'd still hit the Tysons headquarters hard enough to scatter the chickens, as Turner had put it, but they'd let things play out more slowly once AXIOM occupied its secondary location.

Slowly, as in they'd notify James of the Wisconsin Avenue address, letting her know that they'd tracked the head shed to Georgetown, and that she needed to submit another warrant to raid the building, along with every address associated with AXIOM. He felt bad concealing this from her, but he needed to keep the task force's options open. She had agreed to send DOJ lawyers to the US District Court's Eastern District in Virginia tomorrow at nine in the morning to submit a warrant to search AXIOM's Tysons headquarters.

He'd assumed that Gerald McCall, AXIOM's CEO, had infiltrated the court system somehow, and even if he hadn't, Mayer's crew had detected an enhanced countersurveillance effort inside the AXIOM building. So, if the FBI mounted an undiscovered raid later that morning, assuming that the warrant was approved, McCall and Jeremy Powell would presumably scoot to Georgetown. The FBI would have no authority to stop them from leaving, or even follow them, without risking a fatal flaw in their case against AXIOM later down the line.

She'd do the same at the District of Columbia District Court, after McCall and Powell fled to the Georgetown location—if the task force chose the less aggressive of the two approaches in taking down AXIOM. If they went with the hard, Mann didn't want the FBI or the courts to know about Georgetown until his group took care of business.

They'd identified McCall through the FBI's facial recognition database. A longtime trust fund baby entrepreneur, coming from a wealthy northern Virginia family, he had no criminal record or history of shady dealings. Until now. Powell was a different story altogether. As in, he had no story—according to the FBI. But Raul had kindly filled in the gaps, informing Audra Bauer that Powell, a.k.a. Mr. Clean, had been a senior manager at the New Mexico facility when the CIA ran it under the name SINKHOLE, and that AXIOM kept him on the payroll when it took over.

Since SINKHOLE had been a CIA operation, she did a little digging at Langley. The kind of digging a former National Clandestine Service deputy director could wrangle. And damn if she didn't hit pay dirt. She didn't even need to use the photographs Mayer's team had so kindly provided. The SINKHOLE file gave him up readily. Jeremy Powell. The man who had spearheaded the CIA's "black site" program around the world, for nearly a decade, was directly connected to SINKHOLE, LABYRINTH, and AXIOM. It was almost too good to be true.

ARTEMIS—which, as far as he was concerned, included everyone present—had to make a choice between the two options presented. Burn it all down, possibly suffering third-degree burns in the process, or do the "right thing" and let the system decide AXIOM's fate. Arrests. Investigation. Charges. Trials. Acquittals and convictions. Basically, how the system was supposed to work. Except they were three and a half months away from an election, and the system moved at a snail's pace.

If AXIOM's domestic network of cartel soldiers remained in play while the justice system crawled along, the consequences for the country could be dire. If Karl Berg's and Audra Bauer's suspicions were correct, the cost could be our democracy. Or at the very least, an abrupt and unceremonious end to a barely functioning government that currently hung on by a thread. Followed by a slower, but inevitable, end to democracy.

"So. Where do we stand?" said Mann.

"Burn it to the ground," said Serrano. "It's the only way to be sure that this doesn't rear its ugly head later and bite your country in the ass."

Everyone seemed to agree.

"Counterargument?" said Mann. "If we take the scorched-earth option, there's no turning back. We either succeed and emerge as unsung heroes, or we fail and go to jail—making the headlines."

"I say we burn it down," said Turner. "I'm willing to pay the price to take this group down."

The FBI agents who were present, minus the Special Surveillance Group investigators and Chad Lianez, who watched over the two AXIOM locations, nodded in favor of Turner's proclamation. None of them looked overly enthusiastic about going hard against AXIOM, but that was to be expected.

They were sworn law enforcement officers who had already pushed against the limits of their authority. What he was asking them to do tomorrow far exceeded those limits. In other words, he was asking them to participate in an operation that clearly violated the law. By agreeing to take part, they were acknowledging the likelihood that they'd lose everything.

Same with Serrano, who nodded at her crew, all of them signaling their agreement in one way or another. Few of them looked any more eager than his own agents. They understood the consequences of choosing the "go hard" option. It significantly increased their exposure on the street, which similarly magnified their chances of an encounter with the police, which could go in any of several directions. None of them good.

The best-case scenario being arrest, imprisonment, and eventual deportation back to Mexico. The worst being killed by police responders or
held on charges serious enough to negate any chance of deportation.

If they made it back to Mexico, they still had the hope of receiving
their share of the bowling bag money. He'd made sure of that by placing
the bags in a storage unit yesterday and giving the lock combination to
Audra Bauer and Karl Berg, who promised to distribute the money to
Serrano's team, or their next of kin, if tomorrow went entirely sideways.

"Burn it down," said Serrano.

He turned to Melendez and Miralles. "Do I even need to ask?"

"No. But just in case," said Miralles, "we're in."

"Then we go hard, and shut AXIOM down for good," said Mann.
"At the same time, we need to be mindful of our Mexican friends' legal
status. I don't think they should enter the Georgetown building."

"We'll be fine," said Serrano.

"We're going to make a lot of noise on the street prior to hitting
the building. The police response will be quick, particularly with the
Russian embassy a little more than a block away."

"He's right about that," said Audra Bauer. "DC Metro Police might
even have a satellite station nearby. Several high-profile embassies are in
the area. We should do some research on that."

"Our teams on the street will have a hard enough time escaping the
area," said Mann. "But there's almost a one hundred percent chance that
anyone who goes into that building will remain trapped in it until we
negotiate a surrender with local, and possibly federal, authorities. If they
surround the building before we finish the job and escape—that's it. We
won't be employing any kind of force to get out of there. Similar rules
apply to the street teams. If you're caught or things are looking dicey, do
not engage law enforcement. You'll have no weapons on you, or at least
you shouldn't. Just raise your hands and follow instructions. Director
James and I will do everything in our power to fix your situation."

"I'm going in the building," said Serrano.

"I assumed that was the case," said Mann. "But we shouldn't slip any more of your team inside."

"AXIOM has been going back and forth for a day," said Serrano. "And we haven't been watching the building as closely as the Tysons headquarters. They could have imported another team that arrived in the middle of the night. They could have an army in there."

Melendez raised an index finger.

"Yes?" said Mann.

"We'll be fine with the seven we have," said Melendez. "A small, compact group that knows how to shoot in a close-quarters environment is all we need. We sweep the building. Put Anish to work on the geek shit. We're good to go."

Kerri Wallace, formerly one of the head members of Chicago field office's SWAT team, raised her hand. "I can ride in the back compartment. Give you another shooter in case things get wild."

"Another shooter is always welcome," said Miralles, giving a thumbs-up.

"Are you sure?"

"Absolutely," said Wallace.

"That's eight on the inside," said Mann. "Assuming our street-level plan works."

"And if it doesn't," said Karl Berg.

"The only way it doesn't work is if they determine it's a trick," said Mann. "Then they're faced with a hard decision. Drive on and hope to shake us, possibly relying on law enforcement or AXIOM reinforcements to take us out. Or drive into the Georgetown building and hole up, hoping to hold us off long enough for help to arrive."

"Do they have a communications array on the rooftop?" said Bauer.

"We can't fly overhead," said Jax. "Not with the Russian embassy that close. They have drone detection radar, and would report it immediately, putting the entire area on alert. The Russians take drones very seriously."

"I imagine. Ukraine has probably embedded a fear of drones in their collective DNA," said Mann. "But let's put a quadcopter up and look as soon as we start the fireworks. I'd like for your team to destroy any communications gear on that rooftop."

"Easy enough," said Jax.

"Any last thoughts?" said Mann.

Gupta raised his hand, and Mann nodded.

"Ideally, we take down the entire head shed in the garage," said Gupta. "But if not, we need to move as fast as possible to the top two floors. It's impossible to say why they're paying so much attention to this building, but we have to assume it's a backup plan. Some kind of continuity-of-operations thing."

"We've seen this before," said Berg.

"If they flee to the Georgetown building, it's not to hide," said Gupta. "It's to perpetuate their diseased mission. I suggest we take out their ability to transmit from Georgetown, the moment they turn into the building. Once they realize their backup location is compromised, they'll send that disease somewhere else, and we'll be back to square one. Even worse, actually. Most of us will still be tied up in the US legal system while they pull off their plan."

Mann nodded at Anish, the two of them sharing a knowing look.

"Anish is dead right," said Mann. "We're going for broke tomorrow. We won't get another chance before it's too late."

PART IV

CHAPTER 48

McCall hung up the phone and immediately dialed Powell. He'd just received word from one of his contacts in the US District Court located in Alexandria, Virginia, that Department of Justice attorneys had just submitted search warrants for the AXIOM building. The details of the warrant were still a bit sketchy, but the request had been fast-tracked for reasons of "national security." To make matters worse, Executive Assistant Director Camilla James had hand-walked the request through, alongside the DOJ lawyers. It was more than fair to say at this point that the Tysons building had been compromised. Powell answered immediately.

"Do you want me upstairs?"

"There's no time," said McCall. "The feds will likely hit this building within the next hour or two."

"Warrants?"

"Yes," said McCall. "Send DOMINION to Georgetown via satellite comms and prepare the SATCHEL. We need to be on the move within ten minutes."

SATCHEL referred to the physically transportable version of DOMINION, installed on a portable server in the war room that received constant data updates. It could be unplugged and placed in a specially designed duffel bag that contained a forty-eight-hour power source and the interface cords necessary to plug it into the Georgetown annex system or the tertiary backup location.

"Got it. Anything else?" said Powell.

"Once DOMINION is transferred, wipe the servers. And double our spotters here. I don't want to drive into an FBI task force on the way out. Understood?"

"Doing this now," said Powell.

"See you in the loading bay no later than ten minutes from now," said McCall, hanging up.

His next call was to Litman.

"Ready the vehicles and executive security team for departure. We have about an hour before this place is swarmed by FBI agents."

"We'll be ready to roll in under ten," said Litman. "Five vehicles. You and Mr. Powell in the third. Me and the team leader in the second."

"I'd rather you were with us," said McCall. "The SATCHEL will be in our vehicle."

"Understood. I'll be in the front. I have our best driver assigned to the vehicle," said Litman. "I assume we're headed to the Georgetown annex?"

"Correct," said McCall. "Unless we suspect it's compromised."

"Our spotters here and in Georgetown haven't seen anything out of the ordinary, but we're constantly monitoring the situation," said Litman. "Looks like the FBI is playing this close to the vest. We haven't caught a whiff of trouble over the past few days."

"I suspect they just got what they needed to hit this building," said McCall. "Reach out to Georgetown and make sure they're on high alert."

"Yes. That'll be my first call," said Litman. "I need to get moving, sir."

"Don't let me hold you up," said McCall.

He left the SCIF and entered his office. What a shame to leave this mahogany wood masterpiece behind—for now. He'd be back eventually, when DOMINION shifted the sands of fortune back in his favor. This upcoming January, if all went well during the November election, and they didn't lose DOMINION in the next few hours. Once

DOMINION's potential was demonstrated, they'd have an unending list of clients, domestic and abroad. They'd already drawn up blueprints for similar LABYRINTH-like strategies throughout the European Union, Asia, and South America.

McCall made his way to the bar and poured a few fingers of his most expensive Scotch. May as well enjoy it. Once the dust settled here and around DC, he'd sneak away to the ranch estate he owned in Montana, along with his executive team—where he'd run DOMINION on behalf of his client. The alternate location, housing the DOMINION software, sat deep in the hills of his 2,500-acre property. The Georgetown annex primarily served as a temporary refuge in the case of an emergency, like right now.

He'd talked about it as their main secondary location, but anyone who put a moment or two of thought into that concept would realize it wasn't realistic. If all their houses, apartments, favorite restaurants, and friends came under FBI surveillance, life confined to two floors of a building in the heart of the DC area for several months would become unsustainable. No. They'd initiate phase one from Georgetown, which should be enough to distract the FBI, before slipping away to Montana.

McCall took a sip from the glass. Exquisite. He'd bring the unopened bottle in the cabinet below with him to Georgetown. He didn't have time to empty the crystal decanter into another container. Or did he? The contents of this decanter had been a gift from a good Scottish friend living in London. One who had the connections to put him in touch with a group of patriots in both England and Scotland, who had played a key role in Brexit. Damn. He didn't have the time. McCall opened the doors below and removed the bottle he'd purchased himself.

A few minutes later, his leather Italian travel bag stuffed with an assortment of sentimental and practical items collected from his office, McCall took one last look around—the opulence tugging at him.

"Until we meet again," he said, before walking out.

CHAPTER 49

Chad Lianez sat up in his chair. Jax tensed. This could be it. The timing was right. Director James had just notified Mann that the warrants were headed to a judge. The radio frequency detector they'd installed on the rooftop adjacent to the AXIOM building had just lit up. While they couldn't possibly intercept the transmission, they could detect activity with a nearby receiver. And this wasn't just a quick burst. This had the electromagnetic signature associated with a significant data transfer.

"Jax. It's time to shut AXIOM's array down," said Lianez. "The radio frequency detector just lit up. Not a quick burst. A significant data transfer is taking place."

They had installed an RF receiver on the adjacent building's rooftop. While they couldn't intercept any transmission, they could detect any significant bleed over electromagnetic frequency activity. Jax popped out of her seat and took a quick look at his screen.

"Yep," she said, before contacting the drone team.

"Neva. Launch the drone and burn the comms array," said Jax over the radio. "Gloria. Report any movement in the loading bay. Looks like this is the beginning of the end for AXIOM."

The two former Mexican state police officers had taken over surveillance in the building next to AXIOM. Neva had positioned herself on the rooftop with a quadcopter, while Gloria sat in the third-floor office, watching the loading bay. The drone had been equipped with a thermite incendiary grenade instead of an explosive device, to avoid attracting unnecessary attention to the area.

Neva would maneuver the drone to the AXIOM rooftop and set it down on the satellite communications array, where the grenade would burn at four thousand degrees Fahrenheit, melting through the base station and destroying it. The only catch was that they couldn't remotely detonate a thermite grenade. Neva had attached a twenty-five-yard length of light metal fishing wire to the grenade's pin, the other end secured to an antenna fixture on her rooftop. A quarter of the way to the target, the pin would be pulled, giving her about five seconds to maneuver the drone into place.

The timing was ridiculously tight, but she'd practiced on the ground yesterday, making it happen with a few seconds to spare. Moving at eighty miles per hour, she'd be over the AXIOM rooftop within two seconds, leaving her a few more to drop right down on top of it. Jax had watched her do it a dozen times, without the thermite grenade. That was the wild card variable here, and why they'd limited the fishing line to twenty-five yards. They'd tried seventy and a hundred yards, a hundred being roughly the distance between the two buildings, and the wind on the ground pulled the simulated pin during a few of their test flights. All their tests with a twenty-five-yard line had succeeded.

"The drone is inbound," said Neva.

Jax didn't respond. She wanted Neva's full concentration on the drone. She started the countdown in her head. Five. Four. Three. Two. One.

"Looked good from my end," said Neva.

Lianez pumped both fists in the air. "Yes! Signal strength is zero!"

"Neva. We're getting zero signal strength from the communications array," said Jax. "Nice job. Get down to the third floor."

"On the way," said Neva.

"Gloria. You're our eyes," said Jax. "We expect them to depart—"

"A convoy of five large SUVs just pulled up to the fenced area outside the loading bay," said Gloria.

"Copy. I'll leave you to it," said Jax.

Gloria knew the deal. Identify the key players and their place in the convoy.

CHAPTER 50

Powell's phone buzzed while he waited for the elevator. He carried the SATCHEL in one hand, his phone in the other. Two of Litman's personal protective officers stood behind him, facing the office's interior. They carried FN P90 submachine guns, holding them low and to their sides. The P90 was an ideal choice for vehicle security teams. Compact enough to easily maneuver in tight quarters, while packing a rifle-like punch with its 5.7mm, body armor–piercing ammunition. On top of that, its unique top-loading magazine held fifty rounds, requiring fewer magazine reloads.

The remaining DOMINION staff, those not deemed critical to continuity of operations, either didn't notice them or pretended not to. He'd do the same under similar circumstances. Security rarely carried weapons in the open.

"Powell," he said, answering the call.

"Mr. Powell. This is Jason. Rooftop security. Someone just landed a drone on top of the communications array. The array is destroyed."

Odd. He hadn't heard or felt a detonation.

"Explosives?"

"Negative. Thermite device," said Jason. "Melted the core of the array within moments and disappeared into the roof. It's still burning through. I wouldn't be surprised if it cut all the way through to the top floor."

Powell imagined it dropping out of the ceiling and landing on McCall's lap. Too much to hope for, he supposed.

"Copy. Did you see where it came from?"

"It came from the direction of the building to the northeast, but nobody saw it launch," he said. "We were more focused on the surrounding streets and parking lots."

"Understood. How does the surrounding area look?" said Powell.

"Nothing unusual, except for a drone coming out of nowhere," said Jason.

"They could have flown that from anywhere," said Powell. "Keep your eyes peeled."

"We're definitely on high alert up here," said Jason. "Sorry we couldn't intercept the drone. The thermite ignited the moment it touched down. Took us all by surprise."

"I have to go. Pass this along to Litman," said Powell, before ending the call.

The door opened to reveal McCall, carrying some kind of fancy leather travel bag. *Must be nice.* He stepped inside while placing a call to the war room's communications section, just a few rooms away. The door closed as Jenkins answered. He was one of the two remaining communications team members in the building. The rest had been moved to Georgetown.

"Jenkins. Did we just lose the array?"

McCall interrupted him. "What did you just say?"

He held a finger up to McCall, something he'd wanted to do for years.

"Yes. I'm not sure what happened," said Jenkins. "I was about to contact rooftop security."

"Don't bother. The array is gone," said Powell. "What is the status of the database transmission?"

"Thirty-two percent," said Jenkins.

"God damn it, Powell. What the fuck just happened?" said McCall.

"Understood," said Powell. "I'll be in touch shortly."

He disconnected the call.

"Only thirty-two percent got out before our communications array was melted by a drone-delivered thermite device," said Powell, before raising the SATCHEL. "This is it right here. Our only copy of the database."

"FBI?" said McCall. "That doesn't sound like an FBI tactic."

"I have no idea," said Powell. "Could be a new tactic. Maybe they didn't want to use an explosive kamikaze drone with our security personnel on the rooftop. Apparently, the drone materialized out of nowhere, landed on the array, and burned a hole through it."

"Shit," said McCall. "How do we prevent the same thing from happening in Georgetown?"

"We don't let anyone follow us to Georgetown," said Powell. "If we detect anyone on our tail, we'll dispatch a vehicle to take them out. Terminate with extreme prejudice."

"I like the sound of that," said McCall. "Make sure Litman understands that he's authorized to do whatever it takes to make sure our vehicle gets into that parking garage. That's all that matters."

Did he really say that in front of two security officers who might not be in the only vehicle that "matters"?

Litman was waiting for them when the elevator door opened in the loading bay.

"Sir. I just heard about the array. Our rooftop spotters do not detect any FBI or other unusual activity on the ground around the building," said Litman. "My vehicle surveillance teams located at key chokepoints around the business park report the same. Nothing out of the ordinary. I believe we are clear to drive out of here."

"Nothing unusual except drones dropping thermite bombs," said McCall, looking around annoyed. "Where's my ride?"

"We're lined up outside the gate. Five armored SUVs. We'll be in the third vehicle," said Litman. "Can I take your bag?"

"No. I'm fine," said McCall, before stepping off toward the convoy. "How many security officers in each SUV?"

"Six in vehicles one, two, four, and five," said Litman. "Four, including myself, in ours. Twenty-eight highly trained protective officers. Traffic is mostly light. We'll have you inside the annex within thirty minutes, where we have fifteen additional protective officers. A small army to keep you and DOMINION safe."

Powell did some quick math. How the hell would they be able to house and feed more than forty security officers, in addition to the dozen or so staff already on-site? He suspected that once the threat abated, more than half of the security team would be let go. And by "let go," he meant brought to the garage, shot in the head with a suppressed pistol, and stacked in the windowless panel van McCall had asked him to buy and park in the garage. He couldn't imagine any scenario in which McCall let any of them leave while DOMINION was being run from Georgetown, regardless of whether he kept them on the payroll or released them from employment. Something to keep in mind if he was ever summoned to the garage unexpectedly.

CHAPTER 51

Mayer pulled out of the Galleria parking garage and turned south on Tysons Boulevard, pointing toward International Drive. Ray Mills had just received a text from Gloria, confirming that the AXIOM convoy had made a right turn onto International Drive. They were headed to Chain Bridge Road, part of Route 123, which could take them all the way to the Chain Bridge, where they'd cross the Potomac River and approach the target building from the north.

A left turn onto International Drive would have strongly suggested that the convoy planned to take the Dulles Access Road and possibly cross the Potomac farther south, at the Francis Scott Key Memorial Bridge. This route would ultimately take them straight up Wisconsin Avenue and require ARTEMIS to spring their trap south of the Russian embassy, which posed additional law enforcement risks.

They couldn't kick off the active part of the operation north of the embassy because of the short distance between it and the target building. They ran the risk of spooking the convoy into skipping their backup location and heading out of town. Depending on the ever-evolving traffic conditions on both sides of the river, it was still too early to predict whether they'd take the northern or southern approach to the target.

She hoped they'd choose the Chain Bridge and weave their way to Wisconsin Avenue, giving the task force ample space and opportunity to scare AXIOM into seeking refuge in the target building. Things could still go wrong with the northern approach. If they ducked into some of the tight streets west of Wisconsin Avenue, they could engage in an endless number of countersurveillance turns before emerging a block away from their destination. That scenario would leave the task force with a difficult choice. Mayer prayed it didn't come to that.

Mills looked up from the laptop resting on his thighs.

"They should be crossing the intersection—now," he said.

Five identical black SUVs raced east on International Drive a moment later. Mayer slowed for the red light.

"Not bad," said Mills. "Location looks dead on. We have signals in all five vehicles. McCall, Powell, and Litman in the third vehicle, as confirmed by Gloria."

He was seated in the front passenger seat, tracking the convoy's location on a laptop provided by Anish Gupta. The computer had been loaded with software that converted the cell phone signals intercepted by the connected Kingfish device into location data. Over the past twenty-four hours, Gupta and Lianez had positively identified the specific phone signal data of five AXIOM VIPs by directly correlating visual sightings with hijacked signals.

Gerald McCall appeared to be the ringleader, always traveling alone with a security detail. And prior to a few minutes ago, the only person they'd seen use the loading bay to come and go from his personal residence. Even Mr. Clean, a.k.a. Jeremy Powell, who accompanied McCall on a trip to the Georgetown building, walked in and out of the front door at the beginning or end of the day. Based on the CIA profile Audra Bauer had provided to the team, he'd specialized in running black site operations for more than a decade, which made him the most likely AXIOM executive to have overseen the New Mexico facility.

The roles of the other three were far less defined. The team had seen Gary Litman barking orders at the personal protective officers who accompanied McCall, so they assumed he filled a high-level security position. He wore a black, over-the-shoulder arm sling on his left arm, which suggested he may have been present during the shoot-out at Alejandro's Minnesota lake house. Baker had reported hitting one of the operatives shooting from the dock in the shoulder—before the thick chemical cloud created by the escaping group's smoke grenades completely obscured the task force's view of the waterline.

Kerry Conway and Oscar Marino, both identified through the FBI facial recognition database, remained somewhat of a mystery. They'd both served in the Army, before essentially dropping off the grid one year apart. Gupta did a deep dive into their pasts, coming up with nothing but a few PO boxes, utility bills, and credit card accounts connected to the greater Washington, DC, area. The task force had not yet accessed their military records, which remained classified. What they did know was that neither graduated from college with a computer or technical-related degree, so it was safe to say that they didn't sit behind a desk in the Army or the private sector and stare at screens. They were "boots on the ground" types.

Mayer pulled up to the intersection, and the light turned green a few seconds later. She spotted the convoy as soon as she straightened their sedan on International Drive. Gupta's gear made her job infinitely easier. She ran almost no risk of losing them, and zero chance of being detected.

The handheld Kingfish device was also linked to a Harpoon signal amplifier and Amberjack direction-finding antenna. The Kingfish and Harpoon sat inside a milk crate in the footwell behind Mills's seat, the wire for the antenna running out the right passenger window to the low-profile, disk-shaped antenna affixed to the rooftop. The entire rig was powered by a sizable battery in the footwell behind Mayer, constantly recharged through a cable running to the auxiliary power outlet, known decades ago as a cigarette lighter.

All she had to do was keep her vehicle within a third of a mile of the last SUV, nearly five football fields away, and they could track the entire convoy with pinpoint accuracy from a safe and undetectable distance. The only scenario in which they could lose contact with the convoy was if their sedan got into an accident that disabled the vehicle.

"They're taking a left onto Chain Bridge Road," said Mills.

She glanced at the dashboard navigation screen.

"We'll see what they do when they reach the Dulles Access Road overpass," said Mayer. "The system is showing the southern route as one minute faster now. It was four minutes slower the last time I looked. Must have cleared a stalled car or something."

"I'd go with the southern route if I were them," said Mills. "Busier, higher-profile roads. Closer to the Capitol. Not to mention the Russian embassy."

"Don't curse us," said Mayer. "I'm team north."

"Sounds like a *Game of Thrones* motto," said Mills.

She turned onto Chain Bridge Road, which was pretty much a one-mile-long, forty-five-mile-per-hour straight shot to the Dulles Access Road.

"We'll know what's what pretty soon," she said.

Within a minute, the jury rendered its verdict.

"They just took the on-ramp onto the access road," said Mills.

Mayer pounded the wheel with both hands. They could always change their minds and turn north on this side of the river to the Chain Bridge, but it would add a lot of time to their trip. They'd just received word that a warrant had been issued to search their Tysons building. The last thing they'd want to do was delay their arrival at what they perceived to be a safe harbor.

"Pass the word," said Mayer. "Looks like a southern approach. Will advise if that changes."

Mills nodded, before passing her message over the push-to-talk satellite phone system.

CHAPTER 52

Chad Lianez followed Mayer's progress via GPS tracker. One mile until handoff, then he'd take over tracking the convoy, allowing Mayer to peel off and reposition her vehicle less than a block north of the target building. Using both the Hailstorm device in his van—Gupta's van—and the Kingfish in her vehicle, they should be able to create a near-three-dimensional representation of the resistance Mann's team would face inside the building.

They'd managed to pull the schematics for the building from the deepest recesses of the internet, facilitated by a little illegal probing by Gupta. That, combined with the location data provided by the two cell phone intercept devices and a software program that blew Lianez's mind, created a real-time, multidimensional map of cell phone signals.

Even without the Kingfish in Mayer's car, he could accurately report that Kerry Conway, Oscar Marino, and three of the security officers they'd previously "tagged" were on the western side of the building's top floor. But that was just the tip of the iceberg. Since arriving yesterday, they'd marked nineteen additional, heavily encrypted cell phones in the building, all located close enough to the top of the building.

The encryption was the dead giveaway. Gupta's system couldn't completely hack their phones and listen in on their conversations or intercept texts, but it could poke far enough inside to grab the information needed to mark the phones and track them. Once Mayer rolled into position, a street parking space his team had cordoned off with traffic cones connected by cone bars, they should be able to pinpoint the position of every cell phone they'd previously intercepted.

Lianez didn't envy the team breaching the building. Nineteen potential hostiles, plus whatever made it into the building. Hardly a fair fight, but from what he'd been told about the New Mexico operation, they were up to the task. Plus, they had some highly skilled help, compliments of the CIA, or whoever they were. Gupta was one of them, and he hadn't said a word about their background, other than to randomly and subtly dangle the prospect of "work on a different level" if Lianez was interested. "A more level playing field" being the only other description offered, and based on the gear Gupta had at his fingertips, he didn't doubt it.

An appealing prospect, assuming the work didn't pit these tools against the good guys. Lianez understood the concept of the gray area. He wouldn't be here if he hadn't been willing to stray a little too far into that zone, but there was a big difference between gray and black. He had no interest in working for criminals, whether private or institutional. Something he'd need to flesh out with Gupta before he considered a change of employer.

A window opened on the wide-screen monitor in front of him, immediately followed by a chime. The convoy had just appeared on the map, strong signals amplified by a series of signal boosters they'd placed on the tops of rental cars parked along the southern route. The team had rented several vehicles and spent a few hours waiting for street parking to create a series of relays. They had a similar network to the north, on Wisconsin Avenue, and inside the neighborhood to the northwest of the target building. Twenty-two rental cars in total, parked along the approaches.

"Target hit the two-minute mark," said Lianez.

"Got it," said Jax, the satellite phone in her hand going to her ear as he contacted Mills.

"I have strong signals in all five vehicles. You can break contact," said Lianez.

"Copy," said Mills, then ended the call.

"Mann acknowledged," said Jax. "Everything's in motion."

Everyone understood the deal right now. Brevity and precision. Confirm your information and pass it along quickly. Even Mills, a criminal investigator and forensic expert with no field surveillance experience, had performed brilliantly. The entire exchange had taken less than five seconds.

"I assume one of you can drive this van?" said Javier.

"Why?" said Jax.

"If things start to go sideways inside that building, I'm not sitting here behind the wheel of a van," said Javier. "I'm more useful there."

Lianez glanced between the two of them. "Honestly. If it gets to the point where Javier needs to head over, we'll be way past the point where these screens will help. We'll all jump in."

"No, my friend," said Javier. "You're our eyes and ears as we move through the building."

"If you go, I go," said Jax.

"I don't advise that," said Javier.

"I don't care," said Jax.

"Time to shut up and focus! Do whatever you need to do, whenever you need to do it! Just let me concentrate on my job," said Lianez.

"There you have it," said Jax.

"Put on your body armor and prep a weapon," said Javier. "I don't have a good feeling about this."

"Sniper rifle," said Lianez.

"I'm not a sniper," said Jax.

"No, but Javier is," said Lianez. "And if they're going to need help, it's going to be on the roof. Remember my site briefing? I identified a nearby apartment building rooftop with sight lines to the eastern and northern windows, plus it's two floors higher than the target building's rooftop. If things start to get bogged down inside that building, I think that rifle will make a difference."

"How do we access the rooftop?" said Javier.

"Fire escape in the alley to the top floor. Kick down a few doors, I assume," said Lianez.

"Sounds easy enough," said Jax.

"Famous last words," said Lianez.

"Is there any reason we shouldn't do this now?" said Javier.

"Oh, I don't know. Maybe Jax still needs to fly the drone and disable the comms array!" said Lianez.

"Sorry," said Jax. "How far to the fire escape?"

"Two minutes," said Lianez. "Another three to five to get into position, assuming you don't run into a serious obstruction trying to reach the rooftop."

"I'm heading out now," said Javier. "The two of you have this under control."

"I'll join you after I deliver the drone," said Jax.

"Be careful accessing the rooftop," said Lianez. "They have at least two armed spotters on the roof."

CHAPTER 53

Mann studied the laptop screen, which had been synchronized with Gupta's, who was receiving a live feed from his van several blocks to the north.

"Thirty-second mark," said Gupta, the report reaching Mann through his headset.

He shut the laptop and placed it in the footwell. Gupta had the timing under control.

"You good?" said Mann, nudging Turner.

Turner eased his grip on the steering wheel, taking a few breaths before responding, "Just peachy."

Someone put a hand on Mann's shoulder before he could turn his head.

"You don't have to ask all of us," said Serrano. "We're ready."

He just nodded. No reason to distract anyone with words right now. They were seconds away from commencing their run through a gauntlet of explosives, bullets, and whatever the hell else awaited them on the street and inside the target building.

"Twenty seconds," said Gupta, who sat by himself in the SUV's third row.

Miralles and Melendez sat next to the doors in the second row, Serrano squeezed in between them. Wearing full tactical ballistic gear, including helmets, they each carried a short-barreled, suppressed rifle as their primary weapon. A pistol-grip Remington 870 Police Special fourteen-inch breaching shotgun sat in Melendez's lap, the business end pointed at the door.

He'd use the shotgun to rapidly breach locked doors to keep the team moving through the building. If that failed, Miralles, Melendez, and Turner each carried several small, pin-pull-activated C4 charges with three-second fuses.

Miralles cradled a Genesis Arms Gen-12 MBS—a short-barrel, semiautomatic 12-gauge shotgun—loaded with a fifteen-shell drum. She'd use that to expedite clearing the parking garage and any choke points inside the building that presented a problem. The mission's success relied on speed, continuous momentum, and firepower.

Turner and Serrano would fulfill the firepower role, each of them carrying one of the heavy-barrel, drum-fed HK416s into the building. They'd detached the bipods, substituting foregrips that could be used to manually steady their fire or brace against wall corners or doorframes.

Everyone, except for Gupta, carried at least three of the round fragmentation grenades taken from the New Mexico facility; Melendez, Miralles, and Turner each carried at least six. They'd decided not to bother with flash-bang grenades. There were no friendlies on the top two floors of the target building.

"Ten seconds," said Gupta. "Fuego Alpha?"

"*Sí*. I have the convoy in sight. The street is clear of friendlies," said Tianna.

The three teams deployed along Wisconsin Avenue had dressed as Washington, DC, Department of Public Works personnel, emerging roughly ten minutes ago to set up "sidewalk closed" barricades to keep pedestrians out of the kill zone.

"Tianna?" said Gupta.

"Ready," she said.

"Deploy smoke," said Gupta. "Fuego Alpha. You're cleared hot."

Mann swallowed hard. What the hell had he just unleashed?

CHAPTER 54

Tianna didn't bother looking. She trusted the voice in her earpiece and started pulling the pins on the smoke grenades. She rolled two under the BMW next to her, then sent two more across the street, where they hit the curb between two parked vehicles, before grabbing the AK-47 rifle propped up against the car next to her.

Mann's SUV was parked three spaces south, on the northbound side of the road—the opposite side of the road from her. The plan was insane, but it would work. And she'd make her way back to Mexico with enough money to ensure that nobody in her family would have to live in fear again. She lay stomach-down on the sidewalk next to the BMW, the AK-47's barrel braced against the front bumper, aimed slightly upward.

◆　◆　◆

Maria took a knee in the middle of the side street west of Wisconsin Avenue and shouldered the AT4 antitank weapon. Sofia crouched behind the front passenger door of the SUV parked just to the left of her, about fifty feet away, poking her head a few inches above the windows. Just far enough to observe and gauge the convoy's approach. Everything relied on Sofia at this point. Maria was just a trigger puller.

Sofia extended her arm to the right, her hand flat, palm facing the sidewalk. Five seconds. That was the hand signal. Maria removed the rear safety pin and shoved the cocking lever forward and over the top of the launcher, readying it for launch. She leveled the AT4, aiming it between the two vehicles flanking the side street, and flipped the safety lever upward—her thumb resting on the red trigger button.

She'd fired these several times in the Mexican Army, all practice against targets more than two hundred meters away—just over two hundred yards. The projectile, an 84mm unguided high-explosive, armor-piercing warhead, traveled at 950 feet per second, which seemed like a near instantaneous hit on the firing range once she pressed the trigger button. In a few moments, she'd fire it at a target barely fifty feet away. The only way she could miss is if she jerked the launcher upward or to the side while pressing the spring-loaded trigger, which she wouldn't. The projectile would reach her target, the last vehicle in the convoy, less than a tenth of the second after she depressed the button.

Sofia would feel a rush of air to her right, but that should be the extent of her discomfort, aside from the explosive impact. The warhead would penetrate the side of the armored SUV and detonate inside, limiting most of the damage to the interior of the vehicle—which would be barreling up Wisconsin Avenue fast enough to carry the explosion away. Or so she hoped. The entire string of events would happen almost instantaneously, which was why Maria had cautioned Sofia to stay low once she gave the "fire" signal.

Sofia's hand shifted sideways, giving her a thumbs-up. Maria counted the vehicles crossing the gap. One. Two. Three. Four. She pressed the trigger, the front of the rear SUV appearing in the gap between the vehicles parked on Wisconsin Avenue the moment AT4 fired. She never saw the result of her work. The warhead detonated several feet up the street, the sound of the launch dampened by her sound-canceling earbuds. She tossed the smoking launcher to the street and took off running; a hard crash followed by screeching tires echoed off the apartment buildings towering above her. Her earbuds crackled.

"Direct hit," said Sofia. "Let's get out of here."

Sofia caught up to her by the time they reached Thirty-Seventh Street. Less than a hundred feet away. The two of them were built very differently. Sofia was a speedy twig. Maria was more of a lumbering hulk, which was why her Mexican Army company commander had handpicked her to be a part of the company's heavy weapons platoon. She'd lugged everything from belt-fed machine guns to light mortar tubes across high desert terrain.

They hopped into the car parked on the corner of the street and took off, headed north, to pick up Tianna and the second AT4 team, led by Juan Patillo, ex–special forces. After that, they'd head west and melt away.

◆ ◆ ◆

The sharp crunch of the AT4's warhead detonation rattled Tianna. The ground vibrated. The BMW next to her shook. She kept the AK-47 steady through the mayhem unfolding less than fifty meters to her left. The lead SUV roared by. Her signal to open fire. She pressed the trigger and didn't release it—sending thirty 7.62mm bullets into the passing convoy. None of the bullets would penetrate the vehicle's armor, but that wasn't the purpose of her barrage. The point was to create the illusion that the convoy was under attack—forcing AXIOM to seek shelter in the target building, where Mann's team would take them down.

The smoke grenades ignited around the same time as her barrage, pumping billows of grayish-white smoke into the street. Her earpiece crackled.

"Tianna. Friendly vehicle passing."

She triggered her radio's transmit button. "Copy. I'm headed out."

A black Suburban, identical to the convoy vehicles, raced through the cloud of smoke.

Tianna crossed herself and whispered, "Godspeed."

CHAPTER 55

Turner couldn't see a damn thing for a few seconds. When he emerged from the smoke screen Tianna had laid down, he was in the southbound lane. He applied light pressure to the brake pedal and turned the steering wheel right, just missing an oncoming sedan. He'd slightly overcorrected, scraping against a few of the parked cars along the northbound side of the road before he straightened the SUV. He accelerated to catch up with the rest of the convoy.

A few seconds ago, he'd been parked on the right side of the road, waiting for the first AT4 launch—and hoping the targeted SUV didn't career into his own nearly identical vehicle after the warhead detonated. The team had accepted that possibility, which would have been a showstopper. An acceptable risk, given the potential reward. The gamble paid off, the last SUV in the convoy swerving left moments after it exploded, its flaming chassis T-boning a parked car and coming to a complete stop after pushing the car over the curb and onto the sidewalk.

The rest of the convoy had passed a moment later, and Turner had waited until the last vehicle disappeared into the expanding cloud of smoke just a few feet down the road before pulling out of the parking space. Automatic gunfire had erupted as soon as he hit the accelerator, then ended before he lost all visibility.

The hope was that the occupants of the fourth SUV in the convoy wouldn't be able to tell that he'd swapped places with the now-destroyed fifth vehicle. The convoy SUVs were bullet resistant, the sides capable of stopping heavy-caliber machine gun fire, the windows able to withstand sustained rifle or pistol fire.

The task force's SUV was the same make and model, but Hertz didn't rent armored vehicles, so they'd carefully damaged the windshield with the pointed end of a handheld pickaxe, making it look like the windshield had been sprayed by shrapnel, but not penetrated. Same with the hood, front grille, and headlights. They'd even punctured the front right tire, which made his job even harder. Trying to drive a Suburban with a flat front tire at fifty miles per hour wasn't a treat. The thing wanted to pull him off the road.

One of the security officers in the back row of the SUV directly in front of him leaned over the back of his seat. He tapped his right ear repeatedly, which Turner interpreted as, *Why aren't you answering your radio?*

"They're trying to signal us," said Turner.

Mann tapped his ear, before raising both hands and shaking his head. They'd also applied a thin, translucent layer of charcoal soap to the windshield and hood, to hopefully mimic the blast effects of a near-miss explosion—and conceal their faces.

"You really think they're going to buy that?" said Turner.

"We just need this to work for a few more blocks," said Mann. "Start tapping your ear and shaking your head."

"Fine," said Turner, before mimicking Mann.

And this was the easy part of the plan.

CHAPTER 56

Gary Litman looked over his shoulder to address McCall and Powell, who were seated in the SUV's middle row captain's chairs.

"We still can't establish communications with the fifth vehicle," he said. "I recommend that we bypass the Georgetown annex. Someone obviously knew our route, so it's safe to assume they know where we are headed. I'll coordinate with the police and arrange a local law enforcement escort. Mann won't risk killing police officers. We'll be safe while we work on a backup plan."

"But the fifth vehicle survived the attack, right?" said Powell.

"Barely," said Litman. "The windshield and front of the SUV took the brunt of the blast. It's running on a flat tire. Front passenger side."

"That adds twenty-eight shooters, not including yourself, to the fifteen at the annex," said Powell. "How much safer could we be? We'll get the police to surround the building and escort us to the closest airport."

"They fired some kind of rocket at our convoy," said Litman. "What if they fire more at the annex after we arrive?"

"I'm leaning toward bypassing—" started McCall.

A sharp crunch reverberated through the SUV, immediately followed by a pressure wave that rattled the armored Suburban. The lead vehicle burst into flames, before tumbling left, into the oncoming lane.

"Keep going!" said Litman to the driver. "Push through."

They passed the upside-down, flame-engulfed metal chassis that used to be an armored Chevrolet Suburban 3500. Eleven thousand pounds tossed like a trash can to the side of the road. Automatic gunfire raked their vehicle, adding several more hand-size, opaque white splotches along the right-side windows. His earpiece squawked, the other vehicles reporting at once. He wasn't sure if he heard vehicle five, but four came through clear.

"Vehicle four taking gunfire," said Litman, trying to peer between the bullet strikes against his window without success.

The passenger side of the SUV was basically a complete blind spot to him now, unless he rolled down the window, which would be insanity given what had just happened. They didn't stand a chance against one of those rockets. At least they could insulate themselves in the building and throw more than forty heavily armed security officers at the problem.

"We're going to the annex," said Litman. "This is out of control."

"I couldn't agree more," said McCall.

"I'll radio ahead and get a team to the garage to guard the gate when we enter," said Litman. "We'll hunker down and call the police."

"Once the police get a look at the hardware in that burning wreck, they might have some questions," said Powell.

"They can't enter our building without a warrant," said Litman. "And we don't control what kind of firearms our outsourced teams carry. They were hired for vehicle escort duty only. That's the story. If they want to dig deeper, they can get a warrant. We'll be halfway to the secondary backup location with the SATCHEL by the time they produce one."

"I'll line up a jet," said Powell.

"Arrange it for Reagan if possible," said Litman. "We'll work our way west to the Chain Bridge, then down Washington Memorial Parkway to the airport. The route will mostly keep us out of urban shooting galleries like this one. The trip to Dulles isn't any more dangerous, it's just twice as long."

"We should have options at both," said Powell.

"Whichever gets us in the air faster," said McCall.

They sped past the Russian embassy, a cluster of buildings separated from the street by a multicolor stone wall topped by a black metal fence and mostly hidden from view by a thick spread of trees lining the street on both sides of the wall. *They must be shitting their pants in there.* A thought confirmed when they passed the main vehicle gate, located at the northeast corner of the embassy grounds. Two black SUVs raced into position inside, blocking the gate. *That was fast.*

He hoped the police responded just as swiftly to their call, though he wondered if they should hold off on that, while they assessed their situation. The quicker the police arrived, the sooner their "get on the jet" timer started ticking. Several mercifully uneventful seconds later, the vehicle ahead of them slowed for the turn into their building's parking garage. They followed the lead SUV down the ramp and past the three-person security detail standing guard over the gate, which would be locked into the closed position until they were ready to leave. Nobody would be allowed in the building. Not even the residents. He'd post security teams inside at every door to allow people to leave, but it would be a one-way trip until they departed for the airport.

CHAPTER 57

The moment the first vehicle turned into the parking garage, Mann contacted Lianez.

"Breach imminent. Launch the drone," he said, before pressing the button that lowered his window.

Jax would awaken the quadcopter sitting on top of Gupta's van and pilot it to the satellite array on the target building's rooftop, slagging it like the array at AXIOM's Tysons headquarters. After a long discussion with Bauer, Berg, and Gupta, he'd walked away convinced that there was only one way to exterminate whatever AXIOM hoped to deliver to True America 3.0, or whoever planned to use the cartel army they'd created. Kill the head shed and cut off any chance of them spreading their disease before the final blow was delivered. The head shed sat in vehicle three, according to the team in Tysons.

"They just turned into the parking lot," said Melendez. "Safeties off."

He flipped the sector switch on his suppressed rifle from safe to semiautomatic. The SUV directly ahead of them slowed for the turn into the building. Turner slowed to match their speed. Mann analyzed the entrance as they approached the turning point.

"Three guards. One to the left. Two to the right," said Mann. "Weapons are down."

The sentry team was in plain view of the street, which was why they kept their weapons low. If someone spotted one of their rifles or submachine guns and reported it to the police, they'd have a problem on their hands. Not that it mattered right now. Their biggest problem was about to drive right inside the parking garage. Turner eased them into position behind the SUV ahead of them, which sped down the ramp once it cleared the gate. He kept their speed steady as they approached the gate.

Mann didn't know who these people were and didn't care. Maybe that was wrong of him. Probably was. But given what was at stake, he didn't have the luxury of caring. When their SUV pulled up to the gate, Mann aimed through the window and fired two bullets at near point-blank range through the second guard's forehead. The woman's only reaction to the sight of his rifle was a widening of her eyes. Miralles's rifle did the same to the other sentry, who stood a few feet to his target's right. The close-range shots knocked their heads against the cinder block wall behind them, leaving watermelon-size bloodstains. Melendez's rifle fired once, presumably achieving a similar result.

"Floor it!" said Melendez.

Turner hit the accelerator, catapulting them toward the next vehicle in the convoy. He hit the brakes in time to screech to a halt a few feet behind the SUV. Melendez and Miralles were out of their doors before Mann had even grabbed the door handle. Turner shifted the transmission into park, opening his door moments after Melendez slipped by.

"Frags out," said Miralles, over the radio net.

They'd gone over this during the numerous rehearsal drills. Grenades first. Then gunfire. Mann opened the door as Melendez and Miralles started sending short rifle bursts at the security team that emptied out of the SUV in front of them. The two who emerged from the rear passenger door dropped to the concrete immediately, the door window behind them instantly turning crimson red. While Miralles made short work of the security team, Mann retrieved one of the fragmentation grenades from the pouch attached to his vest, pulled the pin, and tossed it toward the lead SUV as he rushed forward.

Miralles spun and grabbed his vest, pulling him behind the SUV moments before their first salvo of grenades detonated a few vehicles down from them—well within fragmentation range. Bits and pieces of metal ricocheted off the concrete wall and ceiling, tapping against the hood and windshield of the vehicle they'd just abandoned, and thumping the roof and sides of the SUV they currently used as cover. She kept him pinned against the back of the SUV for another few seconds, the grenade he'd just thrown detonating and blasting the vehicles with fragments.

"Go!" said Melendez, disappearing down the SUV's left side, followed by Turner.

Miralles let go of Mann and took off down the right side, only to return a moment later, diving to the concrete behind him. Dozens of bullets pounded the passenger-side corner of the vehicle as she scrambled to her feet and crouched next to him.

"Rico. I'm blocked," she said over the radio.

"Yep. Working on it," he said. "Send a few more frags downrange. Most of the security team emptied out on your side. They're working their way to the stairwell."

Mann produced another M67 fragmentation grenade and pulled the pin. Miralles was on her feet, crouched next to him, grenade in hand.

"Do what I do," she said.

He nodded and watched as she underhanded the grenade without exposing more than her hand to the incoming gunfire. She peeled away and he took her place, hesitating for a few moments before mimicking her grenade toss. A bullet zipped across the meaty part of his hand, just below the thumb. He withdrew his hand and examined it. Barely a graze.

"I'm good," said Mann.

She yanked him to the deck, another round of fragments zipping through the compact parking garage. Miralles hopped to her feet.

"Emily. Stay where you are," said Melendez over the radio. "We're engaging."

Several seconds of intense gunfire ensued, before the parking garage went silent.

"A small group, maybe six, retreated into the stairwell next to the elevator," said Melendez. "I can confirm that one of them is McCall."

"Copy. Moving forward," said Miralles. "Garrett. Back me up."

He followed her around the corner of the SUV, moving into position a few feet behind and to her right, where he could fire past her at any targets that emerged. What he witnessed next challenged everything he'd been taught about right and wrong—black and white.

Miralles moved through the tangle of bodies in front of her, firing a single bullet, point-blank, into each of their heads. She paused only to turn her rifle into each vehicle door she passed. When they reached the stairwell door, he looked back. Eight men lay twisted and prone along the passenger side of the convoy, victims of their grenades or gunfire. He guessed the same scene had played out on the other side.

"Let's move Anish up," said Melendez.

CHAPTER 58

Gerald McCall stopped on the second-floor landing. They still had two more flights of stairs to go before they reached AXIOM's supposed safe haven—which didn't feel that safe anymore.

"We need to keep moving," said Litman, grabbing his arm.

He shook his arm free. "Not until we know exactly what the fuck is going on!"

Powell tried to say something, but it came out as a bloody gurgle, his hands wrapped around his neck like he was choking himself. Blood rhythmically surged between his fingers.

"The police are on the way," said Litman. "We need to get upstairs immediately."

No shit, Sherlock.

"I understand that!" said McCall. "What the hell happened down there?"

"They swapped one of their vehicles with the last in our convoy," said Litman. "The smoke screen. The gunfire. The second rocket attack. It was all a big distraction, orchestrated to bring us here."

Street-level tactics weren't his strong suit. He was a big-picture guy who outsourced those details to other people so he could make the big moves that paid the bills and padded everyone's bank accounts. Especially his.

"How long until the police arrive?" said McCall.

"Soon."

He slapped Litman. "*Soon* is not a measure of time. How long?"

Litman looked him straight in the eye. "Unknown. Sir. They don't provide exact times. Hit me again, and I'll fucking kill you. I hired these—"

McCall nodded at one of the security officers, who placed the barrel of his rifle against Litman's head and blasted his brains against the wall—then kicked him down the stairs. He'd long ago inserted a mercenary on the security team. A man paid five times as much as the rest of Litman's goons. An insurance policy in case anyone on the executive team decided on a "hostile takeover."

"We need to move, sir," said the mercenary.

"You're in charge of security now," said McCall, before glancing at Powell, who had taken a knee on the landing.

"What just happened?" said Powell, his voice weak.

"Sorry. Jeremy. But you're deadweight at this point."

The mercenary who had just executed Litman raised his rifle and fired a single shot between Powell's eyes.

"Let's go," said McCall, grabbing the SATCHEL.

When they reached the door to the fourth floor, a sharp detonation echoed through the stairwell. McCall ordered the three remaining security officers back to the landing.

"They're headed up! You're our eyes and ears now," he said, slapping the mercenary on the shoulder. "Engage any group headed up the stairs, then immediately retreat. Don't get into a drawn-out gunfight. They're not shy about using grenades. There's nothing you can do to counter that."

"Yep," said the mercenary, before ordering the others to follow him down to the landing.

Oscar Marino opened the door leading to the fourth floor. "What the fuck happened down there?"

"Someone knows about the annex. Litman and Powell are gone," said McCall, stepping inside. "They hit us in the parking garage, and they're on the way up the stairs."

"Should I recall the teams at the ground-floor access points?" said Marino.

"How many are out there?" said McCall.

"Four. Two teams of two," said Marino. "One team at the front door. One at the door leading to the mechanical room, which can be accessed from the alley."

"I don't see how we can get them up here," said McCall.

"The elevator hasn't moved," said Marino. "They could gather on the first floor and take the elevator up."

"How many do we have up here?" said McCall.

"Eight," said Marino.

"That's not enough," said McCall. "Send them to the elevator and keep in touch with them the entire way. If anything doesn't feel right, open fire the moment the elevator doors open. These fuckers are crafty. They hit our convoy with explosives and somehow slipped in during the chaos."

"Got it," said Marino, before issuing the order over his handheld radio. "What about those three? I can post someone here to let them in if they retreat."

McCall shut the door. "They either repel the attack or die in the stairwell. And make sure the fifth-floor door is locked."

As much as he appreciated the executioner's one-time, on-the-spot loyalty, the last thing he needed around him was a trigger-happy zealot.

"It's secure. Both doors are reinforced and bullet resistant," said Marino. "We can do the same with the internal staircase connecting the fourth and fifth floors—plus the rooftop."

After AXIOM purchased the top two floors of the building for a ridiculous eight-figure price, they immediately filed for the permits necessary to turn it into a two-floor penthouse. Several greased palms later, their plan was approved; the rooftop-access ladder remained a secret.

"Evacuate everyone to the fifth floor and lock it down," said McCall. "Jam the elevator open after the rest of the security team arrives. Or blow the goddamn thing up. I don't care."

"Hostiles are working their way to this floor," said Marino as a team of four security officers rushed to the elevator lobby.

"Then let's get out of here," said McCall. "There's no telling what will happen when the elevator opens."

CHAPTER 59

Serrano approached the blast-scorched, open stairwell door with Mann, the sounds of a vicious gunfight a few floors up echoing into the parking garage. A single, explosive blast rattled the floor beneath her feet. Her radio crackled a few moments later.

"Stairwell is clear," said Melendez. "We found Litman and Powell on one of the landings. Single bullet holes through their heads. Executed."

"Jesus," said Mann. "McCall is cleaning house."

"Why?" said Serrano.

"He thinks he can vanish," said Mann. "And keep the prize."

"How?" said Melendez.

"By holding us off and waiting this out," said Mann. "The police can't be more than a minute or two out."

"Given the chaos we just unleashed on the street, and the reports of gunfire in this building," said Melendez, "they won't enter for another hour."

"True," said Mann. "But if AXIOM manages to barricade themselves for a few hours, we'll be out of options. And I'm not shooting at cops, so don't even go there."

"Same for me," said Serrano.

"Same for all of us," said Miralles. "We don't kill cops or federal agents. The moment we find ourselves in a situation that could go there—hard stop."

"Then we're all on the same page," said Serrano. "So where do we go from here?"

"Try to get this done before the police shut us down," said Mann.

"I'm worried about the rooftop," said Melendez. "The schematics we pulled showed an internal spiral staircase connecting the fourth and fifth floors. A recent addition approved by the city. But this stairwell no longer goes to the fifth floor. According to the permit, they sealed it off, permanently. My guess is they really want to protect something on the fifth floor."

"We've seen sentries on the rooftop. How do they get people up there if this stairwell doesn't go past the fourth floor?" said Mann.

"They must have installed some kind of rooftop access, except through a ceiling hatch on the fifth floor. Something they didn't get approved by the city. I assume it's equipped with some kind of extendable ladder, but if they somehow disable the ladder—we won't be able to get to them. They could sit up there all day."

Gupta broke into the conversation. "Javier is headed to a building across the street. Lianez thinks he can use the fire escape behind the building to reach the top floor unobserved, then kick a few doors down to reach the roof. He brought a sniper rifle. He could force them back down to the fifth floor. The rooftop is two stories higher, so he should be able to prevent them from accessing the rooftop entirely. Jax is on her way to join him. That's two guns. I wouldn't poke my head up there."

"Then it's time to breach the fourth floor," said Melendez. "Anish. Stay behind Mann and Serrano."

"These shitheads better know what they're doing," said Gupta over the radio.

"Just don't trip over your computer case and crack your head open," said Serrano.

"Sounds like she has your number," said Miralles.

"She kind of scares me," said Gupta.

"She *should* scare you," said Mann. "Cata has more at stake here—personally—than any of us, which is why you're in the best hands imaginable. She has more invested in your safety than mine or anyone else on the team."

"Are we done with the therapy session?" said Melendez. "I have a door to breach."

"Do it. We're on our way up," said Mann, taking off up the stairs.

Serrano turned to Gupta, who held a Brügger & Thomet MP9 submachine gun in one hand and a Pelican computer case in the other. He wasn't messing around. Maybe she'd underestimated him.

"Sorry about that comment," said Serrano.

"No need to apologize," said Gupta. "That's how we roll. It's a 24-7 insult factory. Sometimes it stings, but you sting right back. You're a natural. They're going to try to recruit you if you survive this mess. I have no doubt about that."

Serrano shook her head. "I just want to bring closure to this nightmare."

"I know," said Gupta. "We better get moving."

They followed Mann up the stairwell, reaching the tight landing that turned 180 degrees to face the last flight of stairs leading to the fourth-floor door. Serrano thought she had seen it all, before the landing came into view. She'd processed dozens of crime scenes with ARTEMIS, along with several gruesome cartel murders in Ciudad Juárez. But nothing compared to what lay in front of her.

Three fresh bodies ripped to shreds. Faces mostly erased. Limbs twisted at unnatural angles. A few hands and feet blasted away. The bullet- and fragment-pitted walls painted bright red, speckled with darker pieces of internal organs. She looked away, her eyes settling on Gary Litman, who lay completely intact at the foot of the staircase below them—spared the savagery of the grenades tossed by Melendez, Miralles, and Turner. Not that Litman had deserved any mercy.

"Hold here," said Gupta, pushing past Serrano to grab Mann's tactical vest. "They're about to breach the door and clear the hallway."

Mann gave him a thumbs-up, before crouching. Serrano knelt next to him, Gupta backing up and disappearing behind the wall. She considered joining Gupta, until she saw Melendez, Miralles, and Turner take a few steps backward down the stairs and hunker low. A few seconds later, the explosive strip Melendez had run along the doorknob side of the door detonated.

Melendez dashed up the stairs and tossed a grenade to the right. Miralles released the trigger lever of her grenade and handed it to Melendez, who leaned into the hallway, reached around the splintered door, and sent it to the left. Two detonations later, the three of them spilled into the hallway, Turner peeling off to the right. Serrano's earpiece crackled.

"Clear," said Melendez. "I think they moved to the fifth floor. Bring Anish up, but don't enter the hallway until we sweep the entire floor."

Mann started up the stairs, his rifle pointed at the mangled door.

"This is creepy," said Gupta.

"But you've seen this kind of thing before, right?" said Serrano.

"I've never seen primary targets killed like that before," said Gupta. "Both of them were executed. Something is off."

"Did you hear that?" said Serrano, tapping Mann on the shoulder.

"I did," he said. "And I agree. But we have no choice but to push on. That's the only way we finish this."

Serrano considered his words. He was right, of course. If they backed off and slipped out before the police locked the building down, the plot AXIOM had hatched in New Mexico would survive—unopposed. ARTEMIS would be finished. Actually, it was already finished. They'd crossed too many lines. Not even Director James could save them at this point. It was all or nothing now.

"Let's finish this," said Serrano, pushing Mann forward.

CHAPTER 60

McCall took the SATCHEL to the war room and set it down next to a nameless operations technician seated in front of the main control station: a wall of computer monitors connected to the server loaded with the DOMINION program.

"Load the database and send it to SPACE," said McCall.

SPACE was the code word for sending the database forward to a secondary backup location in Montana. The tech didn't know where the database was headed. His only job right now was to connect the SATCHEL to the system and transmit the data. But the man just stared at him, a conflicted look on his face.

"Did I not make myself clear?" said McCall.

Kerry Conway appeared in the doorway on the opposite side of the room.

"The array is dead," she said. "Melted. Just like the array in Tysons."

"Then we need to hold on long enough for the police to surround the building and force Mann's team to back off," said McCall.

"They're on the fourth floor," said Marino.

McCall pointed at the black duffel bag on the floor next to the terrified operations technician.

"All we need to do is get that bag out of here intact, and on a flight to our backup location," said McCall.

"I thought this *was* the backup location," said the young man Clara Furst had sent to observe their faux continuity-of-operations drill.

McCall knew only his first name. Evan. He'd purposefully declined to meet with the man when he arrived at the Tysons building, to spite Furst. If she insisted on inserting one of her lackeys in his business, he certainly wasn't going to roll out the red carpet.

"Evan. I don't know what to say," said McCall. "Our situation has unexpectedly deteriorated this morning. But your product is still intact. We just need to get it out of here."

The man pointed at the duffel bag. "So. That's it? That's the only remaining copy of the database?"

"Yes. This is the fail-safe backup," said McCall. "A hard copy of the database that would survive a sophisticated electronic attack—like this."

"I'd hardly call this an electronic attack, or sophisticated," said Evan. "They landed two drones armed with thermite grenades on each of your communications arrays. Kind of a low-tech attack, in my opinion."

"That's the world we live in," said McCall. "And why we employed a low-tech solution to preserve DOMINION. We just need to hold out until the police arrive."

"The police are already here," said Evan. "One floor below us. All they have to do is flash their badges and tell responding officers that this is a federal raid. You can call and cry all day about rocket attacks on the street and gunfire in the building, but until someone at the FBI connects the dots and realizes this isn't an official operation, we're stuck here fending off some bizarrely resourceful agents."

"Where are you going with this?" said McCall.

Evan checked his phone. "I've arranged a helicopter to pick us up on the roof. ETA five to ten minutes."

"In DC airspace?" said McCall.

"It gets us out of this mess," said Evan. "And preserves that bag and its contents for my client. We can deal with the fallout of an FAA investigation."

"Good point," said McCall.

"I can hold off Mann's team until the helicopter arrives," said Marino. "The intrafloor staircase is an open-spiral design. We've already dropped three seriously heavy metal bookshelves over the opening, piling everything that isn't nailed to the floor or walls into them. They'd have to push those off somehow, while we're firing at them."

"Don't forget their grenades," said McCall.

"If they toss those at us, they'll have to lower the shelves, or risk getting hit by their own shrapnel," said Marino. "We can take cover and resume firing after the grenades detonate."

Evan nodded. "Sounds like a solid plan. Should buy us more than enough time to get out of here."

"How many can the helicopter take?" said McCall.

"Six," said Evan.

"Oscar," said McCall. "Pick two security officers and bring them to the rooftop-access ladder. Don't say a word about the helicopter extract."

"What about everyone else?" said Marino.

"Once we're in the air, pass the word over the tactical net that they should surrender," said McCall.

CHAPTER 61

Mann studied the top of the stairwell, agreeing with Melendez. The only way up was to move the metal shelving units. The elevator was stuck on the fifth floor, presumably jammed open. Not that they'd use the elevator, which would be a certain death trap. Aerial surveillance conducted yesterday hadn't identified any fire escape stairs leading to the fifth floor or the rooftop. He hated to use the term *Mexican stand-off*, but that was where things stood. Neither side could move, and the Metropolitan Police Department was on its way.

Unfortunately, the MPD would be the tiebreaker when they eventually entered the building. Mann's FBI badge versus whatever story McCall concocted. Or maybe not. He pulled out his phone and called James.

"I'm surprised you found the time to call," she said.

"Yeah. It's a little hectic up here," said Mann. "I need you to submit the warrants for the Georgetown address. We're looking at a protracted standoff. There's no way to access the top floor of the building without sustaining serious casualties, and MPD won't wait forever before entering. Especially if McCall starts crying over the 911 line."

"I'm at the District of Columbia District Courthouse with a team of lawyers," said James. "I had a feeling you might need a lifeline."

"You have no idea," said Mann. "Thank you."

"I'll email you the warrant when the judge signs off on it. That should buy you the time you need," said James. "And don't forget.

You're an FBI special agent. You can prevent MPD from entering the building."

"After the warrant is approved," said Mann.

"No. You followed the suspects from Tysons, Virginia, after that warrant was approved, which was about twenty minutes after they fled the building," said James. "Then all hell broke loose on the street, and you followed them into the parking garage, where all hell broke loose again. This is your crime scene."

Mann had lost sight of his authority, given every law he'd broken over the past thirty minutes.

"This is going to be one hell of a cover-up," said Mann.

"I don't know what you're talking about," said James. "Sounds like a routine investigation gone haywire."

"If you say so," said Mann.

"I do," said James. "Keep me posted."

He turned to Melendez. "Is there any way for us to breach?"

Melendez shook his head. "I don't have enough explosives to blow that barrier clear. I have lock poppers. A few more door strips like the one we used on the fourth-floor stairwell. And some C4."

"The C4 might dislodge those shelving units," said Mann.

"We can try," said Melendez. "But we'll most likely just create a jagged gap or two that we can barely crawl or squeeze through. Those shelving units aren't going to just disappear. C4 punches through shit. It doesn't lift objects and toss them aside."

"Can we smoke them out?" said Mann.

"We didn't bring any smoke grenades," said Miralles.

"Can we light a fire?" said Serrano. "A trash bin or something?"

"I don't think that would create enough smoke to force them out," said Melendez.

"Can we light the fifth floor on fire somehow?" said Serrano.

"I suppose we could siphon some gas from the SUVs and create a Molotov cocktail bomb," said Miralles. "Lift the shelving unit up enough to roll one through."

"And take a burst of lead to the face in the process," said Melendez.

"Yeah," said Miralles. "That's a distinct possibility."

"Then we wait this out," said Mann. "James is requesting a warrant to search the building. Once that's approved, we can count on every law enforcement officer in DC to back us up. Helicopters. Drones. The works."

"Funny you mention helicopters," said Serrano, cocking her head. "Do you hear that?"

Mann closed his eyes, like it would somehow help him hear better. Nothing. He removed one of his radio earbuds to see if that made a difference. The wired headset negated sharp, hearing-loss-level sounds, such as gunfire and explosions, while slightly amplifying everything else. Now he heard it. A deep thumping. Barely audible.

"I hear it," said Turner. "Helicopter inbound."

"One of ours?" said Miralles.

"Nothing I arranged," said Mann, before replacing his earbud and contacting Javier and Jax, who should've been in position across the street. "Jax. This is Mann."

"Copy," said Jax. "I just reached the rooftop. Javier is already in position."

"Is there any activity on the rooftop?" said Mann.

"This is Javier. No unusual activity. I see two spotters with binoculars. Both armed with rifles, but the rifles are hanging slack by their sides, pointed downward."

"Do you hear a helicopter?" said Mann.

"I can't hear shit," said Javier.

"I hear a helicopter," said Jax. "Can't tell if it's inbound or passing by."

"This area is a no-fly zone," said Mann. "If a helicopter approaches the target building, let me know right away."

"Copy that," said Jax. "How are things inside the building?"

"We're stuck on the fourth floor," said Mann.

"Maybe we can shake things up a little," said Jax. "Hit some of the windows?"

"Any help would be greatly appreciated," said Mann. "Just don't overextend yourselves. Play it safe. Take out the rooftop sentries first. If they have an inbound helicopter, the fewer shooters up there—the better."

"Are you clearing us hot to engage anyone on the rooftop?" said Jax.

"Affirmative," said Mann.

Gupta crouched next to him. "I think I found a way up to the next floor."

"I'm not crawling through air ducts," said Mann. "This isn't *Die Hard*."

"That's not what I was about to suggest."

"Good," said Mann.

"It's even worse."

Melendez laughed.

"Why are you laughing?" said Gupta.

"Because we've been here before," said Melendez. "This is where you suggest something insane that might work."

"You're still alive, right?" said Gupta, patting Melendez's shoulder.

"What are you proposing?" said Mann.

"Chad Lianez has mapped out the fifth floor for us, compliments of the data provided by Mr. Hailstorm and Mrs. Kingfish," said Gupta. "Six hostiles surrounding the blocked stairwell. One by the elevator. McCall, Marino, and Conway—plus three more cell signals that we assume are security personnel—bunched up in one spot just west of the elevator. We assume this is the rooftop-access point. They're probably waiting for the helicopter."

"Javier?" said Mann over the radio net.

"*Sí?*"

"Do not engage anyone on the rooftop until the helicopter lands. We don't want to scare them off. Once the helicopter touches down, you're cleared hot. If you can nail the pilot, go for that first."

"Copy," said Javier. "We can see the helicopter."

"Looks like a Sikorsky S-76," said Jax.

343

"Heavy duty," said Turner.

"Yep," said Mann. "So. What's the plan, Anish? We're running out of time."

"Nobody is anywhere near the southeast corner of the building," he said. "Someone could climb up that side of the building."

"We don't have grappling gear," said Melendez.

"Javier. Jax. Can you help me here?" said Gupta. "My previous surveillance runs lead me to believe that the exterior can be scaled without gear. It won't be easy, but I think it's doable. And nobody will hear you."

"He's right. You don't need climbing gear. Just a little balance and the ability to do a pull-up," said Jax.

"There might be a little jump involved," said Gupta. "The pull-up thing comes after the jump."

"Of course it does," said Mann, heading toward the southeast corner of the building.

Melendez grabbed his arm, stopping him in his tracks.

"I got this," said Melendez.

Before he could respond, Serrano knocked Melendez aside and pushed Mann against the wall. She shot him a serious look. Probably the most severe one she'd ever sent his way.

"I got this," she said to Mann. "I'll let you know when the elevator is back in business and the stairwell is clear."

"Cata," said Mann. "You don't have to do this."

"I know," she said. "But you're in charge of this operation. Your place is here."

"I can do this," said Melendez.

"I don't doubt it," she said. "But you need to focus on getting to the roof and stopping McCall. I'm good at what I do. But not that good. We need you, Emily, and Luke to break through and follow Garrett's orders. That's my only job."

"Carry on, señorita," said Melendez.

Mann followed her to the corner of the building, where she removed her body armor, retaining the pistol in her thigh holster and the rifle slung across her back.

"What if you can't break the glass?" he said.

Serrano drew her pistol and fired twice at the window in front of her, the bullets punching through but the glass remaining in place. She hit the window between the two holes with the pistol, creating a small opening.

"This isn't going to work. Is it?" she said.

"You really want to do this?" said Mann.

"What do you think?"

Mann pressed his radio button. "Jax. Can you open fire on the fifth-floor windows? Spread the lead around but focus on the southeast corner. We're sending a team up."

"Copy. But that's going to alert the rooftop team," said Jax.

"I rescind my previous order. Javier is now cleared hot to engage anyone on the rooftop," said Mann. "Just watch out for that helicopter. Never know what they'll bring to the fight."

"Copy," said Jax. "Javier?"

"Music to my ears."

CHAPTER 62

Jax pulled back the charging handle of her rifle, and let it slam home. Round chambered. She thumbed the selector switch to semiautomatic. Ready to go. Javier scooted to the north corner of the building, staying low. When he reached the corner, he backed up a few feet and gave her a thumbs-up. The helicopter was getting closer. Might be nothing. Might be everything. She nodded at him, and they both rose at the same time, resting their rifles on the three-foot wall that surrounded the rooftop.

Javier's rifle barked first, one of the AXIOM spotters dropping in place, a red mist hovering above him. His next shot spun the second spotter 180 degrees to face away from them. Jax adjusted her aim and pressed the trigger twice, while Javier cocked his rifle. The spotter dropped to his knees, before face-planting.

"Hit the windows," said Javier. "The helicopter is getting close."

Jax gave him a quick thumbs-up, before methodically pressing her trigger. She spread the rest of her magazine, twenty-eight bullets, between every window along the entire eastern face of the building. After reloading, she focused all her gunfire on the two windows closest to the southeast corner—eventually shattering the lower panes completely.

"Cata. This is Jax. I took out the two windows directly above you. The rooftop sentries have been neutralized."

"Copy. I just saw the glass fall. Thank you," said Serrano.

"We can see about ten feet into the building through the rest of the glass," said Jax. "If anyone rushes your breach point, we'll knock them on their asses. But if they stay back, out of our sight—there's nothing we can do."

"Understood," said Serrano. "I'll climb back down if the situation is shit."

"This whole thing is shit," said Jax.

"You know what I mean."

"I do," said Jax.

"Heading up," said Serrano.

Jax watched her climb out the fourth-floor window and assess the side of the building above her. She had a few suggestions.

"Cata. Reach up with your left hand. You should feel a protruding brick."

Serrano reached up and found the brick, yanking hard a few times.

"Feels solid," she said.

"Looks solid," said Jax. "Pull yourself up with your left arm and swing your right hand upward. You should be able to easily grab the brick windowsill on the fifth floor. I see some glass fragments up there, so you might want to use gloves."

"I can't climb with gloves," said Serrano.

"Yeah. I get that," said Jax. "Give it a try, and if your hand hits glass, keep your left hand engaged on that brick and lower yourself back down."

"Got it," said Serrano.

Serrano swung her right hand up and grasped the brick windowsill. Jax held her breath as Serrano hung there for a moment.

"I'm good," said Serrano.

"Next move," said Jax. "Let go of the brick with your left hand and bring it to the windowsill. You will feel glass. Don't grab the windowsill. You got lucky with the right hand. Bring the hand up and sweep the sill, then grab. Then put your left foot on the brick you just let go of. Does that make sense?"

"Yes. It's like those rock climbing walls Garrett took us to," said Serrano.

"Exactly," said Jax. "There's a method to his madness."

"Thank you," said Mann. "You got this, Cata."

"Cata, the helicopter is a few seconds away," said Jax. "We have to take cover. It's coming in from the west. They won't see you, but—"

The helicopter turned in place over the target building, revealing a door gunner, who stood behind a rifle held up by a lanyard attached to both sides of the door opening.

"Get down!" said Javier, a fusillade of bullets striking the top of the parapet or snapping directly overhead.

Jax reloaded and popped up to fire a few rounds at the helicopter but was immediately suppressed by automatic fire. She glanced at Javier, who shook his head.

"Don't try it," he said over the radio.

"Cata? How are you doing?"

No response. *Shit. She fell.* Jax crawled several feet to her right and rose again, aiming at the helicopter and pressing her trigger until her magazine ran dry. She ducked below the parapet wall. Javier poked his head up for a moment, before gunfire raked their rooftop. He shook his head.

"Nice try," he said.

"Did you see Cata?" said Jax.

"No."

"Cata?" said Jax over the radio.

"Can't talk now," whispered Serrano.

"But you're inside?"

"*Sí.* Moving toward the elevator."

"Cata. This is Gupta. You need to be really careful and quiet. One group is guarding the blocked stairwell. You should be able to bypass them completely, without drawing their attention. But the group waiting for the helicopter is just down the hall from the elevator to the west.

Just around the corner. If one of them takes a few steps backward, they'll be in the hallway with a direct line of sight to the elevator. And you."

"Copy," said Serrano.

The helicopter's engine pitch changed. She glanced at Javier, who took off for the other side of the building.

"Here they come!" said Javier.

Jax peeked over the top of the wall and found the helicopter now pointed directly at her. *Shit.* She scrambled for cover, toward the stairwell shack they'd used to access the rooftop. She met Javier at the open door.

"Down the stairs. Now!" he said, the two of them descending the concrete stairs as the shack above them turned into splinters.

CHAPTER 63

McCall grabbed Evan by the arm. "What are they shooting at?"

"Sniper team on the rooftop across the street," said Evan. "Door gunner drove them back inside."

"FBI?" said McCall.

"Don't know. And don't care," said Evan. "Time to climb to the roof."

"Did they eliminate the snipers?" said McCall.

"The snipers fled the rooftop," said Evan. "Time to get you out of here. Set up your security on the roof, facing the building directly across the street."

Marino sent the three protective agents up the ladder, ordering them to take positions along the eastern wall of the building.

"Can anyone see the shooters if they return?" said McCall.

"We'll be at a slight disadvantage, since the other building is two floors higher, but they won't be able to fire on us or the helicopter until we take off, unless they want to lose their heads. Once we lift off, the door gunner can drive them back again. I suggest we move quickly," said Evan, nodding at the attic stairs in front of him. "And stay low."

McCall handed the SATCHEL to Marino, before climbing the foldable stairs they'd installed to reach the rooftop without using the main stairwell. The moment his head broke the surface of the rooftop, the heat baked his face like he had just opened an oven to check on a roast. He hated DC in the summer. Nothing but a humid sweatbox.

One of his security officers ushered him to a covered position behind an HVAC enclosure. The helicopter was on its way back from across the street. Sirens wailed in the distance, barely audible over the thumping of the helicopter blades.

Evan crouched next to him. "We'll get you out of here. Don't worry."

The security officer turned to McCall. "Are you good, sir?"

"I'm good," said McCall. "Thank you."

The man took off to join his colleagues along the eastern wall of the rooftop as the Sikorsky S-76 slowed to a stationary hover above them. Marino and Conway arrived, Marino returning the SATCHEL to him. McCall shielded his eyes with his unoccupied hand, the helicopter's rotor wash kicking up small pieces of debris and the years of dust and dirt that had settled in the rooftop's corners and crevices.

He wasn't sure how they were going to land that thing up here. The S-76 was one of the larger executive helicopters on the market, and their rooftop wasn't exactly spacious. The helicopter slowly eased to the north and descended to the only flat space on the rooftop that could possibly accommodate it—about twenty feet away. A tight fit. The pilot deserved a bonus for that landing. When the helicopter touched down, Marino got up.

"Not yet," said Evan.

"What are we waiting for?" said Conway.

"Confirmation that the rooftop across the street is clear." A few seconds later he pressed his earpiece and nodded. "We're good. Go!"

McCall took off, getting halfway to the helicopter before he realized there was a problem. Between the blazing sun, the deafening rotor noise, and the dirt pelting him, he scarcely felt the warm spray that hit his neck. Almost ignored it—nearly all his attention focused on boarding the helicopter and getting out of there. But something told him that this was different.

When McCall rubbed the back of his neck, then examined his blood-smeared hand—he knew he'd been played. He turned to face

Evan, who pointed a pistol at his head; Marino and Conway lay dead at Evan's feet, a bloody knife tossed on top of Marino. Blood pumped out of their necks, a thick pool spreading out underneath their heads.

"The database is useless without—" said McCall.

"The software I stole from you over the past twenty-four hours?" said Evan, holding up a pack of cigarettes. "It's a hard drive. Concealed to look like a pack of cigarettes. Nobody on your team even noticed that I never took a smoke break."

"Help!" yelled McCall. "Help!"

A pointless attempt over the rotor noise. Evan motioned with his head, and the door gunner and a second heavily armed man hopped down from the helicopter and pumped bullets into the three security officers positioned against the parapet wall. Only one of the security guards even managed to turn around before he was riddled with bullets.

"Was this the plan all along?" said McCall.

"Actually. No," said Evan. "But you screwed this up so badly, I had to take control of the situation. DOMINION is too valuable."

"You're Jackson's son," said McCall. "Aren't you?"

"Harrison Greely. In the flesh," said the young, dark-haired man. "You might have figured that out if you hadn't been too busy to meet with me yesterday. Things have been a little hectic here. Clara said she'd send a representative from your biggest client over. True America is your biggest client."

True America? Jesus. No.

"Is there any way I get on that helicopter?" said McCall.

He never heard the answer.

CHAPTER 64

Serrano paused at a door leading into the main hallway. More shooting on the rooftop. Barely audible with the helicopter right on top of them. She hoped they didn't send more guards up there.

"Chad. This is Serrano," she whispered. "Any change to the AXIOM security posture?"

"No. You are clear to proceed," said Lianez. "I'll let you know if that changes."

"Copy. I'm moving out," she said, before opening the door far enough to peek down the hallway.

A body armor–clad sentry equipped with an FN P90 submachine gun stood halfway inside the elevator door, leaning against one of the sides to prevent the doors from closing. Every time the door attempted to shut, it jostled him for a moment. She timed her entry with the elevator door activation, slipping into the hallway the moment it moved. He didn't notice Serrano until it was too late, a suppressed burst from her rifle knocking him most of the way into the elevator. She fired once more, striking him in the forehead—just to be sure. She kicked his feet inside and let the doors close.

"Elevator on the way with a dead guard inside," said Serrano over the radio net.

She crouched inside the recessed elevator doorway and aimed back the way she had come. The second door on the left led to the internal stairwell. If AXIOM sent guards down from the rooftop, she'd have plenty of notice and it would take them a while to get here. The security officers guarding the spiral stairs were just seconds away, on the other side of that door.

"Mann. This is Jax. The helicopter landed on top of the target building."

"Copy. We can hear it. We're on our way up. Serrano reached the elevator," said Mann. "Sounds like some more gunfire. You guys good?"

"We're fine," said Jax. "But something is wrong on the rooftop. Looks like McCall, Marino, and Conway are dead. Shit. The helicopter is taking off."

"Get to cover," said Mann. "We got this."

"We just popped off a few rounds at the pilot," said Jax. "We're out of here."

"One of the pilots is KIA," said Javier. "But we're back on the run."

"I'm headed to the rooftop," said Serrano.

"Cata. Wait a few seconds. We're on the way up," said Mann.

"The helicopter is airborne," said Jax. "They just turned and are drifting in our direction."

Automatic gunfire erupted.

"Javier is down," said Jax, the gunfire louder over the radio net than inside the building. "I'm heading over to pull him out—shit—I'm hit. I don't think we'll—"

"Jax?" said Mann. "Javier?"

Nothing. *Fuck!*

"Cata. Please wait for backup!"

"See you on the rooftop," said Serrano, removing her earbud and tossing it to the floor.

She sprinted down the hallway, where they'd detected McCall and his people before the helicopter arrived. Turning the corner at the end of the hallway in a full sprint, she collided with the attic staircase and was momentarily stunned. A few moments later, she was headed up the ladder, the ding of the elevator door barely audible as she emerged onto the roof.

The helicopter hovered over the building across the street, its starboard side exposed to her at a forty-five-degree angle. A shooter in the helicopter door fired an automatic weapon down at the rooftop. She didn't hesitate. Standing in the open, she raised her heavy-barrel, drum-fed HK416, centered the rifle's red ACOG reticle on the gunner, and fired a short burst.

The shooter dropped to his knees and fell out of the helicopter, disappearing from sight. The helicopter immediately spun to expose the full door to Serrano, a second shooter dropping to a prone position on the floor inside. She flipped her weapon's selector switch to automatic and emptied the remaining fifty or so 5.56mm bullets in long bursts toward the helicopter, while running for the cover of the nearest rooftop HVAC unit.

CHAPTER 65

"Dammit, Serrano," said Mann, the one-floor elevator journey feeling like an eternity. "She's going to get herself killed."

"Emily and I will peel left and neutralize the guards around the internal stairwell. Anish. You follow us," said Melendez. "Garrett and Luke, head right and get up to the rooftop. I know I don't need to tell you this, but shoot for the tail rotor. Just fucking obliterate it."

The door slid open, Melendez slipping through with a half inch of clearance on each side of him. Turner did the same, peeling right. Mann's earpiece crackled.

"Clear to the left."

"Right is clear," said Turner.

Mann and Miralles exited at the same time, going their separate ways, followed by Gupta. A series of suppressed gunfire bursts reached Mann's ears halfway up the foldable stairs leading to the rooftop.

"Internal stairwell area clear," said Melendez.

"Breaching the rooftop," said Mann, moments before Turner disappeared above him.

"Serrano is down," said Turner. "Helicopter is escaping."

By the time Mann climbed onto the rooftop, Turner had already braced his HK416 against the nearest HVAC unit, where Serrano lay, and started firing—his bullets sparking off the rear rotor area. The helicopter was already smoking, Serrano's gunfire obviously having done some damage to the engine. But the tail rotor was the key to taking the helicopter down.

Mann took a knee and sighted in on the rotor as it passed from right to left, the helicopter starting to lean forward, which meant its pilot had just pressed the cyclic forward and tilted the rotors for a rapid escape. He aimed at the tail and started pressing his trigger. A few moments later, the helicopter started to spin, smoke now pouring out of the tail. Jesus. This thing was going to drop right in the middle of Georgetown on a summer day, killing dozens of people on the street.

While Turner reloaded, he scooted over to Serrano, who had taken bullets to her upper left arm and lower right leg. Other than that, she looked okay. She squinted, the sun burning above them.

"Is the helicopter down?" she said.

A devastating crunch, followed by several seconds of screeching metal, ensued, answering her question. He glanced over the top of the HVAC unit and saw a thick plume of smoke rising a few blocks away. Thankfully no explosion. Helicopters rarely exploded after crashing. She turned on her side and nodded at the three bodies several feet away.

"Someone killed McCall, Marino, and Conway," said Serrano, recognizing their faces from the surveillance footage she'd reviewed over the past few days. "Someone they trusted. Marino and Conway were knifed in the neck. McCall shot in the head."

Turner jumped up. "We can figure that out later. Right now we need to get to Jax and Javier."

"Jax. Javier. This is Mann," he said over the radio net.

"We're still here, but Javier needs help really bad," said Jax.

"Emily and I will take care of it," said Melendez.

Now that the helicopter's rotors and the gunfire had stopped, it sounded like the entire city's police force was en route.

"Turner and I will throw smoke grenades down on the street to keep the police from getting too close for now. You just need to get into the alley behind the building," said Mann, already on his feet and headed toward the side of the building facing Wisconsin Avenue.

"We're on our way out," said Melendez. "Toss the grenades and get down to the fifth floor. Gupta is in what looks like their operations center. It's just west of the spiral stairs."

"I'll head down," said Turner, handing him two cylindrical canisters. "Throw one as far as you can south and north. Then toss yours a little closer."

"Drop the rest right in front of the building," said Miralles. "We're not coming back. You need to buy us all as much time as possible."

"Got it," said Mann.

He took Turner's grenades and sprinted for the front of the building. The moment he arrived, two police SUVs screeched to a halt, blocking Wisconsin Avenue a hundred feet north of the building. Four police SUVs approached from the north, a little farther out. He pulled the pin on one grenade and sent it sailing north. A second to the south. Pistol fire erupted below, bullets zipping overhead. A few smacked the stone building facade below him. He tossed two more directly below, thick grayish-white smoke billowing in an even pattern on the street. It was another windless, miserably hot day in DC. Through the smoke, two shadows crossed the street and ducked into the alley next to the coffee shop.

Mann returned to Serrano, who had pulled herself into a seated position against the humming HVAC enclosure, a pack of Delicados with a lighter tucked into the plastic wrap in her hand.

"Give a lady a light?" she said.

He lit her cigarette, before going to work on her wounds with the contents of both of their individual first aid kits.

"What do you think happened here?" said Mann.

"I don't know," she said, before taking a long drag. "But whoever killed McCall had bigger plans for DOMINION. I don't know if their plan went down in flames in that helicopter, but we better hope so."

"Since when did you care about US politics?" said Mann.

"Since your government is going to fast-track my citizenship," said Serrano. "I think it's fair to say that that's the least I deserve. Plus some of that money."

"Now you're interested in the money," said Mann, cracking a grin.

"You're damn right," she said. "Have you seen the latest interest rates? I don't plan on renting for the rest of my life."

They both broke out laughing, Mann taking a seat next to her. "I better call James. She's going to need to pull a few strings to get us out of this."

"A few?" said Serrano. "More like a mooring line holding a battleship against a dock. But I have an idea. It kind of came to me while I was lying facing up, hoping that helicopter didn't head over here and finish me off. It's a little far-fetched, but I actually think it'll work—as long as nobody thinks too hard about it."

"My guess is that the US government will want to put this mess in the rearview mirror as quickly as possible," said Mann. "Which means nobody will dig too deeply into a plausible-sounding story that explains the past week or so."

PART V

CHAPTER 66

Mann squeezed Serrano's hand. "I need to get to Walter Reed. O'Reilly and Jax are recovering in a room normally reserved for secretary-of-something types. James wants to have a meeting there to get our story straight."

"It's a good story," said Serrano.

"I have to admit," said Mann. "I think it might work. It gives everyone just enough wiggle room. You good here for now?"

"*Sí,*" she said, sounding exhausted. "How's Javier?"

"Resting," said Mann. "But Dr. Drummond insists he'll make a full recovery."

She turned to look at Javier, who lay on a hospital bed next to her. "He doesn't look good."

"Dr. Drummond is a surgeon," said Mann.

"A black-market surgeon," said Serrano.

"A black-market surgeon for this off-the-books team," said Mann. "Plus, Rico and Emily will be here the whole time to make sure things don't take a turn for the worse. If they do, they'll transport both of you to the nearest hospital."

"We got you and Javier covered," said Melendez. "And this doctor is solid. We've worked with our share of underground medical providers. He's good to go."

"I guess," said Serrano, before grabbing Mann's hand. "Don't let them send me back to Mexico. There's nothing there for me."

"I won't," he said. "Director James said she'd look into pulling some serious strings. Get you fast-tracked for citizenship. Might even put a good word in for you at the FBI."

"I don't want to be a special agent," said Serrano.

"Special Surveillance Group investigator, like Mayer?" said Mann.

"I'd give that some thought," she said.

"I'll be back with some Taco Bell in a few hours," said Mann.

"Taco Bell?" said Miralles.

"She loves that shit," said Mann, shrugging. "I don't judge."

They all shared a quick laugh, before Mann got up and put a hand on the doctor's shoulder.

"Can I talk with you for a minute?" said Mann.

"Of course," said Drummond.

When they got into the hallway, Mann passed him a thick envelope with fifty thousand dollars in it. The doctor opened it and thumbed through the bills.

"I can't take this," he said. "I owe you this debt. And I'm hoping you don't burn my business to the ground."

"I have no intention of ruining your business," said Mann. "And if anyone from the FBI ever comes around asking about these two, you never saw anything. And if they really pressure you, you treated two Hispanic males in their early thirties—and you certainly never saw my face. No matter what they threaten you with."

"I thought you were the FBI?" said Drummond.

"We're the other FBI," said Mann. "The one that doesn't play by the rules."

"Understood," said Drummond.

"I hope so. Because the two agents assigned to watch over my injured friends are not the forgiving kind, if you catch my drift."

"I completely understand," said Drummond.

He patted the doctor on the shoulder again. "Good. Because those two can be very good for your business or very bad. Sounds like they're a fan of your work. Handy, given what they do."

Mann started to leave.

"Sir?"

"Yes?" said Mann.

"What about that other guy? The one I led you to."

"You won't have to worry about him for a while. He's in federal custody facing two dozen murder counts and the attempted murder that landed him at your doorstep," said Mann. "That said, it might not be a bad idea to consider a change of venue within the next few months. Maybe sooner."

CHAPTER 67

O'Reilly's entire body ached. Mostly from lying in this stupid hospital bed. The deep stab wound in her stomach didn't exactly feel great, either. Or the knife wound that passed clear through her calf. Or the bullet wounds that peppered her legs. But being forced to lie on her back for close to a week had felt like torture. They'd transferred her to Walter Reed National Military Medical Center, a far more secure facility, after the attack on the Fairfax hospital.

"You okay?" said Mann, seated next to her bed.

"I need to get out of this bed," said O'Reilly. "Can they put me in a wheelchair or something?"

"It's gonna be a few more weeks. Maybe a little longer," said Mann. "The knife tore up your insides pretty badly."

"Wonderful," said O'Reilly. "And what's going on with that piece of shit?"

"Hard to say," said Mann. "He rolled the dice and chose federal custody over me feeding him to the wolves."

"They better not give him a deal," said O'Reilly.

"He knows a lot about AXIOM's DOMINION operation and was hoping to testify against them for a deal," said Mann.

"A deal that would get him out of killing dozens of FBI agents and trying to kill me?"

"I'm not sure what he was thinking, but you could see the wheels turning," said Mann. "The problem is that there's nobody left alive to testify against. All the main players at AXIOM are dead, along with his hope of a deal. Now we just need to link him directly to the bombing in Sacramento. Circumstantially, it's an easy link, but the forensic teams are having a hard time finding the kind of physical evidence that would make the case a slam dunk."

"How's Jax doing?" said O'Reilly.

Jax was asleep in a bed on the other side of Mann, recovering from a sucking chest wound that Rico and Emily had miraculously triaged on the rooftop, plus a few deep grazes along her thigh. Serrano's gunfire had saved her life, knocking the door gunner out of the helicopter and onto the roof, where Jax emptied her rifle magazine into his crumpled body.

"The doctors say she'll be fine," said Mann.

Director James poked her head into the room. "We're ready. We'll be back in a few, Dana."

"Any way I can listen in?" said O'Reilly.

"I think we can arrange that," said Mann, pulling out his phone.

He FaceTimed James, who reached into her suit pocket to retrieve her phone. Mann set his phone on the tray in front of O'Reilly. James left the room.

"Can you see and hear me?" she said.

"Loud and clear," said O'Reilly.

"We'll be just down the hall," said James.

"Thank you."

"Want anything when I return?"

"A shot of tequila," said O'Reilly. "Preferably the whole bottle."

"We all heard that," said James.

"You were supposed to, ma'am."

They started the meeting with the "story." Serrano had cooked up a good one, which they all agreed wasn't exactly airtight, but would give the Department of Defense and the FBI director the latitude they needed to shut the book on the events that had transpired over the past few weeks. Whether it worked remained to be seen. Once they got their stories straight, the group moved on to the aftermath of the

Georgetown building raid and the fate of everyone involved. Gupta kicked off that part of the meeting.

"I spent as much time with the Georgetown building servers and computers as was practical. The AXIOM tech team at the site successfully killed most of that system. They must have started deleting the servers the moment we hit them in the garage, possibly when the convoy was attacked. I found one computer with a few interesting screenshots on its hard drive. Looked like some kind of database interface. Clickable communications channels, map options, geo-movement tracking window, and what appeared to be a logistics order window. It's impossible to say definitively, but this looked like the kind of software program that could be populated with a database containing all the DOMINION network's information and used in an operations center to direct the network's activities nationwide. Not exactly a complicated software program, but definitely purpose-built."

"You had more luck than the digital forensic teams at the Tysons building," said James. "Servers were erased. Computer hard drives erased. They had more time to work on getting rid of the evidence."

"Would the database have been installed on the server in each location?" said Mann.

"The Georgetown location appeared to be unoccupied until the other day," said Gupta. "So, I'm going to venture a guess and say no. I think that was an emergency backup location. Somewhere undisclosed to all but critical personnel and close enough for them to occupy quickly and discreetly. Essentially a shell with the software loaded for continuity of operations, but I don't think its servers would have been loaded with the database. The database would be constantly uploaded with the LABYRINTH army's movements, status reports, logistical requests, communications. In my opinion, this would require a twenty-four-hour-a-day operations center. It didn't look like they were running two at the same time."

"They probably have a few more backup locations," said Berg.

"In the city?" said Mann.

"I doubt it," said Berg.

"One of my spotters saw Powell carry a substantial-looking black nylon duffel bag into one of the armored SUVs," said Mayer. "Maybe they were transferring the database by hand, since we fried their fancy satellite array."

"That's entirely possible," said Gupta. "They could have arranged the system so that all the data runs through and is stored in a high-capacity memory device. If their comms go down and the shit hits the fan, they just detach it and bring it to the backup location. If you can get me into the Tysons building, I could figure that out."

"I'll pass the idea along to the digital forensic teams," said James. "I need to keep all non-FBI agents off the radar for now."

"Understood," said Gupta.

"I'll also make sure the forensic team investigating the helicopter crash site searches for anything remotely resembling a duffel bag, though I highly doubt they'll have any luck," said James. "One of the fuel bladders burst upon impact with the ground and caught fire, creating enough heat to ignite the metal. By the time the fire department put out the fire, the main part of the helicopter was little more than a charred skeleton. Speaking of skeletons, they did pull four bodies out of the helicopter. Two pilots and two passengers. I strongly suspect that one of the passengers was Harrison Greely."

Berg and Bauer glanced at each other, their faces instantly neutral, if not grim.

"That's bad news," said O'Reilly over FaceTime.

"Just slightly," said Berg.

"Mayer's surveillance teams spotted him entering the Tysons building yesterday," said James. "We didn't know who he was at that point, but Powell transported him to the Georgetown building. We ran his face through the FBI system and came back with a match this morning."

Berg nodded. "This is starting to make more sense now. I assume you looked into the Greely connection, Director James?"

"I did," she said. "I think we dodged a major bullet here."

"That may be the understatement of the decade," said Berg.

"I'm not up to speed on this," said Mann.

"I'll buy you lunch and catch you up," said Berg. "But for now, we need to make sure no transmissions got out of either site after Director James submitted the warrants. Harrison Greely is Jackson Greely's son."

"Jackson Greely," said Mann, the name finally connecting. "The True America lunatic?"

"One and the same. Harrison vanished after one of the teams under my charge vaporized the contents of his father's skull," said Berg. "His involvement in this conspiracy is very bad news. The last thing this country needs is a revenge tour, or a reimagining of Jackson's vision for the country."

"Is there a file I can read?" said Mann.

Berg glanced at Bauer and shrugged.

"Maybe," said Bauer. "Let's see what's what first. Anish?"

"Limited data left the Tysons building, before Jax's drone slagged it. No data left Georgetown before Jax took out that array," said Gupta.

"Harrison killed McCall and tried to escape with the database," said Mann.

"Exactly," said Berg. "But we need to be sure. This may sound extreme, Director James, but the FBI needs to search every rooftop in the vicinity of the crash. If Harrison knew that helicopter was going down, he may have pitched it."

"But he'd need the software," said Mann.

"He had twenty-four hours to steal the software," said Berg. "Ask Anish how hard that would be."

"I infiltrated the National Counterterrorism Center's entire network using a virus I transmitted via a cell phone that didn't get past security. I daisy-chained it."

"I'll make sure they're thorough," said James.

"Are you sure you can't sneak me into the crash site?" said Gupta.

"Do you really think you can do a better job than our people?" said James.

"Yes," said Gupta.

"Fine. I'll get you in there," said James.

"Pair me up with Lianez," said Gupta. "He knows what he's doing."

"Done," said James. "All right. Let's get this moving along."

O'Reilly spoke. "Can I chat with Mann, Berg, and Bauer for a minute?"

"I don't have your tequila," said Mann.

"Funny," said O'Reilly.

James got up and stared at Mann for a few seconds, before shaking his hand. "I'd like you to run CIRG in Dana's absence and come on as her deputy assistant director when she's back on her feet."

"I accept. Assuming they don't fire the three of us within the next few weeks," said Mann.

"Obviously," said James.

When he returned to O'Reilly and Jax's room, Bauer and Berg had arranged chairs around O'Reilly's bed. Mann took his phone, the FaceTime call already finished.

"Can you—"

"Shut the door?" said Berg. "This isn't my first rodeo."

"What's up?" said Mann. "Other than the tequila request."

"I just wanted to ask, off the record, how Cata's crew is doing. Is there anything we can do to help them?" said O'Reilly. "They went above and beyond the call of duty."

"I agree," said Bauer.

"We can help them get back to wherever they want to go," said Berg. "I have some connections."

❖ ❖ ❖

Mann sighed hard. He'd have to tell her eventually. "If I tell you something, do you promise not to hold it against Cata's crew?"

"Oh boy," said O'Reilly. "I do."

"We found some serious cash in LABYRINTH. Money and pre-paid credit cards AXIOM planned to distribute to the class of graduates that they ended up gassing. Elena was the only survivor. I agreed to split that money evenly between all of them. One share per survivor and the next of kin of those that have fallen."

"How much are we talking?" said O'Reilly.

"Roughly seven point five million dollars, split sixteen ways. About four hundred fifty thousand dollars each," he said. "But there's a catch. They won't take the money unless it's also split with every FBI agent that's been involved, or their next of kin. Except for Rocha's."

O'Reilly muttered a few choice words. "I can't stop the trustee of this scheme from distributing money to Serrano's people—"

"That would be me," said Berg. "I agreed to help."

"But I do not approve of giving any of that money to any active FBI agents," said O'Reilly. "That would be like seizing evidence and keeping it."

Mann read between the lines. She was fine with their next of kin receiving money. He'd put money for each of the families in a safe-deposit box and give them the keys. He'd do the same for the rest of the agents but hold on to the keys until they either retired or quit.

"None of the agents will be given any of the money."

For now.

"We're under enough scrutiny as it is," said O'Reilly. "And if you're going to be running CIRG for a while, you need to clean up your act a little."

"Understood," said Mann.

"What are you looking at?" said O'Reilly, her question directed at Berg.

"The pot calling the kettle black," said Berg.

"Funny," said O'Reilly.

After Berg and Bauer had walked out, Mann checked on Jax before leaving. Her vitals were steady. Just sleeping off one hell of a morning.

"Garrett," said O'Reilly.

"Yes?"

"Not today, but maybe tomorrow or the next day," she said, "I'll give you the combination to a small indoor storage locker I keep. Hidden in the back, you'll find a safe where I've stored some files regarding True America. Old files, but I'd like you to sift through them. Hearing the name Greely again gave me goose bumps. You might find something useful in there, based on what the forensics people pull from the helicopter or other locations."

"Will do. Rest up," said Mann. "And don't hesitate to let me know if you need anything. Other than tequila. At least for a few more days."

She gave him a thumbs-up before he backed out of the door. His most pressing mission for now being Taco Bell.

CHAPTER 68

Nine days after the Georgetown raid, Mann, James, and O'Reilly were summoned to the US Department of Justice building, on the other side of Pennsylvania Avenue, directly south of the FBI Headquarters building. A lot had transpired since then, but nothing earth-shattering to push their investigation into the fate of the DOMINION database, software, and "sleeper" network of cartel soldiers forward. They were all beginning to think—more like hope—that the whole thing had essentially "died on the vine" at this point.

Mann pushed O'Reilly's wheelchair down the tiled hallway, following their escort to the conference room assigned to their hearing. Once seated along one side of a long, wide table, they waited in silence for several minutes, before one of the doors in front of them opened. A few men and women wearing sharp navy-blue suits, the official uniform of the Department of Justice and Federal Bureau of Investigation, carried briefcases and files into the room, pulling the four seats in front of them back.

James Teller, the FBI's head of the Office of the General Counsel, entered first, taking the seat to Mann's far right. Lana Goss, inspector general of the Department of Justice, followed, landing next to Teller. The next attendee was a bit of a surprise: Gene Ebert, chief White House counsel. He moved to stand behind the far-left chair. Upon seeing that, everyone else stood up and did the same. Who was next?

The president? Worse. Susan Shale. Director of the Federal Bureau of Investigation. When she took her seat, the rest followed suit.

Shale's presence meant the meeting would be quick, which could be a good or bad thing. They were either about to be fired, or given a quick warning followed by new marching orders. Shale opened the folder in front of her, sort of glancing at it. Theater. She knew exactly what was about to go down.

"Ms. Goss. Do you want to start?" said Shale.

"Yes, ma'am," said Goss, not even bothering to open her files. "I'm not going to lie. I think the whole story is bullshit."

She let that linger in the air for several seconds, nobody on Mann's side of the table biting off on her taunt.

"Nothing to say about that?" said Goss, once again waiting a few seconds. "Well. I guess the good news is they got their story straight. One less thing to worry about with the press all over our asses."

Mann turned to O'Reilly. "Are you comfortable?"

She gave him a *what the hell* look.

"Special Agent Mann. Am I boring you?"

"No, ma'am. Just making sure that my boss isn't in too much pain after being stabbed in the stomach, stabbed through the calf, and shot twice a couple of weeks ago," said Mann. "It's already been a long day for her."

James leaned her head forward and shot him a look. FBI Director Shale showed the slightest hint of a grin before Goss continued.

"While Special Agent Mann's ARTEMIS task force's methods are anything but orthodox, they have proven effective. And we haven't uncovered any direct or circumstantial evidence to suggest that you launched the AT4 attack on Wisconsin Avenue or massacred the people at 2711 Wisconsin Avenue. Witnesses describe a coordinated team of Latino attackers, who fled the scene and have since vanished. There was obviously some kind of internal massacre inside the Georgetown building, which matches your story about pulling into the garage and finding extensive grenade damage and casualties. The FBI doesn't use fragmentation grenades or antitank weapons."

"I've never handled anything like that in my career," said Mann.

"Don't push it," said the FBI director.

"Looks like you and Turner stumbled on some kind of Mexican standoff gone wrong on the rooftop. Everyone dead when you arrived," said Goss. "And I use the phrase *Mexican standoff* on purpose, because that was the original report that drew our attention. Someone reported that you had embedded a former Mexican police officer on your task force, parading her around as an FBI agent, and that she helped your task force take down the LABYRINTH facility in New Mexico. Of course, all of the footage recorded by the security system at LABYRINTH was deleted by AXIOM to conceal their crimes."

O'Reilly knocked her knee into his, the signal to stay quiet.

"We contacted the Owatonna Police Department in Minnesota, along with the Steele County Sheriff's Department. Neither of them confirmed the informant's story. I'm tempted to send a team down there to dig a little deeper, but I think that would be a waste of resources."

Another knee tap.

"So. We're left to honor your team's version of events. James filed a warrant to search the Georgetown building based on an informant's testimony. An informant you dutifully and promptly delivered to the FBI, along with a survivor from the LABYRINTH facility."

"That sounds about right," said Mann.

Director Shale subtly shook her head. Message received.

"AXIOM's executives and head of security took off to Georgetown. Your Special Surveillance Group assets followed them, with you close behind. AXIOM was attacked along Wisconsin Avenue, then by a team staged outside the building. All hell broke loose inside the building, moments before you pulled in and sent your nearest surveillance agent to the rooftop across the street. Eventually you broke through to the control room area on the fifth floor and then the rooftop, where you found everyone that worked for AXIOM dead. Did I miss anything?"

"No. Ma'am," said Mann. "That's exactly what happened."

"Oh. And somehow a bunch of smoke grenades landed on the street after the helicopter crashed and everyone at AXIOM should have been dead," said Goss. "But witnesses are unreliable under stress, and we're going to write that one off to the chaos of battle."

He nodded but didn't say anything.

"Which brings us to the helicopter. Your team showed a serious lack of judgment firing on a helicopter in a crowded urban area," said Goss.

"I understand. It was a heat-of-the-moment thing that we all regret."

"Only by the grace of whoever you believe in up there," she said, glancing above her, "was the popular neighborhood café, with ten outdoor tables right under the crash site, closed for the day due to a family emergency."

His eyes watered up. Mann wasn't acting. He was sincerely thankful.

"Director Shale?" said Goss.

She shook her head, maintaining a neutral expression. "I know shenanigans when I see them. They worked out this time. I'm not big on second chances, but I'm good friends with Ryan Sharpe. Consider this your last warning."

"Yes, ma'am," said James, speaking for all of them.

"Deputy Director O'Reilly?" said Shale.

"Yes, ma'am?"

"How the hell did you survive that attack?"

"Ankle holster," said O'Reilly.

"We banned those years ago," said Shale. "Corrupt agents used them as throwdowns or plants."

"Old habits die hard," said O'Reilly. "Not the corruption part. Just the comfort of a backup pistol."

"Maybe we'll bring them back," said Shale, before glancing around the table. "Anyone else?"

Gene Ebert raised his hand. "This doesn't have to happen now, but I'd like to hear more about the True America angle. Hearing that Harrison Greely was involved in this is beyond disturbing."

Shale nodded. "I'll let you work that out. And please keep me in the loop if there are any developments related to Greely and True America. Sharpe made it clear that their movement was one of the most dangerous domestic terrorism networks he'd ever encountered. Hopefully this was their last gasp."

"Will do, ma'am," said James.

When the head shed cleared the room, they all sat silent for a few minutes.

"So. We all still have our jobs?" said O'Reilly.

"Apparently. Somehow," said James. "But you're all on short leashes. Like, two-foot-long leashes. Maybe shorter."

"Fair enough," said Mann.

"How's Cata doing?" said O'Reilly.

"Funny you should mention her," said Mann. "I'm headed over to pick her up a little later. We have a date with an old friend."

"Raul?" said James.

"Yeah. Some new evidence has surfaced that I don't think he's going to like," said Mann. "And while we're talking about LABYRINTH, what's the status of the investigation into Elena?"

"Nothing popped up," said James. "Elena Rodriguez was low level at best within the Juárez Cartel. She's looking at another two to four months here, while they get everything possible out of her related to what AXIOM taught and told her within LABYRINTH."

"Please keep me in the loop on that. Specifically, her release. She's far from an innocent soul back in her world, but she's cooperating because of a promise I made her."

"I'll make sure she gets your card, and that you're notified of any significant changes to her status," said James.

"Thank you."

"Don't let us hold you up from your date," said James. "Cata doesn't sound like the patient type."

"She isn't," said Mann. "I'm out of here."

CHAPTER 69

Mann surrendered his service pistol and cell phone at the initial check-point of the DC Central Detention Facility, both of which were placed in a small locker, the combination printed out and given to him on a slip of paper. He then walked through a metal detector and submitted to a metal detection wand search that came a little closer to his privates than he'd ever experienced before. He glanced back at the sixtysomething woman who had examined his ID and badge, which he had slid through a small slit in her bulletproof enclosure—catching what he swore to be a thin grin.

"She doesn't like you," said Serrano.

He pointed at his eyes and then turned his fingers toward her and mouthed, *I'm watching you.* The lady laughed, before turning around to harass the next person entering the center. Could've been just a random ribbing. Wouldn't be the first time. The job was so boring they had to have fun somehow.

"You sure about this?" said Mann.

"The last member of *La Triada*? Yeah. I need to see him. Need to see every ounce of hope leak out of him."

"This should be fun," said Mann.

"Not really," she said.

"Sorry."

They waited in a holding room filled with several benches—a diverse assortment of lawyers, family members, girlfriends, wives, and mistresses. Mann nudged her, waking her out of a shallow sleep.

"We're up," said Mann. "Just be careful what you say. These conversations are recorded."

They got up, Mann helping her to her feet. She limped forward with him, his arm supporting her right side.

A few minutes later, they sat across from Raul, separated by a thick glass window. Times had changed, and they all communicated through headsets now. No more olive-green phones from the seventies.

"I was wondering when you'd show up," said Raul, glancing at Serrano. "Looks like a battle occurred, and you won. Good news for all of us."

"Well," said Mann. "That's the problem."

"Problem?"

"*Sí,*" said Mann. "A third party got involved, and killed McCall, Powell, Marino, Litman, and Conway."

"Bullshit," said Raul.

"It's true," said Serrano.

"Who's this bitch?"

"Bad choice of words, not that it matters," said Mann.

"My mother was killed by *La Triada*," said Serrano. "I've been working with Special Agent Mann for over a year to find Alejandro and you."

"Congratulations. What does that have to do with my deal?"

"Do you remember Felix?" said Serrano.

"Never heard of him," said Raul, looking worried.

"One of your *Triada* amigos in Ciudad Juárez. Someone castrated him, while he bled out from several stab wounds. Remember that?"

No response.

"The first one of you to pay for those fucking murders? It panicked the rest of you. Caused you to make mistakes that landed you right here."

"I agreed to be a part of *La Triada* because I had no choice," said Raul. "I was the number one sicario in the cartel. My boss demanded I take part. I didn't do any of that insanity down by the factories."

"Yes, you did," said Cata. "Maybe on a very limited level. But you had to take part. Or the other two would have turned on you. I heard the stories. I may have been a low-level traffic cop at that point, but we all . . . heard the stories. You were there."

Raul raised his hands. "So what? I have a deal. You and I can settle this later."

"That's the problem, Raul," said Mann. "I don't think there's going to be a later. Are you a coffee fan? Espresso with a thin slice of lemon perched on the rim?"

Raul's eyes narrowed to reptilian slits, his true nature showing.

"Because we came across some footage at the coffee shop across the street from O'Reilly's apartment building."

"Yeah. I tried to kill her. This is all part of the deal we're working on. I had nothing to do with the Sacramento bombing. But yeah, I was hired by AXIOM to kill O'Reilly. Why are we going over this again?"

"First. AXIOM is gone," said Mann.

"But I led you to them," said Raul. "Without me, they'd still be out there running their cartel army."

"True. And possibly worthy of a deal or reduced sentence related to O'Reilly's murder," said Mann. "But the camera at the back of the coffee shop across the street from her apartment shows you pressing a button on your phone at the exact same time your house in Sacramento exploded."

"Terrible coincidence," said Raul.

"I agree," said Mann. "But the security camera is a little more high-resolution than most. The coffee shop owner is kind of a geek, and a little paranoid. The footage shows you watching FBI agents approaching your house, and waiting for them to enter, before pressing the screen."

"We had a deal," said Raul.

"Exactly. Nothing has changed," said Mann. "Except for this new evidence that might keep you in jail for the rest of your life. Or get you the death penalty. Can you believe that progressive California still has the death penalty? Crazy."

"I'll kill you for this," said Raul.

"Is this being recorded?" said Mann. "Am I a federal law enforcement agent?"

Four federal prison guards burst into the room and approached Raul, who pulled a pen out of his pocket, pointing it at the guards. Alarms sounded as they wrestled Raul to the ground, a blast of arterial spray hitting the shatterproof window.

One of the guards stood up and put the bloodied pen on the table where Raul had sat a few moments ago, briefly making eye contact with Mann. The guards backed away from Raul, who was on the ground, not visible to Mann and Serrano from the civilian side of the visitation bay, calling for help—his voice barely audible through Mann's headphones. He tried to remove Serrano's headphones, but she knocked his hand away.

"I want to listen," she said.

He waited until Raul's gurgled protests died out, before taking off her headphones and placing them on the counter. They didn't speak until they were in the detention center parking lot.

"Thank you," she said.

"It was the best I could do," said Mann. "Sorry you didn't get to do it yourself."

"*La Triada* is dead," said Serrano. "That's all we ever wanted. Me. And the rest of my team. And the hundreds of families who lost their daughters and wives in Ciudad Juárez to these monsters. You made it happen. That's all that matters."

"We both made it happen," said Mann. "Mostly you."

"True," she said. "Which is why you owe me a vacation."

"Cabo San Lucas?" said Mann.

"You're joking, right?"

"Spain? Madrid. Then the Mediterranean Coast?" said Mann.

"Now you're talking," said Cata. "But I'm not going to be your translator, if that's what you're thinking."

"I speak Spanish just fine," said Mann.

"*Ehhh* . . . not really."

ABOUT THE AUTHOR

Photo © 2022 Bellomo Studios

Steven Konkoly is a *Wall Street Journal* and *USA Today* bestselling author, a graduate of the US Naval Academy, and a veteran of several regular and elite US Navy and Marine Corps units. He has brought his in-depth military experience to bear in his fiction, which includes *A Clean Kill* and *A Hired Kill* in the Garrett Mann series; *Wide Awake*, *Coming Dawn*, and *Deep Sleep* in the Devin Gray series; *The Rescue*, *The Raid*, *The Mountain*, and *Skystorm* in the Ryan Decker series; the speculative postapocalyptic thrillers *The Jakarta Pandemic* and *The Perseid Collapse*; the Fractured State series; the Black Flagged series; and the Zulu Virus Chronicles. Konkoly lives in central Indiana with his family. For more information, visit www.stevenkonkoly.com.

Printed in Great Britain
by Amazon